'T[illegible] separate stories are grad[illegible] skilfully merged together and bring this readable, enjoyable thriller to a melodramatic finish.'
Literary Review on *Why Did You Lie?*

'A masterpiece of plotting and suspense.'
i Paper on *Why Did You Lie?*

'The stories share an underlying menace that is at once disturbing and compelling.'
Daily Mail on *The Undesired*

'A gripping thriller with enough mystery and horror to keep you sitting on the edge of your seat while you try to work out what happened.'
Peter Robinson on *The Silence of the Sea*

'Nordic noir at its very best.'
Irish Independent on *The Silence of the Sea*

'I can see why so many people are enthusiastic about Yrsa's work. It's very engaging, fresh and exciting.'
James Patterson on *The Silence of the Sea*

'A chiller-thriller of immense scariness . . . Not to be read alone after dark.'
The Times on *I Remember You*

'Put simply, it's terrifying. And brilliant.'
Stylist on *The Day is Dark*

'Iceland's answer to Stieg Larsson.'
Daily Telegraph on *Ashes to Dust*

'Stands comparison with the finest contemporary crime writing anywhere in the world.'
Times Literary Supplement on *Ashes to Dust*

'The numerous twists and turns are worthy of Agatha Christie [illegible]ry end.'
[illegible]*st*

Also by Yrsa Sigurdardóttir

The Thora Gudmundsdóttir novels

Last Rituals
My Soul to Take
Ashes to Dust
The Day is Dark
Someone to Watch Over Me
The Silence of the Sea

Standalones

I Remember You
The Undesired

About the Author

Yrsa Sigurdardóttir works as a civil engineer in Reykjavík. She made her crime fiction debut in 2005 with *Last Rituals*, the first instalment in the Thora Gudmundsdóttir series, and has been translated into more than 30 languages. *The Silence of the Sea* won the Petrona Award in 2015. *Why Did You Lie?* is her ninth adult novel.

About the Translator

Victoria Cribb studied and worked in Iceland for many years. She has translated numerous novels from the Icelandic, including works by Arnaldur Indriðason and Sjón.

Why Did You Lie?

Yrsa Sigurdardóttir

Translated from the Icelandic by Victoria Cribb

First published in Great Britain in 2016 by Hodder & Stoughton
An Hachette UK company

First published with the title *Lygi* in 2013 by Veröld Publishing, Reykjavik

First published in paperback in 2017

1

A CIP catalogue record for this title is available from the British Library

Paperback ISBN 978 1 473 60504 6
eBook ISBN 978 1 473 60502 2

Typeset in Sabon MT by Palimpsest Book Production Limited,
Falkirk, Stirlingshire

Printed and bound in Great Britain by Clays Ltd, St Ives plc

Hodder & Stoughton Ltd
Carmelite House
50 Victoria Embankment
London EC4Y 0DZ

www.hodder.co.uk

This book is dedicated to Kristín Halla Jónsdóttir and Sigurdur B. Thorsteinsson – I couldn't have asked for better parents.

—*Yrsa*

Pronunciation guide

NB: The stress always falls on the first syllable in Icelandic

Character names (nicknames in brackets)

Helgi – Hel-ghee
Heida – Hey-tha
Tóti – Toe-tee
Ívar – Eee-var
Nína – Nee-na
Thröstur – Thros-dur
Nói – Noh-wee
Vala – Vaa-la
Tumi – Tu-mee
Púki – Poo-kee
Berglind – Berg-lint
Örvar – Err-var
Stefán (Stebbi) – Ste-fown (Stebbee)
Thorbjörg (Tobba) – Thor-byerg (Tobba)
Dóri – Doh-ree
Bylgja – Bil-gya
Steini – Stain-ee
Lárus (Lalli) – Lao-roos (Lal-lee)
Aldís – Al-dees

Places

Thrídrangar – Three-drown-gar
Stóridrangur – Stohree-drown-goor
Skerjafjördur – Scare-ya-fyerth-oor

Prologue

28 January 2014

Control: TF-LÍF, report your progress.
TF-LÍF: Visual with the Thrídrangar stacks. Overhead in five minutes.
Control: Keep your eyes peeled. Since visibility's good, scan the surface of the sea; see if you can spot the missing man.
TF-LÍF: Roger. Is he wearing a life jacket?
Control: Negative, unlikely. He's believed dead.
TF-LÍF: Roger. Negative visual. Looking. Could he have sunk?
Control: Possible. He's been in the sea long enough for the air to have left the body by now. It's too early for him to float up again. The sea's so damn cold – it's unlikely gases will have formed yet.
TF-LÍF: Have they checked the currents?
Control: Affirm. They think he could wash up near Hafnarvík. But Landeyjasandur's also a possibility. Precise information about the time he entered the water is unavailable.
TF-LÍF: Roger.
Control: We have an update: the police car's arrived at the hangar so there'll be a reception committee waiting when you get back to base.
TF-LÍF: [*Static, inaudible.*]
Control: Say again last message, TF-LÍF; you're breaking up.

TF-LÍF: You didn't miss much. We've only got three nautical miles to go and have a very clear visual on the stack.

Control: Can you see the ground party?

TF-LÍF: Negative. Perhaps when we get closer.

Control: How's the policeman doing? Bearing up?

TF-LÍF: Fine, I believe. Conditions could hardly be better. I'll ask. [*Static, inaudible.*] Yes, he's doing OK. Not looking too queasy yet. We'll see after the descent.

Control: Yes. [*Laughter.*]

TF-LÍF: We're reducing speed. There's an object floating less than one nautical mile to the west of the stack. We're going to check it out.

Control: Roger. Though I'd be surprised if it's the missing man. He should have drifted much further by now.

TF-LÍF: I'm looking through the binoculars. [*Interference, crackling.*] It's a body. Damn.

Control: Any chance he's still alive?

TF-LÍF: Negative. Floating face down. No normal movement.

Control: Roger. That was to be expected. It must be the missing man. You'll have to fetch him after you've picked up the ground party. Those were the orders. How do you read me?

TF-LÍF: Loud and clear. We're turning back. He's not going anywhere. [*Interference.*] What the hell . . . Control, control, are you still there?

Control: Affirm. Go ahead.

TF-LÍF: We've spotted another body. By the foot of the cliff; probably snagged on a rock.

Control: What? Are you sure?

TF-LÍF: Quite sure. It's a person. Dead.

Control: Christ. You've only got one body bag, haven't you?

TF-LÍF: Roger. We understood there was only one casualty. How should we proceed?

Control: Pick up both. Use the stretcher for the second body and cover it with a blanket. I'll get confirmation while you're evacuating the ground party. You may have to return to base and make another trip if the passengers object. But two trips would cost more; the finance department will want it done in one.

TF-LÍF: Wilco. Overhead the stack now. I don't know how to tell you this, but there's another body lying on the steps outside the lighthouse. And a second figure kneeling over it. The person on the ground appears to be male; the other's almost certainly the woman. It's not looking good.

Control: Is the man all right?

TF-LÍF: No sign of movement. But he could be asleep. Shit. [*More expletives, interference.*]

Control: TF-LÍF, this is control. Report your situation.

TF-LÍF: The woman's got a knife. She appears to have stabbed the man in the side or chest. I can't get a proper visual. He's still not moving.

Control: When ready, start winching. Lower our man first, the police officer second.

TF-LÍF: Wilco. Stand by; I need to help get the men ready. Holy shit.

Control: What now?

TF-LÍF: There's something seriously wrong with the woman. She's screaming at the sky – at us, apparently. No, hang on. I think she's laughing.

Control: Tell our man to be careful when he lands. To unhook himself immediately and be prepared for the woman to attack. If she's got a knife, he'll need to take extra care.

Brief him that he's cleared to use force if necessary. And remind him that there's very little room for manoeuvre down there. We don't want him falling off. It's vital that he sits tight as long as she shows no sign of approaching. He's not to move from the helipad until the cop's been lowered.

TF-LÍF: Wilco. Gaui's going down first. Then the cop. I'll pass on the rest of the briefing.

Control: Good luck.

TF-LÍF: Thanks. This is seriously fucked up. [*Interference. Communication breaks off.*]

Chapter 1

26 January 2014

Helgi has a sense of déjà vu, as if he has made this journey before. He can only remember snatches of his dream but as the flight progresses more comes back to him. Nothing too weird; just predictable details that his subconscious must have anticipated last night: the sinking in his stomach as the helicopter takes off, the numbness in the soles of his feet caused by the vibration of the metal fuselage, the uneasy feeling that he's forgotten something important at home. But other details don't fit: his fellow passengers, for example, are quite different from those in his dream, though he can't for the life of him recall what they had looked like. Nor can he remember how the adventure ended just before the alarm clock jarred him into wakefulness, still tired and groggy from his restless night. He's not used to rising this early in winter, as there's not much point in a photographer getting up before first light. And it turned out he could have enjoyed a lie-in after all since the flight was delayed several times before they finally got the green light around midday. But his dream still troubles him, perhaps because when he went to bed he had been under the impression that only the two of them would be going – himself and Ívar, the man who had told him about this adventure in the first place. Only at the airport had he learnt that there would be two additional passengers. This odd coincidence following on from his dream bothered him more than he cared to admit.

Now Helgi leans closer to the window and stares out. The noise inside the helicopter has been deafening since the rotors started up in Reykjavík and the ear protectors on the bulky helmet do little to muffle it. He suspects the helmet would be as good as useless in an accident, too; the impact of a fall would be far too great. He fiddles with it in a vain attempt to reduce the din. Perhaps the purpose of the ear protectors is not to keep noise to a minimum but to enable crew and passengers to communicate. Not that there has been much attempt at that so far. The four passengers can hear the pilots exchanging the odd word but none of them have joined in. Helgi hopes they will all feel chattier once they land, but he isn't really that bothered; it'll be such a mind-blowing experience to find themselves on a small rock in the middle of the vast ocean that there will be no need for small talk about the weather.

There's a crackling sound inside his helmet, followed by a faint, tinny voice: 'If you want to take some aerial shots, you'd better get ready.'

Helgi mumbles something that neither he nor the others can hear. He feels self-conscious about his voice carrying over the intercom to everyone on board. He's already had to speak once, just after take-off. The pilot had offered to fly over Skerjafjördur, on Reykjavík's south coast, so Helgi could photograph a police operation that was under way there. Helgi had wanted to decline the offer and ask the man to keep going but he hadn't dared; it would have sounded like ingratitude. The coastguard had already been incredibly accommodating to him. In the end he took a few shots of the flashing lights through the window while the pilot tilted the helicopter for him, and now he's stuck with a bunch of more or less useless aerial photos that he intends to discreetly delete at the first opportunity.

Helgi fumbles for the heavy case on the floor, wishing he hadn't put the camera away earlier. Every time he leans forward the seat strap tugs at his shoulder, as if to warn him that it's safer not to move around. Meanwhile his brain is telling him that if the helicopter goes down, the strap will offer no more protection than the helmet. Yet despite his doubts about the strap's efficacy, he misses the security it offers when the co-pilot clambers back to him, undoes it, hooks him onto a life-line, then opens the door. With unsteady legs he props himself against the doorframe, aiming the camera with trembling hands while trying to hide his fear from the watchful eyes of his fellow passengers. He is profoundly grateful that he didn't have to take pictures through an open door over land. At least he can kid himself that it might be possible to survive a fall into the sea.

Helgi feels a rush of vertigo and at first even drawing breath is an effort. The knowledge that he can't fall out is no help. Looking down at the choppy surface far below, he experiences a hypnotic urge to undo the life-line and let himself fall. The sea would welcome him. But he's not going to give in to it. The blast of the wind and sting of salt on his lips are an unpleasant reminder of what would actually await him – brutal cold, followed by certain death. Helgi gulps and closes his eyes briefly. All he wants is to beg the co-pilot to close the door so he can be back safely in his seat.

He'll just have to tough it out. If he shows any sign of

weakness, there's a risk they'll send him straight home with the helicopter. Maybe his fear will get the better of him and he won't have the courage to make the descent. But if he chickens out now, he's convinced there will be no second chance. It's now or never. Resolute, he releases his hold on the doorframe and raises his camera. Viewed through the lens, the things that so frightened him a moment earlier are tamed somehow, converted into the subject of a picture he must capture. His hands recover their strength and the solid bulk of the camera is steady in his grip. Now he can see only what he chooses to frame.

His anxiety forgotten, Helgi deftly focuses on the pillars of rock that appear to be rushing towards him, as if they can't wait for him to arrive. He takes several shots of all four, then zooms in until the tallest stack fills the viewfinder.

'Have you noticed that there are four? Not three.'

The words wrench Helgi back into a world of noise and peril; he clings to the doorframe and nods at the man who is smiling at him from the pilot's seat.

'Someone couldn't count.'

Helgi smiles awkwardly, then returns to his task.

How could they have been christened Thrídrangar, 'the Three Stacks', these four claws of rock thrusting up from the waves? Perhaps only three were visible from the Westman Islands or south coast, yet at some point people must have realised their mistake because each stack has its own name: Kúludrangur, Thúfudrangur, Klofadrangur and Stóridrangur. There's no mistaking Stóridrangur, 'the Big Stack', but Helgi hasn't a clue which of the others is which.

Stóridrangur rears out of the sea, sheer on all sides, like a slightly lopsided pillar. Helgi wonders how it has managed to withstand the relentless battering of the waves down the ages, not to mention past earthquakes. The rock it's composed of must be incredibly hard – unless the part now visible is the remains of a much larger, more substantial island that the elements have whittled down to its present size and will in the fullness of time utterly destroy.

'I can fly around the rocks and over the lighthouse, if you like. We're in no big hurry.' Again the pilot has turned to see Helgi's reaction, having clearly given up hope of persuading any of the passengers to use the intercom.

Helgi nods again, then concentrates once more on the subject matter. The soft light is perfect; the sea a greeny-blue, decorated with white surf around the feet of the stacks. The surface resembles a velvet cloth with lace at the edges, though nothing could be further from the truth. The lighthouse, which has brought them to these parts, was built there to prevent these rocks from costing seafarers their lives in storms and darkness. It beggars belief that they ever managed to construct the building on top of Stóridrangur. From what Helgi has read about it, work began around the outbreak of the Second World War. There were no helicopters in those days, so all the building materials and workforce had to be transported to the islet by sea, then hauled up the forty-metre-high precipice. Helgi wonders, not for the first time, whether men were made of sterner stuff in those days. Maybe modern men are equally capable of such feats but are simply never called upon to prove it. Up ahead he can see a chain hanging down the rock face. Only under extreme duress could he be persuaded to climb up the cliff with only that for support.

Just when he's thinking that he's got enough good shots

to make this whole extraordinary journey worthwhile, the pilot's voice blares again in his helmet. 'Are you sure there's space for all four of you down there? There's not much standing room.' Helgi doesn't react but concentrates on his photography. He hears mumbling from the other passengers.

The helicopter is hovering over the lighthouse now and there's no denying that it was a reasonable question. Apart from the little tower and the square helipad, built much later, Stóridrangur consists of nothing but sheer drops. On either side of the manmade structures the rock juts out, steep, jagged and apparently inaccessible. The photos Helgi had found online were only a pale reflection of the reality. Yet again, the real world has trumped the two-dimensional hands down, leaving him feeling hopelessly discouraged. How is he to capture this heart-stopping grandeur? To cause people's jaws to drop as his is doing now? He turns the camera slightly to compensate for the tilting of the helicopter and snaps away. He has in the past lost heart in the face of smaller challenges than the one confronting him now, but this time he resolves to push away his fears and let himself by guided by his photographer's instincts. If he messes up, that's tough; he'll still be in possession of a photo series that few others could boast of. The coast-guard rarely allows photographers along on trips like this, and who could afford to hire a private helicopter for the purpose? He'd been so astonished when his request was granted that he'd stared, stunned, at the receiver long after the person at the other end had hung up. Things never usually go his way, so this is great news. As long as the pictures turn out well.

The helicopter is hovering over the islet, obscuring their

view of the landing pad directly beneath them. The only window of the small white building below has been blocked up, so it looks as if it is staring at them with a blind eye.

'Welcome to Thrídrangar lighthouse.' The pilots look round, grinning as if at some private joke. Then, catching each other's eye, they fiddle with various controls on the instrument panel. They almost seem to be suppressing laughter at the thought of the conditions awaiting their passengers. And maybe they're right; the other four stare down intently at this extraordinary place which is to be their home for the next twenty-four hours, and none of them appears to relish the thought of leaving the helicopter. Especially not given that the only available route is straight down. Helgi takes a few shots of the lighthouse but the helicopter is wobbling more than before and he finds it hard to keep the subject steady in the viewfinder.

'We're ready to deploy the winch, so you'd better finish up and return to your seat.' The pilot sounds more authoritative than before. Helgi takes two more pictures, aware, without bothering to check, that he's botched them, then squeezes back into his seat and only then does he unclip himself from the life-line. In its place he fastens the seat strap.

The co-pilot clambers back to them, closes the door and starts busying himself with winch, cables and strops. He slaps the knee of the passenger nearest the door and gets the man to stand up while he fastens the equipment around him. They talk together while the pilot jerks hard on all the ropes of the harness to test them. Then they take up position by the door, which the co-pilot reopens without batting an eyelid. The passenger takes a small, involuntary step backwards and the other man explains what to do with a good deal of gesturing. The next thing they know, the man is sitting in the doorway, his legs dangling. The others avoid looking at each other but all three press themselves instinctively as far back in their seats as they can. Soon it'll be their turn.

The other man goes next, then the woman. Helgi admires the way she copes with her nerves, which are betrayed by the trembling of her slim hands and her pale, hollow-eyed profile. He gives in to the temptation to take some pictures of her preparations and regrets not having done the same for the men. It would have been amusing to compare their reactions. They had puffed out their chests and held their heads high, filling their lungs with air and their minds with imaginary courage. Their playacting didn't end until they began their descent and the last that could be seen of them was a terrified scarlet face and bulging eyes. The woman's expression shows a healthy respect for her fear coupled with a stoical calm that he wishes he himself possessed. Especially as he's next.

Once the strop and cable have been winched up again, the pilot beckons him over and Helgi stands up, knees trembling. Like a condemned man on his way to the scaffold, he allows the other man to truss him in ropes and push his legs into the strop, then flinches as he checks his handiwork. He is overwhelmed by a familiar sense of shame at being fat as the man touches his body, and wonders if the equipment is calibrated for a lighter weight than his. What if he plummets out of control because he's too heavy? But he says nothing, reluctant to discuss his weight with a stranger, and positions himself like the others in the opening, legs dangling above the pillar of rock. Craning forwards, he looks down at the faces of the other three on the helipad. They gaze up at him, waving cheerily as if to beckon him and let him know that the descent is not as bad as expected. They survived it and he will too. Like passengers climbing off a rollercoaster and waving to the next in line.

Then of course the rollercoaster flies off the rails on a sharp bend because one of the passengers is too heavy.

Helgi lets go and starts his descent. He feels the wind rushing up his body and the line seems terribly thin and inadequate. The only thought in his head is whether he's far enough down to survive a fall, when quite suddenly he feels a hard bump and a jerk that runs up his spine like a pianist running his fingers over the keys. He straightens up, grins at the other three and hurriedly undoes the clips on his harness so he won't be dragged back into the air. The worst moment is when he has released all bar one and knows that if he's pulled upwards now, the fastening is bound to give halfway. But at last he's free and watches the empty harness jerking back up to the helicopter.

The noise of the rotors is too loud for conversation, so they all stand staring upwards. No one wants to be on the receiving end of the next consignment to be lowered. From what Helgi could gather before they boarded, the plan is to renew the lighthouse radio transmitter, replace a broken solar panel and touch up the exterior paintwork. They're also going to measure the area around the helipad and gauge the potential for enlarging and strengthening it to make it fit for purpose again. How this is to be done without loss of life is a mystery to Helgi. The platform is built on a foundation of stone and in order to assess the terrain around it, someone will have to climb down and cling by his toes if he is to find a foothold on the sharp, wind-eroded snags. Helgi hopes fervently that no one will ask him to help.

Together they labour to free each consignment as it is lowered, then push it aside so it won't get in the way of the next. Helgi can no longer feel his arms by the time the co-pilot finally winches down to signal that the drop is complete. He is nonchalant on the descent, smiling and waving at them. His breeziness in no way abates once he has landed.

'That's the lot, then!' the man bellows and Helgi can't help wondering if he ever accidentally yells at his wife like that at the end of a day's work. 'You're all sorted, aren't you?' Helgi nods, awkwardly, and the others follow suit. 'The forecast's good so we assume we'll be picking you up tomorrow evening unless we hear from you first. You've got double rations, so if you think you'll need to spend another night, just let us know. Be careful and, you know, try not to get agoraphobia.' The man grins, revealing teeth as white as his helmet. 'And no going for an early-morning jog. It could end nastily.' Still smiling, he signals to the pilot to winch him up and shortly afterwards pops his head out to wave goodbye. The door closes, the helicopter tilts slightly, then describes a swift arc away from them. As it recedes into the distance, the thunder of the rotors fades until finally they can no longer hear it.

They look at each other self-consciously and no one says anything. It is Helgi's acquaintance Ívar who finally makes a move, muttering that they had better stow the gear. The younger man follows him. They search among the small piles on the platform until they find what they're looking for and break open some boxes. Both seem completely unaffected by vertigo, though to Helgi it looks as if they are stepping dangerously close to the edge and it wouldn't take much to lose one's footing on the rough concrete. He considers making another attempt to talk to the two men, but decides against it. Ívar was reluctant to speak to him at the airport; he doesn't seem to remember him, which isn't really that surprising. A few days ago Helgi had struck up a conversation with him in a bar that seemed mainly to attract lonely, friendless types like himself, plus the odd tourist who appeared horrified at the idea that this might be the fabled Icelandic nightlife.

Ívar had been pretty wasted, bragging about a perilous trip he was about to make. After letting him ramble on for a while, Helgi asked if there was any chance he might be allowed to go along to take pictures. Ívar had thumped him on the back, so hard it hurt, and said it might well be possible. Helgi seemed like a good bloke and he would be glad of the company. Helgi should just ring and ask the coastguard, making sure to mention that Ívar was OK with it. Which he had done.

He watches the men laying aside tools in a neat row. They work in silence, having no apparent need for words. Both clearly know what they're doing and their movements are practised and confident. Helgi thanks his lucky stars he doesn't have to participate in the repairs to the lighthouse or measurements of the helipad. He finds it hard to imagine how there can be any room for manoeuvre in these confined conditions and is sure any activity must be extremely dangerous, whatever security measures are taken. He'd be only too happy to stay out of the way – the only condition for his being permitted to go along – but easy as it was to make such a promise, he sees now that it will be almost impossible to aim the camera without bumping into his companions while they work. If he can ever actually summon up the courage to make the move from the helipad to the lighthouse, that is.

It's hardly any distance but that doesn't make it any less daunting. Involuntarily Helgi grabs hold of a pile of equipment to combat his dizziness. Out of the corner of his eye he catches sight of the young woman who is also searching for something to hold on to, and feels ashamed of himself for not being a proper man like the others. To mask his embarrassment, he starts taking photos completely at random until the men seem to have finished their task.

Gingerly he inches after them as they stride, sure-footed, over to the lighthouse. He is aware of the woman behind him but doesn't dare look round. A rattle of loose gravel and unnaturally rapid breathing indicate that she is following close on his heels. He concentrates on the lighthouse, which looks so small you would have thought it had been built for one of Snow White's seven dwarfs. Once there, he heaves a sigh of relief and presses himself against the rough wall. The woman stations herself beside him, her cheeks ruddy, her eyes betraying a hint of anxiety, as if she has been brought here against her will – or her better judgement. She's kitted out like a veteran, in drab green outdoor gear, designed with an eye to protecting her from the cold rather than enhancing her feminine charms. But the clothes are brand new and she looks about as pleased to be there as him.

Helgi opens his mouth to offer comfort, partly as a means of bolstering his own courage, but can't find the right words. Together they gaze in silence at the view from the rock, at the heaving, glittering surface of the sea and almost cloudless vault of the sky. Helgi shoots a glance at the woman whose name, he now remembers, is Heida. He guesses that she is the technician who has been sent, in a last-minute decision, to update the radio transmitter and GPS equipment in the lighthouse. Tóti, the man with Ívar, must be the other carpenter, as no manual worker would have long pink nails like Heida's.

Ívar sticks his head inside the lighthouse, turns and looks at Heida and Helgi for a moment then climbs onto the step in front of the door and stamps imaginary dirt off his shoes. Tóti follows on his heels. Ívar puts his hands on his hips and sighs, then shoves a knife in the leather sheath attached to his belt. Helgi regrets not having brought along his hunting knife to fit in better.

'Right,' says Ívar. 'No point hanging about. There's no time to lose if we're going to finish by tomorrow evening.'

Slowly Helgi detaches himself from the wall and feels as if he's reeling. 'If you like, I might be able to help. I won't be taking pictures all the time.'

The men barely react, though Ívar mutters that he'll bear it in mind. They enter the lighthouse and Heida follows, but the space is so tiny that one person is forced to stand in the doorway. Helgi allows his rapid heartbeat to slow as he listens to the sound of their voices inside. This is incredible. Here he is, standing on a pillar of rock hardly any bigger in area than his flat, surrounded on all sides by the freezing ocean, which seems to be just waiting for one of them to lose their footing. This is no place for a human being to spend an hour, let alone the whole night.

His thoughts return to his dream and although he can

remember little about it, he's pretty sure his imagination fell far short of the reality. He tries to pick out the helicopter on the horizon but it has gone. There's nothing to see for the moment, so he moves slowly over to join the others, clinging onto the wall all the while, and peers in through the doorway over Tóti's shoulder.

Inside, Heida and Ívar are bending over something he can't see. But his attention is drawn not to the people but to the whitewashed walls of this tiny space. More snatches of his dream flash into his mind. Whitewashed concrete, spattered all over with blood. Shiny black pools on a stone floor. All of a sudden he remembers how the dream ended.

There were four people to begin with.

Two returned to land.

It's a pity he can't remember if he was one of them.

Chapter 2

20 January 2014

Few people had any business down in the bowels of the police station. Because of its low ceiling the windowless basement was used solely for storage, not for stuff that was needed but for useless things that no one could decide whether to throw away. Nína switched on the light and one fluorescent tube after another clicked and flickered to life as she descended the stairs. As a rule only the caretaker came down here, but a faint smell of cigarette smoke suggested that other employees used it on occasion. Nína wrinkled her nose and sighed. She would get used to the stale fug; it wasn't the worst thing she'd smelt in the line of duty. She surveyed the assorted junk that covered the floor, then picked her way through it along the zigzagging path created by the caretaker. She pitied the poor man having to sift through this worthless rubbish in preparation for the force's move to a new, more modern headquarters. But it wasn't all junk; somewhere in here lurked filing cabinets crammed with documents that Nína's superiors felt it would be more appropriate for a police officer to empty. The information they contained might still be sensitive.

Dust danced in the air, refusing to settle. Nína rubbed her nose. The silence was total; she couldn't hear the faintest echo of the roar of traffic from Hverfisgata and Hlemmur Square, which constantly got on her nerves upstairs. Extraordinary how much difference a single layer of concrete could make. Down here it was like entering another world, far from noisy distractions and the light of day. She shrugged off her initial disgust at the stale air, pushing away the memory of all those recent newspaper articles about the dangers of mould spores. Not that she was particularly worried about her health. She didn't really care about anything these days. Lately she had gone about her work like an automaton, doing only what was strictly necessary. Her colleagues treated her as if she were made of porcelain or else a hand grenade primed to go off, and her boss seemed incapable of dealing with the situation. That probably explained why she was down here in the basement. He couldn't send Nína back out on the beat because of the furore that had broken out at the station when she'd lodged a formal complaint about the conduct of a colleague – although such matters were supposed to be handled in the strictest confidence.

They had received a report of a disturbance and possible domestic at a block of flats in the east end of town. Nína had been sent with another officer to restore the peace and arrest the troublemaker if it turned out he had beaten up his wife badly enough for her to press charges. On the way there her fellow officer had been grumbling about a recent report that had revealed the shitty conditions endured by policewomen and the prejudice they experienced from male members of the force. Nína had stood up for her female colleagues; after all, she had firsthand experience of the problem. Women still made up a small minority in the police but apparently even that was too much for some of the men. Her male colleague had tried to argue that men were better at the job than women and started regaling her with exactly the kind of bigotry the survey had exposed. It was a pity, really, that they had wasted their money on research when speaking to him would have told them all they needed to know.

Nína had refrained from comment during most of his rant but her patience snapped when he started using chess to prove his point. She asked if he was really that expert at the noble game himself. Extrapolating from the genius of Russian grandmasters wouldn't wash. If chess was a standard of male intelligence, then he and his fellow officers in the police must be singularly unrepresentative; at least, the less-than-enthusiastic participation in the Christmas chess tournament hadn't pointed to the existence of many grandmasters on the force. This and more in the same vein accompanied their progress up the stairs and by the time the door was opened in response to their banging, they were both red in the face and fuming.

The man standing in the doorway didn't look like much of a chess player. Behind him they could hear his wife whimpering. The flat stank of alcohol and old cigarette smoke. The man let them in as if nothing had happened, as if beating up your wife was standard practice. Nína followed the noise to where his wife was curled up weeping. When she looked up, the crimson mark of a blow was visible on one cheek and her face was streaked with mascara. Her top was torn, revealing a red lace bra, and when she loosened her arms from round her knees, it was apparent that her trousers had been dragged down to her pubic bone. The flies hadn't been undone and the skin around her jutting hipbones was badly grazed.

At this point the caveman entered the room with Nína's colleague. The husband drawled that there was no need to get excited – they were married and could do as they liked. Neither Nína nor her fellow officer bothered to try and correct this misconception. Then he offered them a drink, adding that they shouldn't waste time on that bitch, she was a frigiddirtyfuckingboringwhingingcunt. He must have taken exception to the expression on Nína's face because the next thing she knew he was behind her, pressing hard against her back, thrusting his hands inside her open jacket and grabbing at her breasts. He slurred in her ear, asking if she liked it, and to her disgust she realised he had a hard-on. Then he released one breast and forcing her face round, licked her cheek. The foul stench from his mouth must have been caused by a rotten tooth. Out of the corner of her eye she could see that her colleague was not lifting a finger to help. A mocking smile played over his lips. Her attempts to twist round and stamp on the man's toes were in vain; she couldn't free herself. This seemed only to increase her colleague's amusement.

Suddenly the wife rose from the sofa, roaring like a lion, claws out. At first, so bizarre were the circumstances, Nína feared she was going to attack her for trying to steal her husband. But the woman's fury was directed at him. He loosened his grip as his wife's nails raked across his fleshy cheeks. When Nína turned, the man looked as if he'd tried to disguise himself as a Native American: four bright red parallel lines scored each cheek from ear to ear.

The visit ended with them handcuffing the man for assaulting his wife and resisting arrest. On the way back to the station Nína asked her colleague what the hell he had been thinking of and he retorted that if she was equal to a man surely she should have been strong enough to look after herself. He didn't see how he could have helped.

Her first action on reaching the station was to make a formal complaint about his conduct and demand that he should receive a reprimand. How could he work as a police officer if he couldn't be trusted to come to the aid of a colleague? If a crazed woman had attacked him, Nína wouldn't have stood by and watched. Bickering in the car was one thing, but the dangerous situations arising from their work were quite another. Then officers had to back each other up. Or so she had always believed.

The following day there had been a huge fuss. Nína was asked to withdraw her complaint as it would seriously damage the man's career prospects in the force. Instead, he would receive an informal dressing-down. She was also asked to delete the description of the husband's assault on her from the report. It was for her own good, she was told; she would hardly want the incident to become common knowledge. As if she had willingly colluded in it or been at fault! Nína had refused both requests and threatened to take the matter further if it wasn't handled properly in-house.

Suddenly she was a pariah: no one wanted to work with her; she couldn't be trusted. Even the other female officers gave her the cold shoulder, one commenting that now she had really made their lives unbearable; now they would all be branded as snitches. And she had let them down by not being able to free herself unaided. Nína had been speechless.

When she was taken off the beat until further notice and assigned special duties instead, she hadn't raised any protest. In fact it had been a huge relief. The assault by the drunk had shaken her more than she was willing to admit to herself or her superiors. She had no desire to risk winding up in the same situation again, so she welcomed the monotonous but safe chores that were now dumped on her. Her calm reaction disconcerted the duty sergeant who had obviously been ready for a showdown. Instead she had stood before him, nodding meekly as he outlined her latest assignment, which was even duller than the last.

And now her fortunes had undergone an even greater transformation. Her superiors must have congratulated themselves when they had the brainwave of removing her uncomfortable presence from the office by dispatching her down to the basement. The archives were apparently so extensive that she could expect to be stuck down there for days, even weeks. Meanwhile they could put off making any decision about her future in the force. Her complaint was still being passed from pillar to post and no action had been taken over her accusation against the husband, as it would only expose her fellow officer's breach of conduct. As a result, it looked as if the wife-beater would get away with it, and this made Nína even more determined to stick to her guns, despite the developments in her personal life that had been the final straw. These days she walked around in a daze and would no longer trust herself to behave responsibly at the scene of a crime even if she was returned to ordinary duties. She was well out of the way down here, in her own opinion as well as that of the male chauvinist pigs upstairs.

Nína picked up a heavy roll of black bin bags and struggled to fit as many flat cardboard boxes under her arm as possible. Though thin, she had always been strong, but recently she had become positively haggard. Her cheekbones jutted out of her face and her ribs were like a washboard. At least there were no mirrors in the basement.

Staggering under her load, she made her way towards the archives. Long ago someone had hung a sign, now yellowed with age, on the door, which read: 'Old Sins'. After a struggle Nína managed to open the door without putting down the bags or boxes. She entered the corridor, laid down her load and stood there panting. There were six doors, each of which, the caretaker had told her, led to a separate archive. She spotted a switch but before she could turn on the overhead lights the door swung shut behind her and all at once she was standing in pitch blackness. Nína cursed herself aloud for not anticipating this but the walls seemed to absorb her words.

It was a long time since Nína had been in total darkness; there wasn't even a faint gleam from the cracks around the door. She felt for the wall, then fumbled her way back towards the entrance. As she did so she tried closing her eyes and discovered that it made no difference.

She thought about her husband, Thröstur. Was he aware of the lightless world in which he now existed? As she groped her way along, she hoped fervently that he wasn't. Perhaps he could still see, and everything would be all right, in spite of the pessimistic prognosis. But she had been standing beside the doctor when he'd aimed his torch at her husband's eye and the black pupil had continued to stare blankly at the ceiling.

The doctor had told her that if Thröstur could see, his pupils would contract, adding – as if to rub salt in the wound – that his other senses had probably failed as well. Although he didn't come right out and say it, the implication was that her husband was no better than a living corpse.

When Nína pressed him, the doctor wouldn't confirm that this was a hundred per cent certain, so she had allowed herself the tiny hope that Thröstur was in some way aware of his surroundings. But a more likely explanation was that there was no such thing as certainty in medical science, any more than in other areas of life. If you weren't dead, you were alive. But if the doctors' dire predictions proved correct, she ought really to hope with all her heart that Thröstur wasn't aware of the changes that had taken place in his life. It would be more merciful if he could sense nothing at all, but just felt as if he was sleeping, floating on the wings of beautiful dreams. But her innate pessimism told her that his dreams were probably as bleak as his prospects.

Gripping the cold handle, Nína opened the door again, trying to suppress this line of thought. Yet she couldn't shut out the questions: how could she ensure that Thröstur never found out what sort of state he was in? Never woke up to find himself trapped in a useless body? The only way, in the end, would be to follow the doctors' advice and switch off his life support. Nína felt the blood rushing to her cheeks. Why the hell did *she* have to make this decision? What were the hospital staff, with all their specialist training, for? Couldn't they just tell her what to do? Light spilled in from the corridor and Nína took a deep breath. Don't think too much; that was best. Activate cruise control and go about your life without thinking. That hurt less.

Almost every other fluorescent bulb in the corridor turned out to be working. The walls, once brilliant white, were now discoloured and grubby, and the doorframe was chipped from where people had carelessly bashed it when carrying objects through. The unforgiving glare also revealed how filthy her trouser legs were, and she automatically tried to brush off the worst of the dirt. She had waded heedlessly through the slush on her way to work this morning, after spending the night in a chair by Thröstur's hospital bed. Nowadays the nursing staff had given up shaking her and telling her to go home for a rest; they knew better than anyone when it was best to say nothing. It wasn't difficult, after all. It was always best to keep one's mouth shut. No words were capable of dulling her pain. The silent sympathy she sensed from the doctors and nurses was enough for her, and it was a relief not to have to explain anything; they understood that she would not go home unless compelled to. The flat was an empty shell of what it had once been. All that remained, it seemed, were things whose sole purpose was to remind her of what she had lost.

Nína stood with her hand on the light switch, lost in thought, while the door swung slowly shut as if guided by an invisible hand. As if it wasn't bad enough that the ceiling was so low, the floor sloped as well. She didn't turn away until the door had finally closed. It must have been her imagination but she could have sworn she had seen the handle move.

In front of her were the rows of doors leading to the archives, three on each side. There was no need to waste effort on wondering where to start as all the storerooms were presumably full of old files. The obvious course would be to begin at the back or front and work systematically to the other end. Yet it was to one of the doors in the middle that she headed first. She didn't know why; there was nothing behind her decision but an inexplicable certainty that this was where she should start. The door handle was warm, as if welcoming her, as if inside she would receive long-desired peace. Odd.

She hadn't been paying much attention but as far as she could remember the handle of the door leading to the corridor had felt cold to the touch.

She was met by a smell of dust and old paper. Mindful of what had happened before, Nína took care to switch on the light before entering. As she'd suspected, it was crammed with files, the rows of shelves packed in so tightly that there was barely space to squeeze between them.

She decided to take a better look around before embarking on the sorting and throwing away. The idea was to scan in anything important, then destroy the hard copy, so the task mainly consisted of assessing what should go straight into the bin and what should be digitised. If this job wasn't the most exciting, the scanning would be absolute hell. Nína wouldn't be at all surprised to learn that it was her next assignment once she had finished clearing the basement.

She wandered around, reading the labels on folders and boxes at eye level. *Traffic Offences: January 1979*, *Burglaries: May – September 1980*. Her movements were stirring up dust and again she rubbed her nose to stop herself sneezing. The further inside she went, the dimmer the light, thanks to the high shelves, and she resolved to bring a floor lamp down with her next time.

Nína was about to worm her way out again when her gaze fell on an open file lying on top of a row of upright folders at the back of the room. She blew on it carefully, then noticed there was no dust. Turning it over, leaving it open at the same page, she read the spine: *Suicides: February 1982 – October 1985*. Her blood ran cold and her heart beat with slow, heavy strokes, so insistently she could almost hear it in the silence. She gave herself a moment to recover. Of course she had known suicide was a police matter; she had been on both sides of the desk herself.

Before Thröstur decided his life was meaningless, Nína had been involved in the investigation of such incidents. And lately her thoughts had kept returning to a widow she had spoken to more than two years ago. The woman had gazed at Nína with wide eyes, muttering repeatedly that there had been nothing wrong, her husband would never have done anything thing like that; he had no reason to take his own life. Nína had been filled with sympathy mingled with doubts about the woman's sanity. It had never entered her head that she herself might one day gaze, face puffy with weeping, into the eyes of a police officer and make an almost identical speech. The only difference was that Thröstur had survived his suicide attempt. He was still alive, if you could call it living.

The folder weighed heavier and heavier in her hands. Nína tried to see where it belonged but there were no gaps in the neighbouring shelves. She found one completely empty shelf in another row but the square, dust-free patch on it indicated that it had contained a box or some other object much larger than a folder. She wondered whether to leave the file open on top of the others but thought no, chucking it straight into the bin bag would be a good start. Reports of suicides from thirty years ago could hardly be considered relevant now, as she knew from personal experience. It was only eight weeks since Thröstur had tried to kill himself, yet few shared her interest in finding out why. Apart from his father and sister, no one wanted to know. She could read in the eyes of her close friends that they wished Thröstur could be allowed to go so they wouldn't have to keep pussyfooting around the question of how he was doing or why it had happened. In thirty years' time they would barely remember the incident. She hoped the same would be true of her.

Nevertheless, once she had moved back into the light, Nína couldn't resist the temptation to take a closer look at the contents of the folder. Without wanting or intending to, she began reading the text from the point where she had found it open. There would be no going back.

It turned out to be the final page of a report about a case that had presumably been described in the previous pages since it was impossible to work out the circumstances from the paragraph in front of her. The date was in the top right-hand corner: 18 April 1985. Nína turned back to see how it began, only to discover that the previous pages were missing. It was preceded by a completely unrelated report, which was complete and stapled together. The single page showed evidence of having once been attached to others; the small, triangular scrap of paper left under the staple suggested that the previous pages had been torn away carelessly. She leafed through the file but couldn't find the first part of the report anywhere. Turning back to the paragraph that had shaken her so badly, she stared at the black typewritten letters as if she expected them to have changed. But they hadn't. It was the same concluding paragraph stating that Milla Gautadóttir had signed on behalf of her underage son to witness that his statement was true and correct. This was followed by a brief note confirming that the taking of the statement had been concluded at 10.39 a.m. The name of the son was printed under the mother's name: Thröstur Magnason, born 1 March 1978. Her husband.

Nína closed the file and clutched it to her chest. There was no question that it was her Thröstur. His mother's name was uncommon and it was impossible that she could have had a namesake with a son of exactly the same name and age, and a husband called Magni to boot. Impossible. Closing her eyes, she tried to breathe calmly. Someone must have left the folder out so she would find it. Someone who wanted to hurt her. Her friends – if she had any left on the force – would never have done such a thing. To slip a report dating from her husband's childhood into a file on suicides . . . Nína squeezed her eyes tighter shut and streaks of light, ghosts of the former brightness, danced before her. She didn't want to see anything, didn't want to think at all. If she let herself, she would start tuning into the noises she thought she could hear at the back of the storeroom, from the shelves she hadn't yet examined. As if someone was standing there, breathing heavily. Perhaps the person who had left the folder out was still down there. She could only assume that sound would carry as poorly out of the basement as it did into it. If she screamed, it was unlikely anyone would hear her. Except the person hiding behind her, among the dusty old archives.

Chapter 3

23 January 2014

The weather seemed unable to make up its mind whether to rain, sleet or snow, and the Reykjanes highway gleamed blackly in the glow of the headlights that could do little to penetrate the spray. The family members were using the drive home from the airport to ruminate on their holiday. They sat in silence, Nói behind the wheel, Vala beside him and their teenage son Tumi in the back, staring out at the endless lava-field. Two large suitcases had been stowed beside him since the boot didn't have room for all their baggage. They hadn't planned to do much shopping but, carried away by the low prices in America, had ended up lugging a mountain of stuff home across the Atlantic. Only time would tell how wise some of these purchases had been. They had got no further than the Leifsstöd terminal before Vala remarked that their new clothes didn't look quite as smart as they had in the States; somehow they didn't go with the miserable grey weather. Nói had to bite his lip to stop himself exploding.

'Strange to think we've got to go to work tomorrow.' He focused on the road ahead through the frantically labouring windscreen wipers.

'You were going to go in today, remember? Just be grateful I talked you out of it.' Vala twisted round. 'Are you asleep?'

'No.' Tumi continued to watch the world outside the windows.

Vala opened her mouth to add something, then turned back. Nói understood her change of heart; Tumi was taciturn by nature and when he was tired you might as well try to hold a conversation with the radio.

'God, it'll be so good to be back in our own bed.' Vala closed her eyes and put her hand on Nói's thigh. He wanted to ask if she'd forgotten how much she had been looking forward to leaving home only two weeks ago but checked the impulse. It was best for him to say as little as possible when he was tired as he had a tendency to come out with something regrettable.

'Weird to think strangers have been sleeping in our beds.'

They had done a house swap with an American couple who had been staying at their place while they were using their summer house in Florida. The money they had saved had gone on the contents of their suitcases. And more. Their credit card bill was going to be eye-watering, but then Nói had been aware of what would happen as soon as he let himself be cajoled into agreeing to this trip. It was lucky they were comfortably off; he ran a small software company that turned over a decent profit and Vala, who was a sought-after personal trainer, also earned a decent salary.

'Hope they were satisfied. It's a bugger about the barbecue.'

The American couple had also had access to their holiday chalet and had sent an e-mail mentioning that the barbecue wasn't working. Nói had answered immediately, running through every solution to the problem he could think of. He had received no reply. Vala interpreted the silence as meaning that the couple had got it working again, but Nói was worried they had been offended.

'Oh, it can't have made any difference to them.'

'Unless they turned up at the chalet with a pile of steaks.'

'They could have chucked them in a frying pan. It doesn't matter now, anyway.' As usual, Vala's attempt to stop him worrying had the opposite effect.

Nói tried to pretend he wasn't particularly bothered but his tone emerged sounding aggrieved. 'Maybe not. But I'd have preferred it if they'd sent us a final e-mail to say thanks and goodbye. We did.'

'We're not them. Perhaps they were too busy sightseeing to send us a message. Or the internet's stopped working at home.'

'There's nothing wrong with the internet.' Nói the IT expert couldn't stand any interference in his domain.

'OK, fine. There's nothing wrong with it.'

They spoke little for the rest of the drive. Not because they were angry with each other but because when their conversation descended into sniping like this it was better to shut up. Besides, there was nothing to discuss. Nothing more to be said about the internet or the foreigners' behaviour. There'd be time enough for that later. Fortunately they had always been able to sit in companionable silence, even when first getting to know each other; a time when people usually dread running out of things to say.

Predictably, they hit heavy morning traffic in Hafnarfjördur and had to crawl all the way into Reykjavík. Only when they reached Sudurgata in the west of town did they escape the rush-hour congestion and turn off to their own suburb of Skerjafjördur, which lay by the sea, almost at the end of the domestic airport runway. By the time they got there the heavens had emptied themselves. Nói turned off the squeaking windscreen wipers and the absence of noise left a strange emptiness in the car for the last few hundred metres home. The sight of their familiar street evoked an odd mixture of happiness and gloom in their hearts: they were home; their holiday was over. Nói suspected that all the happiness lay on his side and the gloom on his wife and son's. Now it was back to school for Tumi and work for him and Vala. The sultry heat and retail frenzy were a thing of the past.

Nói parked in the drive beside Vala's car, which they had lent to the Americans. Climbing out, they inhaled the bracingly cold, fresh air.

Tumi stood like a spare part, staring vacantly at nothing, while his tired and irritable parents busied themselves unloading the car. He made no move to help until snapped at by Nói, at which point the boy came to. If anything, he seemed even dreamier than usual. Nói put this and his clumsy movements down to tiredness, yet he suspected that something else was troubling his son. After all, he was the only one of them who had managed to sleep all the way across the Atlantic, dead to the world in a long-legged huddle before they had even taken off. There was something odd, too, about the way he kept staring up at the house. As if he expected to see the American couple waving at them from the windows: *Welcome home! We're thinking of staying put!*

'Are you OK, Tumi?' Vala had halted behind her son, who was blocking her way. He stood as if rooted to the spot, suitcase in hand, gazing at the upstairs windows.

'Mm? Yeah.' Tumi shook himself as if he had fallen asleep on his feet.

'Something wrong with the house?' Nói looked up, searching in vain for anything out of the ordinary. The curtains were in place; in fact the couple seemed to have drawn them all, even in the sitting room where the window dressings were only really for decoration. Home, sweet home. Nói smiled at the thought that popped into his head as he inspected the two-storey wooden house. When they bought it the intention had been to tear it down and replace it with a modern structure of concrete and glass, with door handles and cupboard fittings of brushed steel. But the homely atmosphere of the old house had won Nói over and in the end he had managed to persuade Vala to abandon her vision of a tastefully grey-toned interior. Instead they had done up the old place, extended the kitchen and knocked through some of the rooms. The result was a triumph in Nói's opinion; his childhood dream of a cosy home come true. Vala had seemed content too and Tumi didn't let the upheaval bother him. As long as the house had an internet connection, nothing else mattered to him.

'I can't see anything. What's the matter?'

'No. Yeah. I don't know.' Tumi lowered his gaze and started walking.

'You're just dazed from the journey. It's hardly surprising.' Nói wished his son could have pointed to something concrete – a broken window or a bird on the roof. Anything. He scanned the house again but still couldn't see anything amiss. Lethargy and fatigue gave way to an inexplicable sense of dread.

Together they managed to ferry all the luggage from the car to the front door. Their suitcases seemed to have grown heavier on the trip and as they stood there in a heap they gave the impression of containing an infinite amount of stuff that would now have to be found a home. Nói shook his head; they hadn't needed anything to start with, so they would probably end up having to throw away perfectly good stuff they already owned to make room for all this new gear. He sighed under his breath, then reminded himself that he was home at last and that this was a reason to celebrate.

When they went inside, Nói's pleasure faded slightly. There was an unfamiliar smell in the air and their home seemed indefinably alien, as if the foreign couple had made it their own during the two weeks they'd been living there. Perhaps the same was true of their place in Florida; perhaps there was a lingering trace there of his family's presence. If so, he wished he could go back, fling open all the windows and give it an even more thorough clean.

Nói fumbled for the light switch in the hope that the brightness would dispel his unease. The entrance hall was lit up and he saw the familiar cupboards and shoe rack, looking unnaturally tidy. Before leaving they had blitzed the entire house, including the chaos in the hall. The pairs of shoes were placed neatly in a row, side by side, as if to show that an unusually tidy family lived there. Which was not so far from the truth, if you ignored Tumi's room.

Vala gathered up the pile of letters and newspapers that they had stepped over on their way in, and, yawning, handed them to Nói. She often said that good news never came in the post. He flicked quickly through the envelopes and placed a late Christmas card on top of the pile. Vala bent over him, trying unsuccessfully to identify the handwriting. It didn't actually matter who the card was from as they hadn't sent any this year because they had been too busy preparing for their trip. No doubt they would be crossed off several people's lists as a result.

Before leaving, they had taken down only some of the

Christmas decorations. This had been a source of concern to Nói as he was afraid the couple weren't Christian and might be offended. Besides, Christmas was over and it seemed tasteless to leave them up. Vala had asked if he was all right in the head: who on earth would be offended by Christmas decorations? She wouldn't mind the decorations of other religions herself. Anyway, it looked much more homely with them up and the couple would enjoy that. There hadn't been so much as a pine needle in their house in Florida.

'Puss, puss, puss!' Vala hung up her new jacket, which looked shockingly garish among the sober coats in the cupboard. 'Kitty, kitty, kit!'

'What? Don't say they locked the cat out?'

He usually appeared immediately the front door opened, even if they had only taken out the rubbish. Had something happened to the poor creature? That might explain why the foreigners hadn't answered Nói's e-mails. Perhaps they were traumatised because they'd killed or lost their pet and didn't know how to own up. If that was the case, Nói damn well hoped the Christmas decorations had caused mortal offence.

But at that moment a pathetic mewing was heard from inside the house and shortly afterwards Púki appeared and rubbed himself against the doorframe. The concrete box they had originally planned to build would have required a greyhound. A tabby cat wouldn't have gone with the tasteful monochrome colour scheme.

Vala picked up the cat in her arms and buried her face in his soft fur. 'Gosh, he's lighter and thinner than I remembered.'

This pleased Nói as they had long been planning to put Púki on a diet.

'Did you miss us?' Vala murmured into his fur and was rewarded by a mouthful of cat hair. But instead of putting him down, she hugged him tighter. 'If you two bring the cases in, I'll make sure Púki doesn't get underfoot.'

In no time Nói and Tumi had almost filled the hall with luggage. 'That's the lot.' Nói smiled weakly. They took off their coats but after hanging his up, Nói pulled a man's coat out of the cupboard. 'Recognise this?' Vala shook her head. The garment was short and dark, and looked too big for Nói.

Vala put the cat down and inspected the coat narrowly before handing it back to Nói. 'No. Never seen it before. Can they have forgotten it?' An image of the couple's house ran through her mind with all the countless places they themselves could have left something.

'Unless it was left behind after the party.' The weekend before they went abroad they had thrown a thirty-fifth birthday party for Nói, inviting their wide circle of friends. Some of the guests had left the party late, rather the worse for wear, so it wasn't impossible that one of them had headed out into the night in his shirtsleeves. But no, that couldn't be right, and Vala corrected herself immediately. 'Except that I sorted through the cupboard before we went to America and I'd certainly have noticed it then.'

'Oh, great.' Nói hung it up again. 'I suppose we'll have to post it to them. Though I guess it would make sense to wait and see if we come across anything else of theirs.' He looked round irritably. 'Where are the keys? Weren't they going to leave them on the mat?'

'There was nothing on the floor but post and papers.' Vala was right; a bunch of keys would have been visible among them. 'It looks as if they've just let it all pile up on the mat.

How extraordinary. You'd have thought they could have picked it up. We tidied up theirs.'

'Un-bloody-believable.' Nói shook his head.

The cat perked up when they went into the kitchen and wouldn't stop yowling until Tumi had filled his empty dish. The visitors had departed the previous day and Púki had obviously gobbled up all the food they'd left him. His water bowl was dry as a bone but the cat didn't seem as interested in that when it was filled. This wasn't surprising as he generally preferred the water left in the bottom of the shower tray.

'Here they are.' Vala picked up the car keys from the kitchen table where they were lying beside a neat stack of letters and newspapers. Apparently the Americans had picked up the post for the first part of their stay, then let things slide. She tapped the pile. 'But the other bunch is missing. With the keys to the house and chalet.'

Nói had cheered up but groaned when his satisfaction proved short-lived. 'Jesus. The instructions about the bloody keys weren't exactly complicated. We didn't just chuck theirs in the corner.' Vala often complained that he had a tendency to obsess over things that got on his nerves. It looked as if the Americans were going to prove an endless source of inspiration.

'Well, obviously *they* didn't do that with them either. But it doesn't matter. The keys'll turn up and, anyway, we have a spare set.' Vala yawned. 'Let's forget it and go to bed. I'm dying on my feet.'

'I'm off to bed.' Tumi left the box of cat food untidily on the table. 'I'll wake up when I wake up. Don't disturb me.' Neither of his parents bothered to take note of this instruction. When the time came to unpack their cases he would be woken up whether he liked it or not. They watched him go into the hall and listened to his thunderous progress up the stairs, two at a time as usual.

Once they had heard the door to his room close, Nói broke the silence. He was staring at the bunch of keys in Vala's hand. 'Do you think this is their revenge for the barbecue? Deliberately losing the keys to the chalet?' No sooner had he spoken than he realised he was too tired to think straight.

'I'm sure it is.' Vala smiled, then pulled him to her when she saw his eyes straying to the computer in a corner of the kitchen. 'Don't check on that now. It can wait.' But Nói wouldn't be dissuaded. Gently freeing himself from her arms, he sat down in front of the computer, turned it on and waited impatiently for it to start up.

'I just want to check everything's OK. Supposing they've left the keys in the door and some idiot's got in.' He logged into the chalet webcam. Nói had installed the surveillance system after a wave of break-ins at the holiday colony a year or so before. The camera showed the open-plan living room and kitchen area, as well as most of the decking outside the window. The system had a built-in motion sensor; although the camera was always on, it only saved the footage that included some kind of movement, plus ten seconds before the movement and ten seconds after it. The system could be switched on or off as required.

'What are you going to do if it's been trashed?' Vala stood behind him, watching the screen. 'There's no way you're charging up there now.' Vala hadn't been quite as sold on the idea of buying a holiday chalet in the countryside as he had. It struck him that she might even be pleased if it was broken into.

'I just want to check. If necessary I could ring someone or go to bed now and head up there later.' Nói was glad Vala didn't ask who exactly he was planning to call. There was no caretaker on site and their chalet stood some distance from the main colony to which it officially belonged. His worries proved groundless, however. Everything looked fine when the picture appeared on screen. The old three-piece suite in the living room, which they really should replace, the clunky TV and DVD player, the small kitchen area. Everything was as it should be, intact and untouched. Nói couldn't hide his relief and Vala shared it, though for different reasons. 'Brilliant. Now can we go to bed?'

Nói stood up, having recovered his good mood at last. He was even happier when they saw their bed. The Americans had changed the sheets and although Vala was a little put out by the non-matching linen they had used, she was too relieved to complain. Nói had stripped off and was about to collapse into bed when he announced that he had forgotten to turn off the computer. Vala sighed and told him to relax. It worked. He lay down and conked out even before she did.

The family were all sound asleep when the computer in the kitchen suddenly came to life, so the cat was the only witness when the webcam picked up a movement. He watched the dark picture, then hissed at the screen. Darting out of the kitchen, he bounded upstairs and halted before the open door to the master bedroom. There he sat down on the threshold and mewed plaintively at his sleeping owners.

Chapter 4

20 January 2014

The Christmas bauble resembled a small, fat Santa Claus. It grinned merrily at Nína from where it hung from the curtain pole in the hall, but drew no answering smile from her. She felt an urge to smash it. Thröstur had chosen December to try and kill himself, and although Christmas was over, she still had to clear up after it, deliver the few gifts they had bought people and take down the corny decorations. She didn't know why she couldn't galvanise herself to get on with it, since the shiny tat did nothing but reopen the wound every time she laid eyes on it. One consolation was that they hadn't put up many decorations, so when she finally got round to it the job wouldn't take long. But she couldn't drum up the energy. All she had done was drag the Christmas tree out onto the pavement in mid-January, still dressed in its baubles and fairy lights. It had tumbled around out there for a week before vanishing, and Nína suspected the old man on the ground floor of having something to do with that. Pity he didn't have a key to her place, if he was that keen.

The flat was almost as airless and dusty as the archives at the police station. Even though she'd hardly spent any time at home recently, it was well overdue a clean. Well, that would have to wait. Nína threw off her jacket, missed the peg and left it lying on the floor. This would only be a brief stop. She would have gone straight from work to the hospital but her sister had announced she was coming round. She was obviously worried and Nína wanted to reassure her that she was all right. Task of the day: look normal. Sad, of course, but not unhealthily so. She hoped this would deter Berglind from any further attempts to try and cheer her up. She just wanted to be left alone.

While the coffee was percolating, Nína drew back the kitchen curtains for the first time since Thröstur had been admitted to hospital. She had wanted to spare the neighbours the unedifying sight of her sitting howling at the kitchen table, and also to avoid seeing the garage. She would pull the curtains across the windows again the moment Berglind had gone, though fits of weeping in the kitchen were a thing of the past. She hadn't set foot in the garage since Thröstur had left it in an ambulance, and as far as she knew no one else had had any reason to go in there since the detectives had finished their examination. If Nína had had access to a bulldozer, the low-rise building would have been flattened by now.

In hindsight, she should have noticed something was wrong when Thröstur's attitude to the garage changed almost overnight. When they'd bought the flat six months ago, his behaviour had been perfectly normal. At first he hadn't been particularly keen on the property as prices in the west end of town were on the steep side. But when she managed to persuade him to view the flat, he was infected by her enthusiasm, and from what she remembered the garage had played no small part in that. At the time she had assumed he was planning to tinker with the car or start collecting tools, though he had no real interest in either. The garage had stood more or less empty for the first few months while they were busy doing up the flat. But from the middle of November Thröstur had taken to staring at it out of the window for long periods, as if he expected a figure to appear in one of the garage windows, or was afraid someone would try to break into it.

Nína had assumed he was feeling daunted about having to start work on it just when they had finally got the flat straight. She'd told him she couldn't care less if he left it for now, but her words seemed to have no effect. He would stand for long periods at the window, silently contemplating the building. A week before he did the deed, she had come across him standing in the middle of the garage, lost in thought. He pretended nothing was up when she nudged him and led him out, but was quiet and distant for the rest of the evening. Now, Nína kept wondering if he'd already made up his mind then; whether his evasive gaze had been nothing to do with the problem of how to make use of the building, but a sign that he was calculating the strength of the steel tracks that supported the hefty door. It was one of so many things she would never know. What they hadn't told one another would never be put into words now. For example, she had never told Thröstur about her problems at work, for fear he would go ballistic. He would have been quite capable of beating up her colleague or – worse – writing about the incident in the papers. But now there was no question of changing her mind and confiding in him, as she would have done in the course of time.

Nína watched the coffee drip down. With every drop the kitchen smelt more homely and she inhaled deeply in the hope that it could somehow invigorate her soul. Nína would never have admitted as much but she had a suspicion that the bloody garage itself had somehow planted the idea of suicide in Thröstur's mind. She knew she wasn't alone in thinking that there was some kind of curse on the building. Twice she had seen children from the neighbourhood dawdling along the street, only to break into a run as they passed the garage, eyeing it fearfully. No sooner had they reached a safe distance than they slowed down again, though some glanced round as if to make sure no one was following them.

About a week ago a plastic ball had landed by the garage door as Nína was parking her car. The woolly-hatted heads of the neighbours' children had popped up above the fence but the smiles were wiped off their rosy faces when they saw where their ball had fallen, and after exchanging glances, they had made themselves scarce.

Reluctant as she was to pull back the curtains and let in the grey afternoon light, it would be worth it if the kitchen seemed more inviting as a result. The solo performance of *Woman Making a Slow but Steady Recovery* was to be staged here for the benefit of a single audience member – Berglind – but in the gloom with the curtains drawn it would be almost impossible to play a sane woman convincingly.

Nína gathered up the post and newspapers she had been throwing on the kitchen table for weeks and flung the whole lot in the bin without so much as reading the envelopes. She put a few dirty plates in the dishwasher and set it going, and the low humming and sloshing it emitted sounded comfortingly mundane. Next she arranged some fruit in a glass bowl so the rotten bits wouldn't show. Luckily there was an unopened milk carton that ought to be OK, though it was past its sell-by date. To be on the safe side she poured the milk into a cream jug and placed it with two cups on the kitchen table. Surveying the scene, Nína felt the overall impression still left something to be desired. Removing the Christmas candlestick from the top of the fridge made a slight improvement. After that she sat down and waited.

Her eyes strayed to the window and a chill ran through her but she wouldn't let herself look away. It was a garage. A square, concrete box that had stood there for decades. It wasn't the building's fault that Thröstur had tried to kill himself in there; the decisive factor had been the presence of a suitably sturdy support from which a rope could be slung. That was all. Nína continued to stare out of the window. The sooner she accepted that the problem had lain with Thröstur not the garage, the sooner she'd be reconciled to the building.

As if to dispute this, the brightly coloured plastic ball was still lying there in the slush. But it wasn't only the ball that made her uneasy: high up in the garage wall, two rectangular windows squinted like black eyes. On one of the sills was a flower pot, the shrivelled plant like a skeleton in silhouette. Nína tried to force herself to look at the windows but couldn't, she was so afraid of seeing a movement inside. Perhaps Thröstur had felt the same when he stood here staring at the garage as if mesmerised. She pushed away the thought. She was not going the same way as him, that much was certain.

The big, ugly cracks in the pebbledash wall put her in mind of the broken veins on the cheeks of the man who had shared a ward with Thröstur for the first week. In the end she had plucked up the courage to ask if her husband could be moved to a single room so she could be alone with him. To her surprise, he had been moved two days later and she no longer had to cope with other visitors or patients. But having her wish fulfilled turned out to be a mixed blessing. Now there was nothing to distract her, so she sat alone for the most part, listening to the beeping and sucking of the machines Thröstur was hooked up to. Occasionally one of the nurses would pop their head round the door, but otherwise they might have been alone in the world, Nína and the empty carapace that had once been Thröstur.

Dusk slowly filled in the cracks in the garage wall. Her sister was already a quarter of an hour late. This was unusual, as normally you could set your watch by Berglind. But it didn't really matter; she wasn't going anywhere except up to the hospital, and Berglind only had home waiting for her. In spite of this, Nína was keen to get the visit over with as quickly as possible.

She opened the kitchen window a crack. It was as if the wind had been waiting to pounce because instantly a violent gust blew the curtain in. Old notes and photos of her and Thröstur tried in vain to escape their moorings on the fridge door. Then all was still again. The faint rumble of traffic blended with the noise of the dishwasher and Nína felt a little better. Silence was a constant reminder of what she had lost. Thröstur used to turn on the football the moment he walked in the door. But it didn't cross her mind to let the excited sports commentators loose in the room, any more than it did to lay the table for Thröstur and pretend he still lived here. The television sat unused in the sitting room and Nína averted her eyes from it on the rare occasions she went in there. If she gave it half a chance the reflection in the black glass screen would unnerve her by showing odd shadows and movements, just as the garage windows did.

The doorbell rang shrilly and Nína stood up. At last. She paused briefly in front of the hall mirror and swore under her breath when she saw how haggard she looked. There was no point pretending she was in good spirits if she had black rings under her eyes and wild hair – Berglind would think she had finally tipped over the edge or was overdoing the meds. Nína had in fact refused all the pills she was offered, whether they were to help her sleep or stave off depression, though with every day that passed the thought of such solutions became increasingly attractive. She was held back by stubbornness and the certainty that dulling her senses wouldn't help in the long run. Any more than drawing the curtains would cause the garage to disappear.

Nína licked her fingers and wiped her eyes in a vain attempt to hide the signs of exhaustion. The image the mirror presented her with was unchanged: a familiar face imprinted with shadows. She slapped her cheeks to make them pink, which slightly improved the overall effect.

The doorbell rang again and Nína hurriedly answered it. 'Is the bell broken?' People often said the sisters looked almost identical, but right now few would have thought so. Berglind was the picture of health, a natural glow in her cheeks. Her long blonde hair swirled around her head in the wind and she had to pull a thick strand from her lips. 'Aren't you going to let me in?'

Nína stepped aside and Berglind entered the hall with a sigh of relief. Nína received an icy kiss on the cheek and watched as her sister tried to tidy her hair.

'Should I just throw my coat on the floor?' Berglind eyed Nína's jacket. As she looked up her gaze encountered the Santa Claus and Nína regretted not having smashed the bloody thing after all. Berglind was regarding her anxiously. 'You look terrible. Worse than last time, and that's saying something.' She frowned. 'And what on earth's wrong with your cheeks?'

Clearly her attempt to bring a little colour to her face had misfired. 'Nothing. I'm just tired.' Nína led the way to the kitchen, eager to go in there as soon as possible so Berglind wouldn't have a chance to look around. The kitchen was her stage and that was where the audience member was to sit. 'Coffee?' Behind her she heard Berglind say yes to a small cup. The element was on the blink in the coffee-maker and no steam rose from the cups when Nína poured them. She sat down facing her sister. 'Sorry, it's not very hot.'

'Doesn't matter.' Berglind took a sip and put down her cup. She didn't take another. 'How are you doing?' She glanced around, apparently more satisfied with the kitchen than the hall. Nína's efforts hadn't been wasted. 'I haven't heard from you for ages.'

'I'm always up at the hospital. Or at work.'

Berglind nodded. 'I see.' She opened her mouth to say something else but thought better of it. She looked down at the table as if for inspiration, then raised her eyes again, her expression sombre. 'How long can you carry on like this?' Nína could feel her own face hardening. Her sister took her hand. 'I'm not suggesting you should stop visiting Thröstur. Only wondering if you could cut down your visits a bit so you can start living again – give yourself time to do something else apart from just working.'

'It's not as if he . . .' Nína always had trouble finding the words for what Thröstur had done. If he had died it wouldn't have been a problem, then she could say he had committed suicide, killed himself, taken his own life, topped himself, done himself in, passed away . . . But he was neither alive nor dead. 'It's not as if he's been like this long. It takes time to get over it. To accept it.' But Nína didn't want to accept it. She wanted everything to go back to how it had been.

'It's been nearly eight weeks, Nína.' Berglind squeezed her hand. 'No one's expecting you to be on top of the world but you've got to start looking to the future. A little bit at a time. You could start by breaking up your hospital routine in some way. If you just go on like this, working and sitting with Thröstur forever, it can only end one way. Try going to the gym, or swimming, or to the cinema. I'll go with you.' Berglind squeezed her hand again. 'At least take some time off work – surely they'd understand? If you like you can stay with me and Dóri for a while. I quite understand that you can't face being here. In fact, what the hell, why don't you move in with us properly? Just because Thröstur chose death doesn't mean you should give up on your own life.' The superficial tidy-up had obviously failed to deceive her. 'We can put you up in the den. It's not as if we use it much.'

'It's very kind of you to offer. But there's no need. I'm starting to get on top of things.' Nína did her best to appear convincing: don't smile too much or too little. 'Please try not to worry about me. I'm in a horrible place right now but the end's in sight.'

'Are you sure about that?' Berglind knew her too well to be taken in.

'Absolutely positive.' Nína didn't drop her eyes, didn't give in to the temptation to look out of the window. Even the hateful garage was better than Berglind's penetrating gaze. 'I'm getting there. Honestly.' She freed her cold hand from her sister's warm one. 'Anyway, can you imagine what it'd be like if I lived with you?' Nína's smile was suddenly genuine. 'It would be a nightmare. Remember how furious you used to be if I went into your bedroom when we were kids? No, I really can't picture it.'

Berglind laughed. 'I don't have any posters for you to scribble on these days, so we should be OK. But no, perhaps it *is* a bad idea. At least let's go to the gym together or something, though. It would do me good too.'

Unlike Nína, Berglind was one of those people who loathe exercise. The fact that she was prepared to go to the gym for her sister's sake spoke louder than words. While friends were quietly dropping off the radar, Berglind kept phoning and coming round. With her, Nína never felt as if she was ruining the atmosphere simply by being there. 'Are you sure you want to go to the gym? Why don't we just go to the dentist together and have our old fillings drilled out and replaced?' Now it was Nína's turn to squeeze her sister's hand. 'I suggest we do something else when I'm finally feeling more human – something you'd enjoy. And I promise it'll be soon. Just not quite yet.' For a moment Nína wondered if she should tell her sister about the old case she had come across in the police archives earlier that day; that as a seven-year-old Thröstur had been involved in an inquiry which apparently related to a suicide, and that she suspected this was the explanation for what he had done all these years later. Recently she had been racking her brain for a possible reason, without success, and this explanation was no more foolish than some of the others she had grasped at. She was no expert in psychology but she'd learnt enough about people through her job to realise that their behaviour could be governed by the most unexpected things.

The problem was that Nína didn't know what the old inquiry had been about. She had skimmed through other files in the archives in a vain search for further information but the page seemed to be the only one extant about the incident. She didn't know whose suicide it was or even if the case was concerned with a suicide. The report could have ended up in the wrong folder by mistake, or perhaps the page had become separated from the rest and gone astray.

'A penny for your thoughts?' Berglind was frowning. They weren't accustomed to sitting in silence. As far as Nína could remember, her sister hadn't shut up since she'd first learnt to talk. When they shared a room as children she had even talked regularly in her sleep. At the time Nína had thought it was because the day wasn't long enough for her to get everything off her chest. And because Berglind had talked non-stop when they were growing up, Nína had been forced to cut in every time she wanted to speak, which had left her with the bad habit of interrupting people. It had got her into trouble more than once when talking to her superiors at work.

Berglind tried again: 'Tell me what you're thinking about.'

'Nothing. Well, actually I was remembering how much you used to talk as a kid.' In an attempt to appear casual, Nína took refuge in a mouthful of cold coffee. No, it would be a bad idea to mention the old case to Berglind – at this stage. She was bound to want to chew over it endlessly and Nína wasn't ready for that; she needed more information first. To start with, she meant to have a word with Thröstur's father, who ought to remember the incident, although it was a long time ago. His mother had died of breast cancer five years ago, so she wasn't around to ask. But if Nína managed to extract some information from her father-in-law, she would probably be able to use it to find out more. Information was never far away, especially if you had access to various systems and national databases through the police. She hoped she wouldn't be sacked or forced to take leave before she'd had a chance to try. 'I'm just tired and sleepy. Let's stop talking about me and my problems. I'm so bored of myself it would do me good to change the subject.'

They remained chatting there for a while until it became glaringly obvious that Berglind was avoiding any mention of her own husband. Nína had noticed this tendency in others; it was as if women found it inappropriate to say anything in her hearing that might remind her that their husbands were alive and well. As if it might make her envious. It was typical that when Berglind finally showed signs of making a move, she was careful not to say she had to get home to Dóri but rather that 'duty called'. It was kindly meant, like so many wrong-headed ideas. But in spite of this they hugged each other affectionately as they said goodbye on the front steps. Nína had promised that they would go out and have fun together some time in the next couple of weeks. Do something that wouldn't result in stiff muscles.

Berglind seemed satisfied and didn't notice her sister's expression as she released her. Nína's eyes had accidentally fallen on the garage while they were hugging and she couldn't help noticing that the plastic ball had vanished.

She almost ran into the kitchen to close the window and draw the curtains again before heading off to the hospital. She had no wish to linger here any longer than necessary.

Her stomach churned as she caught sight of the garage in the instant before the curtain fell into place. She wanted to be sick.

There, beside the old flower pot on the garage windowsill, was the plastic ball.

Chapter 5

26 January 2014

The fog closes in with alarming suddenness. One minute they can see ocean to the south and land to the north, the next nothing but a stony grey blankness that shifts and stirs in an oddly languid manner whichever way they look, as if the world has decided to consign the rock to oblivion by sweeping it under a carpet of cloud. The effect is so unreal that Helgi's feelings veer back and forth between pleasure and anxiety as he is adjusting to the transformation. Although he's no fan of classical music, it seems to him that the sound of violins would be peculiarly appropriate at this moment. But in the absence of plangent strings he has to make do with the roaring of the waves far below. In the fog the noise is oddly intensified, as if the sea wishes to remind them of its presence now that it's no longer before their eyes.

Shortly after the fog descended, Ívar had shouted to Helgi to come back to the lighthouse; it would be safest until visibility improved. Helgi, who was perched on the edge of the helipad at the time, had felt relieved. He had chosen the spot to keep out of the others' way while they worked. The echo of their voices carried to him, increasing his feeling of isolation as he sat there as if alone in the world, the grey cloud before his eyes.

So far Ívar has avoided speaking to Helgi if he can help it, and the other two seem to be unconsciously following his example. At least, they have no reason to snub him, whatever Ívar's motives. Helgi guesses the man is still wondering what he said or did that evening they met in the bar. This suggests he doesn't always behave himself when he's drunk, which doesn't surprise Helgi as sober Ívar is not exactly a charmer. Still, he hopes the man is becoming reconciled to the idea of his being here, as he'd like to be allowed to join in their conversation once it gets dark.

Helgi swallows the last bite of his sandwich. Their cool-box had looked full when they opened it but already there's worryingly little left. The remaining food will have to stretch to all tomorrow's meals until the helicopter picks them up in the evening. They decided to have an early supper while the fog was blocking their view and are now sitting in a quiet huddle by the lighthouse, eating and listening to the noises around them. Full but not satisfied, Helgi decides to break the ice. He was careful to eat less than the others, conscious that if they run short of food, they're bound to look at him, the fat man, and wonder if he took more than his share. 'Did we bring a lifebuoy with us or is there one lying around here somewhere?' The last part of his question is redundant. Since the helicopter vanished from sight three hours ago, Helgi has seen everything there is to see on the rock, every stone, every blade of grass. It's unthinkable that he could have failed to notice a lifebuoy.

Tóti is the first to answer. 'No.' He swallows and dislodges the crumbs of his sandwich from his teeth before continuing. 'Are you wondering what'll happen if we fall off?'

Helgi nods. He folds up his sandwich wrapper and puts it

in the rubbish container. 'I thought it would be useful to have one to hand. Just in case.'

'There's no point throwing a lifebuoy to a dead man.' Ívar rubs a hand over his balding scalp as if to check whether a bird has landed on it while he was eating. Two gulls, drawn by the smell when they took out the food, are now hovering overhead, invisible in the fog. From time to time they swoop down like missiles out of the greyness, swerving just above their heads and disappearing again. At some point in their lives they have learnt to be wary of humans and Ívar underlines this lesson by lobbing stones after them. 'The sea's shallow at the base of the rock. If anyone falls off, that'll be the end of their worries.'

So far Helgi has had little to do with the woman, Heida, who has been inside the lighthouse, installing the new transmitter, so the huskiness of her voice comes as a surprise when she finally opens her mouth. 'Can't we talk about something else?' She doesn't address anyone in particular but peers out into the fog, as if talking to someone floating in mid-air.

'Sure. Talk about whatever you like. I'm not stopping you.' Ívar leans against the whitewashed wall, closes his eyes and rests his hands comfortably on his stomach. They are weather-beaten, with skin as coarse as that on his face. Helgi can't help thinking that these would be the perfect hands for committing atrocities; these are fingers that long to maim. As if reading his mind, Ívar shoves them in his anorak pockets as he speaks again. 'For God's sake not politics, though. It could end badly, this close to the edge.'

Heida's expression indicates that she doesn't want to discuss politics any more than she wants to discuss the rocks at the bottom of the cliff. Helgi can't tell if she's uncomfortable about being the only woman among a group of strange men, or unnerved by the precipice. He's ill at ease himself, though he's never been especially bothered by heights. He casts around for some subject to cheer her up. 'How's the technical stuff going? Everything up and running?' It's as lame as talking about the weather. Suddenly the sandwich feels like lead in his stomach and he wishes he hadn't bolted it down so fast.

'The equipment's in place but not connected yet. The installation and tests always take ages. Generally much longer than you expect.' Her cheeks are flushed but otherwise her face is chalk-white, which makes her dark eyes appear black in contrast. The effect is to make her look nervous, as if she's on the verge of confiding some fact of vital importance. Helgi wouldn't mind taking a few snaps of her without her knowledge. But there's no chance in the present circumstances; she couldn't fail to notice his big, cumbersome camera. 'Some things you just can't hurry.'

'Do you all work together?' Helgi assumes they do, yet they don't behave like colleagues around each other. While he was taking pictures earlier, he couldn't help overhearing the echo of their conversation, and as far as he can tell this is the first time Heida has opened her mouth. The men were working outside, of course, but even so you'd have thought they'd exchange the odd word in passing. Perhaps she's naturally shy and retiring.

'No.' It's Tóti who answers. 'I was only called out at the last minute. They obviously didn't trust you to do the job on your own, mate.' He throws the scrunched-up clingfilm from his sandwich at Ívar, who is evidently not amused. The rubbish is caught by the breeze and flies over the cliff.

Heida breaks the momentary silence. 'I work for the firm that imports the radio equipment.' She wraps up the rest of her sandwich, which she has barely touched, and puts it in her pocket.

'Have you been there long?' Tóti wriggles over to the lighthouse and, following Ívar's example, leans against the wall and closes his eyes.

'Years.' Heida clearly isn't going to volunteer any more information.

'Strange I haven't run into you before,' Ívar comments. 'I usually go along when they have to do maintenance on the transmitters.' He picks a yellow stalk of grass and puts it in his mouth. It waggles up and down as he chews it.

'I've always been based in the office.' Heida fiddles with the ring-pull from her can, then crushes it in her small, neat hand.

'You must know Konni then?' Ívar spits out the grass stem and it blows back in his face.

'I'm his daughter.' Heida stares at Ívar's closed eyes but he merely nods. It seems to Helgi that Tóti gives more of a reaction; he twitches, but that might just be because he's falling asleep.

They sit like this for a while, Ívar and Tóti dozing, Heida and Helgi chatting about the weather and the gulls. It becomes increasingly difficult to keep the stilted conversation going and by the time they finally abandon the attempt Helgi is scarlet in the face. He's never been particularly socially adroit and with women the small ration of conversational ability God gave him tends to desert him completely.

Heida stares in the direction of the helipad, squinting now and then, as if trying to discern something in the dense cloud.

Helgi follows her gaze but can't see anything. 'Is there something up there?' He can't imagine it'd be anything but a gull.

'No.' Heida lowers her gaze. 'It's just so creepy somehow. You can't see, and yet you can. If it was just solid grey it would be different, but it's always shifting, so you keep thinking something's about to appear.'

Helgi stares into the fog and immediately understands what she means. The constant movement of the tiny drops of moisture makes it impossible to focus on one spot. 'How long can fog last out here?'

'No idea. Perhaps they know.' She jerks her chin towards the dozing workmen. 'It wasn't forecast, but then I've heard that weather models can't cope with fog. I suppose it's completely unpredictable.' She no sooner stops speaking than the fog lifts slightly. Instead of smiling at the coincidence, Heida shudders and there is a remote look in her eyes. 'I've always found fog really creepy. It disorientates you and makes the world seem different. Perhaps it's because fog doesn't follow any rules. The truth gets lost. Do you know what I mean?'

Helgi looks into Heida's glowing dark eyes and doesn't know how to answer. The truth has never seemed particularly clear to him, with or without fog. Experience has taught him that most things in life are too complicated for easy distinctions between right and wrong. But he doesn't feel up to trying to expound his personal philosophy in the present circumstances. It's not especially profound, after all. It's based on the idea that life is tough and the sooner you accept the fact, the less painful your failures will be. 'Yes, I think so.' The spark in Heida's eyes is extinguished and Helgi realises he has disappointed her, though he can't work out how.

She turns and strains her eyes south to where the ocean is hidden behind a grey curtain. 'My uncle used to work on a fisheries development project in Africa and they told him there that if fog stays around for a long time it signifies bad luck. If it lasts more than half a day it means that some important person will die, presumably the village headman.'

'Which of us fits the description – if the fog sticks around that long?'

'Ívar, I suppose.' Heida glances at the man sleeping propped against the wall. His jaw is slack, his mouth half open. 'He's the oldest, anyway.' She turns back to Helgi. 'And the bossiest.'

Although Ívar is plainly sound asleep, Helgi is not quite so sure about Tóti. His eyes are closed but his alert expression suggests that he has not quite dropped off. Helgi would love to agree with Heida and ask if she too finds the guy sinister, but changes the subject in case Tóti's eavesdropping. 'How do you suppose superstitions like that come about?'

Heida shrugs. 'Maybe a headman died after a fog and people connected the two.'

'People die every day, headmen included. You'd have thought it would take more than that to convert an incident into a full-blown superstition.'

'Are you implying that it might have some basis in reality? That fog is an evil omen?' Heida smiles scornfully. It doesn't suit her. But the expression vanishes when he starts speaking again.

'No, of course not. But perhaps it happened more than once in short succession. It must take quite a lot for a whole people to adopt something like that as a superstition.' Copying Ívar, Helgi puts a blade of dry grass in his mouth and waggles it to and fro. It's ludicrous to think this African belief might have any substance to it. But irrational as it is, the longer he sits there, the more he can't help wondering. The cloud seems to be thickening, which only enhances the effect.

'He also said they believed the dead would appear in fog if they had a score to settle with the living. How do you explain that?' Heida sounds as if she actually wants to hear his opinion.

'I can't. Ghost stories rarely have any rational explanation. Maybe that's why they're so tenacious.' Helgi peers in the direction of the helipad in the hope that visibility is improving after all. An icy chill runs down his spine when he spots a dark shadow where the platform ought to be. He squints to get a better view. It must be a rock he hasn't noticed before. That's odd though, because it appears to be quite a large boulder or pillar of stone, roughly the size of a human figure. The fog closes in again and the shadow disappears. Yet Helgi's eyes remain fixed on the spot and when a light gust of wind sweeps the cloud away, he can see nothing but the square helipad and irregular crag beyond. Nothing that can explain the shape he thought he saw.

Realising how fast he's breathing, Helgi concentrates on trying to calm down. He has been warned that Stóridrangur can have a bad effect on the inexperienced. People can lose their heads and if that happens the only solution is to sit down and focus on taking deep, even breaths. At the time he was told this he'd smiled at the idea, but now he is far from amused. The simple advice helps. Breathe in. Breathe out. What he thought he saw was all in his head. Breathe in. Breathe out. Slowly.

Then he looks at Heida. She is staring fixedly at the same spot, apparently equally shaken. Her eyes meet his and she says in a low, breathless voice: 'What the hell was that?'

Helgi can't answer her, any more than he can explain what he's doing out here, balancing precariously on a pillar of rock in the middle of the ocean. He shouldn't be here. There's no longer any doubt in his mind: the fog has come bearing gifts. But surely there can't be any truth in what Heida said about the dead having a score to settle with the living? If there is, there aren't many of them to choose from.

Chapter 6

23 January 2014

It was midday when Nói finally awoke under the baking-hot duvet. He shook off his drowsiness and the remnants of a dream involving a dark night at the chalet. He had no wish to recall the details. Reaching for Vala, he encountered thin air, and vaguely remembered an unappealing invitation to get up and help her unpack their cases. The hopelessly clashing sheets, which they hadn't used since they'd first lived together in student accommodation, irritated his skin when he moved. He couldn't remember noticing anything wrong with them in those days and reflected ruefully that once one had become used to smooth, expensive, high-thread-count cotton, there was no turning back.

He made a mental note to change the sheets before evening. Poverty held no charms for him; it was too reminiscent of the relentless struggle and privations of his childhood. It had motivated Nói to pull out all the stops from his very first day at school, despite the lack of support from home. Fortunately it had been instilled in him as a small boy that those who were diligent in their studies went on to get good jobs and become rich, so he had done everything in his power to avoid ending up a feckless alcoholic like his mother. Now that he had realised his dreams there was no question of looking back through rose-tinted glasses. The sheets were going in the dustbin and he wouldn't listen to any talk from Vala of using them for rags.

The face that confronted him in the large mirror of their en-suite bathroom was puffy from sleep, with pronounced bags under the eyes. There was a rasp of stubble as he rubbed his cheek. He splashed himself with cold water, glad to be free of the chlorine smell you got in America. He would have liked to let the pure, icy stream play over his face and rinse away the tiredness but decided to jump in the shower instead. As he washed, the longing for a mug of strong coffee became so insistent that he could almost taste it on his lips in the cloud of steam. He was fed up with knocking back American dishwater from giant cardboard cups. His relief at being home was suddenly so overwhelming that he wanted to emit a holler of triumph like a hunter who has brought down a lion. He felt an urge to run downstairs and put the family's passports through the shredder so they would never be tempted to go abroad again. The sound of movement in the bathroom interrupted his domestic bliss and spitting out soap bubbles he called out to Vala.

No answer.

'Vala, is that you?'

There was no sound but a furtive rustle. Nói turned off the tap. 'Tumi?' No response. The rustling had stopped. Foam dripped down his forehead, stinging his eyes, and he turned on the water again. It must have been Púki, though usually the cat avoided the bathroom like the plague if someone was in the shower.

When he stepped out of the cubicle, the cat was sitting outside the bathroom door, yellow eyes glaring, following his every movement. Although Púki had never bitten or scratched, Nói could have sworn that he was preparing to pounce and sink his claws into him. Anyone would have thought the cat had read his thoughts about lion hunting and wanted to take revenge for his distant kin in Africa. Nói closed the door and thought he heard Púki hiss. The cat was nowhere to be seen when he emerged shortly afterwards.

Down in the kitchen he was met by the aroma of coffee from the brimming jug and was again filled with a heart-warming sense of being back where he belonged. He wandered out in search of Vala, still in his dressing gown; he was in no hurry and savoured the sensation as the caffeine began to take effect. By the time he found her cramming dirty clothes into the washing machine in the utility room, he was feeling restored. He kissed her on the nape of her neck, wishing he could tempt her back into bed, but didn't speak the thought aloud.

'Afternoon, sleepyhead.' Vala smiled at him. Her teeth were strikingly white in her attractively tanned face. The Florida sun had obliterated all trace of Icelandic winter pastiness. She was wearing an old, threadbare top that she'd owned for donkey's years and only brought out for doing the household chores. It was like a red flag. if Vala appeared in this shirt, both father and son knew to do as they were told. Yet in spite of this Nói liked the top; it had worn so thin that you could see the outline of her pert breasts, and the baggy neck revealed her sharp collarbones. Ever since he had first set eyes on her, Vala had been slim, but because she worked as a personal trainer he had no idea if she was naturally slender or owed her figure to constant exercise. It used to fill him with pride when they were in company to see that she was in better shape than all the other women her age and most of the younger ones too. She made sure that he kept fit as well, dragging him out running with her and insisting that he attended her gym three times a week. Before he met her it had never crossed his mind to do any exercise. When he was a boy there had been no money to pay the membership fees for sports clubs, let alone buy the necessary gear, so he had never developed the taste for it. It gave no tangible rewards and merely took up valuable time when there were more important goals to be met. Were it not for Vala he probably wouldn't even own a pair of trainers.

She'd had less success with their son. Tumi had never been persuaded to take up any sport or show his face at her workplace, as his weedy figure attested. Of course, his gangling frame would fill out one day, and Nói hoped this would happen sooner rather than later. Still, before long an interest in girls was bound to spur him on to making more effort with his appearance and becoming more sociable.

Tumi and his friends still seemed happiest in each other's company, spending long hours hunched over computer games, mowing down figures jerkily seeking refuge. They spoke little among themselves; in fact the only words his small group of friends seemed to exchange were monosyllables like 'fuck', 'shit' and 'man', which they yelled at the games as they crowded round the large TV monitor in Tumi's bedroom. It was something of a relief to Nói that all his son's friends were social misfits to a man. He took it as proof that Tumi's indifference to anything except computers couldn't be blamed on his failings as a parent. Since Nói had never known his own father, he tended to worry that he wasn't performing well enough in the paternal role. He had nothing, either positive or negative, to measure himself against.

'Where's Tumi?'

'Asleep.' Vala upended a plastic bag of dirty clothes on the floor and sighed. 'Why didn't we wash this back in Florida?'

'The weather outside was too tempting, remember? And we were supposed to be on holiday. I don't know about you, but in my opinion laundry and holidays don't go together. Neither does sweltering heat, actually, but that's another story.'

Nói dodged as Vala threw a dirty sock at him. Coffee slopped out of his mug and he dried the splash with the sock that he had caught in mid-air.

'Would you mind waking him? I need you two to help.' She made a face. 'I want to blitz the whole house today. Get rid of everything associated with those people.'

Nói tutted. 'Are you thinking of the coat? We hardly need to go through the whole house; they're sure to let us know if they've forgotten anything else.'

'I doubt it. They left a bag of dirty laundry by the washing machine. I feel like throwing the whole lot in the bin. I'm certainly not going to wash it.'

It was Nói's turn to grimace. Other people's dirty clothes revolted him as much as a clump of a stranger's pubic hair. If it were up to him they would set fire to the bag. 'What kind of idiots are they?'

'Don't ask me. Maybe they overslept and had to leave the house in a hurry. I can't find the sheets that should've been on our bed either. And when I looked under the bottom sheet I noticed that the mattress protector's missing too. It's not in the laundry basket, anyway. And Púki's litter tray was absolutely disgusting, as if they hadn't let him out the whole time they were here. I almost threw up when I emptied it earlier.' She sounded aggrieved. The house swap had been her brainwave: Nói had been utterly opposed to it at first, although he had caved in eventually. Impersonal hotels with clean towels and minibars were more up his street. All the time they were there he had lived in fear of opening a cupboard in search of a glass and finding something excruciatingly personal, like a sex toy or a leaflet on living with prostate cancer. Things he would rather not know about.

The only reason he had given in was that Vala had been in such a state before the trip. Her sudden decision that they should go abroad had come in the wake of a bout of depression she'd suffered in the run-up to Christmas. She hadn't seemed to care that it would mean taking Tumi out of school after term had started. Nói hadn't wanted to rock the boat, and in the event he was glad he had gone along with her wishes because she was soon back in her usual good mood. She was the perfect woman in his perfect life and he was prepared to go to great lengths to keep her happy.

'There's no way they can have overslept. The flights to America leave in the late afternoon.'

'They were travelling onwards to Europe.'

'Jesus. Then I hope you haven't invited them to stay here on their return journey. Is that why they left all their stuff behind?' Nói felt overwhelmed with dismay. If that was the case, he would soon be getting that minibar and room service after all – he would damn well stay at a hotel if these people were going to make themselves at home in his house again.

'No, you idiot. Of course not. They'll only be stopping over to change planes.'

'Couldn't we take their crap out to the airport, then? Surely the airline can put out an announcement for them to come and fetch their dirty laundry.'

'Yeah, right. The airport has a dedicated team for that.' Vala slammed the washing machine shut. 'Don't be such a fool. Of course they don't – they blow up any luggage that gets left behind.' She stood up. 'We'll just have to post it to them. Collect all the bits and pieces we find when we spring-clean the house and chuck them in a box.'

Nói sighed to himself. 'Spring-clean the whole house?' There was always a chance he'd misheard.

'From top to bottom. There's an odd smell I want to get rid of.'

Nói sniffed the air and though he couldn't remember what the house normally smelt like, it was still there, that faint, alien taint that had greeted them on their arrival this morning. It was neither acrid nor nasty, but disconcerting nevertheless. Still, he could live with it; he didn't know how one got rid of smells but assumed it would involve a major – and tedious – operation. The simplest solution would have been to spray air freshener in all the rooms but Vala was allergic to synthetic scents, so that was out of the question.

Nói made do with shaking his head, then finished his coffee and went to rouse Tumi.

Púki was lying curled in a ball in front of the bedroom door, tail wrapped around as if to hold himself together. His ears flickered slightly when Nói approached, then he raised his head and stared at him, unblinkingly. It was as if the cat expected something of him or wanted to convey some message: *It wasn't me in the bathroom.*

'Who was it then, old boy?' muttered Nói. The cat didn't stir when he opened the door so he had to step over him.

Inside the lights were off and the curtains were still drawn. There was a musty smell and their son had managed to strew his belongings over the floor and half the desk, though they had only been home for a few hours. Before evening the room would be as much of a pigsty as it had been before they went to America.

Tumi's tan looked even deeper against the white sheets; the unaccustomed colour suited him. More familiar was the sight of the open laptop beside him. Nói was about to close it when he decided to grab the opportunity to take a quick peek at the webcam in the chalet. Vala would be annoyed if she caught him using the computer in the kitchen. He perched on the side of the bed, taking care not to wake Tumi. His son muttered something without opening his eyes or stirring.

To his surprise, Nói saw that three new files awaited him on the holiday chalet webpage, all from that morning. Selecting the oldest, he fast-forwarded through the first few seconds that showed a still of the living room and open-plan kitchen, as it should. He tried enhancing the brightness but the video was still too dark for him to see properly. Yet he thought he could detect a faint movement at the end of the decking or just beyond it, though there was no telling what it was, no matter how Nói tried to enlarge the image or tilt the screen this way and that. Eventually he gave up and opened the next video clip. The timer showed that the camera had been activated almost immediately after the first recording, so it was equally dark. Again he fast-forwarded through the first part, then slowed down a few seconds in when the movement appeared. He did his best to watch the whole screen and flinched when something white suddenly appeared under the door that led to the decking. He zoomed in until it was clear that there was a crumpled piece of paper or letter lying on the floor. Nói pulled back a little from the screen and racked his brain to remember if they had ever received any post or flyers at the chalet before. He zoomed in again in a vain attempt to read what was written on the paper but it appeared to be blank. It was impossible to be certain in the poor light, however; the paper could just as well have been a hand-drawn advertisement for the local women's institute cake sale, or a notice from the electricity company that they were turning the power off for maintenance work. The thought reassured him. Of course, it must be something like that.

He checked the third recording, reassured by this innocent explanation. The footage had been captured a little after the last one, but by now he had grown accustomed to the grainy image and could see what it showed more clearly. As a result he had no problem making out the figure walking along the decking – presumably the postman. The face of the black silhouette was invisible and all he could really tell was that it was human. Nói frowned when he realised that, instead of leaving, the figure was walking across the decking, past the large window, to vanish round the corner of the chalet in the direction of the shed and barbecue. Then all was still until the figure reappeared, passed the window, then stepped down from the decking and melted into the darkness.

Nói stopped the video at the point where the shadowy figure was in the middle of the window. It was impossible to tell whether it was a man or a woman, but he was fairly sure the person was wearing a dark-coloured anorak with the large hood pulled up. He stared at the frozen image with a vague sense of misgiving that he couldn't explain. Perhaps it had something to do with the way the figure moved, head lowered to its chest, as if something ominous awaited it beyond the decking.

Tumi stirred and rolled over on his side. Nói just managed to grab the laptop before it slipped onto the floor. 'What are you doing on my computer?' his son mumbled huskily from the depths of his pillow.

'Good afternoon. So you're actually awake.' Nói closed the webpage, snapped the computer shut and left the question unanswered. He didn't want to bother Tumi with his no doubt groundless worries. Some things were not for kids. 'Your mum's on the warpath downstairs. Time to drag yourself out of bed and lend a hand.'

'I'm still tired,' groaned the boy.

'You're always tired.'

'What's the rush? We've only just got home. Can't it wait for a bit? It's not as if the cases are blocking the way into the house.' Although Tumi showed no signs of leaping out of bed, he was at least sitting up. His tousled hair was blonder than usual and under the heavy fringe you could see his mother's large blue eyes and his father's strong square jaw.

'You may not have to go to school till after the weekend but your mother and I have got to go to work in the morning.' Suddenly Nói was filled with the same urge as Vala had described – to obliterate every trace of the American couple, for their son's sake. Tumi would be alone at home tomorrow and Nói didn't want any hint of their presence left in the house. 'On your feet.' He slapped his thighs and stood up. 'Jump in the shower, then come straight down.' A voice inside his head whispered to him to tell the boy to leave the bathroom door open but he couldn't bring himself to say it out loud – it was too ridiculous. He made do with smiling at Tumi, then left the room.

'Shit, I really don't feel like going to work tomorrow.' Nói pulled off the rubber gloves, which were damp inside. He couldn't wait to wash off the unpleasant odour. He blew out a breath, proudly surveying the results of his hard work. The kitchen was looking pretty good. Admittedly there were marks here and there on the stainless steel, but he was too knackered to let it bother him.

'Well, I'm looking forward to it. I can't wait to have a proper workout.' Vala collapsed onto a chair. 'I'm tired of not being tired, if you see what I mean.'

'No.' He had given up hope of ever developing the same passion for physical exercise as his wife. He made the effort to stay in reasonable shape for her sake, but nothing more.

'Drop by after work and I'll show you what I mean. I promise you'll be stiff for the rest of the week.'

'Sounds tempting, but no thanks.' His hands shone as he rinsed off the washing-up liquid; he would smell like a pine tree but it was better than the foul stink of rubber. The sudden memory of the figure on the decking wiped the smile off his face.

'Don't think I'm going to let you off. If you don't come tomorrow, it'll have to be the day after.' Vala stretched and her shoulder joint clicked. 'You'll recover from your jetlag sooner if you're physically tired.'

Nói had planned to go to sleep physically tired that night, but not from the gym. 'I promise.' But even the thought of sex with Vala wasn't enough to distract him from the nagging feeling that there was something amiss at the holiday chalet. 'By the way, have the keys to the chalet turned up?' He tried to sound casual.

Vala shook her head and dropped her arms. 'They're here somewhere. We may have cleaned the whole house but we still haven't done a proper search. I spent most of my time scrubbing the stairs and the wall beside them. I don't know what they've been doing but it was disgusting. Absolutely disgusting. It just goes to show how tired we were this morning that we didn't notice. I could swear there was urine on the stairs.' She closed her eyes and rolled her head in circles. 'If they've accidentally taken the keys with them, they'll post them back to us.' Her head came to a standstill but her short blonde ponytail continued to swing. 'You can use his coat as security.' Then she opened her eyes and smiled at Nói. 'Did you see the bed? I changed it and put on the valance. It looks fantastic.'

'Great.' Nói didn't want to spoil her pleasure but the ruffles around the bed reminded him of an old lady's tablecloth. In fact, the less they said about the bed, the better. Neither the sheets nor the mattress protector had turned up and he was cross enough about that. Nói scrunched up a piece of kitchen towel after drying his hands. The bin turned out to be full so he took out the bag. 'Have you had any messages from them? I haven't heard a thing.'

'No idea. I haven't been on the computer.'

'Haven't you checked your e-mail on your phone?' He and Tumi had given her an extremely expensive smartphone for Christmas but Vala would only use it for making calls.

'No. Why?'

He had no good answer to this, so he knotted the bag and carried it out to the dustbin.

The cold that met him at the front door came as a shock. He had adjusted to the Florida heat straight away and now missed being able to wander in and out without having to put on a coat. It seemed too much hassle to pull one on now, so he took a deep breath and dashed out in his T-shirt and indoor shoes.

For some reason the outside lights were off but he could see by the glow of the lamppost in the street. He cursed as he passed one of the bollard lights lining the drive and saw broken glass lying on the paving. He hadn't noticed it when they arrived this morning and Vala hadn't mentioned it either. The same applied to the next post, and also the third and last before the parking space. None of the lights lining the parking spaces were working either: all the bulbs had been smashed. Vala was right; they must have been half blind with exhaustion this morning.

Nói rubbed his freezing upper arms. Up to now their neighbourhood had been left in peace by vandals, though it wasn't that far from the town centre. He supposed there was no point ringing the police, and anyway he was too tired to be bothered with all that right now. He would buy new bulbs tomorrow – better replace them before Vala came home as there was no need to start her fretting about yobs. Maybe it would be a good idea to install a security camera at home as well. He hurried to dispose of the rubbish but when he opened the bin his anger flared up again. There was a pizza box in the bottom. Those bloody idiots! He had written them clear instructions that no cardboard or paper was to go in the rubbish bin or the dustmen would refuse to empty it. He had also left them the phone number and address of the nearest pizza place, and the box was proof that they had at least taken that information on board. So it wasn't as if they hadn't seen his notes.

Nói found himself hoping uncharitably that the couple's bags had gone missing on the way to Europe, that they had been subjected to an intimate search at airport security and that it would rain non-stop for the rest of their trip. And that strikes would pursue them the length and breadth of the Continent. He realised he was overreacting: he must be more tired than he'd thought. Cold, tired, pissed off and in no way ready to return to work tomorrow. He fished out the box to transfer it to the correct bin. To his surprise, it was heavy and when he opened it he found a whole, untouched pizza inside. A margherita. This evidence of their lack of sophistication did nothing to improve his opinion of them.

Nói headed back to the house. His skin prickled at the thought of the dark parking area and rubbish store behind him. It felt as if someone were watching him and he couldn't have been more relieved to get back inside.

Only then was his mind calm enough to register what he had glimpsed beneath the pizza box in the bin. Nói opened the cupboard and took out his coat.

Chapter 7

26 January 2014

The sun has gone down and the damp is creeping into their bones. Helgi has to make a superhuman effort to stop his teeth chattering. He put down his gloves earlier when changing the lens on his camera and, as bad luck would have it, one of them blew over the cliff. He could see it floating on the gentle swell, fingers splayed, as if a hand were reaching up to the surface from below. Then it sank into the depths and a large air bubble appeared and burst as if the sea were belching after swallowing this morsel.

Instead of favouring one hand over the other, Helgi has taken off his other glove too and is burrowing both hands into his pockets against the chilly wind. There is little else he can do to keep warm. Heida and Ívar are inside the lighthouse but he doesn't like to squash in there with them. He could put on more clothes but doubts this would help much. To make matters worse, the area of flat ground on top of the stack is so small that there's no real way of stretching one's legs except by jumping on the spot. Helgi makes do with this, realising, as he does so, how absurd it is for a fatso like him to be bouncing up and down, hands in pockets, on a rock in the middle of the ocean. He slows down and eventually his feet are barely leaving the ground, which makes him look even more foolish. Tóti is watching him, but looks away briefly when Helgi comes to a standstill. Then their eyes meet, and although they are standing as far apart as is humanly possible on Stóridrangur – Helgi on the helipad, Tóti by the lighthouse – Helgi can detect the contempt in the other man's face.

Helgi puffs out great clouds of breath. He hasn't a clue what to do now that dusk is falling. Of course he could photograph his travelling companions going about their tasks by the light of their work lamps, but he feels drained after the events of the day and experience has taught him that there is little point taking pictures when he's not in the mood. It would be better to save his batteries.

The torch at his feet flickers but, to his relief, the beam grows stronger again when he bangs it. The scramble to the lighthouse with sheer drops on either side would be even more alarming without any light. Nor does he wish to be alone in the darkness on the helipad after what he and Heida saw earlier in the fog.

Of course it must have been a trick of the light or else there must have been some other natural explanation for the dark shape. Yet he can't shake off the feeling that there wasn't. Perhaps he should discuss it with Heida, but so far they have done little more than exchange a glance, inhibited by the presence of Ívar and Tóti. This made it easier to ignore the experience. Now, however, armed only with a torch against whatever might be lurking in the darkness behind him, he can no longer pretend it never happened. What had Heida said? That the dead appeared in the fog when they had a score to settle with the living? If so, he's sure the shadow must have come for Ívar. Surely not for Heida – or

Tóti, even though the younger man is a bit of a jerk. At least he doesn't give off the same aura of malevolence as Ívar. Helgi's shivering grows worse and he starts to pick his way over to the lighthouse.

'Had enough of skipping?' Tóti swings his hammer, grinning at Helgi.

'Yes.' Helgi feels there is no point explaining the real reason or he would appear even more pathetic. The other man's mocking look fades and his hammer pauses mid-swing. Helgi relents. 'How's it going?'

'Not bad.' Tóti surveys the battered wall of the lighthouse where numerous patches of fresh grey concrete bear witness to the repairs. Helgi thinks it's probably like tidying up; the condition has to get really bad before anything is done about it. 'The weather's a bugger, though. It wasn't supposed to be this cold. I'm hoping it'll warm up tomorrow so I can fill in all the holes.' Tóti bends down and switches off his work lamp. The two men are left standing in the faint illumination from the lighthouse. 'Otherwise we're in deep shit. I shouldn't really have started on this with the weather like it is. It'll probably be a total disaster.'

Helgi nods as if he's well acquainted with the problem. 'It's bound to warm up a bit. They didn't forecast falling temperatures, did they?'

'Dunno. But if the wind picks up, it could turn even colder.'

They have slipped into discussing the weather and Helgi is relieved when Heida emerges from the lighthouse to stretch her limbs, looking profoundly grateful to be outside in the fresh air. 'Are you done?' Helgi hopes she'll say yes, so he won't have to be alone with Tóti.

Heida drops her arms and rubs one shoulder. 'I suppose

so.' She looks around. 'God, it's got dark quickly.' She shivers. Her hazel eyes pause on the helipad and Helgi thinks he knows what is passing through her mind. 'What time is it, anyway?'

'Nearly seven.' Tóti lights a cigarette. The flame illuminates his face and in the play of shadows he looks like a zombie. The smoke overpowers the briny smell of the sea for a moment and for the first time in his life Helgi finds it pleasant.

A muffled ringtone drifts over from inside the lighthouse. They hear the sound of Ívar's voice and snatches of a conversation about food, weather and rain. Then Ívar falls silent and tuts before appearing with a frown on his face. 'Fucking hell.'

Tóti takes a drag and leans more comfortably against the wall. 'What?' He seems unmoved by his workmate's curses.

Ívar brandishes his phone at them – a small, pink, oddly feminine clamshell model. 'That was the coastguard.' Realising that Helgi and Heida are staring at his phone, he hastily returns it to his inside pocket. 'The fucking chopper's developed a fault.'

The four of them stand there in a huddle. After photographing countless people for nearly a decade, Helgi reckons he has a pretty good eye for body language. Although he can't see himself, he assumes he is displaying the same symptoms of stress as his travelling companions: the fixed gaze and half-open mouth. Heida is the first to break the silence. 'Developed a fault? How can it have developed a fault?' It's not the most intelligent question but nobody points this out.

'It just broke down. I don't know what's wrong but they say they were forced to do an emergency landing on Snæfellsnes.'

The Snæfellsnes Peninsula is miles away.

'What does that mean?' Tóti asks, the cigarette trembling between his fingers. 'Fucking Snæfellsnes.' Helgi opens his mouth to point out that the peninsula is hardly to blame, but Ívar gets in first.

'I gather they'll have to transport it back to Reykjavík. Once it's there the mechanics can get a better idea of what's wrong and sort it out. The guy I talked to didn't like to hazard a guess about how long the whole thing would take – depends on spare parts and what have you.'

'Surely they could send another chopper to fetch us? What the hell's the problem?' Heida is getting more worked up with every word. 'My child's with a babysitter. I can't stay here forever.'

'The coastguard only have three choppers. One's undergoing a routine service that takes several weeks and the third was hired out to do a job in the Faroe Islands that's running a bit behind schedule.'

'Behind schedule? What do you mean "behind schedule"?' Heida looks ready to throttle Ívar. 'If they've hired out the helicopter until a certain date, they should damn well return it then. What the hell does it matter if the job's behind schedule?' She speaks without pausing for breath, then breaks off, panting, and gives Ívar a murderous glare. Then she seems to come to her senses, her fury evaporates and her expression relaxes. She drops her eyes and kicks at a stone that bounces a short way before shooting over the edge. 'What about other helicopters? Couldn't they borrow one to come and get us?'

'Choppers with winching equipment are few and far between. And I, for one, have no intention of being pulled up by hand into some old rust bucket.' Smoke pours out of Tóti's mouth with every word. 'It won't be a problem. So there's no point getting your knickers in a twist.'

Heida glares at Tóti but doesn't rise to this. Helgi admires her self-control; although quick-tempered, she's clearly no fool. There's absolutely no room to quarrel here.

'Won't we just have to resign ourselves? At least we've got phone reception. Couldn't you get the babysitter to stay a bit longer?' Helgi attempts a friendly smile.

'I suppose so. Do I have any choice?' The anger hasn't entirely left her voice.

'It'll turn out all right in the end,' said Ívar. 'We'll just have to tough it out. If the worst comes to the worst we can ask them to send a boat for us and hope the chain gets us to the bottom of the rock in one piece. Though I don't recommend it, except in an emergency. The fastenings must be seventy years old. So I'll let you lot go first.' Ívar zips up his anorak in an effort to appear nonchalant but Helgi detects a hint of fear or uncertainty in the man's manner. 'We'd better go easy on the food.' He accompanies this with a glance at Helgi, making no attempt to disguise the fact. Helgi flushes scarlet.

Tóti chokes on his smoke. 'Hang on a minute. How long do they reckon it'll take to rescue us? Are we talking about one more night or two?' He is staring intently at Ívar. 'Three? Four?'

'I'm not sure and neither are they, as far as I can tell. All I know is that they asked me about our supplies and when I told them roughly how much we had, that's what they said.' He breaks off and sucks his teeth, then takes his big knife out of its sheath and starts scraping imaginary dirt from under his fingernails. After that he lays down the knife on top of the cool-box and starts rooting aimlessly in the box beside it. 'They also advised us to start collecting rainwater tonight.'

'Jesus Christ.' Tóti flicks his cigarette butt out into the darkness.

Helgi is desperate to roll over on his thin sleeping mat and find a more comfortable position on the hard concrete floor but it's impossible. It's a miracle as it is that he and Heida have both managed to squeeze inside the lighthouse and lie so as to touch as little as possible during the night. If he so much as rolls over onto his back, it will mess up the arrangement. Perhaps, being so much smaller, Heida's more comfortable.

'Are you asleep?' Heida's voice is muffled, as though she's pulled the sleeping bag over her head.

'No.' Helgi stops himself from adding: 'You?'

'I hate it here.'

'Hopefully we'll be able to go home tomorrow.' Helgi feels like a teenager again. He doesn't know quite what to say and can't remember ever being in such an awkward situation with a member of the opposite sex. When the time came to split up for the night, Ívar ruled that Heida should sleep inside and choose who she wanted to share with. The other two would sleep up on the gallery, or narrow catwalk, that ran around the lantern room. Heida picked Helgi almost before Ívar had finished speaking, and he got the impression that Tóti was annoyed by this, though he tried to disguise the fact. Helgi had been surprised himself as he had assumed she would regard Tóti as the best of a bad lot. Perhaps she feels Helgi is the least likely to try anything. She's probably right.

'It's not really about the babysitting. My little girl's in safe hands with my parents. That was just all I could think of at the time. I didn't want to admit how I feel about this place. There's something sinister about the atmosphere.'

Helgi draws a deep breath. 'Isn't it just the confined space and the danger of falling off? Otherwise it's no different from anywhere else.' He says this quite against his own instincts because he knows exactly what she means. As he stares at the open doorway, his longing to turn over intensifies, as though he is afraid of seeing something dart past or the shape of a figure standing out there motionless, watching the lighthouse, waiting for them to fall asleep before moving closer, coming inside . . .

'Where are all the birds?' From the sound of her voice, Heida must have stuck her head out of her sleeping bag. She sits up. 'They were making a constant racket earlier.'

Helgi listens and has to admit that she's right. The only sound is the breakers at the bottom of the cliff. 'I expect they've gone to sleep. Or flown away.' He hopes she'll say something else to distract his attention from the noises outside but no such luck. There is a rustling, then she says goodnight, her voice muffled inside her sleeping bag again.

Helgi waits for sleep to claim him, with nothing but the sound of the waves in his ears, but his mind seems intent on keeping him awake, just in case. Weariness wins out in the end, though, so he is oblivious to the commotion up on the gallery later that night.

Chapter 8

21 January 2014

The office was windowless. The only other such rooms in the building were used for conducting interviews, as store-rooms or for coffee-making facilities. Nína had been allotted this cubbyhole when she joined the police and had never applied to move, even when other offices became available. She couldn't face the thought of packing up all her stuff; it had taken her less than a year to fill the shelves and accumulate piles of papers that she didn't dare throw out without going through them first. Besides, she rarely spent any time at her desk, so the claustrophobia and airlessness weren't a problem. Yet now she regretted not having applied to move. She longed to see the sky and felt as if her office walls were closing in on her, as if it were an extension of the basement.

The file containing reports of suicides from 1982 to 1985 was lying on her desk. She had trawled through it again and again, read every single word, but found nothing else about the case Thröstur had been linked to. Even so, she couldn't quite bring herself to put it in the black bin bag that was sitting, still more or less empty, in front of the archives. She knew it was crazy but she couldn't bear to throw away a single file in case it turned out to contain the information she was looking for. It made no difference that she had already had a quick flick through all the folders; a gnawing fear that she might have overlooked some crucial detail prevented her from getting on with her job. What she really wanted was to take all the files upstairs and examine every page at her leisure. But people would notice if she started lugging stacks of old folders up and down the stairs and someone was bound to alert her boss that Officer Nína, that whinging telltale, had finally lost the plot.

She had sneaked this one file into a cardboard box of video tapes that were probably recordings of old interviews. The box had been sitting on a shelf at the back of the storeroom, covered in a thick layer of dust, and its bottom was so weak that Nína was afraid it wouldn't survive the journey upstairs. For all she knew it might contain something worth copying. The problem would be to track down a VHS player in the building, but, if she could, it would make a nice break from the basement to sit and watch the tapes. Not that she expected their contents to be particularly uplifting. Any material the police thought worth recording was bound to make for depressing viewing.

Nína reached for her mobile phone that had been lying on her desk since this morning. She hadn't bothered to take it downstairs with her as she wasn't expecting any calls, and it was good to have a respite from the outside world now and then. She had popped into the canteen at lunchtime, so her colleagues wouldn't start wondering where she was, but the moment she walked in and encountered their silent stares, she realised what a foolish thought this had been. She had toyed with her food, sitting alone for fear that people would get up and leave if she tried to join them. Maybe she was being paranoid, but she didn't dare put it to the test.

Her stomach rumbled and she wished she had eaten more; she couldn't expect anything better at the hospital – a sandwich from the vending machine, with yellowing mayonnaise, washed down with lukewarm coffee.

The scratched screen showed three missed calls. One was from her sister, another from a number she didn't recognise, and the third from the hospital. She knew the number of Thröstur's ward by now and she felt her heart begin to pound. It was rare for her to receive calls from the hospital. When her husband had first been admitted, she had rung them at hourly intervals, but now she had little telephone contact. Gradually it had sunk in that there was unlikely to be any change, so she made do with slinking in and out of the ward, unseen. Thröstur's condition was stable, as if his body had paused on a ledge on its way over a cliff and probably wouldn't stir from there of its own accord.

For the past two weeks the staff had been dropping hints that it was time to make a decision. At first they had been subtle but when they realised she wasn't going to take the bait, they became more direct. Now would be a good time to switch off the machines that were keeping Thröstur alive, if you could call it alive. The phone call was almost certainly about that. Perhaps they would give her an ultimatum: if she didn't give in, they would be forced to cut the power supply to his room. For an instant she pictured herself dragging a small diesel generator to the ward but dismissed it immediately as madness.

As Nína was calling the hospital back the door opened and her boss stuck his head in. Hastily, she hung up. The very last thing she wanted was for someone to overhear the conversation. Police officers weren't supposed to cry at work.

'How's it going?' Örvar left the door open as if to ensure he could make a quick getaway. He had less than a year left until retirement and lately it had seemed to Nína that he was ageing with every passing month. It was rumoured that he had been diagnosed with cancer and, if his gaunt frame was anything to go by, he probably wouldn't be much of a burden on the pension fund. His black uniform hung off him, as if it had been purchased from a fancy-dress shop.

'Fine. Sort of. There are an awful lot of files.' Nína hoped he hadn't been downstairs to check up on her. The nearly empty bin bag outside the storeroom, and the flat cardboard boxes that had yet to be assembled told their own story. 'But it's slowly coming along.'

'No one expected you to finish it in your coffee break.' Örvar's face registered a twinge of pain as he sat down. 'Just remember, Rome wasn't built in a day.'

Nína suppressed a grimace. She couldn't stand that kind of platitude. She gave the cardboard box a light kick. 'I found a load of old tapes. Do you know if there's a video player in the building? It may be worth saving some of the material. I don't like to chuck it away without going through the recordings.'

Örvar bent forwards slightly to see the box. It was plain he thought Nína's job was of no importance but didn't want her to realise. He put on a thoughtful expression that didn't suit him. 'They're almost certainly recordings of interviews. I remember we experimented with taping them all when video machines first came in. Luckily, that didn't last long or the basement would be overflowing. But talk to the technical manager. He's bound to have an old VHS player somewhere in his storeroom.' Örvar straightened up, surveying her office with an embarrassed air, as if ashamed of the conditions she was expected to work in. 'I've been meaning to drop by and see you.'

'Really? Any particular reason?' This was disingenuous of her. They both knew perfectly well that Nína's situation was unresolved, and there was no point pretending otherwise. 'Sorry, I don't know why I said that. I'm perfectly aware what you want to discuss.'

Örvar nodded, looking almost comically relieved not to have to beat about the bush. 'There are a couple of reasons, actually. One is to check whether you've by any chance changed your mind about the complaint – in light of your circumstances.'

'Circumstances?' Nína felt her face tightening into a mask of anger.

'You know what I mean. But if you want me to put it more bluntly, I simply mean that you've got enough on your plate at the moment without having to cope with any extra stress.' Örvar heaved such a deep breath you'd have thought he wanted to suck all the oxygen out of the room. 'Anyway, I don't mean to pry into your personal affairs. We all need space to deal with our problems in peace. And the other reason was that I just wanted to check how you are and whether you'd like to take some time off. There's no shame in it, you know.'

Nína looked away from his dark eyes, which were so deep-set they almost disappeared into his head. Nothing would delight her colleagues, Örvar included, more than her absence from the station. She smiled through her rage, realising she must look half demented. 'Thank you but I don't need a holiday. Things are getting better – I gather I'm over the worst part. My complaint won't put me under any extra strain, if that's what you're worried about,' she lied with a straight face. The thought of not being able to take refuge in work was unbearable. What was she supposed to do all day? Sit beside Thröstur twenty-four/seven until she became rooted to the chair?

'Do you have someone to – er – talk to? A counsellor or . . .?'

'Yes.' It was easy to carry on lying once you had begun.

'Here at work?'

'No. At the hospital.' Nína knew Örvar would be able to check up to see if she had used the counselling service at the police station. 'If you don't mind, I'd rather not discuss it. But you can rest assured that I'm getting there. I'll soon be up to putting all my energy into pursuing the complaint.'

Örvar swallowed, his Adam's apple rising and falling in his sinewy throat. 'Right. Good.' Doubtless there were few things less consistent with his definition of 'good' than the idea of Nína tearing like a hurricane through the police station hierarchy in pursuit of justice. 'Leaving aside the complaint, naturally we're all looking forward to having you back on top form.' About as much as they looked forward to their flu jabs in October. 'We could do with more officers right now.' This was a feeble attempt to cheer her up and convince her that she was still part of the team. But Nína was aware that she had never been a particularly effective officer and doubted it would make any difference to the station whether she was back to her usual self or not.

She had been full of enthusiasm when she joined the police but her zeal had soon faded when it came home to her how little she could really achieve. The drunks carried on drinking; the thugs carried on beating people up. It didn't help that her colleagues had reservations about her because she was a woman and, to make matters worse, married to a journalist. Every time sensitive information was leaked to the press she sensed that suspicion fell on her, whether Thröstur worked for the media outlet in question or not.

'You know you have all my sympathy, Nína, and I'm not the only person here at the station who feels for you – we just find it hard to put it into words. But our thoughts are with you. In spite of this business of the complaint.'

She fought back a contemptuous smile. It would have been more natural for them to gloat over her misfortune, given that she had dared to shop one of the team. How very noble of them not to. 'I don't know what to say. I'm touched.' Nína adjusted her features to disguise the sarcasm. 'If you get a chance, do please pass on my gratitude to them for their thoughtfulness. I can't tell you how relieved I am not to have to spend my whole time fending off expressions of sympathy. That would be unbearable.' Better to let them think she appreciated their indifference and misinterpreted it as kindness.

Örvar's eyes had been lowered to the desk during this speech and had fallen on the folder. Nína cursed herself for not having shoved it in a drawer or at least turned it to face her. Putting his head on one side, he read the spine.

Silence.

Nína tried to look unconcerned.

'Is this from the basement?'

'Yes. I brought it upstairs just now without thinking. I'll take it back down tomorrow morning.'

Örvar nodded slowly. Nína hoped this blunder wouldn't keep him here any longer. When it had sunk in that she intended to stick to her guns and wasn't shattered enough to agree to go on leave, he prepared to stand up. But the folder containing the old suicide reports was obviously a sign that she was still obsessing over what had happened to Thröstur. 'Have you been through it?' he asked.

Nína wondered if she should carry on embroidering the truth but couldn't be bothered. 'Yes.'

'And?' Örvar drew the file towards him and Nína pushed it over, as if she didn't think it mattered. He leafed through it, pausing sometimes but saying nothing. Then his face darkened, he snapped the folder shut and slid it back across the desk. He'd got a paper cut and sucked and shook his finger. 'You won't find the explanation for what happened to your husband in other people's lives.'

Nína contemplated the folder. 'As a matter of fact, I came across a case in which Thröstur was interviewed as a witness. When he was a child.' She tried to swallow but her throat was suddenly dry. 'For all I know it may be connected.' She had no need to elaborate.

'It wouldn't be the first time something like that has happened.' Örvar frowned, his eyes seeming to sink even deeper into his head. 'Was it a sexual abuse case? They can leave scars that never heal.'

'I don't know what sort of case it was. I only found one page. But it was in this folder, so I assume it related to a suicide.' Nína met Örvar's gaze, much as she'd have preferred not to. He dropped his eyes first, running a hand through his thin white hair.

'That doesn't necessarily mean anything. Reports are always ending up in the wrong folders.'

'But . . .' Nína wanted to object but couldn't find the words. Of course he was right; many of the things that disrupted people's lives turned out to be nothing but coincidence.

'You shouldn't be going through old suicide reports. It's not healthy for you to obsess over them when you're going through this tragedy with your husband.'

'I just happened to spot his name when I was leafing through. I wasn't intending to spend any more time looking at this file than any of the others down there.'

'No, maybe not.' Örvar looked unconvinced. 'But I recommend you don't give it any more thought now. You can look into it later when you're feeling better. Besides, we don't pay you to spend your time rooting around among cold cases. As an employee of the police you're supposed to be devoting your time to the tasks assigned to you. And if you can't do your job, you should take sick leave. It would be better for everybody.' So sick leave was back on the agenda. Nína wondered if others like him were waiting outside in the corridor, eager for news that she was going to take a holiday.

'I'm doing the job I'm supposed to be doing.' This wasn't entirely true but she had lost her temper.

'And you should remember another thing, Nína.' Örvar rose to his feet, his knuckles whitening on the arms of his chair and the corners of his mouth turning down, though he tried to hide the fact. He didn't finish the sentence until he was standing up, then looked not at her but at the folder. 'People who choose to die that way don't give much thought to those they leave behind. Don't let your husband's decision ruin your life. That can easily happen if you're not careful.'

Could her sister Berglind have been talking to Örvar? The advice was almost identical to what she had said yesterday evening. Mind you, it was a conventional sentiment in the circumstances: chin up.

Nína watched Örvar walk out into the corridor. He didn't say goodbye or add any further comments on the subject. By the time it occurred to her that his eyes had been resting on the file when he referred to people whose lives had been destroyed, it was too late to ask if he had anyone specific in mind. Had he come across a case he remembered, while he was leafing through? An instance where the surviving spouse had been crushed by grief? If so, it could hardly have been the case Thröstur was concerned with as there was next to no information in the scrap that remained of the report. The brief paragraph would hardly have been sufficient to pierce the fog of thirty years of amnesia. Then there was his comment about selfishness, which showed that he had no understanding of depression. But he was unlikely to have been referring specifically to Thröstur as he barely knew him and so had no basis on which to judge Thröstur's motives or lack of consideration. Nína had deliberately avoided work parties where partners were invited along, so Örvar had never seen them together at police dinner dances or other gatherings. She had been afraid her colleagues might start having a go at Thröstur once they'd downed a few drinks. An investigative journalist, known for sparing no one, would have been as welcome at a police annual bash as a Muslim cleric at a feminist convention. All Örvar knew about Thröstur was that he was a journalist. And however much her boss might dislike reporters, she doubted he regarded them as totally devoid of feeling. No, he couldn't possibly have been referring to Thröstur.

Nína turned the pages until she found Thröstur's statement and noticed a tiny smear of blood at the top of the page that hadn't been there before.

Örvar's paper cut. He had been looking at the report.

Instinct told Nína that his comment about selfishness and destroyed lives had been in reference to this case. Örvar's police career stretched back decades and he would have already joined the force by 1985. Perhaps he was on the ball enough to remember the case, despite the scanty details. So why couldn't he have admitted the fact? What the hell was wrong with the man?

She stood up to go and track down a video player. She would call the hospital back later. There was no way she was ready to face a difficult conversation just now.

Chapter 9

21 January 2014

The shelves sagged beneath the weight of obsolete equipment that looked clumsy and antiquated where once it must have seemed state of the art. So museum-like was the atmosphere that Nína wouldn't have been surprised to spot a traditional carved wooden bowl among the clutter or a butter churn in the corner. She had been given a place to sit just inside the little room opening off the technical manager's office, where he had hooked up a video player and small boxy TV set for her. He had handled both with such loving care you'd have thought they were priceless artefacts. Fortunately, however, he seemed less keen on people than gadgets and made no attempt at small talk. The only words they had exchanged from the moment she turned up with a box full of VHS tapes until he left her to get on with it, were her request to use a video player and his parting warning that she wasn't to muck around with the controls. If anything went wrong, she was to give him a shout immediately.

Apart from the grating squeak emitted by the machine as she fast-forwarded, there was silence in the room. On the screen in front of her, a young man was squirming on an uncomfortable-looking plastic chair. His long dark hair fell over his eyes, helping him avoid the policeman's gaze. If you ignored the haircut and clothes, the recordings could have been made yesterday. Evidently human nature didn't change. The guilty manipulated the truth and the police, undeterred, continued mechanically firing questions at them. It proved wearing in the long run to listen to strung-out suspects entangling themselves in ever more intricate webs of lies, so Nína had removed the headphones after the first tape. The lips of the man on screen moved noiselessly as he answered questions about an old misdemeanour that no longer mattered. Nína had soon realised that this was a complete waste of time, yet she carried on watching anyway. She lacked the initiative to press the 'Off' button, say goodbye to the crooks of the eighties and get the hell out of there. It was always possible the tapes might contain something worth keeping, though what that might be was impossible to say. Perhaps one of the officers would suddenly lose his rag and attack the suspect. It wasn't unheard of. She really would be popular if she uncovered evidence of excessive force employed in the line of duty, however far in the past.

The long-haired man returned his hands to the edge of the table after gesturing for emphasis. Soon he was twisting his fingers together, as if he meant to tie them in knots. It was the sign of a liar. Nína had been in the police long enough to see through people without the need to turn up the volume. The suspects' mannerisms and eyes often inadvertently gave them away. If she were listening she would no doubt have heard the man going into far too much detail when describing events, which was always a dead giveaway, or repeating the police officer's questions – a well-known method of buying time.

As she fast-forwarded in search of the next interview, the

movements of the suspect and the policemen facing him appeared absurdly jerky. Then she pressed play and read the name, date and case number written on a piece of paper and held up to the camera. The date of the interviews seemed to be the only system to the recordings, which meant that cases were not dealt with consecutively; instead people trickled in to be questioned about a whole variety of different incidents. The technology had been new at the time and perhaps the received wisdom had been that it was better not to keep changing the tape. She remembered the fuss there had been the time her father managed to snarl up a rented video in their family VHS player, back when they first became popular. She and her sister hadn't dared go near the machine for months for fear of destroying another tape.

When she read the handwritten sign, Nína did a double take. She paused the frame with clumsy fingers and stared, stunned, at the white sheet of paper almost filling the screen.

Thröstur Magnason, witness
18 April 1985
Case no. 1363-85

She leant back as far from the television as she could. She hadn't for a minute expected to find the interview of Thröstur as a child among the recordings, let alone on the second tape she watched. She read the text again to assure herself that she wasn't imagining it.

There was no mistake: it was him.

She was dying to watch the recording but simultaneously felt a panicky urge to leap up and run out of the room. To calm her nerves, she plugged in the clunky headphones and put them on. It was like plunging her head under water; she could hear nothing. If she pressed play, her body would remain in the present while her mind was transported back to 1985. With Thröstur.

Her hand moved towards the 'Play' button. Her fingers trembled slightly as they hovered in front of the machine, as if they couldn't make up their mind whether to go all the way. Then suddenly her index finger went for it and pressed the button.

The white paper was removed and a tall policeman opened the door of the interview room. He moved into the gap, talking to someone outside in the corridor, then showed the person in. He was careful not to turn his back on the interviewee, as per the regulations, but the procedure seemed laughable when a small boy appeared. He was accompanied by a woman in a buttoned-up coat, holding her handbag in front of her like Moominmamma. She looked about as likely to cause trouble as the boy, and he barely came up to the man's waist. Not that Nína took much notice of the woman. Her attention was riveted on the boy as he walked warily over to the interview table and took up position behind a chair, glancing nervously round the room. His face could only be seen in full when his gaze passed over the camera. Nína's heart lurched.

It was her Thröstur. She recognised the child's face from the framed photos on the dusty piano that nobody played any more in her father-in-law's house. But even if she had never seen them, she would still have recognised him. His features were the same, though the overall impression was much softer. There was no hint of shadow in the round face and the strong jawline, still unformed, was barely detectable.

He was still blond, though later his hair would darken so much that no one would have guessed he had once resembled a Swede. His complexion, too, was very fair, and it looked as if all the colour in his face was concentrated in his bright red lips. Nína felt again that sharp stab in her heart that people often talk of but she had up to now regarded as a mere figure of speech. It felt as if she'd picked up a pencil and jabbed herself in the chest.

Only when the boy Thröstur finally turned to the woman in the coat did Nína tear her gaze from him and look at her. She recognised her face immediately, now that the woman had moved closer and was facing the camera. It was her late mother-in-law, Milla Gautadóttir. Although she had inevitably changed less than her son in the intervening years between this recording and the time Nína had first met her, it was strange to see her looking so young. Nína had only got to know her in middle age and had never stopped to wonder what she had looked like as a girl. To her mind her mother-in-law had simply sprung into being as a middle-aged woman – who was never permitted to grow old. The breast cancer that had got the better of her in the space of just two months had at least spared her from having to witness Thröstur's fate. Not that this in any way lessened the tragedy of her early death.

'Take a seat. It doesn't matter who sits where.' The police officer waited until mother and son were sitting down. Both looked as if they expected the chairs to collapse under their weight. Thröstur's mother put her bulky handbag on her lap and smiled apprehensively at the policeman. Thröstur stuck his hands under his thighs and swung his legs. He looked around again, still wide-eyed.

'I'd like to begin by thanking you for coming in.'

Milla nodded, still smiling awkwardly. She didn't speak.

'It's not often that boys your age get the chance to come in here, you know.' The man placed his hands on the table, one on top of the other. Beside them was a notepad and pen. 'So I need to make absolutely sure I do everything right. I don't want you to think the police are mean or bullies.'

Thröstur turned to the man and shook his head vehemently. His hair was much longer than was the fashion nowadays and his golden locks swung. 'I don't think that.' His expression shone with sincerity; the ingenuous child's face was irresistible. The sharp pain in Nína's heart intensified and she was pierced with sadness that she and Thröstur would never have children. Their son might have looked like this.

'I'm glad to hear it. Do you understand why you were asked to come in?' The policeman's voice was firm but friendly. In spite of this, Thröstur's manner showed a trace of anxiety or fear. He darted a quick glance at his mother but when his profile reappeared he looked as confused as before. 'I think so. I'm not sure.'

'This isn't a test and there's nothing to be afraid of. You're what's known as a witness. Witnesses are ordinary people who've seen something that the police are interested in. We can't be everywhere, so it's important that people help by telling us the truth if they see something that might be a crime.'

'A crime? What's a crime?' Thröstur stopped swinging his legs. 'I know what a criminal is. It's a thief.'

'Quite right. When somebody steals from another person that's a crime and he's a criminal. But stealing's not the only crime. For example, it's against the law to hurt people.' The policeman leant confidingly over the table. 'Crimes are bad, especially for the people hurt by them. So when people see a crime, they're supposed to tell the police. Then we can arrest the criminal.'

'Even if nobody told me, I'd still arrest the man if I was a cop.'

'But first you'd have to be sure the man was a thief, wouldn't you?' The police officer received no answer but Thröstur appeared to be considering the matter. The man continued: 'Wouldn't you tell if you saw somebody stealing?'

Thröstur looked back at his mother who met his gaze but didn't speak. He chewed at his bottom lip and began swinging his legs again. 'Yes. I'd ring the police. When I got home.'

'Good. I knew you were a sensible boy. Now I'm going to tell you another thing that's just as important. Sometimes we have to talk to a witness to make sure there *hasn't* been a crime. Again, it's terribly important for the witness to tell the truth.'

'I don't understand.' Thröstur frowned. 'Do I have to ring the police if I don't see a criminal?'

'No, not exactly. In the sort of cases I'm talking about, the police would come round and ask you some questions. Like the other day, remember?' Thröstur nodded and the policeman continued. 'A police officer came round to see you and your friends and asked you what you'd seen.'

Thröstur's frown deepened. 'I know.'

'Now I'm going to ask you the same questions again in case you remember something you forgot to tell us then. I'm also going to ask your friends who were with you. But I'm talking to you first.'

'I'm the oldest. I was born in March.' Thröstur sat up

straighter, which had the effect of making him appear even younger and more vulnerable. Nína realised she had been holding her breath and let it go noisily. Suddenly it felt uncomfortable to be looking back in time like this, seeing Thröstur at such a young age. It would have been different if he hadn't been lying on his deathbed. She would have gone home and teased him about his stripy polo-neck jumper and the anorak he was growing out of – that is, once she had finished interrogating him and scolding him for not telling her about this. But now all she could do was go up to the hospital and sit beside his soulless, insensible body. It was peculiar to think that the last words she would hear Thröstur speak were uttered thirty years ago. Foolish as it was, Nína couldn't help wondering what the boy would say to the camera if he knew that his future wife would one day be watching the recording. He'd probably ask her to promise never to cook anything containing mushrooms or onion.

'Indeed. Clearly I was right to talk to you first.' Nína turned her attention to the police officer. It was less painful. She thought he was doing an extraordinarily good job. He was every bit as skilful as his modern colleagues who were sent on all kinds of training courses before being allowed to interview children. She wondered why the task had fallen to him and guessed he was probably the officer who had the most children of his own. He certainly knew how to talk to them. Or perhaps he was going out of his way to perform well because the interview was being recorded.

She watched the man as he reached for the notepad. 'Now, think carefully before you answer – we're in no hurry. Give yourself time to remember what happened and make sure you tell the truth. Your mother's here with you and you wouldn't want to hurt her by telling a lie. I expect you're very fond of her, aren't you?'

Thröstur hung his head. From the movement of his mop of hair, he appeared to be nodding. 'I don't want anything bad to happen to Mum.'

Milla put a hand on her son's shoulder. She removed it almost immediately, as if she thought demonstrations of affection were inappropriate in the middle of a police interview.

'Of course not. Nothing bad will happen to her, son.'

'I know.' Thröstur didn't look up but stared in fascination at the zip of his pale-blue anorak. Nína frowned. She was no expert when it came to children but there had been something odd about the little boy's reaction when the policeman referred to his mother. Did the incident relate to her somehow?

The policeman slapped his hands on the table with a bang. 'Good. Why don't we get started then, so we can let you go back outside in the sunshine as soon as possible?' He picked up a pen and held it poised over the pad, ready to note down the boy's answers.

Thröstur looked up and met the policeman's eye. He pulled his hands from under his thighs and laid them on the table in front of him. Then he leant forwards. 'I'm ready.'

'Good. Me too.' The policeman smiled and shot a brief glance at Thröstur's mother. Milla nodded as if to say: *We're ready; get it over with so my child and I can leave and never have anything to do with the police again*. Nína smiled faintly. She should be so lucky.

'Right. Let's begin by reminding ourselves where you were and how long you were sitting there.'

'We were sitting on the fence by the grey house. The fence is grey too. It's made of concrete. You can sit on it. You can't sit on wooden fences. They hurt.' Thröstur looked at his mother, who smiled. 'But I don't know how long we were there. I can almost tell the time. But I haven't got a watch.'

'That's all right. But you sat there quite a long time? Didn't you?'

'Yes. We were there a very, very long time. I wrote down fifteen number plates. That's a lot, you know, and one was an ambulance too. My book's almost full now.' Nína vaguely remembered this craze from her own childhood. Her best friend's brother had had a little book in which he used to collect car registration numbers, but she had never understood the appeal, either then or now. The brother hadn't, to her knowledge, ever done anything with them, he had simply recorded the numbers in a book. So Thröstur had been sitting on the wall with his friends, noting down car licence plates.

'Did fifteen cars go past while you were sitting there?'

'No. Lots more. But I couldn't write down all the numbers. Some zoom past but we can't write quickly enough. And it's hard to remember the numbers while you're writing them. We could only really write down the numbers of the cars that stopped.' Thröstur pointed to the pen in the policeman's hand that was skating nimbly over the page. 'But you could definitely get the numbers of the cars that zoom by. You write so fast.'

'Yes, maybe I should try.' The officer smiled at Thröstur. 'You were sitting right opposite the house, weren't you? There was nothing blocking your view, no lorry parked in front of it or anything like that?' Thröstur shook his head. He opened his mouth to say something, then clamped his lips shut. The policeman picked up on this. 'Perhaps you remember now that there was something in the way which you forgot when you talked to us before? It's all right if you didn't remember the first time. We can always change it.'

'No.' The child spoke in a small voice. 'There was nothing in the way. I'm sure.'

'All right. But is there any chance you weren't watching all the time? You must be busy writing when a car stops for long enough for you to get its number. Perhaps lots of cars came at once and you couldn't look up from your books for a while.'

'We took it in turns to look across the road.' Thröstur's eyes were lowered; his shoulders drooped. 'It's a bad place.'

'Bad? How do you mean?'

'Just bad.'

'Can you explain that a bit better for me? Why do you think that? Did you kids maybe go inside and see something frightening?' Nína pricked up her ears. She wanted to yell at the screen to make the policeman explain what was going on.

Thröstur looked up and his eyes seemed to have widened. He answered with sudden vehemence. 'No. We didn't see anything. Nothing at all.' Then he dropped his gaze again and when he resumed speaking it was on an indrawn breath. 'But that's not why. I just know it's a bad place. Everyone says so.'

'Everyone? Who's everyone?'

'The other children.'

'All right.' For the first time in the interview the policeman seemed at a loss. He didn't have any question prepared and tried to disguise the fact by pretending to read back over his notes. Then he cleared his throat, rubbed a hand across his forehead and stared at Thröstur. Eventually the boy looked up and met his gaze. 'So you're sure you watched the whole time and that what you told the police the other day was correct?'

Thröstur licked his lips. His fingers, which had been resting almost motionless on the table, were suddenly fidgety. He squirmed in his chair, then glanced away, his face turned towards the camera, as if he wanted to address his words to Nína, thirty years later. 'No. I don't want to change anything. I told the truth then. We didn't see anything.' His eyes roved around in search of something to fix on; he wriggled in his seat, clenched his fingers and licked his lips.

All the signs of a liar rolled into one.

The picture vanished and the screen filled with electronic snow. It was the end of the tape.

Chapter 10

24 January 2014

Vala had been right. He should have taken an extra day's holiday to recover. His body was stuck in another time zone and he simply couldn't concentrate on adapting the accounting software to the needs of the client. Endless lines from chunks of different programs danced on the two screens but seemed to retreat whenever he tried to read them. Steam was rising from the mug on his desk, but Nói felt repulsed by the smell. How many coffees was that already this morning? The caffeine had stimulated him at first but by now he felt he must have more coffee than blood running through his veins.

Nói tipped his head back and closed his eyes. He was in a tetchy mood, and exasperated with himself for being so perverse. When he turned up this morning he had expected to be confronted by all kinds of problems that his staff had been unable to solve in his absence, but that wasn't the case. Apparently everything had gone like clockwork without him. Of course he should have been pleased by this, not cross. To make matters worse, he could tell from his employees' expressions that they hadn't missed him and might actually have preferred it if he'd stayed in America for good. He'd rather they had heaved a sigh of relief and handed him stacks of projects that no one had been able to sort out without him.

As it was, there was nothing for him to do. To disguise the fact that he was wandering aimlessly around the office, he had grabbed a minor project that had come in yesterday and shouldn't cause him any headaches. And now here he was, stuck.

His thoughts wandered back to yesterday evening, the dustbin and broken bulbs in the outdoor lights. It wasn't quite the homecoming he had dreamt of during the cramped indignities of economy class. His mind had conjured up a picture of home in which peace and quiet reigned undisturbed but the reality had been quite different. All it had taken to destroy his peace of mind were a few shards of broken glass. Before coming to work this morning he had even checked whether next-door's exterior lights had been vandalised in the same way. They hadn't, and while Nói certainly didn't bear his neighbours any ill will, he would have preferred it if they had been targeted too. It was unsettling to think that his house had been singled out for this treatment, especially since destroying the exterior lights in an out-of-the-way private garden was such an odd thing to do. Why? Nói could think of only two possible reasons: either some silly kids from the neighbourhood had run amok, or someone had wanted to make their garden dark. The latter explanation was far more worrying as it raised the question: why, for goodness' sake? Pushing the thought away, Nói had tried to convince himself that it must have been local teenagers and that the next thing on the agenda would be to spray the house with graffiti. But deep down he knew the local kids were harmless and that he wouldn't be coming home to find the place decorated with neon-coloured penises. There must be some other explanation for the vandalism.

Then there was the dustbin. Underneath the box containing the untouched pizza he had found the household's large pair of scissors. They had been hunting high and low for these ever since they'd unpacked and wanted to snip the labels off the clothes they'd bought. Nói had taken the least interest in the search since he suspected they would never actually wear most of these clothes. The scissors appeared to have vanished off the face of the earth – until he spotted them in the dustbin. They had been lying, perfectly clean, under the pizza box, and it was impossible to guess why the house guests had thrown them away. They were too large and heavy to have got mixed up with the other rubbish by mistake.

Nói had retrieved them from the bin and showed them to Vala, but unlike him she had been unmoved. She didn't think the discovery could be significant because the scissors were clean. Judging by her expression, they would have to have been covered in blood, preferably with an eyeball impaled on the tip of one blade, before she thought there was any cause for concern. Disappointed by her reaction, he had told her about the pizza, but this had provoked even less interest. She had stared at him in surprise and said their guests had presumably ordered a takeaway and decided they didn't want it when it arrived. No doubt as a result of language difficulties. She was unimpressed by Nói's objection that the Americans must have known what they were doing when they ordered a margherita; it would have been different if they'd ordered something with an indecipherable Icelandic name. She shook her head and refused to discuss it any further. When Nói suggested ringing the police, she burst out laughing and asked sarcastically if he was going to demand the couple's extradition for the crime of throwing out a pair of scissors and an untouched pizza. Or perhaps he thought putting the recycling in the wrong bins was a criminal matter. At that point he gave up.

Nevertheless he had placed the scissors in a plastic bag and put them to one side in case anything else came to light. He was aware that he was overreacting but couldn't rid himself of the persistent feeling that something was seriously wrong. He almost wished something really bad would happen, so he could rub Vala's nose in it.

Nói opened his eyes and heaved a low sigh. Leaning forwards, he tried to concentrate.

'You going to finish that?' One of his colleagues was standing in the doorway of his office, a pair of smeary reading glasses pushed up into his scruffy hair. You would have thought that Nói, as owner and boss, could have insisted on certain standards of dress and personal hygiene, but when he had suggested this, the head of human resources had gaped at him in astonishment and pointed out that there wouldn't be many people left if he did; in fact, he might as well shut up shop. Just as well the woman wasn't in charge of the country's flight attendants. Nói, for one, would have been disgusted if the fingernails of the air hostesses bringing him coffee had been as dirty as those now resting on his door handle. He actually had to avert his eyes.

Nói cleared his throat. 'Yes, sure. No problem. I'll be done by four.' His tone disguised how unlikely this was to happen. It was nearly lunchtime and he had achieved practically nothing.

'How was Florida, by the way?' The man folded his arms and leant against the doorpost. 'You don't look as if you've had much of a rest.'

The bloodshot eyes and dark shadows had obviously not faded since he'd looked in the mirror this morning. 'It was great. I did manage to relax – I'm just jetlagged. We got back at the crack of dawn yesterday.'

'How did the house swap go? All fine, I hope? The car hasn't clocked up an extra hundred thousand kilometres?'

Nói was too tired to enter into this conversation. Besides, he was in no hurry to share his concerns with his staff for fear of encountering the same indifference as he had from Vala. 'The house was fine. Car too.'

'Oh, OK.' The man's expression suggested he had been half hoping for a tale of woe. 'Well, you were lucky. A friend of a friend discovered that the people he did a house swap with had used his car to commute all over the country. They drove back and forth every day to avoid having to pay for hotels – Akureyri, Snæfellsnes, Jökulsárlón, you name it. Back and forth. The car'd been driven more in those three weeks than in the three years since the guy had bought it.'

Nói made a show of smiling. 'The people we exchanged with obviously didn't go in for that sort of thing.' In fact he had no idea if they had. The car had been standing in the drive when they came home and neither he nor Vala had looked inside. 'They didn't trash our car any more than we did theirs.' Nói wished the man would go. He didn't like being reminded of the house swap. And why did the guy have to mention the business of the car? Now he wouldn't be able to relax until he had gone home and checked the clock. He felt a strong urge to ring Tumi – to make sure he was all right. Ridiculous. No doubt his son was sleeping like a baby, as was his custom when on holiday. Nói looked at the screen, then back at the man in the doorway. 'Anyway, I'd better get on. If I relax too much there's a danger I'll crash out on the keyboard.'

The man unfolded his arms and took himself off. The moment he had closed the door Nói reached for the phone, knocking over a photo in his clumsiness. It had been taken on the morning of Tumi's first day at school, and when Nói set up his software company Vala had suggested he put it on his desk. It would set the tone for how his staff should decorate their workstations. The advice had proved completely useless. There were more pictures of Darth Vader in the office than of all the employees' children put together. In fact the photo of Tumi was probably the only one.

Nói propped the picture up again. Knocked flat it only intensified his needless anxiety about his son. He studied the toothless grin and the school bag that looked several sizes too big for the skinny little body. Of course nothing was wrong. All the same he dialled home.

To Nói's surprise the phone only rang twice, though it was clear his son had only just woken up. From the tinny sound he must have answered in his bedroom, on the novelty phone shaped like a car. 'I was just going to call you. I can't get hold of Mum.'

'She's at work. We went in together this morning. What did you want her for?'

'I thought it was her downstairs. I heard a noise. Did you come home just now?'

'No.' Nói glanced at the car keys on his desk and his fingers started inching towards them. 'Sure it wasn't just the postman shoving something through the letterbox? Or Púki rattling around in the kitchen?'

Tumi didn't answer straight away but Nói could hear his rapid breathing. 'No, Púki's here on my bed. And it wasn't the postman.'

'Perhaps your mum popped home to fetch something.' Nói hesitated. 'What kind of noise was it?'

'It just sounded like someone moving about downstairs. I don't know, I can't describe it.' He sounded resentful, as he always did when asked to clarify something. Nói didn't know why but the boy seemed incapable of expressing himself. He was inclined to blame the school system. It was easier than admitting that it might be his and Vala's fault.

Nói stared at the screen in front of him. The rule of thumb that a software designer should write an average of ten lines of code a day suddenly seemed absurd: he would be lucky to finish one. What had he been thinking of to say he'd be done with this by four? He checked his e-mail distractedly but there was still no reply from the Americans. Why weren't they answering their messages? Did they think he was just going to forget about the keys if he didn't hear from them? And weren't they at all bothered about getting the man's coat back? He could understand if they didn't care about the dirty washing. Perhaps he had pissed them off by writing again this morning to ask about the scissors. But damn it, surely they couldn't be that touchy? The only acceptable excuse was that they hadn't had a chance to check their e-mail yet. Nói closed his eyes and massaged them. 'I'm thinking of knocking off early. Why don't I just come home now and bring us a couple of burgers for lunch?'

'Yeah, that'd be great.' Tumi seemed relieved; the resentment had vanished from his voice. 'I'm starving and I don't feel like anything from the fridge. There's nothing but the stuff those people left and I don't want that. It seems disgusting somehow.'

Nói just managed to stop himself from agreeing wholeheartedly. 'What nonsense. I'll be home in an hour at most.' He hung up and tried to focus on work. But the black text of the software program kept retreating before his eyes and in the end he decided to call it a day. Why wait? He wasn't going to achieve anything in the next half-hour. On the way out he paused by the secretary and told her he wouldn't be back this afternoon. For an instant he could have sworn she looked pleased, though she was usually better at controlling her expression. Still, this annoyed Nói less than the beer cans he had spotted here and there on people's desks. Evidently a degree of anarchy had reigned in the office during his absence and he suspected that the problems he was sure must have been piling up had simply been swept under the carpet. Or thrown out. But he didn't say anything – plenty of time for that after the weekend.

While queuing at the window of the drive-in burger joint he tried to ring Vala but wasn't surprised when she didn't answer. She was rarely able to take calls at work. He texted her: *Ring when free – decided to go home*. Then he tossed the phone on the passenger seat and wondered what to say if she called and asked why. He knew she felt he had a tendency to read too much into things – but then her habit of assuming everything was fine got on his nerves too. Like now. She had snapped at him yesterday evening when he couldn't stop talking about the scissors, and this morning she had sighed loudly when he tried to raise the subject of the Americans again. He'd had the sense to shut up. He could just picture her face if she found out the real reason for his leaving work early. He would never let on that he'd hurried home to Tumi because he had a sense of foreboding. Tightening his grip on the steering wheel, he restrained the urge to pull out of the queue and race home. His tension eased a little when his turn at the window finally came.

Nói felt his heartbeat slowing to normal as soon as their house appeared at the end of the street. But it missed a beat when he entered their drive and noticed the front door standing ajar. Switching off the engine, he stared at the door as it swung gently to and fro in the breeze as if controlled by an invisible hand. Nói sat paralysed in his seat, watching to see if the wind would slam the door shut. Then he came to his senses, grabbed the food and got out of the car. As he walked towards it the door continued to swing gently, pausing just short of the frame when he reached it. There it remained, as still as if it were shut. He pushed it wide, stepped inside and inspected it thoroughly before closing it behind him, as if he expected to find an explanation for why it had been open.

But of course there was nothing to see, except that it was time to varnish the wood again. He couldn't think of any sensible explanation, unless Vala had left the door on the latch when they'd gone out this morning. Or Tumi had opened it and forgotten to shut it again. But that was hard to believe.

Nói called out to his son and received an unintelligible yell from upstairs in reply. Shortly afterwards Tumi appeared looking undisturbed, with Púki in his arms. He was barefoot, in jeans and a T-shirt that hung lopsided from his shoulders. The cat closed its eyes, opened its jaw and yawned, revealing a ridged palate and sharp canines. Then it grew restless and jumped down on the floor.

'Did you get hold of Mum at all?'

Nói put down the bag on the kitchen table. The food seemed to have shrunk to a small lump at the bottom. It smelt of frying fat. 'No, she didn't pick up. But I think I know what you heard. The front door was open. We can't have closed it properly when we left this morning. Unless you opened it?'

Tumi frowned. 'Duh . . . no. And it wasn't that kind of noise.' He put a limp chip in his mouth. 'I know exactly what the door sounds like. The computer started up too.' He pointed with a chip at the black monitor in the corner.

'Did you turn it off?'

'No. I haven't been down. Not until you arrived just now.'

'The computer's off, Tumi. You can see that for yourself.'

'Isn't it just hibernating? This was a while ago.'

'No. There's no light showing. You must have been hearing things or dreaming.'

Tumi stared hard at the computer as if he could activate it with his eyes. 'I wasn't hearing things. I know the Windows start-up sound. And I wasn't dreaming either. There was someone downstairs. It must have been Mum. Or some burglar or crackhead.'

'Breaking in to use the internet? I sincerely doubt it.'

'Well, what about the people who were staying here? Are you sure they've left the country? Perhaps they came back to fetch their stuff.'

'Of course they've gone.' Nói didn't even like talking about it. The last thing he wanted was to become obsessed with the idea that their guests were still prowling around. He would rather blame it on the wind but if Tumi insisted it was a burglar, they would just have to agree to disagree.

Listlessly, Nói removed the wrapper from one of the burgers, which turned out to be even less appetising than he had feared. Suddenly his hunger was gone. 'The wind must have blown something in through the open door.'

'Uh-uh.' The sweating burger seemed to hit the spot with Tumi. 'It definitely wasn't the wind. It couldn't turn on a computer.'

Nói contained himself until his son had finished eating and he himself had wrapped the remaining half of his burger in the packaging and thrown it away. The food tasted odd, like earth. He suspected the smell was in his own nostrils but even so he felt an urgent need to brush his teeth. He must be more exhausted than he'd realised. 'I'm going to put my feet up with the papers.' A pile of newspapers had accumulated during their holiday and if he didn't get a move on and read them, Vala would throw them out. She didn't understand how anyone could be interested in old news. But old news suited him perfectly: no need to waste time wondering how things would turn out – events began and ran their course. The whole story was contained in the heap of papers. Like the annual news round-up but in smaller doses. 'You planning to go out at all?'

'Nah. Not for the moment anyway.' Tumi threw the burger wrapper in the bin. He yawned. There was tomato ketchup in the corner of his mouth. 'I'm going to jump in the shower, then I'll do something.'

Nói watched his son slouch out of the kitchen, hardly bothering to lift his feet, but resisted the temptation to tell the boy to buck up and go out and get some fresh air. Strange how his son could be so relaxed now after his earlier anxiety about a possible intruder. His father's presence clearly filled him with confidence, though Nói had to admit to himself that he wouldn't be much use in a crisis. What would he do if a junkie or a burglar suddenly leapt out of hiding? Search for the scissors in the plastic bag he had put in the back of the cupboard in the larder? On second thoughts, he realised he could probably handle a situation like that better than many.

While he was waiting for the water in the tap to run cold, he contemplated what was left of the snow outside.

A man wearing a long dark raincoat was standing on the footpath between their property and the beach, too far away for Nói to see if he was facing the house or looking out to sea. Nói waited to see what the man would do – perhaps he was Tumi's burglar or crackhead, but he didn't move and Nói's patience ran out. He drained the brimming glass and turned away from the window. The man remained standing in the same spot.

The water took away the taste of earth and Nói felt a little better. He decided to put off reading the papers for a while and check on the car instead. His employee's tale about house guests abusing a borrowed car bothered him, though he thought it unlikely there was anything to fear in this case. Surely it was extremely unusual for people to drive for days in cars they had been loaned. Petrol wasn't cheap, after all. But a seed of doubt had been sown in his mind and he wouldn't be able to relax until he had at least looked at the clock.

The wind was bitter and cut right through his thin shirt. The shrill bleeping of the car's electronic lock shattered a hush that seemed unusual for this time of day: no roar of engines from the airport; almost no traffic passing through the neighbourhood. There was an air of finality about the silence that descended after the brief bleeping. As if he had suddenly gone deaf and would never hear again.

Inside the car was a strange earthy smell that reminded Nói of the taste he'd had to rinse away. He grimaced and a shiver ran through him. The car was spick and span but the smell made him queasy. Hastily he climbed in to look at the mileage. It was within normal limits. Rather less than he had expected, in fact. The most the couple had driven was up to the chalet and possibly to the popular tourist sites on the Golden Circle – the waterfall at Gullfoss and hot springs at Geysir. All he need do was take the car in for a thorough valeting to get rid of the smell, then all would be fine again.

Feeling as if a load had been taken off his mind, he was about to step out of the car when from the corner of his eye he noticed that the man on the footpath was now standing at the end of the street. The bare branches of the shrubs on the boundary cast their shadows on him and his face was hidden by a hood. Cautiously Nói pushed the door open, fighting a desire to turn the key in the ignition and make a hasty getaway. But Tumi was in the house with the door unlocked. Nói got out and when he slammed the car door the man turned unhurriedly away and walked back towards the coast path. His gait was odd, more like Tumi's slouching shuffle than that of an adult. Perhaps it was one of Tumi's shy friends.

Then Nói remembered the video footage from the chalet and couldn't help wondering if this was the same person who had stuck the circular under the door there. But the idea was ridiculous. All they had in common was the hood hiding their face, and everyone wore hoods nowadays, so it would be absurd to draw any conclusions from that.

Nói hurried back to the house. When he was a few paces short of the door it opened. Slowly but surely, with a slight squeaking of the badly oiled hinges. Without his knowing where the words came from, a brief greeting sprang into his mind: *Welcome back, liar.*

Chapter 11

22 January 2014

Nína leant against the doorway of Thröstur's hospital room. She had been woken by backache from her uncomfortable doze in the armchair by his bed but she could feel the pain dissipating now that she was standing up. She couldn't remember the last time she had slept the whole night through or woken refreshed in the morning. Her lids felt heavy, her eyes dry, and she rubbed them before peering down the corridor. As always there were all kinds of trolleys, beds, equipment and other paraphernalia lined up along the walls, as if the architects had forgotten to provide the building with any storage space. A rare peace had fallen; apart from a quiet humming and the odd bleep from the machines linked up to the sleeping patients all was silent. No one was about and the night shift staff were sitting down somewhere out of sight.

The pain in Nína's back intensified as she stretched. Her gaze wandered down the corridor once more before she returned to the room. Of course nothing had changed and everything was in its place. Yet Nína had an odd fancy that the shadows of the terminal patients were lurking behind the furniture in the ward. They had to be hiding somewhere, as there was no hint of them in the rooms where their owners lay supine under the glare of the ceiling lights. Before her imagination could lead her any further astray the sucking noise of Thröstur's ventilator wrenched her back to earth. She closed the door carefully and sat down again in the by now far too familiar chair. What she really wanted to do at this moment was go back to the police station and carry on the search for more documents or video tapes, but this would be noticed. She would be reprimanded for turning up outside working hours, and it might lend support to the arguments of those who were eager to diagnose her as neurotic and force her to take leave. How would she be able to search for the documents then?

Thröstur was as motionless as the equipment in the corridor. This was to be expected; the links between his muscles and brain had been severed when the noose tightened round his neck, and oxygen deprivation had done the rest. There was no hope that he would ever move again. He lay in the same position as always, on his back with his arms above the duvet. Occasionally there was a slight change but that was because he had been washed, shaved or examined. Afterwards one of his arms might be arranged a tiny bit further from his side than before, or his body might lie a little crooked in the bed. There was no other sign of movement. His brain had gone on a permanent holiday and there was no one home to control his muscles. His body was so shrunken that he almost looked like a stranger. The speed at which he was wasting away was the most disconcerting aspect for Nína. People on diets battled for months, if not years, to rid themselves of those last five stubborn pounds but here lay Thröstur, not moving a muscle, withering away before her eyes in spite of the nutrition he received through the drip. Even his face was unrecognisable: his cheeks were hollow, his closed eyes had sunk deep into their sockets, and his lips were as pale as his skin and so dry that she was afraid they might flake off. Gently she applied some Vaseline to them, taking care not to disturb the mouthpiece that connected his blue tracheal tube to the ventilator. As usual the Vaseline formed clumps on his crusted lips and spread to the sticky tape that was holding the tube in place.

Gingerly, Nína picked up her husband's hand. His arms lay so unnaturally straight down his sides that she toyed with the idea of rearranging them, bending them at the elbows or putting one arm up over his head. That was how Thröstur used to sleep. But she resisted the impulse for fear she wouldn't be able to stop. If she tried to arrange Thröstur to resemble a living person it might end with her tearing out the tubes and needles that were keeping him alive. And although they were pretty much waiting for her to give the green light for this, there was bound to be a commotion if she took the initiative herself. So she made do with hiding his cold hand in hers. The cannula in the back of his hand dug into her palm. If only they could stick a similar cannula into his brain and access the information inside. There was so much she longed to know, and the answers could only be found there. Presumably Thröstur's memories still existed, though his brain no longer worked – like data stored on a hard disk. It wasn't lost just because the computer was switched off. But it would be once he was dead. Once his life-support machine was switched off, his memories would vanish forever. One day perhaps it would be possible to transcribe memories, but she doubted the hospital would be prepared to keep Thröstur alive until the necessary technology had been invented. Not judging by the hurry they had been in to get rid of him when she finally returned their call late yesterday afternoon.

Nína's face grew hot at the memory of that phone call. To begin with she had avoided the subject with a long-winded rigmarole about how she was giving it serious thought. But as the call went on and the person she was speaking to showed no signs of giving up, her self-control had broken and she had ended up blubbing like an idiot. What did the hospital care if Thröstur was not only her beloved husband but her best friend too? Would the fact that they had rarely quarrelled and had been perfectly happy together carry any weight when set against the ward's need to save money? Of course not. Conversations like these were humiliating. At least, thanks to her snivelling, she had managed to avoid agreeing to a date. For now. The man was no doubt biding his time and either he or another member of the team would ring back soon or ambush her at the hospital.

Nína squeezed Thröstur's hand but his fingers felt like dough. She let it go, leant back in her chair and rearranged the grey fleece blanket, marked 'National Hospitals Laundry', which had creased underneath her. Although it was hot in the room, she shivered. She forced herself to focus on the positive; it seemed she might be on the trail at last, might have finally stumbled on a possible explanation for what Thröstur had done. The video was unequivocal proof that as a boy he had been linked to an incident that could conceivably have eaten away at him ever since and even played a part in his decision to take his own life. Far-fetched? Maybe. But it was better than no explanation at all.

One day he had been wondering aloud if they should join

some other couples they knew on a long weekend away, the next he was standing in their garage, tying a noose. None of their friends had mentioned the trip in Nína's hearing since Thröstur had been taken to hospital, probably for fear that she would still want to come with them. It would be impossible to get into the holiday mood with a bereaved spouse in tow.

Nína brought her thoughts back to the old case. It was infuriating to have such incomplete information and be forced to run through all the possible scenarios. In view of his youth, it was highly unlikely that Thröstur could have committed a crime himself, however odd his behaviour had been during the interview. The alternative was more likely: that he had been the victim of a crime, though it was as a witness that he had been called in to the station. Just about anything could have emerged from the inquiry – or been missed by those investigating. As her boss had rightly pointed out, he wouldn't be the first person to suffer lasting damage as the result of sexual abuse at a tender age. The wounds tended to grow more painful over time, especially if the victims couldn't bring themselves to talk about their experiences. Thröstur had never uttered a word about this case, though she had always believed they trusted one another implicitly. What could have been more natural than to mention that he had been involved in a police investigation as a child? Especially in light of her job, and the fact that he was writing an article about historical cases of child abuse. The more she thought about it, the less likely this explanation seemed. But something had happened, and sooner or later she would find out what it was. Children weren't summoned by the police to give a statement for no reason.

Nína felt warmer but didn't know if that was due to the blanket or the thought that she might actually be on the verge of making some progress. The video had given her the longed-for starting point. Now she needed to dig up the rest of the story, so she wouldn't have to keep brooding over what could have driven Thröstur to this desperate act. Instinctively her eyes sought out the ugly wound still visible on his neck. She no longer felt the need to cover it with the sheet. Things were moving in the right direction. Whatever the story from his childhood turned out to involve, the explanation had to lie there.

Nína drew her legs towards her and wrapped the blanket more tightly around herself. She closed her eyes and emptied her mind but sleep refused to come. No matter how much she tossed and turned, she couldn't drop off. There was too much to think about and she had to come up with a plan. The information she needed must exist somewhere. But where? And who could she ask? She'd been unable to find the rest of the interview on the other videos, or indeed any other interviews connected to the case. Thröstur's mother, Milla, was dead and a brief phone call to his father, Magni, had achieved nothing. The man had been nonplussed and said he had never heard of the incident. It didn't sound as if he was concealing anything from Nína. At first he suggested she must have been mistaken – the boy must have been some other Thröstur.

When she told him about the recording in which his wife was clearly recognisable, all he could think of was that he must have been away at sea at the time and that Milla had forgotten to tell him about it afterwards. Nína found this hard to believe, though she didn't like to contradict him. But her doubts must have been obvious because her father-in-law then came up with another, slightly more plausible, explanation. His wife had done her best to shield him from problems during his shore leave, keen to present him with a picture of the perfect family life: clean, well-behaved children, a spotless home. Perhaps she had thought it better to keep him out of the matter. This was more credible than the idea that an ordinary woman who had never had any other brush with the law would somehow forget that she had accompanied their son to a police interview.

By the end of the phone call Thröstur's father was as eager as Nína to get to the bottom of the matter. Before he rang off, he added that he couldn't stop wondering what could have come over his boy. He seemed convinced that he himself must have failed his son by his frequent long absences when Thröstur was growing up. Nína assured him that this could have had nothing whatsoever to do with Thröstur's decision, but she had been a little relieved as well. It was a comfort to learn that she wasn't alone in entertaining such thoughts. She was also grateful that he evidently disagreed with Thröstur's sister, who seemed to blame Nína for what had happened, though she hadn't accused her to her face. If only she would come right out and say it that would give Nína a chance to defend herself. Until then, she would simply have to bite her lip. It was impossible to lose your temper with someone who wouldn't quarrel openly, especially since the two of them never met up one on one. Yet, in spite of these reflections, her relief at her father-in-law's words was mingled with guilt that she should take any kind of satisfaction in the old man's suffering.

The sucking sound from the ventilator intensified slightly

and Nína poked her head out from under the blanket. The plastic concertina beside the machine compressed and expanded. She had asked the doctor what it was for but hadn't been in any fit state to register the answer – she had only asked in an attempt to stop herself breaking down – so she was still none the wiser as to its function. Perhaps it was to stop the oxygen flowing constantly into the lungs by emulating the action of breathing.

In, out. In, out.

The repetitive movement had a soothing effect on Nína and she couldn't tear her eyes from the concertina that was keeping Thröstur alive. Of course it was time to put an end to this. Her fantasies about the development of some sort of technology for transcribing memories were nonsense and it wasn't fair to Thröstur or their relationship to delay the decision any longer. Every day she saw him lying at death's door the old memories of him were pushed further and further back in her mind. In the end they would vanish. Nína took the decision then and there. A shower of hail rattled against the window. It wasn't Thröstur lying in the bed. He had departed long ago. If she wanted to sit beside him for the rest of her life, she might just as well sit beside a photograph.

Next time she saw the doctors she would request that his life support be switched off.

'I'm so proud of you.' Berglind's smile was sincere. 'Of course it's horrible but it had to be done. You've come to terms with that, haven't you?'

'I don't feel particularly good about the decision but I don't feel bad either. I'm just trying not to think about it.'

The keyhole was covered in snow and Nína was having trouble opening the door. Last night's hailstorm had developed into a blizzard that showed no sign of relenting. As the two women clambered over a snowdrift that had collected in front of the entrance, half of it collapsed inside onto the floor.

Berglind pulled an elastic band from her pocket and tied her hair back in a ponytail. 'Where shall we start?'

'The sitting room, I suppose.' In the middle of her conversation with the doctor that morning it had dawned on Nína that once Thröstur had passed away she would no longer be able to spend her nights at the hospital; she would have to start sleeping at home.

The decision to sell the flat had been taken right then. While the doctor was telling her how relatives usually spent the last hours with their loved one, her mind was occupied with the problem of how to get the property off her hands as quickly as possible.

After that she could begin a new life, far from the old one and far from that creepy garage.

The first step was to ask her sister Berglind to help her clear out the flat, and she had done this the minute her conversation with the doctor was over, partly so she wouldn't have a chance to change her mind. It was also essential to have her sister by her side so she wouldn't have to be alone in the flat, permanently on edge, imagining that every creak and every tiny noise boded evil. Nína smiled at Berglind. 'I don't have any cardboard boxes so we can start by wrapping stuff in newspaper. I've got enough of it. We can fetch some boxes once the shops open.' If they made good progress they might be able to pack up the whole lot today. Berglind was a teacher and had the day off because her pupils had gone on a school trip, and Nína had rung the station and told them she would make up her hours at the weekend. The fear that she might not go ahead with this if she waited one more day was all too real.

Berglind poked her foot at a box on the floor by the wall. 'Have you already made a start?'

'No. That arrived from Thröstur's office with all his stuff in it. I started looking through it but I couldn't face it.' Nína folded her arms and shook her head. 'I don't know why they sent it to me. What am I supposed to do with his old work papers? They just couldn't be bothered to clear out his desk themselves. It looks as if they just swept everything straight into the box.' The man who brought it round had informed her that they were not going to publish the article Thröstur had been working on. He had kept its subject matter close to his chest and as the others were already rushed off their feet, there was no one free to take over and finish it. Nína had shaken her head and faked disappointment, although she couldn't have cared less. But now as she considered the box it occurred to her that the article might have opened an old wound and finally driven Thröstur over the edge. She knew the piece had dealt with paedophiles who had escaped justice in the past. Perhaps he *had* been abused as a boy after all.

'Maybe you'll want to look at it later.' Berglind peered inside the box. 'Or maybe not. Though you should probably go through it before you move. You don't want to start your new life with that hanging over you.'

'No, I guess not. I'll make time for it soon.' Thröstur might conceivably have written some notes about his own case. If so, the box might contain answers. But that was a long shot. Why would he need to make notes to remind himself of his own trauma?

'Is there much stuff in the garage?' Berglind had moved over to the window and was gazing out. 'Maybe we should get Dóri to take care of that.'

Nína managed to control the tremor in her voice. She didn't want to make her brother-in-law go in there. 'No, no need. It's empty.'

This was technically true of the main garage space, but the storeroom at the back of it was full of all kinds of junk, in addition to their skis and the gardening tools they had bought in the autumn sales. The new owners of the flat were welcome to the lot. 'Anyway, I don't want Dóri going in there. There's something creepy about that garage.' To her surprise, Berglind didn't contradict her, merely carried on staring out of the balcony door. When she turned round there was no sign that she doubted what Nína had said.

'Just as well it's empty then.' Berglind rubbed her upper arms, as if to smooth away gooseflesh. Then she grinned. 'Right, shall we get cracking?'

Nína knew her sister too well to be deceived. Berglind had seen something. She went over to the door and looked out. Visibility was poor in the falling snow and great clumps of it were sliding unhurriedly down the glass. Yet she saw at once what had shaken Berglind. The side door of the garage was standing ajar. It had been shut a few minutes ago when they came home. Nína peered at the snow in front of the building but there were no footprints. In her heart she had known there wouldn't be any. She stepped back from the window but couldn't drag her gaze from the garage. The blackness inside the open door reminded her of a gaping mouth, searching for the next prey to devour.

Chapter 12

27 January 2014

The air inside the tiny lighthouse is dank, cold and sour-tasting. Helgi pushes himself up on his elbows, grimacing as his bones make contact with the bare floor. An icy draught is pouring in through the gaps round the door but he is grateful to be able to fill his lungs with something other than the fug inside his sleeping bag. Lying awake in the early hours, he had pulled his head inside it in case it was having a cold face that was preventing him from dropping off. It must have worked because he can't remember anything else until now. While his eyes are adjusting to the darkness, he sits up properly and rubs his sore elbows, then turns his head from side to side, his stiff neck joints clicking. His bed at home with its soft mattress and warm duvet seems light years away.

At his feet Heida is lying curled up in a ball as if to prevent their sleeping bags from touching in the cramped space. Her head is resting on her arm and her curly hair looks as if she has ruffled it with her fingers during the night. She is deathly pale in the gloom. Something black and silver is sticking out from under her sleeping bag and after puzzling over it for a while, Helgi realises it's a torch. His own is tucked inside his bedding, just in case.

Helgi flushes slightly when Heida opens her eyes. How embarrassing to be caught gawping at someone when they wake up. 'Did I disturb you? Sorry.'

'No. I was already awake. I just couldn't face getting up. It's so cold.'

Helgi can't argue with that. The air is almost crackling with frost. 'Want me to pass you your jacket?' Personally he is eager to get out of here; he finds it excruciatingly awkward being alone with a woman he doesn't know and having to behave as if they're old friends. He has the feeling she's waiting for him to come out with something clever or witty, and he seems incapable of rising to the occasion. Why can he never manage that with women? He struggles to his knees and reaches for his anorak. The shiny fabric feels stiff to the touch – from the cold, presumably – and when he has pulled it on he feels even chillier until his body has warmed it up.

Heida watches his actions without moving. 'Is that any better?'

'Not much, to be honest.' Helgi tries slapping his arms against himself for warmth. 'But you don't really have any choice if you're going to venture out of your sleeping bag. I'm guessing there's a hard frost outside.'

Heida sits up and takes the thick jacket he passes her. She bashes the back of her hand against the wall as she is pulling it on but her wince of pain turns to a look of shock once she is encased in the freezing anorak. 'Jesus!' Heida wraps her arms around herself and crosses her legs inside the sleeping bag. 'Are they awake?'

'Don't know. Doubt it. I haven't heard any movements outside.' Helgi gropes for his shoes but can only find one. The other turns out to be under his sleeping bag, which would explain the ache in the small of his back. 'I wonder what sort of night they had? At least we had a roof over our heads.'

'I expect they're used to it.' There is no sympathy in Heida's voice.

Helgi wants to ask if she chose to have him inside with her because she regards him as the biggest pussy of the lot, but stops himself. He doesn't want to hear the answer. Instead, he puts on his shoes and stands up. 'I'm just popping outside.' He doesn't like to say he needs a leak, though it must be obvious. She can hardly imagine he's going for a walk. Just before he reaches for the door handle, he turns. 'You talked in your sleep last night.'

'Oh?' Heida looks startled and Helgi instantly regrets mentioning it. It makes it sound as if he was watching her in the night. But really he wasn't.

'I woke up to hear you saying something. I expect you were sleep-talking. It didn't sound as if you were talking to yourself, anyway. Or to me.'

'What did I say?' Heida seems cross and Helgi kicks himself for bringing it up.

'I didn't understand. It almost sounded like another language.'

Heida stares at him, muttering something under her breath that Helgi can't catch. He seizes this opportunity to go outside.

The instant he opens the door he is met by a gust of wind so violent that he almost loses his grip on the handle. Nature is reminding them who's in charge, in case they had any doubt. He steps carefully outside and manages, with considerable difficulty, to close the door behind him. But the moment he lets go of it he discovers that it's not the only thing round here that's inclined to flap like a sail. It's so hard to keep his balance that he decides against moving far to relieve himself. Holding on to the lighthouse he can move down to the next step, from which, with care, he can reach the third, which ends on the brink, and pee off the edge. It's a precarious feeling, edging his way down, hearing the raging sea below in the semi-darkness, and he's glad to be able to zip up again.

'Mind you don't get blown over.'

Helgi starts so badly that he only just avoids losing his footing. He takes a moment to recover, then turns carefully, once he's sure he looks calm, not like a man in a panic. He came within a hair's breadth of falling. Ívar's face appears in a gap in the concrete handrail of the lighthouse gallery. Helgi coughs and inches his way back up the steps. 'How did you two sleep?'

'How do you think?' Ívar grins, his face scarlet, strands of hair sticking out from under his crooked hat. 'I vote we swap tonight. You two outside, us inside.'

Helgi clings to the wall with bare fingers as he leans back to see Ívar's face. The cold, rough surface hurts his unprotected skin. 'I really hope it doesn't come to that. Surely they'll fetch us later today?' His hands are trembling and he hopes Ívar won't notice.

'An optimist, eh?' The head disappears, then reappears above the rail. Ívar has risen to his knees and is adjusting his hat with gloved hands. 'We should've made them fetch us by boat yesterday. It's almost impossible in weather like this. At least, I can't see you and Heida climbing down the rock and jumping into a boat in a sea like this. Not you, anyway, mate.'

'I meant by helicopter.' The wind snatches the hood off

Helgi's head but he doesn't dare let go of the wall to pull it back up. It is unnerving having to crane his neck like this: the slightest movement could make him lose his footing.

'Like I said. You're an optimist.'

Helgi can't be bothered to stand here arguing; he wants to go back inside. All he's getting out of this is a stiff neck and he doesn't like the undercurrent of their conversation. They don't seem to be able to speak to each other without descending into sniping, as if there's something simmering beneath the surface, something Ívar is not saying but would like to fling in his face. Helgi hasn't a clue what it could be; they've never met before apart from that one conversation in the bar that evening. And since Helgi was perfectly nice at the time, he can't see what he's done to deserve this hostility. 'I'm going to try and make some space so we can all eat inside. We can't risk the food blowing into the sea. You two come down when you're ready.' The joints in his neck click so loudly as he turns his head that he thinks Ívar must have heard them.

It is darker inside the lighthouse. Given the strength of the wind now, it's obvious why the window was blocked off: no glass would be capable of withstanding such a battering, year in, year out. Helgi's sleeping bag takes to the air when he opens the door and falls back to the floor as he slams it behind him. Heida is still sitting on hers. She has put on her boots, hat and padded ski gloves. In the gloom her hands look like those of a robot.

'You're certainly dressed for the weather.' His voice sounds falsely cheerful to his ears.

'I heard you talking. Are they awake?'

'Ívar is. I said I'd make room so we can all have breakfast

in here. It would be crazy to try and eat outside in this gale.' Helgi starts bundling up his belongings. It doesn't take long but he has difficulty rolling up his sleeping bag in the confined space. Out of the corner of his eye he sees Heida tidying her own things away much more neatly; nothing is bundled up or stuffed quickly into her backpack, yet it takes her no longer than him.

'Ívar implied we might have to spend another night here.'

Heida's eyes convey all she thinks about that. She groans, her face grim. 'I just can't do it. I'm scared to.' As though she thought simply saying this would somehow alter their fate.

'Perhaps he's talking rubbish. We'll find out more when he comes down. I imagine he'll ring the coastguard. They're always rescuing people from all kinds of scrapes, so they must be able to pick us up.' Helgi doesn't know what else to say. He doesn't want to spend another night on the rock, though neither does the thought of the winch appeal much in this weather. Hopefully they'll come later this afternoon. By then the wind should have dropped and he'll have had time to prepare himself mentally for being hauled up to the helicopter. They both look up on hearing some sort of commotion overhead. 'Hope they haven't blown away.' Helgi smiles at Heida but she doesn't reciprocate, so he turns back to carry on fighting with his sleeping bag.

The next minute the door crashes open and Ívar sticks his head in. He is even redder in the face than before. 'I can't find Tóti.' He doesn't let go of the door or show any sign of coming inside. The wind sends all the loose objects on the floor flying.

'What do you mean?' Helgi straightens up.

'Hasn't he just gone for a pee?' Heida stands up too, inadvertently treading on a booklet that has blown out of one of the radio equipment boxes. 'He might have climbed out onto the crag for a bit of privacy.'

'Are you soft in the head? There's nowhere to hide here. Do you think I didn't have a look around when I saw he wasn't in his sleeping bag? Are you a complete fucking idiot?'

'What are you saying?' Helgi stuffs his bag into a corner and takes a step towards the door. 'If this is meant to be a joke, it's not funny at all.'

'I'm not joking, you stupid bastard.' Ívar staggers as the wind snatches at the door. 'He's vanished.'

Helgi looks at Heida, who is still standing on the booklet. The pages flap, as if she has trodden on a small bird that is desperately fluttering its wings. 'Wait here. I'm going to find out what's going on.'

By way of reply, Heida zips her jacket up to her neck. 'No way. I'm coming too.' When she lifts her foot off the booklet it flies into the corner, where it continues to flail around in the draught. Helgi fights an impulse to tell her to stay put; she's not his responsibility and what she does is none of his concern. When he asked her to wait, it was because he was afraid the violence of the wind and the limited standing room by the lighthouse could put them in even greater danger. The more people milling around out there, the bigger the risk.

He would much rather stay in here himself.

The moment they step outside the wind seems determined to show off its strength. They stagger around and bump into one another, but finally the three of them manage to climb onto the gallery around the lighthouse.

There's nobody there.

Ívar stands upright, gesturing with one hand while hanging on to the rail for dear life with the other. 'Look. He's not here.' He turns to the crag that rises up behind the lighthouse. 'And there's nowhere to hide.'

They all survey the narrow gallery. There are two sleeping bags on the floor, shiny with sea-spray. On top of one is a sports bag that Helgi assumes belongs to Ívar. The other sleeping bag keeps bellying out and collapsing again, without moving from its place, and Heida pokes at it warily with her toe. Then she peers in through the opening. 'His backpack's inside.'

'Is that yours, then?' Helgi indicates the sports bag that is preventing the other sleeping bag from taking to the air.

'Yes. What the fuck's the matter with you?' Ívar's eyes flash and spittle flies from his mouth. 'Are you doing a stock check or do you think Tóti's hiding inside it?'

Helgi blushes furiously, though he doubts either of them notices. His face must be ruddy from the cold anyway. 'I'm just trying to work it out. I need to think.'

'Think? What about? Tóti's vanished. He's not here and he's not out there.' Ívar waves in all directions. He meets Helgi's eye and adds, as if reciting a nursery rhyme: 'He's not anywhere.'

'We must stay calm.' Helgi tries to mask his own fear. 'There's no point quarrelling. As far as I know none of us has any experience in this sort of thing, so we'll just have to do our best. Was he here when you woke up?'

'No.' The violence has left Ívar's voice and there's a break in it. The man you'd have thought nothing could shake; a strong, weather-beaten tough guy; the type who'd love it if the axle of his jeep snapped during a storm in the depths of the Icelandic wilderness. But suddenly he has got a grip on himself again and rubs his grey stubble. 'I just didn't twig because of the gear in his sleeping bag. It looked like Tóti was lying inside. But when I prodded it I realised he wasn't there.'

Heida picks her way right round the gallery, but there is no sign of Tóti. 'Could he have climbed down the chain? Been rescued before us?'

'Of course not. Do you think he would have gone without telling us?' Ívar snatches off his hat and scratches his head. The wind makes his thin hair stand on end. He licks his salt-crusted lips and takes a deep breath. 'He's not here.' All eyes turn to the sea that surrounds the rock.

The waves rage against each other as if driven by invisible forces. The dark shadows under the crests all look as if they could be Tóti, but they keep disappearing before the eye can make out what is there. It doesn't help that it isn't properly light yet.

'He must have fallen.' Helgi clears his throat and looks away as Ívar glowers at him. 'Maybe he went to relieve himself and the wind knocked him off or he slipped. That's the only possible explanation. I very nearly fell off myself just now. Were you aware of him at all last night? Is it possible he went for a leak and didn't come back?'

'What does it matter *when* he disappeared?' Ívar is shouting now, and not just to drown out the wind.

'If he fell into the sea a short time ago, he may still be alive.' Helgi keeps his voice level.

'Nobody could survive that drop. Are you fucking stupid? I know he didn't fall off yesterday evening. He woke me last night because he was dying of cold. The wind was blowing straight in through the bloody gap in the railing and he couldn't sleep. We swapped places and I saw him get into his sleeping bag. He was alive then. Fuck.' Ívar rams his hat back on his head. 'Fucking, fucking hell.'

Helgi notices that Heida isn't saying anything. Her eyes are fixed on Tóti's sleeping bag and she bends down to it as Ívar turns to face out to sea. Opening the bag, she peers inside and starts back. Then she removes one of her gloves, runs her bare hand over the lining and examines her fingertips, before rising to her feet, her face white.

'I'm going down. There's nothing we can do here.' She avoids looking at Ívar as she begins to climb over the rail and Helgi notices that, instead of putting her glove back on, she shoves it in her pocket.

She lets go of the whitewashed handrail and clambers down the crag that almost touches the lighthouse at this point. Left behind on the rail are two red fingerprints.

Chapter 13

24 January 2014

From her face it was clear that Vala had overdone it. Nói thought she should have followed his example and taken a three-day weekend. She had dark shadows under her eyes as if she'd just been for a swim in heavy mascara, and her drooping lids and slurring voice made her seem a little drunk. 'I just can't think about it now. Tomorrow.'

Nói put his tablet back on the table. The screen showed a freeze frame from the security camera at the holiday chalet. He knew Vala well enough not to bother even trying to persuade her to come over to the desktop. With the tablet he could at least follow her around and force her to look. But the moment she'd walked in he'd known it was a bad idea to share his worries with her. It would have been wiser to wait, give her a chance to relax, have some supper, but he hadn't been able to stop himself. He had been sitting alone brooding far too long for that. And now the damage was done.

'Come on – it's weird. You've got to admit it.'

'Maybe.' Vala heaved a sigh. 'Maybe not. Please don't start banging on about pizza and scissors again – I'm too shattered to care.' She unzipped the jacket she hadn't taken off yet before collapsing onto a chair in the kitchen. 'Anyway, I can't see what difference it makes. You're just collecting anything that fits in with some crackpot theory you're obsessed with. Even if the camera footage shows people behaving oddly, it doesn't tell us anything. Except perhaps that you shouldn't be videoing your guests. I'm not sure we'd come out of it looking too good if people found out. Is it even legal?' She took off her jacket, hung it over the back of the chair and rubbed her shoulders. 'And take that iPad away. I'm not looking at it any more. I feel like a peeping Tom.'

Nói snatched back the tablet. 'It's very strange. And there's nothing illegal about the security camera. They knew about it – it was in the notes we left them, and it's not like it records continuously. The system switches off when all movement ceases for any length of time, and it only films when there's no one in the chalet.'

'But you've got videos of them.' Vala exhaled wearily.

'Yes, but out on the decking, and only when they're arriving. They obviously read our instructions because the first thing he does when they come in is switch off the system. And he switches it on when they go out or to bed.' Nói cast around desperately for some way to convince her, while leaving out the stuff that would annoy her. He knew his worries stemmed from nothing more than a hunch that something was wrong. It had been triggered by a few minor details: the belongings the Americans had left behind, the things they *hadn't* left behind, like the keys, and now this camera footage. Taken separately, unfortunately none of these details was sufficiently unusual to bother Vala, and she didn't seem inclined to put them all together like him. It was easier said than done to convince other people of one's gut instinct, especially when there was no concrete evidence of anything amiss, yet this had no effect on his own conviction. Forget logic: there was something wrong. 'Well, I find the whole thing extremely odd, though you refuse to admit it.'

Nói had gone through all the footage from the chalet from the period when the foreigners were using it. There were quite a few recordings, but each one was fairly short. The first showed the Americans' arrival; them coming inside and looking around, apparently pleased with what they saw. The couple were around the same age as him and Vala, the man rather overweight, the woman slim. Neither was particularly memorable to look at. Both wore brand-new Icelandic fleeces under thick jackets, jeans and walking boots. With them they had two sports bags and several plastic bags of shopping.

Then the man switched off the system and the picture vanished.

After this came several clips in which they were returning from hikes or pottering about on the decking. Nothing remarkable and nothing that suggested there was anything wrong. Nói had deleted the footage he didn't want Vala to see, in which the woman appeared stark naked while fetching a drink of water in the night. It was an unavoidable flaw in the system and there was no need to draw Vala's attention to the fact. This was rather unfortunate since the clip showed the woman peering warily out of the kitchen window as if checking to see if there was somebody outside. She did the same at the large windows facing onto the decking. But it would be pointless to show this to Vala; she would be far too worked up about the infringement of the couple's privacy to wonder why the woman should think there was somebody or something outside.

The two clips he chose to show her were different. One was also recorded at night but this time it showed the man, clad in nothing but ill-fitting checked pyjama bottoms. Vala wanted to avert her eyes from the sight of his large paunch but Nói insisted she watch as the man crept over to the windows just like his wife had the night before – a fact Nói could not, unfortunately, mention. The man tiptoed to the windows, then went to check that the door was definitely locked. After he had gone back into the bedroom the view through the windows showed headlights being switched on somewhere beyond the decking. The lights swung away and disappeared. Vala had simply yawned and refused to admit that this was of any interest, though Nói noticed her fingers drumming nervously after the footage had ended.

The other clip showed the guests returning from a walk and forgetting to turn off the system when they came in. The man fetched some steaks from the fridge, went back out onto the decking and disappeared round the corner in the direction of the barbecue. Then he came back wearing an odd expression, the meat still in his hands. He put it down on the table and appeared to retch. The couple spoke together and although the recording had no sound, it was obvious that they were not discussing the Icelandic scenery or the likelihood of seeing the Northern Lights that night. Then the woman rushed out, disappeared like him round the corner in the direction of the barbecue and reappeared almost immediately, her hand over her mouth.

Then there was confusion. The Americans raced around gathering up their belongings before abandoning the chalet. There were no more recordings until the most recent.

'Please at least admit that the business with the barbecue

isn't normal.' Nói tried to get a grip on himself; he hadn't meant his voice to wobble like that.

'OK. If you'll promise to stop going on about it.' Vala rubbed her forehead as if she had a headache. Looking at his face, she saw he wasn't capable of agreeing to this deal. She sighed. 'Nói. It must have been when they discovered the barbecue wasn't working. I'll admit their reactions were a bit excessive but these people clearly aren't used to things not going their way.'

'No.' Nói shook his head vehemently. 'The problem with the barbecue was the day before; I can tell from his e-mail and the date of the recording. He must have been able to get it working after I sent him the instructions.'

'Perhaps it broke down again or the repair didn't work. How should I know? Please stop going on about it.'

'Vala, I've e-mailed them repeatedly and they haven't answered. Something's happened.'

'Like what? Come on. They're having fun in Paris or somewhere and don't have time to reply to some weirdo in Iceland who keeps bombarding them with messages.'

'I rang and checked with the airlines to see if they'd left the country. Pity I don't know where they were going, only the date.'

'And?'

'And nothing. They wouldn't tell me. Apparently passenger lists are confidential. Then there's the business of the outside lights. Who do you think broke them? Even if the Americans were a bit odd I can't believe they'd have done that.'

'No, I'm sure they didn't. But we do have vandals in this country. It doesn't necessarily mean anything if they target you. For Christ's sake.' Vala rolled her eyes. 'Nói. I'm dying of hunger. If I don't eat something soon I'll pass out. Gudda was sick and I had to take her spinning class on top of everything else.' She glanced around. 'I was hoping you'd have magicked up something to eat.'

'I would have done if I'd realised how late it was. I forgot the time while I was going through the recordings from the chalet. But I'll throw something together. Why don't you have a rest while I'm doing that?'

Vala sighed and let her head fall back. When she spoke again her voice sounded oddly constricted. 'Did you think the scissors would feature in one of the videos? Or the pizza?' She sat up again, regarding him with half-closed eyes.

'No, I didn't.' Nói couldn't keep the defensiveness out of his voice. It was partly triggered by Vala's indifference but also by the fact that he had failed to sort out any supper. 'I've decided to call the police and I wanted to find a video clip that would persuade them to look into the case.'

'Case? What case? There is no case.' Vala groaned again, loudly. 'The two of them are just off somewhere having a good time and can't be bothered to talk to you. I bet you've sent them a million messages about the keys, but they've probably lost them and don't want to admit it. They must think you're crazy.'

He had *not* sent them a million messages. OK, he'd sent a fair few, but he'd rather not go into that. Some people might indeed find his e-mails odd, particularly the most recent one. 'No one's answering the mobile number they gave us. And then there are the videos; it's as though they thought someone was prowling around outside the chalet. I'm beginning to wonder if they got into some kind of dispute with whoever it was.'

'Oh, please, stop it.' Vala shook her head. 'Just because you invent some story it doesn't mean it's true.' She got up and jerked open the fridge. On the half-empty shelves were pots of jam, tomato ketchup and other items that tended to accumulate until the family could bear it no more, threw out the lot and began collecting a new set. 'We didn't leave their fridge this empty. Perhaps they're embarrassed about that as well. I'd have been mortified if we'd left behind nothing but an apple and come home to find our own fridge full of food. I just hope it all goes off while they're in Europe.' She rummaged in the fridge drawers. 'Though I doubt there's any chance of that. Doesn't American food keep forever? They're ashamed, Nói. That's all it is. Remember what a disgusting state the stairs were in?'

'Yes, all right. But at least they left *some* food behind.' Nói wasn't prepared to concede that the explanation might lie with the empty fridge. Or the filthy staircase.

Vala turned, folding her arms across her chest. 'Are you kidding? Open cartons and ancient pots of *skyr* and butter covered in crumbs? They couldn't be bothered to throw this stuff away, that's the only reason it's there.' She kicked the fridge door shut. 'Just accept it. There's nothing going on.'

No sooner had she finished speaking than the family's new automatic Roomba vacuum cleaner popped out of its charger and began its robotic dance across the floor. Practical as he was, Nói hadn't managed to set the timer since they'd taken it out of its box and it started up whenever it felt like it. They stared, transfixed by the behaviour of the vacuum, which seemed unable to make up its mind where to go. When it suddenly made a beeline for Vala, Nói leapt over to switch it off before his wife could kick the expensive gadget. He put it back in its charger. 'Go and have a lie-down. I'll nip out to the shop.'

On the way down the street he saw his neighbour's car approaching and decided to ask him a few questions. It couldn't hurt and – who knows? – he might even have noticed something. The man's expression suggested that the last thing he was in the mood for on his way home from work was a leisurely chat. Their eyes met awkwardly while their windows were rolling down.

'Hi, Steini. I just wanted to ask if you'd happened to notice the Americans who were staying in our house while we were away?'

'Notice them?' The man's gaze flicked automatically to his own house. He looked as tired as Vala. 'As in did I see them coming and going, or did I notice activity in the house? Lights going on and off, that sort of thing?'

'Oh, just if you'd seen them.'

'Yes, I did. Once or twice. I expect they went out early and came back late. As tourists do.'

'Were they all right? Did it look as if anything had gone wrong?' It was a stupid question but Nói assumed the man wouldn't want to prolong the conversation by demanding an explanation.

'Er, I don't know what to say. They seemed OK. They weren't in wheelchairs or on crutches, at any rate.'

Nói smiled weakly. Seeing the man put his car in gear, he hurriedly slipped in another question. 'Do you happen to remember when you last saw them?'

The man looked through his windscreen at his house and drive. 'Not exactly. Maybe a week, ten days ago?' He waved dismissively, rolled up his window and pulled into his drive.

Supper was an uninspiring affair but it hit the spot. They'd had enough of dining out on their trip, so bread, tinned soup, cheese and liver sausage made a nice change. The lettering on the milk carton and the familiar plain packaging of the butter and cheese made them feel that they were truly home at last. It didn't hurt either that the meal required only minimal washing-up, though Tumi still objected to being landed with the chore. His parents left the kitchen, ignoring their son's protests about the injustice of the world, and went to watch the evening news.

Before long, Vala nodded off in her chair. She was obviously even more exhausted than Nói had realised and he wished he hadn't pestered her so hard to discuss the mystery of the Americans. Now he came to think about it, her reaction had been much more heated than usual when they disagreed. It must be due to fatigue. As a rule she avoided conflict and let Nói have the last word. He didn't like to recall their disagreements because more often than not he turned out to have been in the wrong. But this time she hadn't made the slightest attempt to concede that he had a point, not even to shut him up. Odd.

Taking care not to disturb her, Nói got up and turned down the volume. It was unlikely he'd get a better chance to use the computer this weekend. Vala had convinced herself that he was barking up the wrong tree completely, and she wouldn't leave him alone if she saw him messing around with anything connected to the foreigners. If he was going to win her over to his point of view, he would need more compelling evidence than the recordings, the objects in the bin and a vague hunch.

He checked his inbox; there were no e-mails from the Americans. Then the doorbell rang; Bylgja from next door was outside. She was hugging her thick cardigan around her, the wind tousling her shoulder-length hair. Although Nói and Vala had little contact with their neighbours, they had got to know her a bit and found her pleasant enough. Her husband, on the other hand, was a bit of a lout.

'Sorry to bother you, Nói, but Steini told me you'd been asking him about the foreigners who were staying in your house. I was wondering if you wouldn't rather talk to me. He never notices anything – I'm amazed you even managed to get him to stop the car. I'd have expected him to drive straight past.' She tried to smile but her mouth trembled with the cold. 'I hope I'm not disturbing you.'

'No. Not at all. Vala fell asleep during the news and I'm not doing anything much.' He stepped aside so she could come in.

The woman shivered as if to shake off the chill. 'To tell the truth I've been wondering about your guests.'

'Really?' Automatically, Nói bent down to the radiator and turned up the heat. 'Was there something odd about them?'

'No, not at all. They were very nice. A perfectly ordinary couple, not unlike you and Vala.'

Nói felt rather put out at being compared to the big-bellied man; he wished she'd added that he was of course much slimmer.

'I met them a few times and gave them some advice about where to go. They were worried about driving conditions. Perfectly understandable as it snowed quite a bit the first week and I gather they have little experience of winter driving in Florida.'

'Yes, they don't get much snow there.' Nói wondered if he should offer her a cup of coffee but couldn't tell if she was in a hurry.

'If you don't mind, I wanted to know why you asked if we'd seen them. You see, I've been a bit concerned about them and was wondering if everything was OK.'

'Why were you concerned?' Nói was careful to hide his excitement.

'It's nothing major. I just didn't see them the second week. And I lent them our satnav but they didn't return it. I found that a bit odd because they'd struck me as honest sort of people.' The woman turned pink. 'I didn't tell Steini because he'd only harp on about it endlessly. Actually, I was rather hoping you might have come across it.'

Nói shook his head. 'No, I'm afraid not. It could be here somewhere but I doubt it. It wasn't in the glove compartment or on the dashboard.'

'I've already had a look in the car – I tried the door and it turned out to be unlocked. The satnav wasn't there.' She added hastily: 'I pushed the door-lock down afterwards. To be on the safe side.'

'I see.' Had the Americans been a couple of crooks after all? Why on earth hadn't he and Vala requested references before signing the house-swap agreement?

'You wouldn't mind asking them about the satnav next time you hear from them, would you? They might have hired a car and accidentally left it inside. All I'd need is the name of the rental company.'

'I don't imagine they'd have hired a car. They had the use of ours.'

'Really? I thought it had broken down.'

'Why did you think that?'

'It stood here untouched all last week.'

Nói hadn't tried the ignition, so he didn't know if the woman's guess was correct. 'When did you last see them?'

Bylgja furrowed her brow as she tried to remember. 'I saw them now and then during the first two days. Then they went up to your holiday chalet and that's when I lent them the satnav, but I wasn't aware of them after that. The car was back in the drive one morning, though, so they must have come home during the night. But I didn't see them again.'

Shortly afterwards Bylgja said goodbye and Nói remained standing in the hall. Something must have happened to them. He walked over to the computer and on his way past the kitchen window he thought he saw a dark shadow moving at the near end of the garden. He looked more carefully but couldn't see anything. The naked branches of the bushes lining the boundary waved in the wind and the rope on the flagpole slapped in unison. Of course there was nobody there. Nevertheless, he went into the hall and locked the front door.

It occurred to him that there was a key to this house on the ring with the keys to the chalet. What had happened to that? Nói thought about it. The question was not *where* the keys were but *who* had them. He went to the garden door and peered out through the glass. Nothing. Taking out his phone, he tried the Americans' mobile number again. When it began to ring, he went back to his computer, trapping the phone on his shoulder.

So he didn't notice when the blanket of snow at the bottom of the garden was lit up briefly by a bluish glow. It vanished momentarily, then lit up again and went out when Nói hung up in frustration.

Chapter 14

22 January 2014

All the flat's contents below a certain size had been packed into boxes or crammed into black bin bags that were now waiting to go to the dump. It had taken much less time than Nína had anticipated, perhaps because she was throwing so much of it away. She was only going to hang on to essential household items or things that would be expensive to replace. Some of the stuff she was throwing out could, she knew, have been used by other people, but she didn't want any of these things to have a future. That way she wouldn't have to dread seeing someone wearing Thröstur's clothes or come across objects in other people's houses that had once belonged to them. Nína could tell Berglind was unimpressed by her reasoning, but Thröstur's sister Kata didn't even ask her about the black bags littering the floor.

'Did he never mention it?' Nína handed a glass of Coke over the coffee table to her sister-in-law, then topped up Berglind's. The two women were sitting at opposite ends of the sofa, as if it were Nína's job to reconcile them after a long feud. 'Or your mother, maybe?'

Kata sipped her Coke, regarding Nína with wide eyes over the rim of her glass, then dropped her gaze. Since Thröstur had gone into a coma their relationship had cooled and they spoke less and less often, though Nína couldn't quite work out why. She suspected Kata felt she was monopolising the right to grieve. She read as much in her sister-in-law's expression when she came to visit Thröstur in hospital; a shadow had crossed her face when she saw Nína curled up in the chair at his bedside. Nína could understand Kata's feelings. Brother and sister had always been very close – perhaps because of their mother's untimely death – and Kata's grief was genuine, so it must have felt a bit strange to be sidelined like this. Nína certainly wouldn't have been too pleased to find Kata sitting by Thröstur's bedside whenever she arrived at the hospital.

'If they ever told me, I've forgotten. I would have been nine if Thröstur was seven, and I'm afraid I don't remember much that far back.' Kata placed her glass gingerly on the table, as if afraid it would break. 'Is there any chance it could be a mistake? That the boy wasn't actually Thröstur?'

Nína held out her phone. 'There's no question who it is.' As a favour, the technical manager had agreed to convert the video into digital format for her. It hadn't been necessary to explain, though it must have been obvious to him that it wasn't work related. She tried to interpret her sister-in-law's expression as she watched the footage. The voices of the policeman and Thröstur emerged, high and tinny, from the phone.

'Yes. That's Thröstur all right. And Mum too.' Kata watched the video to the end without further comment. She passed the phone back to Nína. 'Can't you find the rest of the recording? Half of it seems to be missing.'

'I've searched high and low but I can't find a thing. I don't think there is any more. Perhaps they didn't realise the tape had run out.' Nína turned off the screen. 'So it doesn't ring any bells? Seeing that?'

Kata shook her head slowly. 'No. Though I do vaguely recall that licence-plate book. Thröstur was mad about collecting car numbers for a while.'

'The book doesn't still exist, does it?' Nína asked, though she found the possibility highly unlikely after all these years and the constant moves that had, by his own account, characterised Thröstur's youth.

'No chance. Dad got rid of loads of stuff after Mum died. If the book still existed, he'd have thrown it away then. We moved out of the west end that summer and I'm pretty sure I don't remember Thröstur having the book after that. He made new friends and maybe they weren't interested.' Kata shifted on the sofa but seemed no more comfortable afterwards. 'Anyway, I don't understand what good it would do you to find the book or any other information about this old case. It was such a long time ago. Aren't there more than enough problems that need sorting out now?' she said witheringly. She didn't need to add that she felt Nína had failed Thröstur.

'Because I suspect this old case may have some connection to Thröstur's decision to commit suicide.' Nína spoke slowly and evenly, and it dawned on her that she didn't actually give a damn what Kata thought. Her sister-in-law's sidelong glances had long ago ceased to bother her.

'That's a bit far-fetched, isn't it?' Kata's look of scorn deepened, though it was mingled now with a hint of uncertainty. 'Why would something that happened when he was seven drive him to do that? I think you're deluding yourself.' Kata's eyes alighted on the bin bags and boxes on the floor, apparently registering them for the first time. 'Why've you packed everything away? Are you planning to decorate?'

'No. I'm moving.' Nína cleared her throat. 'And I've decided to let them switch off the life support.'

'The *life support*? You mean Thröstur?' Kata's voice was choked with pain.

'Yes. I'm going to follow the doctors' advice.' Nína straightened her shoulders, as if to show her resolve. Berglind was doing her best to melt into the sofa.

'Why now? And shouldn't you have told me and Dad?'

'I rang your father earlier. And I'm telling you now.'

'Just because I asked about the boxes?' Realising how ridiculous this sounded, Kata lowered her gaze but couldn't hide her burning cheeks. 'What did Dad say?'

'Nothing. Except that he supported me in this. There's no hope of recovery.' It was all perfectly clear to Nína now. She couldn't understand why she hadn't decided the instant she grasped Thröstur's situation. There had never been any hope and, on reflection, the hospital staff had made this as plain as they could, but she had chosen to put a different interpretation on their words. 'There's no point delaying. Thröstur did what he did and we can't change that. This decision's only a sort of epilogue.'

'When?' Kata looked up and met Nína's eye. Brother and sister were so alike, though her features were a little finer.

'Early next week. Probably on Tuesday.'

'I see.' Kata stood up. 'Are you sticking around here for a bit longer? I'm thinking of going over to the hospital. I'd like to be alone with him for a little while.'

'I'm not going over till later this evening.' It occurred to Nína to ask if Kata would like to stay and finish her tepid

Coke but she knew there was no point. Her sister-in-law wouldn't be persuaded to linger and couldn't provide any answers about the past.

When Nína came back into the sitting room after seeing her sister-in-law out, Berglind was on her feet by the window, watching Kata leave. 'God, I could kill you. Couldn't you have warned me you hadn't told her about Thröstur yet?'

'I really needed to have you here. She might have bawled me out if you hadn't been. I couldn't have coped with that.'

'Why should she be angry with you? It's her brother she should be furious with.'

'It's all so complicated. She can't possibly be angry with Thröstur, so I'm the obvious target.'

Berglind's face softened. She wasn't the type to lose her temper. As a result she had always been popular when they were children, whereas the more stubborn, volatile Nína had had more trouble maintaining friendships. It wasn't until she'd met Thröstur that she had made a real friend – apart from her sister, that is. Like her, he was capable of going off the deep end in spectacular style, but they had agreed about almost everything. After they'd got together Nína's temperament had softened; it wasn't as tempting to fly off the handle if the person you were talking to agreed with you. Most people liked Berglind but her niceness drove Nína up the wall at times. She had to restrain the urge to provoke her sister into expressing some kind of indignation. It was typical that when she had confided in Berglind about her problems at work, Berglind had immediately tried to see the matter from all sides. That was not at all what Nína had wanted to hear. The only side that mattered to her was her own. Other people were welcome to view the matter from all angles and write long academic treatises on human behaviour. Not her. As a result, Nína had avoided any further discussion of the issue with her sister, which meant she'd had no one to talk to at all, and now she regretted not having confided in Thröstur straight away.

'Do you really think the incident from Thröstur's childhood is relevant?' Berglind had her voice well under control now. Her anger had evaporated.

'Yes, I do.' Nína smiled weakly at her sister. 'I hope so. Because then I can stop wondering what *I* could have done differently.'

Berglind opened her mouth to speak, changed her mind and went over and gave her sister a hug. Then she took their half-full glasses into the kitchen.

Surveying the room, Nína saw there was not much more they could do there. Everything had been packed and all that remained was to empty the flat and clean it. But what should she do with the contents? Although she wanted to speed up the move as much as possible and was even prepared to buy a property unseen if necessary, it wasn't that simple. She couldn't complete the purchase of a new flat until she had sold this one. And since it had been in her and Thröstur's name, it would be impossible to sell it without legal hassle. Everything would be easier once he was dead, painful though the thought was.

When Berglind suggested they call it a day, get a Chinese takeaway and take it home to her place, Nína made no objection. She realised her stomach was aching with hunger; for once she actually had an appetite. That must be a sign of improvement.

* * *

They had used the trip downstairs to take out some of the stuff that was destined for the dump. Nína was standing with a bulging bin bag in her arms, preparing to lock up, when the door of the ground-floor flat opened. Her elderly neighbour was standing there. He must have been lying in wait for her as he couldn't have been on his way out, dressed as he was in knitted sleeveless jumper, frayed shirt, corduroy trousers and felt slippers. On his head was a pair of gold-framed reading glasses. Nína would have liked to shove a pipe in his mouth and hand him a leather-bound volume of poetry to complete the picture. Though they'd rarely spoken, Nína knew he was a widower who had lived in the house for years. On high days and holidays the place filled up with his offspring. As she studied the thin figure she couldn't help wondering if this was to be her fate: to live alone for decades. Her circumstances would be even more pitiful than his, though, as she couldn't look forward to any visits from her children's families at Christmas. That reminded her of the Christmas tree. Perhaps he was going to tell her off for failing to take it to the recycling depot herself.

'I'm so glad to have run into you at last,' the old man said. 'I was beginning to think you'd moved. It would've been understandable. I lost my wife when I wasn't much older than you and it was hard enough even though she didn't die by her own hand.'

This struck Nína as rather an unlikely prologue to a ticking-off. 'I've been at the hospital,' she explained. 'Or work.'

'I see. I heard it's not looking good.' The old man stepped aside as if to make room for them in his hall and Nína saw Berglind's horrified expression; she was clearly afraid they would be invited in for coffee.

Nína wondered where the man had heard this but then realised it didn't matter. 'That's right.' She smiled dully at him. 'The whole thing's pretty awful. But it's only right you should know that I've decided to sell up. As you say, it's not really feasible for me to go on living here.'

'No. I understand.' The man shook his head. 'It's a terrible business.'

Nína rubbed her hands together. 'Anyway, we're going to be late for supper.' Out of the corner of her eye she saw Berglind's shoulders relax.

The old man was in no hurry. He nodded slowly, hugging himself to keep out the worst of the chill. He gave the impression that there was something he needed to get off his chest. About the Christmas tree, no doubt. 'It's been on my mind for ages,' he began, 'and I'm not sure we'll have another chance to speak before you move.' A twinge of pain crossed his face. 'When you're my age nothing's certain. But never mind that.' In contrast to his wrinkles, his eyes were youthful, with bright whites and clear blue irises. 'I didn't like to mention it when the business with your husband happened, but since then it's been weighing on my mind. Maybe I'm being ridiculous but I feel you ought to know.'

'Know what?' Nína shuffled her feet. Her stomach rumbled and Berglind was nudging her discreetly.

The old man stroked his cheek. 'It's about something that happened in this street thirty years ago.'

'What?' Nína's voice was hoarse; she wasn't at all sure she wanted to hear any more.

'There was a couple living here at the time who went through almost exactly the same thing as you and Thröstur. Their names were Stefán and Thorbjörg. Stebbi and Tobba.'

'Oh?' The names meant nothing to Nína.

'The man committed suicide. The woman was left behind like you. Though actually they had a child so she wasn't strictly alone, but I don't think that made much difference. She was devastated, as I'm sure you are. And the boy was equally badly affected – he and his father had been terribly close and it knocked the ground from under the poor child's feet. Just as much as his mother's.'

'Let me get this straight: you're telling me that a couple used to live here in the neighbourhood and the man killed himself like Thröstur? Thirty years ago?' Nína's face darkened; she could feel her rage churning. What was this bullshit? She had enough of her own problems without having to hear about someone else's. 'Well, I don't suppose there are many streets in the old part of Reykjavík where there hasn't been a similar kind of tragedy, if you care to look.'

The old man's eyes widened in astonishment. 'Oh, I'm sorry, I obviously didn't make myself clear. The thing is, they lived in your flat.'

Nína started. 'Upstairs?'

The man nodded. 'The man was a journalist like Thröstur.'

'And?' The bag in Nína's arms seemed to weigh more heavily with every detail that the old man added. She wanted to throw it down in the garden and leave it there like the Christmas tree.

'The thing is, he hanged himself too. He didn't take an overdose or walk into the sea. He hanged himself in the garage.'

The world turned black before Nína's eyes. 'In the garage?'

The old man grew embarrassed. He rubbed his hands together, looking from Nína to Berglind. 'I don't know if it makes any difference. But I felt I had to tell you. Perhaps it was wrong of me.' He swallowed. 'And there's more, since I've started. If you'd care to hear.'

Nína put down the bag, pretending not to notice the sour expression on her sister's face. Berglind was shivering with cold. 'Yes, please. I'd like to hear everything you can tell me.'

Chapter 15

27 January 2014

The temperature has dropped again and the cold sneaks in round the badly fitting door with the gusts of wind. It was slightly warmer up until a moment ago but the sleeping bags and clothes they had stuffed into the cracks around the frame for insulation are there no longer. Ívar was like a rat in a trap and had to get out. And there's no point putting it all back only to have to tear it down again when he gives up on the conditions outside and wants to come in.

'Do you think he can hear us?' Heida whispers, as if she believes that, far from being outside, Ívar is hiding under the pile of bedding by the door.

'No need to whisper. The most he'll be able to hear over that wind is the echo of our voices.' Helgi closes his eyes again, leans against the wall and tries not to think about the cold that is clutching at his back. Ívar must be perishing out there, but he insisted on rushing outside when Heida told him what they had seen in the fog. The man flushed dark red and breathed hard through his nose when she started repeating the story about the dead coming back to haunt those who have done them wrong. Fearing Ívar was going to have a heart attack, Helgi wondered what to do. He didn't know any first aid and Heida didn't look as if she was any more clued up than him. When she saw Ívar's reaction, she piled it on even thicker, telling him that it wasn't only fog that summoned the dead but bad weather too. Like the storm that was brewing. At that point Ívar sprang to his feet, flung some comment at her about fucking bullshit old wives' tales, and looked ready to go for her. Then he stormed out of the door.

Helgi listens to the wild screaming of the wind. It sounds as if the weather is seeking an outlet for its fury, though there is no knowing what has caused it. 'This is no ordinary gale. I hope the guy's being careful out there and doesn't get blown off.'

'I can't agree.' Heida raises her voice slightly. 'For all I care he can be blown to kingdom come.'

Helgi opens his eyes and stretches. He looks at Heida, who is resting her face on her knees. She has been sitting hunched up like that ever since she came back inside, as if to avoid any physical contact with her companions. 'I don't believe you really mean that.' Helgi immediately regrets his remark; how should he know whether she means it or not?

'You can try and kid yourself into believing whatever you like but I know what I saw. Tóti's sleeping bag was covered in blood. Ívar must have stabbed him or something.' She has forgotten to whisper but even so Helgi can hardly hear her over the wind. 'I don't care what you think. I know he killed him.'

'There are a number of possible explanations. I find the idea of Ívar murdering him the least likely.'

Heida uncurls and stares at him. Her tousled hair is sticking out from under her hat and her cheeks are a hectic red. Helgi studies her. It's extraordinary how rough the tidiest people can look when the going gets tough. He himself is hardly God's gift but his appearance seems the least affected by the trip. If they are forced to sit here until evening, Heida will end up unrecognisable.

'You come up with a better explanation then.'

'Well, I don't know.' Helgi is finding it hard to think straight. His back is so cold that he can't focus on anything else. 'Perhaps Tóti went walkabout last night and injured himself but didn't realise he was bleeding. He got back into his sleeping bag, then started feeling ill and got up again, then passed out from loss of blood and fell over the rail.'

'And plunged over the cliff into the sea?' The sarcastic look says it all.

'You know what it's like here. If you lose your footing, it's certain death.'

Heida's expression resembles that of a spoilt child. She ignores Helgi's reasoning. 'All right, if you're so clever and have it all worked out, tell me how he injured himself last night? He went to bed at the same time as us.'

'Perhaps he went for a pee and bumped into something.' Helgi closes his eyes and leans his head against the wall. The rough surface hurts the back of his skull.

'There's nothing to bump into here.'

'No. Maybe not.' Helgi decides to change the subject in an attempt to keep the peace. Things are bad enough as it is: Ívar's on the verge of cracking up, and Helgi knows he won't be able to control himself much longer if Heida keeps getting on his nerves. 'Do you know, is it good to shiver when you're cold? Or should you try and avoid it?'

'I don't know,' snaps Heida. From her reaction, anyone would have thought Helgi had made an indecent proposal. 'And I don't care either. I just want to get out of here.'

'You will, before you know it. You'll be right as rain.' Helgi rises to a crouch and pulls out a sleeping bag from the pile by the door. Space is so tight in the lighthouse that everything is within reach. He stuffs the bag behind his back and feels better at once. 'Strange phrase, "right as rain", isn't it? How can rain be right?'

'What the hell are you on about?' Heida lays her head on her knees again. 'I can't cope with your nonsense right now. I'm freezing and I feel terrible.' She glances up briefly to check if Helgi is hurt. 'Sorry. I don't mean to be a bitch but this is doing my head in.'

'It'll be OK. Just you wait and see.' Helgi looks over at the door, which is rattling in the wind. 'They'll come and get us and someone else'll be given the job of finding out what happened to Tóti.'

'But what if they don't come till tomorrow morning? What'll we do tonight? I can't sleep with that man in here. What's to stop him attacking us as well?'

'Why would he do that? Anyway, they're going to fetch us later this afternoon or this evening. The repairs must be finished soon and the helicopter will be ready the moment the wind drops. I guarantee it. In the worst-case scenario we'll have to abseil down the cliff to a boat, but we'll get out of here, one way or another.' Helgi's stomach churns at the thought of the slippery chain dangling down the rock face. He hasn't yet made himself lie on his stomach on the ledge and peer over at this means of descending but he remembers catching a glimpse of it when the helicopter originally approached the lighthouse. He will not be taking that route except in the direst necessity.

'What if he's lying? What guarantee do you have that he was speaking to the coastguard earlier? He could have been playacting.' Heida sits up suddenly, frees her legs and rises onto her knees. She is gaping at Helgi as if frightened by what she has said.

'He made the call. I could hear the other person's voice.'

This does nothing to pacify Heida. After all, Ívar could just as well have rung a friend or the speaking clock and merely pretended to be talking to a rescuer. The fact that Helgi heard someone on the other end means nothing.

'But why would he have pretended to make contact?' Helgi reasons. 'If they don't rescue us, he'll be in the same mess as we are. Our food's running out and there's not a lot of water left either.' On reflection, this was a stupid thing to say but it's too late now: he's given her even more reason to be worried.

'How long does it take to die of thirst? And people hardly live any time without food either, do they? Three days? Two?'

'Now it's my turn to say please stop asking questions.' Helgi smiles, hoping she'll recognise the absurdity of their situation.

Heida hesitates, then returns his smile, showing the merest hint of teeth. But a moment later she's off again. 'I can't stay here any longer. I can tell it's going to turn out badly. What the hell was I thinking of to let myself be talked into coming?'

'It's your job. We're prepared to put ourselves through all sorts of things for work. It's not as if we're here on holiday.'

The door shakes as if someone who has never seen a handle before is trying desperately to break in. The wind has gained force and is battering anything in its path. 'I'm going out to fetch him.' Ignoring the protests from his frozen knees, Helgi stands up.

'Please don't!' Heida gazes at him imploringly and it occurs to Helgi that she might be close to the edge. 'Just leave him. He'll come in when he's ready.' She moves as if to grab Helgi's leg to prevent him from leaving, but stops herself. 'I know it was him.'

Avoiding her eye, Helgi takes tight hold of the handle and braces himself for a violent buffeting. Before he opens the door, he looks round and sees Heida glaring at him as if he is breaking a sacred trust. 'If you're right, other people will deal with him shortly. But we can't let him stay outside alone. We won't feel any better if he has an accident.' Helgi turns the handle and, although he is prepared for the worst, the door flies back with such force that he is lucky not to dislocate his shoulder. After a struggle he manages to close it behind him, unsure if Heida uttered a parting comment.

He gasps as he turns to face into the gale. It fills his mouth with a nauseating taste of salt but he knows if he tries to spit it out, it'll be blown straight back into his face. Disconcerted, he loses concentration briefly and the next gust flings him against the wall. He thanks his lucky stars it didn't blow him down the steps and over the edge. As he clings for dear life to the window recess, he reflects once again that it's obvious why they blocked it off. Yet it would be absurd to imagine this is the worst storm that has ever battered Thrídrangar. Land is invisible; a blizzard appears to be raging just beyond the rock. It will hit them any minute: he must persuade Ívar to go inside.

'Ívar!' Helgi yells as loud as he can but the wind forces the words back down his throat, intensifying the brackish taste in his mouth. The cords of his anorak whip his face until it stings and he tries in vain to push them into his neckline. The storm has given them a life of their own. In the end Helgi has to release his grip on the window so he can tie them more securely under his chin.

Ívar is on the helipad, lying flat on his stomach above the terrifying abyss, and for a split second Helgi thinks the man is injured or even dead. But then he moves, turning his head and stretching. The hood of his anorak inflates, flapping in the wind, so it's unlikely he can hear Helgi. There is nothing for it but to clamber down over the rocks and try to talk him round. Otherwise it is almost a foregone conclusion that Ívar will be blown off the helipad. He's probably fairly safe as long as he lies flat but the moment he tries to stand up he's bound to lose his balance in the squalls.

No sooner has Helgi set off down the rocky slope towards the helipad than it occurs to him to obey Heida after all and leave Ívar to his fate. He has absolutely no reason to sacrifice himself for this man. Yet in spite of that he keeps going, until he is suddenly knocked sideways and has to exert all his strength not to fall. The most sensible approach would be to lie down and crawl but this is easier said than done. He'll be all right if he moves slowly and cautiously enough between the gusts, never taking his eyes off his goal. But if Ívar refuses to come back straight away and the wind grows any stronger while he is trying to persuade him, they'll almost certainly have to crawl back.

Helgi stoops down to Ívar when he finally reaches him and grabs at his jacket to attract his attention. 'Come on.' He practically has to shout. Ívar's face is running with water, his eyes are bloodshot from the salt. 'You must come inside, or the storm will blow you over the edge.'

'I saw him.' Ívar points down into the wild surf below. The waves crash into the cliff; the sea churns and boils around them. 'He's down there.'

After a moment's pause, Helgi lies down on his front beside Ívar. 'Where?' He peers over, clinging to the edge of the helipad, painfully aware of the inadequacy of this handhold. The spray stings his eyes but he forces himself to hold them open. 'I can't see anything.'

'He keeps appearing and disappearing.' Ívar is staring down intently and doesn't notice when Helgi abandons the attempt to identify anything in the boiling breakers below and drags himself further back onto the helipad.

'Come on, Ívar. Even if you do spot him, there's nothing we can do. He can't possibly be alive if he's down there, and we can't haul him up. When they come to rescue us they'll mount a proper search for him.' His voice cracks mid-yell, but he takes a deep breath and manages to shout so that Ívar can hear. 'We don't want them to have to search for you as well.'

Ívar turns and gapes at Helgi in astonishment, as if it hadn't crossed his mind that anything could happen to him. The wind fills his hood again, making it look as if his head is expanding. He glances down once more, then turns back to Helgi. 'What if they don't come? What if we're stranded here?'

'Of course they're going to come. You spoke to them, remember? We just have to sit tight till then.' Helgi rises to his knees and puts an arm round Ívar's shoulders. 'Come on. We'll be hearing the helicopter before you know it.'

'When?' Ívar stares pleadingly at Helgi and for the first time he realises the man is shaking with cold. Come to think of it, he's freezing himself but he's too worried about his companions to pay any attention to the fact. If help doesn't arrive soon, there's a risk that being cooped up together in the tiny lighthouse will prove too much for them.

Helgi tightens his grip on the other man's hard-muscled shoulder. 'Soon. Come on, we can't stay here. The blizzard'll strike any minute. We must get inside before that happens.' He takes one last look over the edge, driven by a desire to see the man below, though all he really wants is to look away. His hold slackens when he glimpses a grey fleece between the crests of the waves. For a split second it vanishes, then reappears, unmistakably this time, as if the sea is trying to return the man's half-submerged body. To Helgi it looks as if the colourless face is turning its vacant gaze heavenwards, the hair black with seawater, the mouth half open. As if Tóti is crying out to his Maker over this injustice. The body is tossed ceaselessly to and fro, which makes it hard to see properly amidst the white foam. Yet Helgi can tell that Tóti's fleece is torn across his abdomen, exposing the white T-shirt and pale flesh beneath. There is no blood; the sea has probably washed it away.

Helgi tries to tear his gaze from the sight. There is something so unspeakably harrowing about the face in the surf. 'Come on.' He staggers to his feet, reeling in the wind's blast, and this time manages to drag Ívar away with him. They hang on to each other as they inch their way towards the lighthouse. Although it is not far, the wind has decided to amuse itself with capricious changes of direction, making their journey perilous in the extreme.

Helgi has an overpowering sense that someone or something is standing on the helipad behind them, watching their progress. He is reminded of what he thought he saw in the fog yesterday and finds himself taking larger, more determined steps. Ívar accompanies him, tightening his grip on his arm. There is no need for words; Helgi senses that Ívar feels the same. When they reach the steps up to the lighthouse, Helgi turns and looks back at the helipad. The blizzard has reached the stack now, the mesmerising, whirling whiteness moving closer and closer. He raises his arm to tear open the door but Ívar is blocking his way, standing rooted to the spot. 'Get inside, man!' Helgi pushes at his back.

'Who did that? Did you write that, you fat fucking pig?'

For an instant Helgi wrestles with the temptation to shove the man away from the door, down the steps and watch him fly over the cliff. 'What are you talking about? Get inside!' Helgi seizes Ívar's arm but the other man doesn't budge.

'Did you write that, you pathetic tosser?' The man is so worked up that his screech drowns out the storm. Again and again he slaps his hand on the wall beside the door.

Using a black marker pen, probably the same one that Helgi saw Tóti use to highlight the damage to the wall, someone has written in large, clumsy letters: *Stefán Egill Fridriksson 1985*. 'No, Ívar, I didn't write that. Don't worry, it'll come off.' Helgi closes his eyes as the blizzard strikes. Again he tries to push Ívar but the other man now seems incapable of moving and allows Helgi to squeeze past him to the door. Helgi drags it open and they both tumble inside without another word.

Chapter 16

25 January 2014

'I told you the police wouldn't be interested.'

Nói sighed in exasperation; his wife's smugness was intolerable. Vala was cutting up a grapefruit after her morning run, still wearing her tight running gear. This made Nói even grumpier since he was sitting there in his dressing gown. Did she ever relax? He had dragged himself out of bed at the same time as her but refused her invitation to come and get his circulation going. As if it required any special intervention to get one's blood to circulate. It wasn't as if it pooled in your body while you slept. Instead he had rung the police and reported his concerns about the foreigners. He had added the detail about the neighbours' missing satnav to make his case sound more convincing.

'Actually they were interested. They've made a note of it and will deal with it as soon as they get a chance. I wasn't expecting them to turn up here with their sirens wailing.' To be honest, he had been hoping for a bit more of a reaction, but he would never have admitted as much to Vala.

'They won't do a thing. Believe me, I know all about it.' As if Vala was an expert in police matters. She had never got so much as a speeding fine in her life. 'They receive all kinds of tip-offs and they wouldn't achieve much if they went around following up any old nonsense.'

'May I remind you that these people stole a satnav. The police are bound to be interested in that, if nothing else.'

Vala tutted. 'Maybe if the satnav had been attached to a car. The police don't go looking for phones or small items like that. They concentrate on the big stuff.' She put down the knife and took a seat facing Nói, her colour high. There were small beads of sweat along her hairline. He hunched over his coffee cup.

'Do you want the other half?'

The prospect only made him hanker for bacon and eggs. 'No, thanks. Definitely not.' He took a mouthful of coffee, casting around for some way of rendering her speechless, but nothing came to mind. 'I'm thinking of popping up to the chalet later. To check on things and look for the keys.'

Vala swallowed a piece of grapefruit. 'OK. But what if the police turn up while you're gone?' She grinned, her white teeth gleaming. 'I'm teasing. Go on then. If it'll make you stop fretting, I'll be only too happy. Want me to come along?'

Nói wasn't sure how to answer. He wanted her there if his theory that something had happened to the couple turned out to be right. But if he was wrong he had no wish to drive home under a barrage of taunts about how she had known all along that everything was fine. 'I was thinking of taking Tumi. It'd do you good to relax and he could use some fresh air.' He was suddenly sure that she had been thinking along the same lines: while she would enjoy discovering that there was nothing wrong at the chalet, she couldn't bear the thought of his gloating if the situation turned out to be ugly.

'Yes. Maybe that would be best. I'll go round to Mum's and give her the presents we bought them. Then we'll have tomorrow to ourselves.'

Nói stood up, retied his dressing gown, and tried not to think about what that meant: running, swimming, gym, yoga or just stretching exercises that would cause him to ache in places he never knew existed. Perhaps he could fake illness and persuade her to make do with watching other people torture their bodies instead. There were some exciting matches on TV tomorrow.

'This car's a heap of shit.' The comment came out of the blue. They had been driving in silence for the last half-hour.

'Oh?' Nói turned off the tarmac road onto the track leading to the holiday colony. It passed through an area of twisted birch scrub that was unlikely ever to grow into a forest. He had no idea who had planted the trees since they had already been there when he and Vala purchased the chalet four years ago. He hadn't noticed any sign of growth over that period. 'It gets us from A to B. And it was cheap.'

'Yeah. That's why it's so uncool. Cheap cars are never cool.'

'In that case we'll probably never own a cool car. Not unless we win the lottery. Which we never will since we don't even buy tickets.'

'Why not?'

'Because we'd never win. Nobody wins the lottery.' Nói slowed down in anticipation of a nasty pothole. The landscape was pale with snow and no one else appeared to have driven along the track that day. 'Aren't you looking forward to going back to school?' No sooner had he said it than he realised that he had already asked Tumi that. Still, better to repeat the conversation than let himself get riled about their crappy car.

'I've already told you: no, I'm not looking forward to it. How much further is it, anyway?'

'Five minutes. You ought to recognise where we are.'

'Not in the snow.'

Nói couldn't even be bothered to be shocked by this answer. 'What do you think? Is everything going to be OK at the chalet, or a mess?'

'A mess. But it'll look OK on the surface.'

Nói glanced at his son's face in the hope of reading his expression but Tumi averted his eyes and stared out of the window. Nói didn't ask any further questions, preferring to interpret this as meaning that he had an ally. Even if there was nothing to see, it didn't necessarily mean that everything was OK.

They sat in the car for a minute or two, studying the chalet. It was exactly like a thousand others: a wooden, single-storey structure with a sleeping loft, surrounded by a railed-in area of decking. It went with the family car – not particularly showy or conspicuous – which suited Nói down to the ground. The modern glass structures featured in glossy magazines held no attraction for him. What he wanted was somewhere cosy and ordinary where a sock left on the floor would not destroy the overall impression. The chalet fitted the bill perfectly and much to his surprise Vala had fallen for it too. The first time they'd visited after buying it, he had realised that the place represented something quite different to her – outdoor life and long walks over the endless moors and up into the mountains. Whereas what attracted him was the thought of barbecuing, lounging on the sofa and enjoying the quiet at night. In the event, however, they had managed to combine the two and both were fond of the chalet.

The slamming of the car doors echoed in the silence, and the gravel crunched loudly under their feet as they walked towards the small building. The air was so crisp that Nói could have sworn it crackled, and he relished filling his lungs after the drive. 'Notice how good it is to breathe here?' He wasn't really expecting any answering enthusiasm, but it was his duty as a parent to open his son's eyes to the glories of nature.

Tumi slipped on the icy ground and just avoided losing his balance. He had fallen in love with a particular brand of trainers that Vala loathed, and always wore them, regardless of the weather. This was his third pair in a row. Smooth-soled and slippery – but cool. 'Seems a bit weird to me. Even the air.'

'How do you mean?' Nói had just been feeling relieved at how normal everything seemed. He had come to the conclusion during their silent drive here that he would rather everything was all right, even if it meant that Vala would crow.

'It's too quiet. There's no birds or anything.'

'They're just being quiet so they don't attract attention. Most of them have gone anyway. In case you hadn't noticed, it's winter.'

'There's always birds here. Even in winter.'

Nói stamped the snow off his shoes onto the decking and shrugged. He didn't want to agree with his son but he had to admit that the hush felt unusually oppressive. Suddenly the thought struck him that it had been a mistake to bring Tumi along. What would he do if they came across a body? Tumi was too old to be fobbed off with the lie that the dead person was sleeping. 'Wait here. I'm going to have a look around inside in case anything's wrong.'

'If something's wrong I want to see. Why else do you think I let you drag me all the way up here?'

'Wait, I said.' The hinges squeaked as Nói opened the door. Had they always done that? Their arrival was normally accompanied by bustle and noise, so the faint squeaking would have gone unnoticed. He experienced the same sensation as he had on their return from America. It was as if a different, alien tang hung in the air that met him, but he couldn't work out what it was this time either. As usual the wooden panelling on the walls muffled all sounds, which made it even quieter inside than out.

The hush had a dense quality.

Nói's first action was to pick up a crumpled letter that was lying on the floor by the door, in exactly the same spot as it had in the video clip. The side facing upwards had a single line printed in the middle of the page, and he turned it over to see if the main text was an advertisement for a Christmas bazaar at the church or something equally rustic. But the back was blank. The message said: *The day of reckoning has come. Why did you lie?* Nói frowned. It must have been delivered to the wrong house. None of them were liars and certainly none of them were expecting a day of reckoning. He and Vala had always stressed the importance of being honest in all their dealings. With Tumi too, though once or twice they'd had to resort to white lies when their son was small and asked awkward questions. *Why's granddad got an oxygen tank? – He's practising to be a diver.* An answer better suited to a five-year-old than the truth about his grandfather: *He's dying of lung cancer, darling.*

Nói folded the paper and put it in his pocket. It was nothing to do with them. Yet a vague memory came back to him of the words that had sprung into his mind the day before, not exactly the same but uncomfortably similar: *Welcome back, liar*. This odd coincidence was unsettling, but then that was the nature of coincidences; you only noticed the ones that disconcerted you. Others passed without your being aware of them. Nói continued his circuit of the house and opened the doors to both bedrooms and the small bathroom without spotting anything untoward. He climbed far enough up the ladder to peer onto the sleeping platform but it was the same story there. Nothing out of the ordinary. In spite of everything he felt a momentary stab of disappointment. He turned on the ladder and called out to Tumi that it was safe to come in, everything was absolutely fine.

'Smells bad.' Tumi walked in, making a face, his hands in his pockets. 'What do we do now? Drive home?' He surveyed the room as if the answer was to be found on the walls.

'I'm going to take a better look around, just to make sure they've put everything away properly. Would you mind hunting for the keys?'

While his son pulled out kitchen drawers, Nói walked over to the living-room window facing the decking. He looked out but could see nothing unusual. No one was lurking in the birch scrub; he could see no other cars or anything that could be regarded as abnormal or strange.

Tumi banged a drawer shut. 'The keys aren't here.'

'No. That would have been too simple.' Nói stretched. He wondered if he should pull the curtains across the window or leave them as they were, and he hadn't made up his mind when Tumi spoke again.

'What's this, Dad?'

'What?'

'Some kind of letter, or note. But it can't be from those foreigners. It's in Icelandic.'

Nói took the folded sheet of paper from his son. 'Where was it?'

Tumi pointed to the kitchen worktop.

In the middle of the page was written: *Why did you lie? The truth will out*. 'What is this rubbish?' He could ignore one note with this sort of cryptic message and convince himself that it was a mistake. But two?

Tumi shrugged. 'I don't know. I didn't write it.'

'I didn't think you did.' Nói put the note in his pocket with the other. It must have been delivered either before the foreigners arrived or while they were here, or it would have been lying on the floor beside the other note. The family hadn't visited the chalet since mid-November and it certainly hadn't been lying on the worktop then. He would hardly have forgotten such a peculiar message. 'I expect the guests picked it up somewhere without understanding it. Maybe it's some kind of weird advertisement.' One more white lie could hardly do the boy any harm.

'Advertisement? What for?'

'Search me. But the note's obviously nothing to do with us. Perhaps it's the name of a play. Or a line from a poem.' Was it possible that the message was part of some peculiar art happening or poem that the poet delivered to houses line by line? Such a thing wasn't unheard of.

They lapsed into silence and continued their search until they were sure the keys were nowhere in the chalet. Nói didn't forget the notes, however, and while he was peering under the beds and running his hands along the shelves he couldn't stop thinking about the strange messages. After checking all the likely and then the unlikely places, they gave up and decided to head home.

On the way back to the car Nói went to check the barbecue in the hope of discovering what had upset the guests. He opened the heavy steel lid. On the rack inside lay a dead cat that looked almost exactly like Púki.

Chapter 17

23 January 2014

Nína kept sneezing but had developed the knack of turning away from the shelves when the fit came upon her so as not to blow up even more dust. As always, once she was engrossed in a project, her physical discomfort ceased to bother her. She would have stayed where she was even if she had sneezed every time she drew breath. At last she had a solid lead: a name, a year and a month, more or less. Her neighbour from the ground floor had remembered them as best he could, and although he had been a little uncertain, Nína was almost sure he was right. She would deal with it later if it transpired that he was mistaken. Or that the whole thing was pure coincidence – which she refused to believe. The date the old man had guessed at fitted exactly with the witness statement Thröstur had given the police as a boy. Turning her head, Nína had seen the wall of the garden on the other side of the street. A grey, concrete fence, Thröstur had told the policeman. All that was missing were the phantoms of children perched there with notebooks, on the eternal lookout for cars. Ashen-faced, she had turned back to the man and carried on interrogating him.

She had bombarded him with such a merciless stream of questions that the old man had backed further and further inside his flat, until the conversation that had begun by the front door had ended halfway down his passage. She could read in his eyes that he regretted ever having brought the subject up and for a while he seemed afraid she might try and shake the information out of him if he didn't answer quickly and confidently enough. Even Berglind looked disconcerted, though she had the sense to stay out of it.

The old man had mainly talked about the journalist Stefán's suicide in the garage thirty years earlier. But Nína also learnt from him that the building already had a bad reputation at the time, as though past generations of children had come to a secret agreement, without the grown-ups' knowledge, that there was something sinister about the place. For example, there had been a bicycle repair shop there that had closed down in the end because the children refused to take their bikes to it. The workshop owner had been forced to pack up and move his business elsewhere.

Nína's neighbour had no idea what basis the children had had for their belief, but the story had lived on among successive generations of kids in the area and even today a hint of their old fear of the garage remained. In the old man's opinion, Stefán's suicide must have had a lot to do with it, and now Thröstur's attempt to follow suit. Perhaps the children imagined that the building itself forced people to kill themselves and were afraid of suffering the same fate.

As the sisters were saying goodbye to the old man, Nína thanked him for removing the Christmas tree. From his expression she inferred that he hadn't been responsible. Whatever happened, it was clear she had to sell the flat.

Nína crammed yet another folder back onto the shelf. Nothing there. She pulled out the next and began leafing through it. Her movements were quick and deft, as she was practised by now. After fine-combing all the files labelled 'Suicide', she decided to widen her search in case the reports on Stefán's death had ended up in the wrong folder. To hell with the fact that she had already gone through most of the files in the basement. She hadn't been in possession of a name then, so it was perfectly possible that she had overlooked the relevant documents.

According to her neighbour, the police had spent a good deal of time on the case. The widow had refused to accept that her husband had taken his own life and insisted there must have been another explanation: an accident or maybe something more sinister. She had threatened to go to the press, but the neighbour didn't remember seeing anything about the incident in the papers. And anyway the widow had been in a state of collapse by the time the police finally closed the case.

He didn't know what had become of the woman but he doubted things had turned out well for her. A year after the incident she had abandoned her attempts to keep up the payments on the flat, not least because, shortly before her husband had killed himself, the tenant renting the garage had handed in his notice.

The old man had talked to Stefán a week before he died. Stefán had knocked on his door to ask if he would be interested in renting the garage from them and admitted that he was dreading having to break it to his wife that their tenant was leaving as they were very hard up just then. His death must have been a terrible blow to the family finances. For all the old man knew, it might have been money worries that had led him to take this desperate way out.

The widow's sufferings were far from over, however. Her husband's suicide left her almost incapable of working and she started drinking heavily. By the time the bank threw her out of the flat, the family was in a wretched state and the impact on her young son had been particularly cruel. If Nína hadn't just listened to this tragic tale she would have been inclined to burst out laughing when the old man earnestly advised her to steer clear of alcohol, at least for the next year.

If his account was to be trusted, the police must have written reports about the case. Nína went on flicking through the files, hardly taking in what she read but aware that subconsciously she was classifying the information with great care. This became evident when she finally came across the woman's name. She gasped inadvertently, the dust-filled air leaving a bad taste in her mouth. Hastily she turned over the pages to find the next report, in the hope that other documents relating to the case would have been filed with it. Not so. Swallowing her disappointment, Nína focused on what she had found.

She felt her lips moving as she read the file, as they had when she was a little girl learning to sound out her letters. The frisson was the same too; she wanted to ensure she didn't miss anything. So she read the page again. And again. Afterwards she laid her hands on it, leant back against the wall and closed her eyes while digesting what the text had contained. Really, it was nothing more than a confirmation of what the neighbour had told her. There was no mention of Þröstur or anything to link him to the incident.

The report was not classified as an investigation into a suicide. That was why Nína had scarcely given it a glance the first time she went through the files. It was just one of countless folders containing reports about unfortunate souls who had suffered a raw deal. The recently widowed Thorbjörg Hinriksdóttir had telephoned to request police assistance at her home – not for the first time. When they arrived, it transpired that she was not in any danger: what she actually wanted was to discuss the death of her husband six months previously. When asked why she had requested police assistance, Thorbjörg responded that she was fed up with never being put through to anyone when she called and constantly being turfed out of the station. Nobody in the police would talk to her any more. The officers pointed out that wasting police time was a criminal offence but she refused to listen. The author of the report added that the woman had reeked of alcohol and that the empty bottles and overflowing ashtrays littering the flat were evidence of a serious drink problem.

The woman wanted to draw their attention to what she described as vital information, but judging from the report this did not seem to include any new facts. It all boiled down to her conviction, repeatedly asserted, that Stefán had had no reason to kill himself and that the police had failed to prove otherwise. The officers pointed out that they could hardly be expected to do so; the job of the police was merely to rule out other eventualities and this had been done. The woman then claimed to be in possession of new information about the garage that she believed was relevant. When they questioned her, however, it seemed there was little substance to this. Shortly before his death her husband had apparently made a big issue of telling their son never to enter the garage or go anywhere near it. When the police tried to explain that this was understandable since the building had been full of dangerous tools on account of the workshop on the premises, the woman had blown her top and in the end they had fled under a hail of abuse and accusations of cowardice and a cover-up. The woman's son had been nowhere to be seen. The report concluded that this situation could not continue and guidance was requested as to how officers should respond to further call-outs. It was also recommended that social services be contacted to check on the boy's wellbeing.

Some chance. She knew from experience that the right of parents to mistreat their offspring was much stronger than the child's right to a safe and happy childhood. If the situation thirty years ago was anything like it was today, the boy had probably been left to fend for himself.

The ticking of the clock on the wall was driving Nína crazy. Her eyes kept straying to it, only to be reminded how slowly time was passing. Her boss, Örvar, was playing the silent card to lure her into filling the awkward gap with some nonsense that he could then refute. But although there were countless things Nína wanted to say, she was not going to give in. She examined her nails, realised how dirty they were and placed her hands composedly in her lap. Then she looked up and made herself smile at Örvar, to convey the message that she could play this game longer than him if necessary – even if she did look as though she'd been dragged through a hedge backwards after her sojourn in the filthy basement.

It worked. 'There are a finite number of ways to commit suicide, Nína. Your husband chose a fairly common . . . way out. The documents in the basement go back decades and, quite frankly, it would be surprising if you didn't come across another case that was similar.'

'There are plenty of ways to kill yourself.' Nína had to

discipline her voice to stop it wobbling. She straightened her spine. 'Are you seriously trying to tell me that it's only to be expected that Thröstur should have attempted suicide in the same way and in the very same spot as a man who lived in his flat thirty years before, who was also a journalist? Are you saying that doesn't surprise you at all? Two men of almost the same age, who aren't known to have suffered any major setbacks that might explain their actions? Don't you at least find it strange?'

Örvar looked unwell; he seemed tired and couldn't hide how much he wanted this conversation to be over. 'Well, of course it's a bit odd. But I don't see what it changes. Do you?'

'I'm just trying to point out that the incidents are weirdly similar and involve a worryingly large number of coincidences. In addition to the fact that when Thröstur was a boy he was mixed up somehow with the first suicide. Surely that must make you a bit curious?' Nína tried to read her boss's face. 'It's all right for me to look into this, isn't it? Into why the other reports are missing, I mean? Judging by what it says here, there should have been lots of them.'

'There could be all kinds of explanations for that. Perhaps they ended up in a file belonging to one of the old hands here at the station. Not everything finds its way down to the archives, I can tell you.' He waved the report. 'Nína, the affair was investigated at the time, you only have to read this to see that it received far more attention than it warranted. But nothing suspicious seems to have emerged, so the police would have turned to more pressing affairs. The idea of reopening the case thirty years after the event is utterly absurd.' He replaced the document on his desk and pushed his face towards hers. Instinctively she drew back. 'I promise you, Nína, we did everything in our power to rule out the possibility of any criminal involvement in your husband's case. You can hardly believe we would fail to look after one of our own?'

Nína had to choke back a laugh. The last thing she wanted was to mix up her formal complaint with Thröstur's case; there was too much at stake, so she couldn't speak her mind. She cleared her throat. 'When Thröstur's death was examined nobody knew about his connection to this old incident. So no one can have looked into it.'

'Connection!' The word emerged with the force of an expletive and Örvar pulled away from her again. 'Why not let our imaginations run wild and try to picture what possible crime could be behind all this?' He cast around as if searching for an answer. 'Hmm. I just can't think of any. Can you? If you can come up with a good idea I'll put someone on the case immediately.'

Nína opened and closed her mouth several times as if she had been ordered to imitate a fish. 'I don't have any theories. If I did, I wouldn't have bothered asking you to reopen the case.' The courage she had summoned up in order to confront her boss in his lair had now drained away. 'I'm trying to do the right thing in the circumstances, by coming to you instead of conducting a private investigation. I'm well aware that I'm not neutral and would run the risk of over-interpreting things.'

'Like now, I'm afraid.' Örvar hesitated. To give him his due, he didn't seem to derive any pleasure from speaking to her like this. Quite the opposite, in fact. 'You're on a wild-goose chase, Nína. You're just putting off the inevitable – the need to deal with your own trauma. Unfortunately, the police's limited finances mean we can't help you in your search for something that doesn't exist.' He glanced at the calendar in his notebook. 'Take some leave, Nína. You could do with it. I'll find someone to take over in the basement.'

Nína licked her dry lips. She did her best to maintain her composure, though she wanted to scream. 'Maybe I will. Especially if I'm left with no alternative but to investigate the matter myself. Then I'll need all the free time I can get.'

Örvar seemed oddly thrown. 'If you go on leave, Nína, you're to do just that. You're not to try and investigate anything.' He coughed and snapped his diary shut. His bony hand lay on top of it as if he expected the book to spring open of its own accord. The gnarled vein in the back of his hand showed a rapid pulse.

'I won't be able to help myself. If no one else is going to look into it, I'll have to do it myself.' Sometimes it was best to be blunt.

Her boss emitted a low sigh. 'This is ridiculous.' He shook his head. His eyes searched her face while his fingers tried to find some means of occupying themselves on the desktop. 'There's no chance this will turn out well, Nína.'

She shrugged. 'I don't believe my situation can get any worse.'

'That's what you think.' The furrows in his face deepened and filled with shadows. 'I'm going to suggest a compromise which I hope you'll accept. It goes against the grain but I've always had time for you. You're conscientious and tenacious when you want to be, and you've often taken on more than your share. I want you to get over this and be yourself again, so I'm going to stick my neck out.' Unable to resist the temptation, he lapsed into silence again, but Nína was not going to fall for that trick. What was she supposed to say? 'Thank you so much'? After a brief pause he carried on: 'I'll look into it myself, though I doubt I can spare much time. Still, I'll do my best. What do you say to that?'

Nína wavered. This was not at all what she had been after. She had been hoping that the police would launch a proper inquiry. 'OK. But I'm not going on leave. I want to carry on working.' She would be in a better position to keep Örvar to his promise if she was at the station – and to carry on digging into the case for herself.

'Fine.' He couldn't conceal his chagrin. 'Fine. We'll leave it at that then. For now.'

Nína rose to her feet and picked up the report. 'Thank you.' She turned in the doorway and their eyes met briefly before she went out into the corridor. She rolled up the report and slapped it on her palm as she tried to bring order to her thoughts. One thing was clear: her boss's shifty gaze and body language had indicated that he knew a lot more about the case than he was letting on.

Chapter 18

27 January 2014

The blood-soaked sleeping bag lies in a crumpled heap on the floor. They sit huddled around, staring at it as if they expect it to speak if only it could find the right words. All they have been able to agree on since this morning is that they must stop the bag from blowing away, in case it holds the clue to Tóti's fate. But an argument broke out over how to touch it, since none of them wanted to contaminate it with their DNA or fingerprints. Finally, Helgi took it upon himself to roll it up, armed with plastic bags on both hands. And now it is lying on the floor between them, as a reminder of what has happened.

'I didn't lay a finger on him.' Ívar breaks the silence. He is utterly deflated now, his momentary madness over. It was the writing on the wall outside that caused him to go berserk; he started yelling incomprehensibly, pointing at Heida and Helgi in turn in his fury. One minute he was blaming them for the graffiti, the next he suddenly seemed to think Tóti had written it. Then he sank down, utterly overcome. 'I swear to you, I didn't touch him.'

'Nobody's saying you did.' Helgi removes his gaze from the sleeping bag and studies his companions instead. Ívar's eyes are flickering around in a vain hunt for something to fix on.

'He must have fallen,' Helgi says. 'Got up to relieve himself and lost his footing. If there's anything else behind it, the police, or whoever investigates this sort of accident, will find out. Let's think about something else.'

'Like what? Hunger? The lack of water?' Heida snaps and buries her face in her knees. She still hasn't forgiven Helgi for allowing Ívar to come in. 'And why's there blood in the sleeping bag if he fell while taking a pee?'

'I don't know. Like I said, it's not our job to find out. All we need to do is sit tight and wait.' Helgi pauses and takes stock of what's happened, still feeling faintly stunned at this turn of events. He seems to be the only one capable of thinking straight. Heida and Ívar are behaving as if they've lost the plot. Both complain of headaches; Heida blaming the lack of air inside, though she won't be persuaded to stick her head out of the door. Ívar also refuses point blank to go outside, as if he's prepared to spend the rest of his life in the lighthouse, if necessary. He seems to be under the impression that some dreadful fate awaits him outside. Clearly he can't stop thinking about the name on the wall.

Helgi avoids any mention of it, for fear the man might go berserk again, though there's no denying that he'd like to interrogate him, watch him squirm. It's an odd feeling, unlike him, and Helgi guesses it must be a consequence of finding himself thrust into the role of leader. His leadership abilities, limited though they are, seem to go hand in hand with other, darker qualities. But he resists the temptation to needle Ívar, reminding himself that in the circumstances he must shoulder the responsibility for their situation.

If someone had told Helgi at the beginning of this trip that he would have to take charge and ensure the group held on to their sanity, he would have laughed in disbelief. He's no leader and in the past the kind of people who possess such qualities have wanted little to do with him, no doubt because of his weight. In dodgeball practice, the kids always used to choose him second to last, ahead only of Regína who had glasses and a crutch. He was invited to parties by the other children in his class only because it was forbidden to leave anyone out. How is he to know what a real leader would do in this situation? Well, he can't bail out now; he'll just have to do his best. There's no alternative. 'Do either of you have a pack of cards? Maybe we could play whist or something to pass the time.'

'You need four people for whist.' Ívar has finally brought himself to look at the sleeping bag.

'You want to play cards? Are you kidding?' Heida raises her head and shoots Helgi a contemptuous look. But her face has at least lost its frozen expression. Perhaps Helgi's leadership abilities consist of being useless enough to shake the others out of their despair.

'It was just a suggestion. We can't sit here in silence forever.'

'I can.' Heida clamps her lips shut and buries her face again.

'What the hell happened? I just don't get it. I don't.' Ívar shakes his head and it appears to Helgi that his eyes are wet. The man who only yesterday had seemed capable of tearing nails out of planks with his bare teeth.

'You're not fooling anyone, pretending to be surprised.' Heida's comment is almost inaudible.

'Pretending to be surprised? What the fuck's that supposed to mean?' Ívar's cheeks are burning and if any tears had crept into his eyes they are gone now.

'What do you think it means?' Heida doesn't look up.

'How many times do I have to say it? I didn't go anywhere near the guy.' Ívar is back to his usual self and Helgi's not sure this is an improvement. His voice rises ominously and his face is contorted with ill-concealed fury. Before Helgi can think of any means of pacifying them, Heida speaks up again.

'How do you sleep at night? Lightly? Deeply?' Although her face is still buried, it's obvious who she's addressing.

'Average. I don't know. How should I know? When I'm asleep I'm asleep; it's not like I can check.' Ívar's face darkens further and Helgi doesn't like the way things are going. He may be a useless leader but clearly he's an even worse peacemaker.

'Listen to me. If you didn't go near Tóti, it must have been one of us two. But do you seriously expect us to believe that you wouldn't have woken up? Space is really tight on the gallery. I couldn't have moved up there last night without risking treading on you, and as for Helgi . . .' Heida rolls her head on her knees. 'So that leaves only you.'

'Stop it.' Helgi is afraid this will end in disaster. 'There's no way we can establish what happened. Maybe Tóti started bleeding internally and vomited blood into his sleeping bag. Maybe someone else came here in the night. There are countless other possibilities. It doesn't have to be one of us.'

'Internal bleeding! Jesus wept,' Heida shouts, exasperated.

All right, the idea is absurd, Helgi agrees, but it was all he could come up with off the top of his head. Now Ívar nods at him with a conspiratorial wink: men against women.

Heida ignores the provocation. 'And who on earth could have been here? If anyone could land, we'd have been evacuated hours ago.'

Helgi decides to stay out of it. All he's doing is making things worse. Instead he tunes in to the wind that is buffeting the lighthouse from every side. The door bangs in its frame. What are they to do if it gives way? Taking out his phone, he checks the clock. It's as if time has slowed down; as if the minutes are refusing to leave the rock to make way for new ones. The fact becomes glaringly obvious in the context of their repeated phone calls to the coastguard. Whenever one of them thinks it's time to check if there's any news of a rescue, it invariably turns out that they have only just rung. They are politely reminded not to waste their batteries. The coastguard will be in touch the moment there's any news. *Don't call us, we'll call you.* The presence of the phone in Helgi's hand makes him long to ring yet again in the hope that a time has been fixed, but yet again it turns out to be far too soon after his last call. He's terrified the coastguard will decide not to fetch them at all if they become too much of a nuisance. Which is absurd, of course, but then the whole situation is absurd.

'If we had a radio we could listen to the weather forecast. It's about to start.' Ívar has also taken out his phone to check the time. His face expresses the same disappointment as Helgi's. 'I'd have packed differently if I'd had any inkling we were going to end up in this bloody mess.'

'I'd have packed a gun.' Heida sounds as if she actually means it. Helgi thanks God she didn't know in advance. When she speaks again, it's on a less inflammatory topic. 'If you want to listen to the forecast you can use your phones. There's an internet connection here.' All of a sudden her hatred and rage seem to have subsided. Helgi wonders if this is because she has resumed her professional role, now that the conversation has turned to communications, and this has brought her to her senses. After all, who would buy the services of a person whose strongest desire is to shove a gun barrel down your throat? Perhaps he should try and persuade her to finish testing and installing the equipment which is still sitting, shiny and new, in the corner, ludicrously redundant in their present predicament.

'My phone's so ancient it can't connect to the internet.' Ívar brandishes the pink Nokia handset, which back in the day boasted the innovative Snake game.

'We can use mine. It may not be the latest but at least you can get online.' Helgi toys with his phone; there's no way of knowing if he'll be able to connect here. He has only ever used it via his router at home or in his rented studio. 'Do you know how to do it, Heida? Do you need a password?' In fact, Helgi reckons he could work it out for himself but he's hoping to distract her. Afterwards he'll encourage her to do a bit of work. Once Heida's focused on her task, it'll leave him free to concentrate on Ívar.

Heida puts out a hand for his phone. 'Are you sure you can spare the battery? You don't have much left.'

'Doesn't matter.' Helgi doesn't know who's supposed to call him. There's no one waiting for him at home. Not yet. He has received two calls during the trip, both from newspapers who had heard about their situation and wanted him to take pictures. Perhaps it would be better if his battery did run out once the news desks get wind of the fact that one of their group is missing. He doesn't want to give in to the temptation to tell them about the photos he took of Tóti's body when he went outside in the storm earlier, at the request of the coastguard, to check if it was still there. It hadn't moved from where it was caught on a rock at the base of the stack. Naturally the pictures would never be published in any of the papers but that wouldn't stop people fighting to get a look at them. The snow made them rather fuzzy but did nothing to detract from the horror. There's no question what they show. When he took them he thought they might prove useful to the police if the body subsequently broke loose and vanished into the sea. But now he doesn't know if he should own up; the police might regard him as a cold-blooded bastard. Which he isn't. He's just never been in a situation like this before.

Heida fiddles with his phone, then hands it back. She seems to have recovered her composure but it probably wouldn't take much to tip her over the edge again. 'There you go. You should be able to listen now.' She stretches, awkwardly so as to avoid touching the sleeping bag, but loses her balance and brushes against the yellow and blue material. She and Ívar both yelp; Helgi sighs under his breath. He feels an urge to yell at them both to behave like adults but instead concentrates on trying to bring up the news website.

'What's this?' Ívar sounds horrified, but Helgi won't grant him the satisfaction of looking up and instead carries on tapping at the far too small letters on his screen. Although the web address is short, it's almost beyond him to enter it; his fat, sausage-like fingers tremble on the tiny keyboard.

'Don't touch it!' Helgi hears Heida shifting back against the wall but remains focused on trying to connect to the news. Serve them both right if he pretends not to hear them.

'It's only paper.' Helgi sees out of the corner of his eye that Ívar is bending over the opening of the sleeping bag. 'Only a piece of paper.'

Finally Helgi manages to connect to the news server and raises his eyes from the phone. He sees Ívar pulling a blood-stained sheet of paper out of the sleeping bag. 'What the hell are you doing? We weren't going to touch anything!' He should have known better than to take his eyes off them.

'But what if it tells us what happened? Wouldn't we feel better if we knew?' Heida speaks as if she and Ívar have suddenly become allies.

'I'm not so sure about that.' Helgi rises to his knees and moves closer to Ívar. 'Put the paper back where it was. It can't say anything that'll help us. I don't believe for a minute that it'll explain anything.'

'But what if it's a suicide note? A goodbye letter?' Ívar's voice betrays a misplaced optimism.

'Yes, let's take a look at it now we've got it out.' Heida inches closer, not even noticing that she's got one knee on the sleeping bag. She watches Ívar as he unfolds the paper with his fingernails. Forensics won't exactly be over the moon about this but it's better than covering it with prints. He makes a clumsy job of it but finally succeeds in flattening it out.

In the middle of the page are four words: *The day of reckoning.*

'What does it say?' The page is facing away from Heida. 'Day of reckoning?'

Helgi notices that Ívar is paralysed. He is staring at the page, his mouth working, as it did when he spotted the writing on the wall this morning. Helgi and Heida do not say a word.

Now that they have stopped talking, they can hear the phone. The announcer is reading with the characteristically odd intonation favoured by newsreaders:

Police in the capital area have yet to release a statement about their investigation into the deaths of four people in Skerjafjördur on Saturday night. According to sources, the incident is being treated as murder. The police are asking anyone with information to come forward without delay . . .

'Turn that bloody thing off,' growls Ívar.

Chapter 19

24 January 2014

All day Nína had been keeping her side of the bargain. She had turned up to work in the morning, had a coffee, then headed down to the basement where she dutifully sorted through obsolete paperwork. She didn't hunt for anything about Thröstur or the couple Thorbjörg and Stefán but gave thought only to whether the documents were worth keeping. She made such good progress that she managed to clear several more metres of shelving than expected. Now the corridor was full of black bags of rubbish and cardboard boxes containing material to be preserved. She didn't envy whoever was landed with the job of scanning it all in. Better not to think about the fact that it would probably fall to her. Some things should just come as a nasty surprise. Really, she wondered why they hadn't simply lugged a photocopier down to the basement to make her life easier. Perhaps it wasn't possible to link it up to the computer system down here. The moment she saw a USB cable running down the stairs to the basement she would know what she was in for.

Apart from half an hour off for lunch, she had worked flat out until her arms were aching. She had gone to the canteen to fetch some food but eaten it in her office. It was easier than sitting alone, watching her colleagues pretending not to see her. So what if the odd crumb spilled onto her keyboard? Although physically tired, she felt as happy as if she had just spent a summer's day at the hot-water beach in Nauthólsvík. At last she had succeeded in purging her mind; it was the first day in ages she hadn't spent hours on end brooding over her wretched situation. Thröstur's case was being reviewed and soon there would be news, for better or worse. There was no need to worry about it for now. All of a sudden she felt wonderful.

This lasted right up until she ran out of bin bags and went upstairs to fetch more. Coming face to face with Örvar in the corridor, she asked if he'd had time to look at the case. The only reason she did so was to avoid having to walk past him in awkward silence. But his reaction opened her eyes: the long-drawn-out umming and ahing, followed by a series of excuses and explanations as to why he hadn't had a chance to get round to it yet.

Plainly the man had no intention of lifting a finger.

He had been hoping to be able to put it off indefinitely. Well, if that was the case Nína regarded their agreement as null and void. If he had no intention of revisiting the cold case and its putative connection to Thröstur's suicide attempt, she would resume her own investigation. She made up her mind while Örvar was still in the middle of explaining how behind he was with his reports, and an inadvertent smile crept over her lips as she nodded and pretended to understand. He frowned as if he sensed that some aspect of their relationship had shifted fractionally, although he couldn't put his finger on what. Beaming at him, she said she'd look forward to hearing from him later.

The question was how to proceed now. Firstly, she would have to pursue her inquiry outside working hours as far as possible, since it was none of her employers' business what she got up to in her leisure time. Secondly, she would have to track down Stefán's widow Thorbjörg. The woman had been waiting thirty years to meet someone who believed that there was more to her husband's death than met the eye, and with any luck she would welcome Nína. If, that is, she hadn't drunk herself into an early grave. What would happen after that was anybody's guess.

Thorbjörg Hinriksdóttir wasn't in the telephone directory. But she was alive. According to the national register she was probably homeless, but Nína was fairly sure she wasn't sleeping rough since she knew most of Reykjavík's homeless by name from working as an officer on the beat. That meant she must be under a roof somewhere, but where? Judging by the descriptions of her problems with alcohol, she was probably either at a treatment centre like Hladgerdarkot or in some other institution. For all Nína knew she could have been in a car crash or had a brain haemorrhage and been admitted somewhere permanently. Her thoughts flew to Thröstur lying there in his coma and she hoped to goodness the woman hadn't been reduced to the same state. If she had, it would be futile to try and ask her anything.

Several phone calls, during which Nína shamelessly introduced herself as a police officer, revealed that Thorbjörg had until recently lived at a halfway house in the Vogar district, but was now in the National Hospital in Fossvogur. It was uncertain what would become of her afterwards as she required constant care, but she would probably be moved to a nursing home.

According to her ID number, Thorbjörg was sixty-one years old. If her husband Stefán had been alive, she would no doubt have been taken up with golf or boasting about her grandchildren to her sewing circle. Not lying in death's waiting room.

Nína wondered how best to approach her. Should she ring the hospital and give advance warning of her visit, or just show up? The woman at the halfway house had been reluctant to disclose what was wrong with Thorbjörg, perhaps sensing that Nína's enquiry was not strictly work related.

In the end Nína decided a surprise visit would be best; that way the woman would have no chance to refuse to see her if the intervening years had dulled her interest in the circumstances of Stefán's death.

Nína took a deep breath before entering the ward. Thorbjörg's bed was halfway down. She appeared to be asleep, lying on her back like Thröstur, her body straight, arms by her sides. Like him she was hooked up to all kinds of machines, but where his body formed a barely visible bump under the duvet, her belly rose in a great mound as if she were about to give birth or was trying unsuccessfully to conceal a basketball from the staff. Since it was unlikely at her age that she was about to add to the human race, either someone must be missing their ball or the woman had an abdominal tumour the size of a human head.

Nína gave a low cough. No response. She was surprised at how smooth and young the woman's face looked, though her colouring didn't suggest a healthy lifestyle. Her skin was as yellow as an old newspaper. Nína had expected the woman to be weather-beaten and scored with wrinkles like the street drinkers she had come across, who looked as if the marks of a harsh life had been carved into their flesh with a knife. She cleared her throat again, louder this time. The woman opened and closed her mouth, then turned her head to Nína and cracked open her eyes. Her youthful face became instantly old: the whites of her eyes were a bright yellow.

'Hello.'

'Who are you? Are you from AA?'

'No. My name's Nína.'

'You look like you're from AA. For God's sake, go and find someone else to bore to death.' Her voice rasped as if someone had run a grater over her vocal cords.

'I assure you, I'm not from AA.' Nína couldn't help wondering what it was about her that gave that impression. AA volunteers came in all shapes and sizes, so the woman must be referring to her manner or expression. When all this was over she would have to sort herself out, both mentally and physically. 'I was hoping you'd be willing to talk to me about a matter that touches us both.'

'Are you from the God squad then?' Thorbjörg screwed up her yellow eyes. 'If so, you can bugger off. I'm beyond salvation and I've no interest in your heaven. You can tell your God it's time He made some changes up there. Hell sounds a lot more tempting.'

'I'm not from the God squad. I'm not selling Herbalife either.' Nína guessed this would be the next accusation. 'I came to discuss your husband's death in 1985. Nearly two months ago my husband tried to kill himself in exactly the same place as yours. And the similarities don't end there.'

'I'd have bought some Herbalife off you. Just so you know.' Thorbjörg's voice had softened and Nína wondered if she was going to break down. She braced herself to see bright yellow tears seeping down the woman's cheeks. But instead Thorbjörg sat up a little in bed. The grotesque belly was completely out of proportion to the woman's emaciated body. Noticing Nína's eyes fixed on the bump, Thorbjörg smoothed the duvet over it. Her nails and fingers were almost as yellow as her eyes. 'My liver's packed in. I'm on a waiting list for a transplant but I'm right at the bottom and that's where I'm likely to stay. The others are far more deserving. I didn't exactly look after the one I was originally given.'

'I see. Well, I hope there'll be one for you.' Nína went to fetch a chair that was over in the corner, as far from the bed as possible, as if to underline the fact that Thorbjörg received no visitors. She sat down, hoping she hadn't misread her welcome. 'I don't know how much you remember from that time but I'd be grateful if you could cast your mind back. Anything would help. All the reports about your husband have disappeared. Or been mislaid.'

'Huh. They'll have put them through the shredder straight away. If they had shredders back then. I can't remember.'

'I think they've simply been misplaced. Thirty years is a long time.' Nína wasn't sure the woman had the strength to talk, so she went ahead and told her all about Throstur, then outlined the little she knew about Thorbjörg's husband. She placed all the details before this poor yellow woman, as conscientiously as if she were presenting a judge with the information for a search warrant application. When she had finished she tried in vain to interpret Thorbjörg's reaction.

'There was no boy involved in the investigation into my Stebbi's death. I'd have remembered.' The woman licked her cracked lips. 'There were no witnesses, unfortunately. That was the problem.'

'Are you quite sure?' Nína was wrong-footed. Was it possible that Thröstur had been involved in a completely different suicide case? Or another case entirely? She had assumed that since the report had been filed under suicide it must have referred to that type of incident. But of course the document could simply have ended up in the wrong folder.

'If there'd been any witnesses I'd have looked them up and spoken to them personally. I was never satisfied with the way they dealt with the case and I did everything I could to investigate it myself. It sounds like the same thing's happening with your husband. History's repeating itself.'

Nína nodded. Then it dawned on her that the woman hadn't been informed. The police had judged, rightly, that she couldn't be trusted to leave the witnesses alone. Especially since the witnesses were children. 'OK. Forget them. It doesn't alter the rest. We live in your old flat and our husbands both decided one day to walk out into that horrible garage and take their own lives.' She didn't bother to repeat that the men had both been journalists. It was irrelevant. 'At the time you believed something untoward had happened and now I'm in the same boat. Perhaps we can help each other out.'

Thorbjörg laughed mirthlessly, then heaved a gusty sigh. Nína thought she could almost smell stale cigarettes, as if the exhalation had released molecules of ancient smoke. 'You're nearly three decades too late, dear. Where were you when I still saw any point in fighting?'

'Playing with my Barbie.'

'Think you'll end up in here? Like me?' The words contained neither mockery nor malice. 'Let me tell you something. I drank too much before my Stebbi died. He drank too. Maybe

I wouldn't have ended up quite the way I have, but I was on the wrong track anyway. And it didn't help that we belonged to that famous generation you may have heard of, who got screwed over financially. We all bought property with index-linked loans, and received index-linked wages, and ended up in terrible debt when the government abolished wage indexation in '83. We were on the brink of bankruptcy but we managed to stay afloat by renting out the garage and tightening our belts. When Stebbi died, more than half the family income disappeared and so did our tenant. Which was understandable really as his business was about as healthy as our finances. One króna in, two krónur out. Anyhow. In less than a year I'd lost my husband and my home. And I dealt with it by drinking. Then drinking some more. The upshot was that I lost the one thing that should have mattered to me more than anything else in the world: my son. In the end he gave up on me and I don't blame him. I'm amazed he hung in there as long as he did.'

Thorbjörg stared down at her belly, then looked up at Nína, her yellow eyes almost kind. 'So, to answer my own question, no, I don't think you'll suffer the same fate as me. You don't look like an addict. More like an AA type, as I said when you came in.'

'I don't have any problems with booze, but I'm not from AA either. Can I ask you a question?'

'Feel free. I'm not going anywhere. And it's fun having a visitor. Though you could've brought me flowers – that would really have shocked the nurses.'

'Since you lost the tenant of the garage, is it possible that your husband picked that spot as some sort of sign that his decision was linked to money worries? That he didn't want to live any more when he saw what was going to happen to your flat? I have to ask, though I know from experience how painful questions like this can be.'

'Stebbi didn't kill himself. I'm as sure of that now as I was at the time. We may have been skint, we may not have been model citizens but he was happy. He loved me, he adored our son, and I've never met anyone who got as much of a kick out of his work as he did. Stebbi was regarded as one of the top journalists in the country in those days. Nobody could touch him.'

Thorbjörg rose up in bed as she told Nína this, but then doubled up with a coughing fit. When she could speak again she added: 'The explanation the police came up with for him choosing the garage was that he'd been irresistibly drawn to the ceiling. You know . . . to the metal tracks the garage door runs along.' Glancing at Nína, she saw that she had no need to explain. It was obvious that Thröstur had used the same support. 'Anyway, they said that suicidal people tend to choose the strangest places. There's no room left in their minds for anything else and they just don't even consider the feelings of the people they leave behind or the shock they'll get from finding them dangling from the ceiling. I was told they're too ill to grasp the impact it'll have on their families. And that was supposed to make me feel better.' She snorted. 'But the tenant had gone, the garage was empty and Stebbi knew that, of course. All that was in there were some tools the tenant hadn't cleared out yet.'

'Were they valuable? Is there any chance your husband could have run into a burglar who knocked him out, then hanged him?' The suggestion was so ludicrous that Nína wished she could unsay it. She hastened to ask something that would sound more plausible. 'Or that someone wanted him dead because of a story he was working on?'

'Stebbi would never have let a burglar get the better of him. He was a big, strong bloke and anyway burglars don't often get into fights with people. They usually run away, don't they?'

'Yes, as a rule. Almost always, in fact. But what about the stories he was working on? Could they have had something to do with it?'

'I don't know. I can't really see how Stebbi could have ended up in the garage with someone he'd contacted about an article. It just doesn't make sense. I knew some of the things he was working on. With some stories he would try out theories or hunches on me to see how they sounded. Sometimes I listened, sometimes I didn't. There are limits to how much you can bear to hear when it comes to crime. We hadn't been together long when I begged him to spare me the worst details, and once our son was old enough to understand what we were talking about, Stebbi pretty much stopped discussing that stuff. At least until the boy was in bed. But though I don't know exactly what he was working on at the time, I can't believe his death was connected to it. After all, Icelanders are past masters at forgetting stuff; if you get bad press for something, in no time at all collective amnesia sets in and people have nothing but a dim memory of hearing something negative about you. No one would bother to kill a journalist to suppress a news story. There's never that much at stake. You don't think *your* husband could have been killed because of a story he was working on, do you?'

Nína started but covered it up. 'No. Though I haven't actually given it any thought. I've only recently begun to consider the possibility that his death might not have been voluntary. Before that I'd mostly been wondering what had been going on in his life that I hadn't noticed – blaming myself.'

'I know the feeling.' Thorbjörg sank back against the pillow, her eyes on the ceiling. 'What you need is a decent cop. I was too stupid to take advantage of it but there was one officer who seemed to understand, and feel sorry for me. He was very concerned about my son, who didn't have many allies at the time. Just a drunken mother and a dead father.' Thorbjörg turned her head back to Nína, looking suddenly exhausted. She closed her eyes and her jaw slackened. 'You seem like you've got your head screwed on and are capable of speaking up for yourself. You should be able to persuade someone, get them interested in taking a closer look. I think you should go for it. You're bound to have more luck than me, with that AA vibe you've got.'

Nína wanted to turn and examine herself in the mirror behind her. But it would have to wait. 'Actually, I'm a police officer myself.' She hadn't mentioned the fact before as she had come here in the capacity of soon-to-be widow meeting a veteran. 'Who was this decent cop, if you don't mind my asking?' She would bet her bottom dollar that it was the man in the video who she had admired for his gentle touch with a juvenile witness.

'He wasn't in charge of the inquiry; he was just a nice, quite young bloke who came round on some of the call-outs. The case seemed to touch a nerve with him. Unlike those other tossers.' The woman turned her head away again. 'Örvar, that was it. Can't remember his patronymic.'

Chapter 20

25 January 2014

'There was a fucking dead cat on the barbecue! What exactly would it take to get you and your colleagues to take me seriously?' Realising how loudly he was speaking, Nói lowered his voice. His experience of agitated clients was that the higher the decibels, the less desire he felt to help them. 'OK, I know I'm a bit worked up; I'll try and control myself. It's just not every day you see something like that.' He moved over to the sitting-room window, drew back the curtains and peered out. The back garden looked bleak and colourless under a light dusting of snow. There was no one to be seen on the path by the sea. 'No. There's no way the animal could have got there by itself. No way.' Nói bent closer to the glass to see in both directions and reassure himself that there was nobody standing by the hedge, watching the house. 'How should I know if the barbecue lid was open and the cat closed it behind itself? Would a cat be capable of that? The lid weighs a ton. Anyway, I reckon it was dead before it was put in there – not that I'm an expert. You must have someone who could verify that. It had a collar on but I couldn't bring myself to touch it to read the tag.'

Vala was sitting on the sofa with Púki in her arms, her eyes on Nói. Finally it seemed to have sunk in that something might be seriously wrong. Instead of dismissing his concerns she was gnawing at her thumbnail, which she only did when she was truly anxious. Nói turned away and concentrated on the telephone conversation. On the way back from the chalet he had thought hard about what to say to the police to persuade them to take him seriously this time. He hadn't wanted to phone from the car out of consideration for Tumi, so he'd had plenty of time to rehearse. To practise being sober and dignified but firm.

Then he'd gone and made a hash of it.

He didn't regret postponing the call, as there had been no reason to worry Tumi unnecessarily. The boy didn't seem affected but the shock might well sink in later, and he must have overheard snatches of this conversation from upstairs, since Nói had raised his voice more than once. 'Yes, thanks. I'd be grateful. I'll be home all day . . . Thanks . . . Yes, this is my number.' Nói gave the police his address again, both for the house and the chalet, then hung up. 'They're going to send round an officer. And someone from the Selfoss force is going up to the chalet.' He sat down beside Vala on the sofa. 'Christ.'

'Do you think *they* did it? Killed a cat and put it on the barbecue?' She tightened her grip on Púki, who mewed in protest.

'I don't know what to think. Except that we can be thankful Púki's safe. The cat on the barbecue was almost identical. Of course, every other cat in Iceland's a tabby, but still . . .'

'Do you think it had been there long?'

'I don't know. It didn't smell too bad but perhaps that was because it was frozen. I can't even think about it without wanting to throw up.'

'Could they have gone crazy because the barbecue wasn't working properly and done this for revenge?'

'They're clearly rather odd, but I can't picture them charging around the countryside, out of their minds with rage, looking for a cat to kill. It would be an absurd way of getting even with us. Mind you, it's crazy for a pet cat to end up on a barbecue whichever way you look at it.'

'And you're sure it hadn't been cooked?'

Nói fought back nausea. 'Positive. It was just lying there. Its fur wasn't even singed.'

'Perhaps they were about to cook themselves a cat when they discovered the barbecue was broken. They eat cats in Asia.'

Nói tipped his head back and closed his eyes. 'They weren't Asian.' He groaned. 'The whole thing's so sick. Why the hell did we get involved with this fucking house swap?' He thought of what his employee had said and pictured the man's expression if he ever found out what had happened. Running up the mileage on the family car seemed pretty trivial in comparison. 'I just want to hand over the scissors, notes and recordings from the chalet and let the police take care of finding our keys and getting to the bottom of it all. After that I never want to have to think about it again.'

'Maybe they didn't kill the cat, just found the corpse and meant to cremate the animal instead of burying it. Maybe that's what people do in America.' Her voice was whiny, as if she was trying to force him to agree. Nói wanted to yell that she should have listened to him from the beginning, but realised this would achieve nothing. The cat would still have been waiting for him on the barbecue. He felt a spiteful urge to get the last word by saying she should try educating herself about other countries while she was pounding away on the treadmill, but he bit his tongue. 'The cops'll sort it out, Vala.' Nói scratched the cat behind its ears but the thought of the dead animal on the blackened rack made him snatch back his hand and wipe it on his trousers. 'Where are the notes?'

'What notes?'

Nói had the feeling she knew exactly what he meant, and couldn't understand why she was engaging in this pretence.

'The notes Tumi and I found at the chalet. The ones with the weird messages. What did you think I was talking about?'

'Oh, them. I put them on the kitchen table.' Vala said this rather too casually.

'You're sure we didn't accidentally bring one from home? It would be stupid to confuse the police with it if we know what it's about. One of the notes could have been delivered before the couple arrived. I know the other one was delivered after they left.' Nói wanted to turn and watch his wife's reaction but resisted the impulse. They were both upset and there was no need to transfer his suspicion of the Americans onto her. She was just tired and in shock like him.

'No. I've never seen that note before. Never set eyes on it.' Her denial was rather too vehement. And her tone somehow unconvincing. Yet he couldn't begin to understand why she would lie. It was hard to imagine that she could have printed it out herself or forgotten that she'd seen a message like that. It just didn't make sense. Without another word, Nói stood up and left the room. He was going to remove the notes so they didn't end up in the bin 'by accident' before the police arrived. It was a pity all three of them had handled the paper, so the presence of their fingerprints wouldn't prove anything.

Hearing Púki miaowing in the sitting room, Nói wondered what would become of the poor creature if anything happened to them. Then he realised how stupid it was to think like this; he'd obviously been infected by Vala's strange ideas about the cat on the barbecue. What on earth could possibly happen to them? It would be more natural to wonder how they would feel if something happened to their pet cat.

The police officers – who looked like a teenage boy and his older brother – sat at the kitchen table, examining the evidence Nói had collected. They did not seem particularly impressed and he had to admit that the overall effect wasn't as compelling as he had hoped. The scissors seemed to be the only item that could prove anything. They were wrapped in a tea towel, the sharp blades gleaming inside the cheerful checked design, and the police were chiefly interested in them. They had yawned during the video footage. 'You're sure you didn't throw them away yourselves? By accident?'

'Of course we didn't. Do you ever accidentally throw away large pairs of scissors?' Nói regretted it the instant the words were out of his mouth. He attributed his irritation to the headache that had crept up on him and was now so bad that he felt almost too sick to keep up his side of the conversation. He wanted to retreat to a darkened room and lie down. But that wasn't an option. First he had to persuade the police to take this stuff away and do something about it. The laughable part was that originally he had been hoping they might want him to help or might ask his opinion, that sort of thing. Now he just wanted these boys out of his house as soon as possible. Extraordinary how one dead cat could change everything. 'They were lying in the dustbin and they weren't wrapped in anything like you might expect if they'd got mixed up with other rubbish. They were underneath a pizza box with an untouched pizza inside.' He omitted to mention the type of pizza. Even in his head it sounded ridiculous to start going on about margheritas.

'Was it yours?'

Nói shook his head.

'You didn't check the date? There's usually a note on the box saying who ordered it and when.'

'No. Maybe it's still in the bin. As far as I know it hasn't been emptied yet.' The two policemen caught each other's eye and one of them shrugged as if unable to decide whether it was worth grubbing around in the dustbin. Nói waited for them to turn back to him. 'Then there's the business of the outside lights.'

'It's fairly common for kids to do that kind of thing, isn't it?' Vala had been sitting in silence, as if preoccupied, and Nói had assumed she wasn't even listening. She seemed desperate to play the whole thing down, although she had been visibly shaken when he first told her.

'What happened to the outside lights?' The older youth was so bored he could hardly be bothered to open his mouth when he spoke.

'Someone broke all the bulbs in them. Either before we flew home or the same day. I was too tired to notice when we got back.'

'Wouldn't you agree that it's not necessarily connected to the rest? Things like that are pretty common, aren't they?' Vala seemed eager for reassurance that it was nothing; that outside lights were put up with the sole purpose of providing entertainment for the country's teenagers. Nói wanted to tell her to keep out of it. This matter was his baby and she shouldn't keep undermining him like this. But his headache was so severe that he couldn't face starting an argument with her. It would look bad in front of the police, too.

'It's not actually that common. At least, we don't receive many reports of that kind of thing. In fact, I can't remember hearing about a single case before. What about you?' The younger officer turned to the elder, who, to Nói's delight, confirmed this. His headache receded momentarily, only to intensify again almost at once.

'I assume you'll want to find out who did it. I swept up the broken glass. It's in a bag in the garage. You can take it with you. I've replaced the bulbs already.' The officers exchanged glances again and the older one smirked. Nói pretended not to notice, though he wanted to grab the boy by the lapels and shake him. 'Perhaps the Americans did it. I'm beginning to think they must have been on drugs, or just wrong in the head. They left stuff behind, took stuff that was ours . . . Our bedclothes and mattress protector have disappeared, for example, and I've already told you about the satnav our neighbours lent them. It seems there was something funny about them. Unless . . .'

'Unless what?' The younger officer pricked up his ears and looked suddenly interested. Perhaps it was a way of stopping himself from falling asleep on the table.

'Well, unless something happened to them. That was what I suspected at first. You saw the recordings.'

'They didn't really tell us much. And anyway, they were tourists, weren't they? Do they have family in Iceland, or any business connections? I can't see why anyone in this country would have a score to settle with them.'

'They didn't know anyone here,' Vala chipped in. 'As far as we're aware. They were just ordinary Americans.' Then she added distractedly: 'Unless they were used to smuggle drugs into the country. It's not as if they'd have told us. We'd never have allowed anything like that to go on in our house.'

'Perhaps we're getting a little ahead of ourselves.'

It was annoying to be patronised by people so much younger than them and Nói wished Vala would pull herself together. She had no right to open her mouth, given the way she had scoffed at his concerns.

'You have a son, don't you?'

'Yes. His name's Tumi. But he's only in his teens and he doesn't know anything about this.'

'All the same, we'd like to meet him if he's at home.' The policemen's expressions were hard to read. 'We'd like to speak to all of you.'

'Tumi!' Nói yelled, stepping into the hall. From upstairs came the sound of clomping footsteps. 'The police want to see you.'

'Me? What have I done?' Tumi looked anything but innocent when he appeared, his illegal downloads obviously weighing heavily on his mind.

'Nothing. Come down.'

Tumi followed his father into the kitchen and stood as far away from the police as he could, hands in his pockets, fringe over his eyes, but his hair wasn't long enough to hide his flushed cheeks.

'Hello. Are you Tumi?' As the police officers regarded his son with grave faces, Nói felt an impulse to joke that their shift was over and this was their replacement. Who did they think he was? But Tumi reacted calmly to the question and nodded, his fringe flopping. 'We'd like to ask you about these items – find out if they have anything to do with you.'

Tumi stepped over to the table and surveyed the objects arranged on top. 'Nope. I know nothing about any of them.'

'What about the cat? Any chance you and your mates put it on your dad's barbecue for a laugh? Or that someone did it to tease you? Are you being bullied at school?'

'Nah. It's nothing to do with me. And I haven't got any friends who'd do a thing like that, or enemies either.'

'May I point out that my son is fifteen years old? So are his friends, and if he has any enemies they're presumably the same age. None of them has a driving licence and it wouldn't be that simple for them to travel all the way east over the mountains to our chalet just to play a practical joke.'

The policemen didn't turn a hair at this. 'So, as far as you're aware, none of this has anything to do with you or anyone you know?'

Tumi shook his head again, his hands still in his pockets, his cheeks scarlet.

'All right. If you change your mind or remember anything, let your parents know. Immediately.'

'OK.' Tumi shrugged nonchalantly.

The police officers were watching him as if they expected him to haul up his T-shirt to reveal explosives strapped to his body. When nothing of the sort occurred, they turned their attention back to Nói. 'One more question. Do you hunt?'

'Me?' Nói realised his look of astonishment was a bit of an overreaction. It was a perfectly reasonable question, as many locals went out shooting ptarmigan or geese. 'No, I don't.'

'You don't keep a gun in the house or garage? Or any other kind of firearm?'

'No. Certainly not.' Nói wondered if he should invite them to look for themselves. 'Why do you ask?'

'About a week ago we received notification that a shot had been fired near here in the middle of the night. I answered that call-out and I was wondering if your Americans could have been involved. The person who rang thought the shot had been fired from the coast path below your house. Presumably out to sea. Maybe someone shooting at gulls. I just wondered if these people could have found a gun at your place and wanted to try it out. If they killed the cat, they could well have been capable of taking pot-shots at seabirds.'

'I don't own a gun. If they were shooting birds round here they must have brought the gun with them.' Nói's headache intensified and he felt violently sick. But he knew that if he rushed out to throw up it would look suspicious. He shoved his hand in his trouser pocket and felt something he had almost forgotten. 'Oh, yes, and then there's these. I don't understand what they mean but they're nothing to do with us.' One of the policemen read the notes Nói had pulled out of his pocket, licked his lips and handed them to his colleague who glanced at the text and raised his eyebrows. They both looked back at Nói.

'Were these at the chalet?'

'Yes. One was lying on the floor – the one that was pushed under the door in one of the recordings I showed you – and Tumi found the other on the kitchen worktop. Didn't you, Tumi?' His son nodded.

The police officers rose to their feet without another word. They put on their gloves and began placing all the items on the table in transparent plastic bags, which they sealed and labelled with a black marker pen. Nói thought they handled the letters with particular care. 'We've all touched the notes.' Better mention the fact.

'That's a pity. If you find anything else suspicious, don't touch it, just call us straight away.' All of a sudden they seemed to be taking the matter a lot more seriously.

'I've also seen a man standing outside, staring at the house. At least I think it was a man. He moved away when he realised I'd spotted him.' Nói heard Vala gasp.

'Ring us if it happens again. Don't attempt to approach him.' The policemen caught one another's eye again, apparently eager to leave. Nói saw them out. He felt too ill to process their sudden, unexpected concern. The fresh air alleviated his headache slightly and he paused briefly in the doorway. Then he closed the front door and decided to go and lie down.

He took one step into the hall, stopped dead as he registered what he had seen outside, then turned and reopened the front door. He could see the rear lights of the police car retreating down the road. But it wasn't the car he was looking at.

The outside lights weren't on, though – as he'd told the police – he had replaced the bulbs. They had been broken again.

Chapter 21

24 and 25 January 2014

The fine flakes of snow were falling so slowly it looked as if they might float up into the sky again. They settled on Nína's eyelashes and when she tried to brush them away her mascara smudged. It didn't really matter; she wasn't expecting to see anyone and she could wash it off later. It might even be an advantage to look like a junkie if she did encounter someone, though, really, who on earth was likely to be in the garage? The moment she turned the door handle, however, her determination to stay calm and rational deserted her. It was unlocked. Suddenly the idea of someone lurking in the darkness inside didn't seem so far-fetched. Although homeless people generally hung around the centre of town, there was nothing to prevent them from wandering out to the west end, so one of them could conceivably have sought temporary shelter or even be dossing down here. She hadn't been inside for weeks and the presence of a squatter would explain the ball on the windowsill and the shadows that she thought she had seen moving behind the glass lately.

Before going in she peered through the haze of snow at the wall on the other side of the street. Presumably that was where Thröstur had sat thirty years ago, scribbling down licence-plate numbers. Through the snow crystals on her eyelashes it was easy to imagine she saw the indistinct outline of a child, pencil poised, waiting for a car to drive past through the slush. She looked away and memories rose unbidden to her mind of Thröstur's reactions to the garage. At first he had been pleased to have a home for their old junk-heap of a car, but then one day he had stopped parking it inside. Presumably the explanation for that was to do with what had happened there in the past. Of course, she had yet to establish beyond doubt that it was Stefán's case Thröstur had been a witness to, but it was hard to imagine what else it could have been.

She was inclined to think that Thröstur hadn't initially recognised the property they were buying. When realisation eventually struck, it must have been difficult for him to overcome his revulsion and use the garage. She wondered whether he had always remembered the incident but forgotten where it took place, or buried the memory completely. She would probably never know.

What could have brought it all back to him? If the garage itself had been the trigger, why had it taken so many months? She hadn't noticed him acting oddly around the building until November, when they had been living in the flat for several months. Something must have sparked the memory. But what? Perhaps it hadn't been any single factor; the memory had simply re-emerged of its own accord.

Again Nína had to remind herself that there was nothing to be afraid of. These concrete walls were not to blame for what had happened to Thröstur, any more than they were for Stefán's fate. Meeting Thorbjörg had opened her eyes. We make our own luck. Thorbjörg could have pulled herself together and taken responsibility for her life but she had lacked the guts or the will power. Of course, the woman's alcoholism had played a part, but people overcame these things with less incentive than the welfare of their child. To be fair, perhaps it hadn't been that easy for her to drag herself out of the pit back then. Nína had never been in her situation; never had to explain to a small child why Daddy wasn't coming home. How were you supposed to do that? *Some people have a pain in their body, darling, others have an illness in their mind. Like Daddy. He was so ill that he thought it was better to die. To leave you and me behind. But it wasn't his fault so we can't be angry with him. He loved us very much, you must remember that. He loved you more than anything else in the world*. That sort of thing.

Of course there was every indication that Thröstur and Stefán had taken their own lives. The garage itself was innocent.

It was as if a curtain had been lifted. The story had taken shape and one of the main characters even had a face: one with sad, yellow eyes. But it wasn't enough. She still needed to venture onto the stage to convince herself once and for all that there was nothing there that could explain Thröstur's fate.

In the end, though, it was the sale of the flat that was forcing her to bite the bullet. How could she hand over the keys to some poor innocent couple if she believed the garage would bring them bad luck? No, better to go inside, inspect the place and reassure herself that there was nothing to fear.

'Hello.' Nína had meant to shout into the empty building but the word emerged as a whisper. There was no reply. Hastily she found the light switch. The bare bulb lit up the interior and Nína breathed easier when she saw she was alone. For a split second she thought of ringing Berglind and waiting out in the car for her and Dóri, then changed her mind. No, she could do this alone. She had to. There was nothing intrinsically malignant about the garage; it simply drew unhappy people to it. The sooner she faced up to that fact, the better.

Even so she almost ran straight out again when she spotted the ball on the windowsill. Taking a deep breath, she forced herself to examine it. The brightly coloured image on its surface, a rabbit, had been blurred in the printing process and the result was not as cute as intended; its teeth were too prominent, its eyes wonky and half crazed. Perhaps she was reading too much into it. She stepped further inside, averting her eyes from the steel tracks that supported the garage door. She didn't want to risk catching sight of the mark left by the rope on the dusty metal. Here and there she could see evidence of the police examination but she didn't dwell on that. They had found a whole host of fingerprints – the garage couldn't have been given a proper clean for at least half a century – but only three sets had been traced to their owners. One belonged to Thröstur, one to her and the third to Dóri, who had helped them carry various bits and pieces when they'd first moved in. The other fingerprints had been left by unknown people some time in the past and the police saw no point in trying to identify them.

The floor was dirty, with drifts of dust lying along the walls and in the corners. There was little to see: a few boxes of junk and a battered desk and office chair that had accompanied Thröstur from his family home. Nína remembered that he had planned to potter around in here, repairing bits of engine. The police had emptied the desk in the hope of finding a suicide note but there was nothing. Although Nína knew people rarely wrote them, she had taken this as further proof that Thröstur had not tried to kill himself. He would have left a note, damn it.

At the back of the garage was the locked storeroom. Nína walked towards it, inadvertently taking bigger strides than usual. Once she had opened the storeroom and taken a peek inside, this belated initiation ceremony would be over. There would be nothing left to do and she could finally leave this place. Between her and Thröstur, and Thorbjörg and Stefán, there had been two other owners who had suffered no misfortune. If there was a curse on the garage, it only seemed to affect journalists.

Nína had to give the door of the storeroom a hard jerk and it shook on its rusty hinges as she released her hold. The bulb inside had blown, so she shone her phone inside to illuminate the contents.

She wasn't prepared for how much crap had piled up in there. When they first moved in she had stuck her head inside and recoiled at how much the previous owners had left in there, but now the situation was much worse. Clutter lay strewn over the floor so there was hardly anywhere to put your feet. She couldn't imagine who it was that had torn through it like a hurricane; Thröstur maybe, or the police? Rusty tools, torn magazines, skis, children's clothes and a broken shovel, ancient drinks cans and bottles – some long-obsolete Icelandic brand she had never heard of. Three children's bikes lay piled one on top of the other under all the rubbish, presumably relics of the bicycle repair shop that had once operated out of the premises. Nína assumed some of the old tools must date back to then too. Apparently the tenant hadn't bothered to collect the rest of his gear. Perhaps

Thorbjörg had refused to open the door for him and he had abandoned the attempt.

The presence of the bikes was more of a puzzle. Surely the children who owned them wouldn't have been resigned to losing them just because some adult was having money trouble? Seeing a bike like the one she had owned as a girl, Nína remembered how attached she had been to it. She would have insisted on getting it back. Perhaps the young owners hadn't been able to afford to pay for the repairs.

The only object that appeared to have been left undisturbed was a squalid-looking folding bed. The torn, stained mattress was covered in a thick layer of dust. There was no question that this place needed a thorough spring clean. But Nína decided not to break with tradition: the new owners would inherit the mess, assuming anyone wanted to buy the flat.

As she backed out she caught sight of a picture on the wall by the bed. It was the drawing of a face, apparently by a child – a girl, she guessed. It consisted of no more than a few lines, of which the pigtail had probably proved the greatest test of the artist's talents. What made the strongest impression on Nína, however, was the large, downturned mouth.

She hurried out of the garage. The light dust of snow was still falling but this time she let the flakes settle on her eyelashes. The cold air and the drips running down her face were somehow cleansing. She felt in urgent need of a shower.

Next morning Nína arrived at work before anyone else. This was partly to escape the hospital before the doctors began their rounds, as she was reluctant to discuss when she wanted Thröstur's life support switched off. She owed them an answer but couldn't make up her mind. Ever since she'd made the decision she'd been preoccupied with other things. No, the main reason for turning up early today was to ambush Örvar. He hadn't told her the truth and she wanted to confront him. She didn't give a damn that she'd promised to leave the investigation to him; no one could be held to a deal based on lies.

He appeared at the end of the corridor, concentrating so hard on not spilling a brimming cup of coffee that he failed to notice Nína waiting by the door of his office until it was too late to pretend he was on his way somewhere else. Struggling to mask his consternation, he invited her to take a seat. He was very busy, he explained, and could only spare her a few minutes. Another lie, no doubt.

Nína sat down and came straight to the point while Örvar was swearing over the coffee he'd slopped onto his desk. Typical that he could carry it without accident all the way from the machine, then mess up just when he was home and dry. 'Never take your eye off the ball,' he muttered, mopping at the stained paperwork. No doubt the curses were directed at her too but she pretended not to notice. Finally he sat down, looking even more exhausted than usual. She knew he'd been finding these weekend shifts a trial, but there was no getting out of them. At least he was weary enough to buy Nína's explanation that she'd come in early now to make up for her day off on Wednesday. She had been afraid he would send her straight home.

'Nína, it's not what you think. I wasn't involved in the actual inquiry because I'd only recently joined the police. If Thorbjörg said that, she was mistaken. I went round a few times on call-out and felt sorry for her and her son. She must have remembered me because I was polite to her, and understanding about how hard she was finding it to accept what had happened.' Örvar sighed. 'I did a little checking for her in-house but there was no evidence – really, none at all – to suggest anything other than suicide.'

'Then why not just tell me that? Why pretend not to know that another woman had experienced exactly the same thing in exactly the same place?'

'Nína, I had no idea where you lived. I've never been round to your house and since we got an HR manager I haven't kept up to speed with my team's private lives. Except when they choose to confide in me.'

'Which I *did*. But you didn't say a word. You must have twigged when I said I'd found a statement taken from Thröstur. There can't have been many suicides where a child was called in as a witness. Didn't the penny drop when his name came up in that context?'

'There were three kids. Boys, if memory serves, all around the same age. And since you ask, I never knew their names as I only heard about it secondhand – I never actually went near the investigation. I hadn't a clue that your husband was one of them. It's thirty years since I tried to help Thorbjörg and since then I've met countless women in the line of duty. Children, too.' Örvar took a sip of coffee and made a face when he saw that he'd forgotten to wipe the bottom of his mug. There was a brown ring on the desk, shaped like a mouth shouting at him. Which was exactly what she felt like doing right now. It was intolerable to have to sit here and watch him squirm. She even suspected him of deliberately spilling the coffee to buy himself time.

'It first began to come back to me when you told me about the video. Then the penny finally dropped – but not immediately.'

Nína didn't believe this for a second but decided to let him continue.

'Since then I haven't had a chance to discuss it with you. I know we've crossed paths in the office but I hadn't made up my mind what to say. It was partly out of concern for you – I didn't want to raise your hopes. I still stand by what I said – no one but your husband was responsible for his actions. But I should have mentioned it to you earlier, I admit that.'

'But you didn't mention it at all – I had to ask you. That's not the same thing.' Nína paused to give Örvar a chance to apologise or protest but he said nothing, so she went on. 'But now you're going to tell me anything of importance you remember, aren't you?'

'Do I have any choice?'

'No, not really. I won't stop asking.'

'What do you want to know? I can't remember it in much detail.'

'The two questions bugging me most are how did Thröstur get involved and what happened to the reports?'

'I don't know *exactly* where the reports are.' Örvar sounded convincing but it was an odd choice of words.

'What do you mean *exactly*?'

'Just that. I can't point you to their exact location, I'm afraid. But I'll ask the old hands to check their shelves. And I'll have a look around my office, though there's no reason they'd be in here. As you'll remember, it wasn't my case, and I had a clear-out not long ago. Besides, I try to deal with everything as soon as a case is closed. Unlike some people, I don't sit on the files for decades.' He glanced round at the overflowing shelves. 'Though, on second thoughts, maybe it's longer since my last clear-out than I remembered. Maybe several years.' Örvar stole a glance at the clock. 'Look, I'm pressed for time, as I said. I've got to be at a meeting in five minutes. What was the other question?'

'How was Thröstur mixed up in it? And the other two boys?'

'Their testimony contradicted Thorbjörg's claim that someone else had been involved in her husband's death. The boys were able to confirm that nobody had entered the garage, so it was clear that no crime had been committed. Thorbjörg wasn't told about them, only that all the indications were that her husband had acted alone.'

Now it was Nína's turn to frown. 'Then I find the way Thröstur was interviewed very odd. Wouldn't a single statement, taken on the spot, have done? It sounded as if the man interviewing him thought he had something to hide. And how did they manage to trace the kids?'

'By coincidence Stefán's body was discovered almost immediately. The boys were still sitting on the wall when the police and ambulance arrived. So it wasn't difficult.' Örvar adjusted his shirt collar and picked up pen and notebook. 'Statements were taken from them on the spot, then they were interviewed again in the presence of a legal guardian and after that the decision was made to question them further. Their statements weren't entirely consistent with the evidence and the police hoped it would be possible to discover why. But they were unsuccessful.'

'Weren't consistent how?' Nína remembered the mannerisms that had indicated Thröstur was lying.

'They claimed they hadn't seen anyone go in. Full stop. There didn't seem anything strange about it in the first statements because they'd been taken at the scene, but when they came in for formal interviews it transpired that they claimed not to have seen anybody at all. Not even Thorbjörg's husband, who was known to have gone in while they were sitting there.'

'How could the police establish that? Kids don't have a particularly good sense of time. Perhaps they arrived after he went inside.'

'No. A driver was parked there, waiting for the woman next door, and remembered seeing the kids on the wall and the man entering the garage. After being shown a photo of Thorbjörg's husband he confirmed that it had been him. Then the woman he'd been waiting for came out and he drove away with her. His testimony also fitted with that of the woman's son. He walked past the garage on his way home and saw Thorbjörg's husband emerging from his house, the kids on the wall and the driver in the car.'

'How was the driver traced?'

'The kids' licence-plate books. It was the last vehicle registration they'd all managed to write down before they recorded the number of the ambulance, so it was obvious that we should speak to the owner of that car. But the kids stuck to their story that no one had entered the garage.' He stood up. 'It was all very peculiar. No explanation was ever found.'

Chapter 22

25 January 2014

When Nói finally surfaced, his headache had gone and he felt as if a boulder had been extracted from his head. Sitting up on the edge of the bed he saw that he had slept for nearly four hours. A low rumbling from his stomach reminded him that it was long past suppertime and he could use a drink too. It was freezing in the bedroom with the window wide open, so he went over and closed it after sweeping out the snow that had collected on the sill.

Everything was going to hell.

Muffled sounds reached the bedroom. Vala must be watching one of her tedious crime serials, unless she'd nodded off over the evening news. That was probably it, since she hadn't come and given him a shake as she usually did when he went for a rest. He couldn't remember the last time he'd been allowed to lie in peace until he got up of his own accord. Under normal circumstances she wouldn't have stopped badgering him until she had dragged him out on a run with her. She never suffered from headaches herself so it was impossible to get through to her that however fast you jogged you couldn't outrun the pain. For her, exercise was the magic solution to everything, whether it was aches, tiredness or just a bad mood. Usually he either gave in or ignored her, but at moments like this he felt his wife's obsession bordered on insanity. What on earth was Vala running away from? She seemed incapable of grasping the fact that sometimes it was all right to be a bit under the weather or take some time out to relax.

Suddenly it occurred to him that the reason she had left him alone was almost certainly to postpone discussing the police's visit. She had behaved very oddly while the officers were there and although he couldn't understand what she had to hide, he'd got the distinct impression that she knew more about the whole business than he did. Could the Americans have contacted her instead? They had her e-mail address too, so it was perfectly possible – but what was it that she didn't want to share with him? It was unlike her to be secretive, especially since she knew how much he loathed that sort of thing. He couldn't even stand surprise parties like the one their friends had thrown for his twenty-fifth birthday ten years ago. He still shuddered when he thought of the flurry of furtive phone conversations she'd had in the days leading up to it.

While these thoughts were running through his head, he remembered that Vala had been in a pretty bad way before they went abroad. She had seemed depressed during Advent, and in the days before they'd left for the States she had suffered from mood swings, one minute hyper, the next jumping out of her skin at the slightest sound. When he demanded to know what was wrong, she had dismissed it as pre-holiday nerves. And certainly once they arrived in Florida she had relaxed and reverted to her normal self, so he had taken her explanation at face value.

Now, however, he wondered if he should have pressed her harder for the truth. Looking back, it seemed possible that she had been upset over something to do with the Americans. She had handled all the preparations for their trip because he'd had to work like crazy to be able to take time off. There had been no opportunity to ask what the matter was.

If he was honest, he would have to admit that he'd been relieved when she didn't want to discuss it. Other people's feelings were not his strong point. His attention span when it came to listening to someone fret over how things should have been done differently was very short, as he preferred to look to the future. Well, he would just have to make the effort if he wanted things out in the open.

Nói went out onto the landing. He hoped there was some supper left, though his wife and son would probably have made themselves separate snacks. The emphasis on eating together as a family was all on his side; Vala and Tumi were happy to give shared meals a miss when he wasn't around. But this didn't bother him as he felt it wasn't a proper family supper anyway if he wasn't there. He walked past the TV alcove on the landing and saw that it was Tumi lying there on the sofa, glued to the screen. He might have known: a war film was on and while he stood there two soldiers were blown into the air by a landmine.

'Move. You're in the way.'

Nói shifted so his son wouldn't miss any flying limbs. 'Where's your mother?'

'She went round to Sigga's. She said you're to heat up the soup in the saucepan for yourself.' Tumi didn't look at his father; all his attention was focused on the battling actors. 'But I'm warning you, it's disgusting. It's . . . *green*.' He shuddered theatrically.

'When did your mother go out?'

'As soon as we'd eaten, luckily – so I could fix myself some proper food. She said she'd be late so we weren't to wait up for her.'

'Oh?'

Tumi shrugged, indifferent as ever when it came to his parents. 'She said you knew.' If so, either Nói hadn't taken it in or the fact had slipped his mind. His headache hadn't exactly helped his concentration, so Vala may well have mentioned her plans, but he didn't think so. Well, if she thought she could dodge his questions like this, she could think again. He would stay up and wait for her, however tired he was.

'Oh, yeah, and the police rang.'

'What did they want?'

'They were just asking if you knew some people. I wrote some notes on the pad by the phone. I didn't want to wake you up, and Mum had left.' Tumi sat upright. 'Did the cop really think me and my mates had put that cat on the barbecue?'

'No. But they have to ask to eliminate all the possibilities.'

'Oh.' Tumi seemed disappointed. 'Anyway, there's a number you're meant to call. I think he said to call tomorrow, not tonight.'

Nói went downstairs to the kitchen, frustrated that the boy was incapable of taking down messages properly. He paused on the bottom step, then called up to ask Tumi if he knew where Púki was. His son said he hadn't seen him. The cat was accustomed to going out at night, which was infuriating because when he finally did come home he would miaow insistently until either Nói or Vala woke up and let him in. And as an extra treat, he brought them presents of mice from the beach. For some reason he never did this during the day. But Nói didn't care about that now; he just wanted the cat safely indoors. He couldn't stop thinking about how like Púki the cat on the barbecue had been. Was it a coincidence?

'Púki! Puss-puss!' Nói called into the dark back garden, then listened. If the cat was nearby he usually came running in the hope of food. But he couldn't hear the familiar jingling of his bell. He raised his voice. 'Púki! Here, kitty!' There was no sound, so Nói closed the door. He peered outside but the light from the house didn't reach far and the darkness hanging over the sea beyond the garden seemed almost solid. No moon or stars tonight. If someone was standing out there watching, they wouldn't even need to hide.

The boy hadn't lied about the soup. The green gloop in the pan was so unappetising that Nói's hunger evaporated. He poured a little down the sink so it would look as if he had eaten some, then turned his attention to the notes Tumi had scribbled down. They conveyed little; there was a telephone number – the police station, presumably – and two male names he didn't recognise. Though scrawled down any old how, the words were just about legible. On the rare occasions when Tumi picked up a pen the results left a lot to be desired.

'Tumi. Come down here a minute.'

'What? I'm in the middle of a film.' His son slouched downstairs, looking anything but pleased.

'What does this mean? There are some names and a phone number here. I gathered from what you said that there was more to the message. Is this the man I'm supposed to ring?' He pointed at the name beside the number.

Tumi frowned at the paper as if struggling to remember. 'No.'

'No? What do you mean?'

'That's not the bloke you're supposed to ring. You're to call this number but I can't remember the guy's name. Gud-something. I didn't write it down. But he'll answer.'

'Tumi, what are these names?'

'They're the names of two blokes he wanted to know if we recognised. One's the owner of the cat on the barbecue. I said I'd never heard of him. Apparently he lives in Breidholt. Oh, and the cat was killed – poisoned. According to this Gud-bloke, anyway.'

Nói didn't recognise the name. He wondered if it was the man who had delivered the notes or the one who had killed the animal. But it seemed unlikely that he'd have killed his own cat just to frighten a pair of strangers. 'What did he say about the other name?' It wasn't familiar either.

'Nothing. Just asked if I knew anything about this bloke. Obviously I'd never heard of him.'

Nói didn't understand what was so obvious about it.

'He's going to ask you about it tomorrow. If you call. Otherwise he'll be in touch on Monday.'

'Didn't he say why he wanted to know?'

'Nope.'

Nói stared at the name. *Lárus Jónmundsson.* He didn't think he knew anyone called Lárus, even in its shortened version, Lalli. 'Did he say anything else?'

'No. Nothing. Nothing I can remember. Can I go back to my film now?'

'No, you can't.' Nói looked back at the paper again, picked up the phone and dialled the number. He could use this opportunity to notify the police that the outdoor lights had been smashed again. After several rings an automatic message told him his call was being diverted to the switchboard. He hung up. Naturally, the man had gone home – it was Saturday night.

He tried calling Vala but she didn't answer either. This made him even more annoyed because it confirmed that she was avoiding him. 'Next time you take a call like that you're to write down exactly what they said. If you have trouble keeping up, just tell the person to repeat the information. Imagine if your mate Jói called and left a message that you were to meet him at the University Cinema at eight and I'd just written "cinema".'

'He'd never call this number.'

Nói was momentarily overwhelmed by anger. 'No, of course not. How stupid of me. How incredibly stupid.' He picked up the piece of paper, trying to force out a smile, and his eye fell on something written on the back. It was an ordinary sheet of A4, exactly like the one Tumi had found in the chalet. On the back was a brief message: *Serves you right, liar.*

'Did you write that, Tumi?'

'Eh?' Tumi took the paper and read the text. 'Nah.'

'Then what's it doing here? Where did this paper come from?' Nói was surprised at how calm he managed to remain.

'It was lying on the doormat.'

'When?'

'The bell rang just after I'd answered the phone and I went to the door while I was talking to the cop. There was nobody there. Then the cop started asking if I could take a message and I grabbed the piece of paper. I didn't notice what it said.'

'Do you think the person who rang the bell pushed the note through the letterbox or was it there already?'

Tumi shrugged his bony shoulders. 'Dunno. Though it definitely came after Mum left. She wouldn't have stepped over it; she'd have picked it up, right?'

Nói agreed. 'Had she been gone long?'

'Yeah, I think so. Maybe half an hour, an hour. Something like that. Though it could've been longer. Or shorter.'

Nói controlled his anger with difficulty. Carefully, using his fingernails, he took the paper from Tumi and laid it on the table, telling his son not to touch it.

He was relieved when he saw on the phone display that it was almost two hours since the police had rung but even so he decided to check that the front door was locked. It wasn't, and overcoming a powerful sense of reluctance, he peered outside to check if there was anyone hanging around. Perhaps the cat was out there.

A young policewoman was standing with her hand poised to ring the bell as Nói opened the door, and he was so startled he could hardly stammer out a word. She seemed equally taken aback and stared at him, open-mouthed and embarrassed. Then she dropped her hand, cleared her throat and asked rather formally: 'Are you Nói Fridriksson?'

Vala hadn't answered her phone. He was flooded with grief and dread, and even as he nodded he knew that the police visit was about her.

Chapter 23

27 January 2014

An obliterating darkness has fallen. Although the wild weather prevented the day from ever growing properly light, a faint greyness had at least filtered in through the cracks round the door and the blocked-off window, as if fleeing the storm. Now, however, they can't see a thing if the lamp is switched off, and the cold seems to gain strength in the gloom. But as they huddle on the hard floor, wearing all their clothes, their fingers and feet numb inside their sleeping bags, the atmosphere is definitely less tense than it was this morning. This is not due to any cessation of hostilities between them but because the coastguard has just delivered the news they have been waiting for and were afraid would never come. The repairs to the helicopter are almost complete; they will be rescued at daybreak. When the phone started ringing they sat gaping at it without speaking. Although they had been waiting impatiently for the call for hours, they were suddenly robbed of the courage to answer. So many things could have gone wrong.

Helgi was the first to reach for his phone. The coastguard control centre seemed to have worked out that he had taken charge. Heida and Ívar sat stock still, intently following his every word. The message was blessedly short, and he hung up and told them the news: they would only have to spend one more night in the lighthouse. If they'd had any alcohol with them they would have drunk a toast.

Tóti's fate no longer seems to matter and no one refers to the acrimonious words that passed between them earlier. Heida and Ívar seem to find it easy to shrug off recent events and act as if nothing has happened, but Helgi has the feeling that the anger is still there, lurking behind the radio equipment in the corner, conserving its energy for the coming night.

'I'm going to have a bath.' The woman's face is a patchwork of dark shadows and bright, pale skin. 'The moment I walk in the door. Then I'm going to crawl into bed and sleep for twenty-four hours. Mum's promised to babysit for a bit longer.' Heida had rung her mother to give her the good news and hadn't spared her the grim details of what they'd been through. Yet it's surprising, Helgi thinks, how few calls or messages any of them have received. None of them appears to be particularly popular. Then again, they have only been here thirty-six hours, just twelve hours longer than originally planned. People probably think they're still immersed in the tasks they came here to perform. Perhaps nobody wants to disturb them in such cramped conditions. There isn't really room to talk privately, after all.

Heida shudders. 'I'm never coming back here. Screw the equipment.' She won't be persuaded to complete the installation, and Helgi doesn't care enough about the assignment to put pressure on her. Besides, he thinks it might be risky to let her loose on an expensive radio transmitter in her current frame of mind. She might decide to cut all the wires or throw the whole lot on the floor.

'I'll need to pack in a hurry when I get home,' Ívar announces, oblivious to the fact that neither of his companions has the slightest interest in his plans. Helgi assumes Heida is equally indifferent to what he himself is going to do since she showed no sign of asking him when the opportunity came up.

'I've got to catch a flight on Tuesday. I'll be seriously pissed off if I miss the plane. The tickets cost a bomb.'

Helgi relents. He knows perfectly well where the man is going; Ívar told him about the trip that time they met in the bar. At such tedious length that every slurred word seemed to last half a lifetime. 'Where are you going, again?'

'Thailand. For two months. Not bad, eh?' Ívar smiles, failing to notice Heida's scandalised expression. She glares and opens her mouth to comment. She's probably about to ask if Ívar's going there for the cheap prostitutes. Helgi's curious to know if he's guessed correctly, but errs on the side of caution and says nothing.

He turns to Heida. 'So, where do you live?' It's all he can think of and anyway he assumes he'll never see her again once this disastrous trip is over. He's unlikely to run into her, though it's strange to think their paths may cross one day at the supermarket or strolling through town. He suspects she'll pretend not to notice him and dive behind a shelf or into the nearest shop. It would be best for both of them. His presence would only remind her of this horrible experience, and if at any point he thought he might like to get to know her, that moment has definitely passed.

'In the west end of town. I can't imagine living anywhere else.'

Helgi nods, hoping his opinion doesn't show on his face. She's obviously one of those people who doesn't realise that not everyone can afford to have a favourite district and stay there. He, for example, has to put up with whatever accommodation he can afford, and her part of town is out of his league. 'Is that where you're from?'

'Yes. Born and bred.' She moves and the shadows play across her face. 'You?'

'Oh, I've lived here and there. Always in Reykjavík but never in the west.' It feels odd to mention the city by name. Out here in the Atlantic it seems so far away, and although the plan is for the helicopter to rescue them tomorrow morning he can't stop worrying that a volcanic eruption or some other natural catastrophe might take priority. Perhaps they'll end their days out here after all. He runs through everything that could prevent the helicopter from coming: a broken rotor blade; an outbreak of food poisoning in the pilots' canteen; the forecast of a week-long storm; a tangled winch line. Any number of other unforeseen eventualities could prolong their stay on the stack.

'I doubt you'll get to enjoy a bath straight away.' Ívar shifts on his buttocks, wincing and pulling up his sleeping bag. There's a note of tetchiness in his voice. Perhaps he *did* clock Heida's reaction when he said where he was going. 'We'll be lucky if we're allowed a shower at the police station before they throw us in the cells. You do realise we'll all be arrested the minute we set foot in Reykjavík? If not right here on the rock, before we're even lifted off.'

'Don't be ridiculous.' Helgi is sick to death of their bickering. 'Nobody's going to be arrested. They'll launch an inquiry and take it from there. It was almost certainly an accident and hopefully they'll tell us what happened once they've worked it out.'

'How do you explain the note, then?' Ívar's pessimism seems to have infected Heida.

'I'm not even going to try. That's a job for someone else.' Yet he can't stop himself from hazarding a guess. It might help to prevent the firestorm that is about to break out. You can almost smell their smouldering anger. 'Perhaps the note was already in his sleeping bag when he came here. Perhaps it ended up there on some camping trip months ago. Who knows? The idea that one of us came out here with the intention of shoving it into his sleeping bag is absurd. Why would we?' Helgi takes a deep breath and exhales a white cloud of vapour that vanishes almost immediately. 'I know I didn't do it, and I imagine the same goes for both of you. Anyway, I don't understand why you're so bothered about this *day of reckoning* business. It doesn't mean anything to me and I refuse to get all worked up about it.'

'*I'm* not getting worked up.' It appears that Heida at least has come to her senses. Helgi hopes everything will be all right again. 'And *I* didn't put it there.'

'Neither did I.' Ívar sounds affronted. Of the three of them he seems to be taking the message most personally, though he refused to admit it when Helgi tried to quiz him.

'Of course not. None of us did. We're ordinary people who don't go around committing murder. Obviously it was an accident and the police will work on that assumption unless they can prove otherwise, which I doubt. At any rate, it's clear the police won't arrest us without substantial proof.' Helgi digs his hands into his anorak pockets to warm them. 'I've never been arrested and I intend to keep it that way for the rest of my life.'

'Does that matter?' Heida's voice is suddenly tremulous.

'No. Probably not. Why?'

She doesn't look as if she's ever been on the wrong side of the law.

'No, it's just . . .'

'Just what? Have you been arrested? Sentenced?'

'No, of course I haven't been sentenced.' She turns pink. 'I was done for drink driving once. Years ago. I was arrested, technically, but it was settled out of court. I got a fine and a ban. They must see there's no way that could have any bearing on what's happened here. If they can even be bothered to look it up.'

Helgi notices that Ívar has gone unusually quiet, where ordinarily he'd chip in with some snide remark. 'What about you? Have you got a police record?' The moment he asks the question, Helgi regrets it. What if the answer exposes Ívar in some way and causes him to go berserk? He could easily overpower and even kill them. They would have a hard job defending themselves in this tiny space.

'Nothing worth mentioning.'

'Go on, tell us. It's only fair. I told you about mine.' Heida leans forward as if she expects Ívar to whisper it to them.

'It's nothing major. I was arrested for being drunk and disorderly. It was bullshit. I got a suspended sentence.'

'Disorderly? Did that involve violence?' Heida's voice betrays her eagerness for him to say yes. Helgi can guess her reasoning: if Ívar has a record of assault, he'll probably be arrested while they are allowed to go free. Then she'll get her bath in her nice house at the fancy end of town.

'It had nothing to do with violence. I said drunk and disorderly. You do a lot of things when you're drunk that you wouldn't do sober. But no one's ever accused me of violence, not once. So don't try and pin it on me now.'

Helgi wishes he could put in his earphones and use music to drown out the quarrel that is brewing, even if it drains his battery, but he doesn't dare in case he needs his phone later. The night is young. 'Stop squabbling. Neither of you is known to the police. For God's sake, try and bury the hatchet.'

They all fall silent and return to staring at Tóti's sleeping bag. Helgi feels as if he knows every inch of the shiny material, every thread and stain. He assumes the same applies to the others. No one speaks until abruptly Ívar scrambles to his feet and says he's going out for a slash. He pushes past Helgi, treading on his foot where it's concealed by the sleeping bag. Helgi winces but doesn't protest; it wasn't deliberate.

Once the door has closed behind Ívar, Helgi's and Heida's eyes meet. He hopes he doesn't look as despairing and frightened as she does. She licks her lips, her eyes widening. 'That man scares me to death,' she whispers. 'We'll have to take it in turns to sleep.'

'I'm up for that.' Helgi rubs his sore foot. 'When he pushed past me just now I was wondering if I should ask him to hand over his knife.' He doesn't dare raise his voice above a whisper, either. Since the weather improved there is nothing to cover the sound of their conversation.

'His knife? The one in his belt?' Heida gulps. 'Has he still got it? I thought the sheath was empty this morning. I thought he'd left it behind with his tools yesterday evening.'

'Then he must have fetched it again. I thought I saw it. He definitely had it earlier when I went outside to bring him in.' Helgi glances around, his gaze coming to rest on the spot where Ívar was sitting. 'Perhaps it's here somewhere.'

Rising to his knees, he rummages in the man's sleeping bag. Nothing. He pulls the lamp closer and conducts a more thorough search. 'I can hardly see a thing in this light, but I'm pretty certain it's not here.' Helgi moves the lamp and continues his search over a wider area. 'Are you sure the knife wasn't there this morning? I'm almost a hundred per cent certain I saw the handle sticking out when he went past me just now.'

'No. I'm not at all sure.' Heida worms her way further back until she is pressed against the wall. Helgi considers pointing out that she is no safer there and that really they ought to swap places. If all hell breaks loose, it would be better to be near the door. But it's too much trouble to move so he says nothing.

'Jesus. You've got to make him hand over the knife. The blood in the sleeping bag must have come from a stab wound. There might be traces on the blade that can be analysed. I don't believe the blood can be washed off completely. Even if he's cleaned it, they'll be able to prove he stabbed Tóti. The knife's a crucial piece of evidence.' It takes effort to whisper for any length of time, and her breathing is ragged after this brief speech. Helgi pictures her standing out on the helipad as their rescuer is being winched down, yelling that Ívar has a knife.

'And another thing: I don't like the thought of him having a knife in here tonight. What if we accidentally fall asleep?'

'I'm sure it isn't the only weapon here.' Helgi realises he doesn't actually know this for certain, not having checked their supplies or sneaked a look inside his companions' bags. 'At least I'm assuming there must be something sharp among the tools they brought along. Or among your stuff, for that matter.' He can't resist needling her a little. He's the only one who has brought nothing with him that could cause injury. At a pinch he could bludgeon someone with the camera. But he would never do that.

'I don't have anything like that with me.' Heida doesn't seem to have taken what he said personally. She clearly thinks he agrees with her about Ívar being the one to fear. Unless she's inventing her suspicions to fool him? If so, she's succeeding brilliantly, but he doubts she's acting: the conversation is too boring to be deliberately manufactured. 'And you saw his face when we found the note. I'm convinced the paper's his. He must have dropped it when he was dragging Tóti's body out of the sleeping bag, and he knows his fingerprints are on it. Are you sure it's still in there?'

Helgi hopes Ívar will come back soon. He's tired of whispering. 'We were all shocked, remember? Not just him, though he was the only one who went nuts. And of course the note's still there.' Nevertheless, Helgi opens the bag with a pen and checks inside. 'Yes, there it is.' He settles back in the same place as before. 'The cops'll get to the bottom of it. Forensics are so advanced these days that they're bound to find traces of DNA on the paper or in the bag.' He pulls his own sleeping bag up over his thighs. 'But if I'd stabbed somebody in such an isolated place, I'd begin by disposing of the weapon. That's logical, isn't it? I wouldn't want it on me when the police arrived. Let's hope he's a bit slow and hasn't worked that out yet. If not, he could be getting rid of the knife right now. And it would never be found.'

At that moment the door is flung open. An awkward silence falls, as it so often does when the person who's being talked about comes in.

'Don't all speak at once.'

Helgi can feel the cold radiating from the man and decides not to go outside himself. It can wait. He sees that Heida is gazing at Ívar as if mesmerised, apparently unable to tear her eyes from the sheath hanging at his belt. It is empty.

Chapter 24

25 January 2014

The estate agent had left with the potential buyers; a young couple with a toddler whose nose they kept having to wipe when they weren't intervening to stop it fiddling with the dishwasher controls. It was impossible to interpret the parents' expressions; they'd exchanged glances from time to time and nodded as cupboard doors were opened or taps turned on. He had seemed more satisfied with the garage than his wife, who had grimaced and picked up the child.

The whole time they were in the garage the estate agent had tapped his pen on his folder, as if counting the seconds. Perhaps he had worked out the minimum amount of time he would have to linger in there so as not to rouse the couple's suspicions. It was obvious that he hadn't told them about Thröstur, and he kept catching Nína's eye as if afraid she would blurt it out.

He and Nína both breathed more easily once they re-emerged into the open air, and she could have sworn that the woman relaxed her hold on the child. Nína had originally intended to start with the garage and end with the flat, to ensure that potential buyers wouldn't leave with a bad taste in their mouths, but in the event she didn't have a chance to inform the estate agent of this plan because the couple were standing right next to them.

In parting the estate agent had said he would be in touch, but gave no hint of whether the couple were likely to make an offer. Then he herded the family into his car and they drove away, slightly faster than they had come.

The doorbell announced Berglind's arrival, echoing in the empty hall as Nína went to let her in. The flat's contents had gone, either to the dump or to her sister's garage. Her brother-in-law's expression had been far from thrilled when it sank in that he would no longer be able to put his car away, and Nína knew she would have to find herself another flat as soon as possible. It would be hard to explain to him why she couldn't use her own garage until the flat was sold, but to be fair to him he hadn't asked or even seemed to have thought about it. But inevitably he would the next time he had to wake up early in order to scrape the ice off his car.

Berglind stood beaming on the doorstep. She had a cake box in her arms, held carelessly at an angle so the cake was almost certainly squashed inside. 'Have you sold it? I bought this to celebrate.' Typical Berglind, always so positive. Ever since she was small she had been unable to buy a lottery ticket without planning how she was going to spend the jackpot. Which she never actually won.

'I'll faint with shock if they put in an offer.' Nína stepped aside to let Berglind pass and took the cake from her. A sweet smell of marzipan filled the hall. 'But they were the first to view it. It would be expecting too much to think they'll go for it. Let's just celebrate the fact that someone wanted to look at it straight away. That must be a good sign.'

'You shouldn't have emptied the flat. It makes you seem desperate. People will make lower offers.'

'I don't care. If someone puts in an offer I'll buy another flat the same day and never look back.'

'Where are you going to sleep . . . when, you know, Thröstur is . . . you know . . .?' One could hardly expect Berglind of all people to find upbeat words for death, the ultimate downer. 'Our spare room's waiting for you, of course, when you can't stay at the hospital any longer.'

'Thanks. We'll see. Worst-case scenario, I could sleep here on a mattress. I don't know what the estate agent would think but I could always hide it when he was showing people round.' Nína put the box on the kitchen worktop and opened it. As she had suspected, the fancy cake was squashed into one corner. She tried to repair it with her fingers but only succeeded in making matters worse.

'You're staying with us. I won't hear of anything else. I'd hate to think of you here in the empty flat, surrounded by bare walls. You'll be much more comfortable at my place.' Berglind peered into the cake box and frowned. 'You'd think they'd pack it better.'

'You would, wouldn't you?' Nína was so relieved at the change of subject that she refrained from pointing out that Berglind was responsible for the damage herself. 'But I'm sure it'll taste the same.' She fetched two paper plates left over from when they had ordered pizza while packing up the contents of the flat, and a knife and two forks from a small cardboard box of essentials which also contained a jar of instant coffee, two cups, three plates, cutlery, scissors, soap and a corkscrew. A corkscrew? It wasn't as if there was much to celebrate in this house.

Berglind lifted out a piece of cake that looked as if the baker had sat on it. Her face brightened when she tasted it. 'Have you taken a look at Thröstur's work papers yet?'

'No. I haven't had time.' She was lying; while waiting for the estate agent she could easily have gone through every last scrap of paper in the box.

'Nonsense.' Berglind stood up. 'I'm going to do it myself. I can tell you'll never get round to it.'

Nína opened her mouth but didn't try to stop her sister. It would have meant having to explain why she had failed to do it and she wasn't sure she could. For one thing, she didn't really understand it herself; for another, she couldn't face telling anyone else what she was afraid might – or might not – emerge from the box. She couldn't make up her mind what would be worse. If it turned out to contain papers showing that Thröstur had been having a hard time at work, she would feel ashamed that she hadn't guessed and offered him the support he needed. But if it contained nothing of interest the blame would be focused back on their relationship – which obviously hadn't provided him with enough reason to live. Neither explanation was desirable, so it would be better simply to avoid going through the box. The trail she was following in relation to his childhood was more appealing. There was no way she could be blamed for what had happened back then.

Berglind banged down the box on the counter by the sink. She cut herself another piece of cake, ate a forkful, and then opened the box. 'There you go. Nothing to be scared of – just paper and pens.' She fished out a sheaf of papers and Nína heard pens rattling in the bottom. Suddenly she lost all appetite for the cake and pushed her plate away. She watched Berglind intently, trying to interpret every change of expression as she read, and was relieved when her sister laid down the first pages, saying they were of no interest. But trepidation flooded her again as Berglind picked up the next batch and began to read. 'These seem to be copies of documents relating to his article. The one you told me about – historical child abuse. Ugh, I'm not sure I want to read any more.'

Nína took the bundle of papers from her without thinking. The case Thröstur had been researching was just one of many that had already been splashed all over the media. There was unlikely to be anything here she hadn't already seen; the names and faces changed, but all were variations on the same disturbing theme. Was it any wonder that Berglind didn't want to think about this stuff? She wouldn't last a day as a cop – ugliness had never had any place in her world.

Nína skimmed the pages and saw that they contained a draft of the first article Thröstur had written on the subject. The story had dominated the news for two weeks, with every media outlet vying to outdo the others with their exposés. There had been no shortage of cases to choose from.

The articles dealt with the abuse of children and teenagers going back decades, from the time when people had thought it better to sweep everything under the carpet in order to spare the victims the shame. As a result, there was quite a backlog of these cases and now that the victims were adults they had started coming forward in droves. Nína remembered being struck by their stoicism and lack of anger, by how quietly they had suffered while their abusers repeatedly violated their innocence. It was extraordinary how successfully these human vermin had used threats to silence the children, and how their victims had managed to lock these vile secrets away in the back of their minds.

Three factors apparently accounted for their silence: the threat of retaliation if they told tales; repeated reminders from the paedophile that if it came to their word against his or hers, a child would not be believed over an adult; and, rather more indirectly, a deep-seated sense of shame that arose from the children's mistaken belief that they were somehow responsible for these horrendous acts. It was repulsive. Nína's skin prickled. It had been far too long since she had felt pity for anyone but herself, and the realisation made her feel disgusted with herself, too.

Clearing her throat, she turned her face away so that Berglind wouldn't be able to read her expression. It was impossible not to wonder if Thröstur had been one of those children. If he had suffered this type of trauma in his youth it might explain why he had lied to the police. It might also explain why he had tried to kill himself as an adult: perhaps dredging up these events and brooding over the harrowing details had proved too much for him. Nína gnawed at her lip. The salty taste of blood brought her up short: in her distress she hadn't realised how hard she was biting. She pushed the thoughts away. This was neither the time nor place to break down. There would be plenty of opportunity for that later, in private.

Towards the bottom of the stack of papers were the original sources for Thröstur's investigation: printouts of e-mails containing the testimonies of named individuals or arrangements for them to meet Thröstur to tell him their stories. She recognised some of their names from the news coverage.

Although Nína was used to such things from her own work, she found them uncomfortable reading, perhaps because the e-mails weren't intended for her eyes. People had written to

Thröstur in good faith, trusting that he would keep what they were telling him confidential. But her guilt was mitigated by the knowledge that most had later published their stories in the press. Even so, this material should never have been passed on to her. She knew Thröstur's employers had been in a hurry to clear his desk for his replacement – the man who delivered the box to her had explained as much. He was too young to realise she might be hurt by the news that Thröstur's shoes had been filled so quickly.

Berglind rummaged around in the box in search of something interesting. 'Here's more for you.' She held out a thick sheaf of papers that Nína took care not to muddle up with the documents she was still perusing. Berglind took out another batch and leafed through them with ever diminishing interest. Perhaps she had been hoping to find a suicide note from Thröstur, an expression of his love for Nína so lyrical and passionate that it would make everything all right again. 'Look. Isn't this your flat?' She handed Nína an old photo of a house. The colours had faded to sepia. It appeared to have been taken many years, if not decades, ago. On the back was a series of letters and numbers: SEF-235-85. Nothing else.

'Yes, it is. Well, I never.' Nína studied the picture that could have been one of any number of properties built at the time: boxy, with a sloping roof and small balconies; clad in pebbledash. But there was no question that it was their building. Taken a long time ago, judging by the size of the trees in the garden. 'It's our flat all right.' She put the photo down after checking the back for an explanation. 'What else have you got there?'

'A picture of a man.' Berglind handed Nína a photo, which also appeared to be fairly old, though with only the man's haircut to go by Nína couldn't date it with any certainty. His perm suggested it had been taken at the beginning of the eighties. 'Do you know who it is?'

Nína shook her head. 'Though I'm guessing from the other contents of this box that he was no choirboy.' She held the photo up to the light. It was also faded and a little blurred. All its sharpness seemed to have vanished as the colours had broken down. 'Though it could just as well be one of the victims. Someone who was going to testify about the crimes committed against him and wanted this picture to accompany the story.' She studied the man's screwed-up eyes and felt there was something repugnant about him. Of course it was only her imagination but it had an effect on her nonetheless. The man appeared to be in his thirties, so on second thoughts he was unlikely to be one of the victims. Clearly the picture had not been taken by a professional and the man's expression suggested that he had been caught unawares. It showed his face and the upper half of his body and had been taken outdoors. Behind him was a street that could have been anywhere, since all that was visible was part of a house. Nína turned the picture over but there was nothing written on the back. She laid it face down.

Berglind passed her more papers. All had the appearance of being quite old. Some were typed, others handwritten, clearly not by Thröstur. They all bore the same serial number as the photo of the house: SEF-235-85, which conveyed nothing to Nína or her sister. 'Where did he get all this old stuff from?' Berglind asked. 'These aren't notes taken during interviews. But they seem to be connected to child abuse. Oh, God, I can't read this.'

Nína took the last of the papers from her. 'They must

come from the newspaper archives. At least they seem to go back decades. Perhaps the number relates to an old archiving system. Whatever SEF-235-85 might mean.'

'Isn't 85 a year, like 1985?' Berglind stared meditatively into space. 'But what could the rest stand for? "Suspect Evidence File"?' She sighed. 'I'd be a hopeless police officer.'

'If it refers to a working title it could mean anything. Or nothing. Perhaps they're the initials of the journalist the files belonged to. That's not unlikely.'

'It should be easy enough to find out.' Berglind picked up her phone and started tapping. 'No. Nothing comes up. I need more.'

'Trying putting in "Stefán Fridriksson journalist". I don't know if he had a middle name.' Nína tried to disguise how odd she was feeling. It didn't help when Berglind gave a triumphant whoop.

'Bingo! Stefán Egill Fridriksson. He was a journalist on the same paper as Thröstur. She fell silent a moment and when she spoke again she sounded rather more subdued. 'He died in 1985. In April.'

'I know.'

'You know? What do you mean?'

'He was the guy who lived here in this flat and hanged himself in the garage like Thröstur. Remember?' Why hadn't she thought to ask Thorbjörg which paper Stefán had worked for? Perhaps because she hadn't been able to believe that there could be any further coincidences.

'Oh, God.'

'Quite.' Nína stared at the papers littering the kitchen counter. She picked up an old document at random but couldn't concentrate. The similarities between Thröstur's and Stefán's cases wouldn't leave her alone. On top of everything else, it looked as if both men had been working on articles about child abuse. The old notes and memos seemed mostly to relate to a paedophile. Stefán hadn't collected as much incriminating evidence as Thröstur, but no doubt that was to do with the era. Few people had spoken openly about such things in 1985. The paedophile's name didn't appear anywhere but she would have to go through the papers again to be certain. She meant to read every single letter of every single document, if only to find out why Thröstur had retrieved this material from the archives and why Stefán had thought a photo of the house he lived in was relevant to a child-abuse story. Perhaps the other photo was of him.

She spotted a piece of paper that had definitely belonged to Thröstur. It was covered in familiar doodles of the kind he used to draw while talking on the phone. Countless circles and drawings of flowers, boxes and tornadoes, along with some phone numbers he had jotted down. In the midst of what looked like choppy waves on an ancient Greek urn he had written: *Lalli? Lárus – Lárus Jónmundsson?* The name rang a bell. Without taking her eyes off the paper she asked Berglind to Google it.

Out of the corner of her eye she could see Berglind tapping the keypad with her nail. 'There's only one. A man your age. A lawyer.' She tapped again, then looked up. Nína turned to her and saw from her face that something was wrong. 'He's dead. Died in December, at home. The police are asking anyone who spoke to him on the day he died to get in touch.'

It was as if the badly painted walls of the kitchen were slowly but surely closing in on them. Suddenly Nína found it hard to breathe. 'Come on. Let's take this stuff and go home to your place.'

She remembered now why she recognised the name. His death had been investigated at the police station and although she hadn't been involved in the case, it had piqued her curiosity. After all, she was bound to be unnaturally interested in suicides for a while. Lárus was believed to have killed himself. First Stefán, then Thröstur, and now him.

Chapter 25

26 January 2014

The bruises on her face were an angry red at the outer edges but starting to darken in the middle. Nói couldn't begin to count them, still less all the ones on her neck. Her cheekbones and forehead were covered in small cuts and abrasions and there were two large half-moons under her eyes that extended down her cheeks. She looked like a poster girl for a road-safety campaign. According to the doctor, the black eyes were caused by her broken nose and would get worse before they got better. Vala would be in a lot of pain once the local anaesthetic and analgesics she'd been given at A&E wore off, so Nói should try to get some liquid painkillers down her. These looked disgusting and oddly viscous, but pills were out of the question since her broken lower jaw had been wired to the upper one and the whole inside of her mouth was swollen and extremely tender.

'It'll be all right.' Nói helped Vala into the car, having slid the passenger seat back as far as it would go. He fastened her seatbelt, taking care not to touch the plaster cast on her right arm. He had helped her to dress in the loose sportswear that the nurse on duty had advised him to bring along and it had cut him to the quick when he saw that her body was as bruised and grazed as her face. Before he rushed off to the hospital, he'd talked to the nurse on the phone and she'd told him that Vala had got off incredibly lightly in the circumstances. When a pedestrian was hit by a car travelling at speed, the consequences were usually much more serious. Vala was lucky to be alive and not to have sustained permanent injuries. Fortunately, instead of landing on the road, she had been thrown up on to the bonnet of her own car, which she had been walking towards at the time. Although no one said as much, Nói thought the fact that Vala was in such good physical shape had probably been a factor as well. He imagined her twisting in the air like a cat, but the image was probably drawn from action movies – it was almost certainly simply pure luck. He couldn't bear to think about the consequences if her head or spine had hit the kerb.

The same nurse escorted them to the door and squeezed his hand in parting, saying that she really hoped the police would catch the driver. Nói bit his tongue to stop himself wasting some well-chosen words on the bastard.

Carefully, he pushed the passenger door shut. As he walked round the car he hoped the cold air would purge the anger from his mind. His rage at the driver was unquestionably justified; less so the portion of it that was directed at Vala. Yet he couldn't control it. How had she got into this mess? And he was livid about the damage to the car, which was now sitting in her friend's street, waiting for him to fetch it and take it to the garage. But what angered him most was that Vala wouldn't be able to utter a word until tomorrow at the earliest. He had so many burning questions but they would have to wait. He couldn't hand her a pen and paper and order her to write down the answers with her left hand, much as he wanted to.

No, he must restrain himself and make sure she wasn't aware of his fury. He told himself it was probably caused by the shock of realising how close he'd come to losing her for good.

'Right. Home we go. Tumi said he was going to wait up but I doubt he'll have been able to stay awake.' It was nearly half past one in the morning. 'Though you never know. It's not so different from his usual bedtime.' Nói smiled at Vala but received little response. Then again, how were you supposed to smile with a broken jaw?

'The police came round. That's how I heard.' Nói couldn't bear the silence in the car and the odd whistling Vala made as she drew breath hurt his ears. 'They sent round a cop as if they thought *I*'d run you over. She wanted to know what you'd been up to, if you had any enemies – then asked where I'd been all evening. It wasn't until she'd finished interrogating me and had a look at my car that I was allowed to leave. That's why it took me so long to get to you.'

Vala turned her head with difficulty and gazed at him with wide eyes. Presumably she had been unaware how much time had passed since she reached the hospital. 'You'll go out like a light once we're home. I'll fetch some extra pillows from the cupboard and prop you up with them so you won't move in your sleep. That should help.'

Vala looked away; no sign of gratitude could be read from her profile. He longed to scream at her. What the fuck had she been thinking of, slipping out while he was asleep? This is what happened to people who went sneaking off like that. But he clamped his lips shut and concentrated on driving. The journey felt as if it would never end; every bump and bend in the road caused Vala to groan, so he took his foot off the accelerator. It didn't help that he couldn't seem to find a topic of conversation that didn't require her to answer. He was burning with a desire to tell her to nod or shake her head in answer to some questions but didn't dare for fear she would start crying. It was bound to sting like hell if salty tears got into the cuts on her face.

He was relieved when they pulled into the darkened drive at home but Vala flinched when she saw the broken bulbs of the outside lights by the parking space. She turned stiffly and peered up the street. There was no one to be seen but that didn't lessen the terror in her eyes, which were almost buried now in her swollen face. Nói helped her indoors as fast as he dared. She limped and her balance seemed shaky. It would be a long time before she went for a run or to work and the thought of her alone at home made him anxious. Perhaps he would be forced to take a holiday from the office, only go in during the afternoons once Tumi had come home from school, or even stay at home while she was recuperating. His staff would probably welcome his absence; after all, they had managed fine while he was in Florida. Perhaps it would be best for everyone. Although the consensus was that the hit and run had been an accident, he wasn't ruling out the possibility that it was connected to the string of peculiar events that had occurred since their return. A person who could kill a cat and stick it on a barbecue was probably more capable than most of knocking down a pedestrian and fleeing the scene.

Tumi was sitting in the kitchen with his laptop, apparently determined to wait up. Púki was curled up in his arms. The boy was tired but his eyes widened with shock when he saw his mother hobble inside with his father's help. 'Holy shit.'

Tumi put down the cat and groped for his phone. 'I've got to take a picture of this.'

The gurgling noises from Vala's throat said it all and Nói snapped at his son. Tumi seemed thrown by their reactions but accepted the telling-off and, chastened, asked his mother how she was feeling. The noise she emitted could only be interpreted as meaning 'bloody awful'. He offered to bring her a glass of water but she refused it with the same inarticulate sounds.

'Did they catch the guy who did this?'

'No. But hopefully they will. As soon as possible.' Nói looked at Vala. 'If it *was* a man . . . Do they know?' She stared at him, then nodded slowly. Of course it was possible she had seen into the car, either as she was flying through the air or after she'd landed.

'Shit! They should lock the bastard up.' Tumi glanced at his father. 'Was he drunk?'

'We don't know yet.' Nói read in Vala's eyes that she wished he had answered differently. Quite against his instincts he added: 'But it was almost certainly a drunk. Or drug addict. According to the police officer who came round.' He smiled at Tumi who earlier that evening had stood in the background, watching as his father was grilled by the policewoman. 'Once she'd established that *I* was at home all evening.' Tumi frowned.

Púki tripped lightly over to Nói and Vala and began weaving in and out of their legs as if they were standing there purely to create an obstacle course for him. Nói pushed him away for fear he would trip Vala up and the cat shot upstairs, deeply offended. After he had gone, Vala stared at the floor and her husband and son stared at her. None of them seemed to have a clue what to do and it was only when Nói noticed that Vala was having difficulty keeping her eyes open that he offered to help her up to bed. She nodded with the least possible movement of her head and moved slowly over to the stairs.

She was limping badly and Nói hurried over to support her. On their way past the kitchen worktop her gaze fell on the note that had been delivered after she went out that evening, and she stopped dead and read the brief text: *Serves you right, liar.* She stood transfixed, her body rigid.

'This came while you were out.' Nói regretted that he hadn't put it out of sight, though in truth he had left it there deliberately to see her reaction. 'It could even have been delivered around the time you were knocked down. Or shortly afterwards.'

The words on the page had gained a horrible significance now. Vala made as if to pick it up but Nói took a gentle hold of her hand. 'We'd better not touch it. I was so shocked earlier that I forgot to mention it to the policewoman. Then I thought it would probably make more sense to talk to the other officers who took the rest of the stuff. We'd better not add any more fingerprints to it. It's already covered in mine and Tumi's.'

'Shit!' Tumi had come up beside them and was gazing at the text. He seemed to be catching on and Nói cursed himself for failing to block his view. 'Shit. Is this from the guy who knocked you down, Mum?' Without waiting for an answer he blurted out: 'Why's he calling you a liar? How does he know where we live?'

Vala made no attempt to answer, not that she could speak anyway. She seemed to have stopped breathing. Nói glared at Tumi to shut him up.

He helped Vala upstairs and into bed. She made it clear that she didn't want to take her clothes off. She closed her swollen, luridly bruised eyes the moment her head touched the pillow. Nói drew the covers carefully over her but even so she winced as the duvet caught on her plaster cast. For a while he stood there gazing at her blood-caked hair spread out on the white pillow, then switched off the light and left the room.

He shooed Tumi up to bed. The boy's face was full of questions but he seemed unable to grasp the enormity of what he was thinking because he didn't put any of them into words. He merely said goodnight and asked his father to make absolutely sure the front door was locked.

Nói went round all the windows on the ground floor to check that none of them was open even a crack. When he tested the back door it turned out to be unlocked, presumably from when Tumi had let Púki in. He locked it and tried the handle. He briefly considered barricading it with furniture but knew he would only regret it tomorrow morning when he had to put everything back.

After fetching some pillows and arranging them between the two of them he crawled into bed with Vala, feeling utterly exhausted. Though he was so tired he doubted he would move an inch in the night, he didn't want to take any risks. He couldn't bear the thought of being woken by a moan of pain from her. As he closed his eyes he felt a great weight of fatigue settling on him. But as he lay there as though pole-axed, the blackest thoughts began to plague his mind until he thought his head would burst. He didn't have the strength to resist them, but finally sleep brought him release from the evening's burden of upset and fear.

Yet he didn't have long to enjoy it. Shortly after he dropped off, he started up at a sound. He couldn't remember what it was but knew that it had woken him. While he was shaking off his drowsiness he strained his ears in case the sound came again. He could hear nothing but the booming of the sea.

Nói coughed and glanced over at Vala to see if she had woken up too. There was no one in the bed. The pillows were all in place but the duvet had been pulled aside. 'Vala?' he called, then realised she would have difficulty answering, so he swung his legs out of bed. The wooden floor felt icy underfoot but he stood up anyway. Perhaps she had gone to the loo or was searching for her painkillers. He was an idiot not to have put them on her bedside table. But their bathroom was empty and Vala wasn't in the kitchen either. The painkillers were still in their paper bag by the sink. Púki was curled up in his bed by the kitchen radiator and rose majestically to his feet, convinced that it was feeding time. He yowled as if he had been starving for days but Nói ignored him; if the cat was fed now he would want to go out and Nói didn't like the thought of him being outside at night. Not now, and perhaps not ever again.

'Vala?' She must be able to make some sound, for God's sake. What the fuck was wrong with her? He listened and thought he heard a movement in the utility room. After a moment's hesitation he followed the noise. Perhaps it would be safer to grab a knife or a rolling pin – if they even owned such a thing – as he couldn't be sure that the sounds were being made by Vala rather than some violent intruder. But Nói couldn't imagine how a knife or blunt object would help him; he pictured himself battering or stabbing his wife by mistake. Steeling himself, he crept towards the utility room and flung open the door. His heart was hammering in his chest.

Inside Vala was standing by the washing machine, bending over a box. She turned slowly but because of the swelling it was impossible to tell if she was surprised. She seemed somehow unreal, as if the Vala he had married was hidden inside a stranger.

'What on earth are you doing?' Nói moved closer to see what was concealed in the box but Vala tried desperately to shake her head. She had something in her left hand and was trying to hide it under her baggy T-shirt.

'What have you got there?' Nói stepped in front of her and she gave up her vain attempt to conceal the evidence. She held out several sheets of paper, then pointed at the box where two more were lying on top of an old pair of trainers. They were the same kind of notes as had turned up in the chalet and in the hall earlier that evening, and the messages were of the same sort: *Why did you lie?*; *The day of reckoning is nigh*; *Just you wait, liar*, and more in that vein.

'When did these arrive?' Nói met his wife's eyes and she mumbled incomprehensibly. He would have to phrase the question better. 'Did they come just now?' She shook her head: *No*. 'Did they come before we went abroad?' She nodded: *Yes*. 'Do you know who sent them?' She didn't react. He stared at her in disbelief. 'Why didn't you tell me? You must know what's going on if you hid these from me, and if so you must know who sent them.'

Another feeble head-shake: *No*. Tears ran down her cheeks. They must have stung but Vala didn't appear to notice. Again she shook her head: *No*.

Chapter 26

28 January 2014

'Is this night ever going to end?' Heida is so hoarse that Helgi passes her the bottle, despite their resolve to drink as little water as possible. They can always melt some snow. Besides, it doesn't matter if they run out because they're going to be rescued at daybreak – if that ever comes. Time is still creeping forward with an agonising slowness. The air in the lighthouse is dank. Since the storm died down the weather has turned frosty and still, but they are able to keep reasonably warm thanks to each other's body heat. They are all pretty stiff by now, though.

'I need to stretch my legs. Are you coming?' Helgi takes back the water bottle once Heida has sipped a little. 'I want to see if the stars are still out; look at something other than these four walls. Even if it's only darkness.'

She looks at him with a hint of hesitation and doubt in her weary face, then nods slowly and struggles to her feet. They are both sitting swaddled in their sleeping bags but haven't dared to lie down. If they do, they're afraid they'll nod off, which would put paid to their decision to stay on guard all night. Ívar did his best to make himself comfortable, then fell sound asleep almost instantly. Neither of them prodded him or made any effort to keep him awake, despite the thunderous concert of snoring that ensued. They have been speaking in an undertone ever since for fear of waking him.

The knife is nowhere to be seen, though Helgi has made rather feeble attempts to get Ívar to admit that he no longer has it. He's a failure both as an actor and as a storyteller. Adopting an exaggeratedly hearty manner he had pretended he needed the knife to fix the zip on his sleeping bag. The excuse could have been better thought out as Ívar immediately wanted to see what was wrong. And of course the zip turned out to be working perfectly. Ívar gave Helgi a puzzled look, then shook his head and returned to his spot. His hand never moved towards the empty sheath. It was fortunate he didn't look in Heida's direction as she could have been posing for Munch's *The Scream*: mouth agape, hands clamped to her cheeks. She had obviously been expecting a fight to break out. Her look of terror had faded once it was clear that peace would be maintained for the moment, but he could tell she hadn't relaxed until Ívar fell asleep.

Ívar doesn't stir as they climb out and close the door behind them.

'I read somewhere that there are fewer stars visible in the night sky than there are Cheerios in a full packet.' Heida gazes up at the heavens. The gale has dragged the clouds away with it, south over the sea, and countless stars are now glimmering overhead. 'Though I find it hard to believe. The person who claimed that can't have been here.'

'No, I suppose not.' Helgi clenches his fists in his anorak pockets and curses himself yet again for losing one of his gloves. 'It's really beautiful. A great improvement on the ceiling of the lighthouse. I feel as if I've been staring at whitewashed concrete for the last ten years. I couldn't take it any more. I'm almost prepared to try and survive out here until it grows light.'

'But it's freezing. You'll die of cold.' From her tone, Heida doesn't seem to regard this as such a bad fate, but she adds: 'Just because something's beautiful doesn't mean it's not dangerous.'

'I know.' Helgi is still gazing at the heavens. He could add that he has never personally experienced true beauty. Whenever he comes across glorious scenery he whips out his camera, which effectively forms a barrier between himself and the subject. And the people who have crossed his path have never been particularly beautiful, either inside or out. But no, his sojourn on the rock must be making him cynical. Of course he's met beautiful, kind people. 'God, I can't wait to get out of here. I just hope I don't develop claustrophobia as a result of this miserable experience.'

'No, I'm sure you won't.' Heida picks her way carefully over to the helipad and Helgi follows. On the way she turns and looks at him, her eyes dark, her face like ivory in the moonlight. 'You haven't taken many pictures since we were stranded here. Why not?'

'I've photographed every single rock, so taking more pictures wouldn't achieve anything. And I don't particularly want photos of us three, squashed in there.' It's none of her business but the main reason is that it will make it easier for him to shake off the press when they start pursuing him after all this is over. He'll lie that his batteries ran out and the only pictures he has were taken before disaster struck. If it is established that Tóti was murdered, he will have no peace from people making him offers for photos of the scene, so it's better not to put himself in temptation's way. He's not entirely sure why he's intending to let such a fantastic opportunity slip through his fingers but thinks it probably has something to do with the feeling that he would be betraying those who shared his predicament. Even though he doesn't really care for them. Especially not Ívar. Maybe he likes Heida more than he realises. 'If you'd like a photo of yourself standing here in the middle of the night, I can fetch my camera.'

'Thanks but no thanks.' She straightens up once she has the concrete helipad underfoot. 'Do you honestly think we'll get home?' She has lost interest in him and his pictures.

'I can't imagine what could prevent us now. The weather seems OK and it can't change that much by morning. And the problem with the helicopter's been fixed, so it looks to me as if we're almost home and dry.' He had received a text message just before midnight informing them that the repairs were completed. He would have preferred a phone call but he could understand why the coastguard didn't want to talk to them. 'It would be bloody unlucky if anything happened to stop it coming now.'

'Luck hasn't exactly been smiling on us so far.'

'I don't know. We're alive, which is more than can be said for Tóti.' Helgi kicks a pebble, which bounces across the platform and over the edge. He listens for a faint splash but hears nothing, despite the hush. The seabirds are either roosting for the night or floating on the sea, somewhere far below.

'Don't talk about him.' Heida's tone is pleading. 'I'd rather not have to hear his name again any time soon, though I suppose I'll have to if what you say about the police turns out to be right.' Her sigh produces a white jet of steam.

Helgi can't now remember what he said when they discussed the possibility of arrest and a police inquiry into Tóti's death. They talked so much that he can no longer recall who said what. Nor does he want to remember. 'I can't work out if I'm more hungry or thirsty. The question is, should we eat the small amount of food we've got left and put up with being hungry tomorrow?'

'Yes.' Heida's eyes are shining. 'Let's. Do you think we can do it without waking Ívar?'

'I wasn't suggesting we should leave him out. It wouldn't be fair and, anyway, it could be risky. I'd rather listen to my stomach rumbling than you two screeching at each other again.'

'I don't screech.' Heida turns her head away and Helgi wonders if he's made her angry again. 'I just don't understand why we should feed a dangerous lunatic like him. It'll only make him stronger. It would be best for everyone if he slept till the chopper arrives.'

'But what if he wakes up hungry in the night? Or the chopper doesn't come? What then?' Earlier that evening Helgi had decided to avoid mentioning anything that could exacerbate his companions' pessimism. Now he has let this slip out, he doesn't know how to recover the situation. 'But of course it'll come – all I meant is, what if he wakes up early and demands his share of the food?'

'We'll leave some for him. Since you insist. I have no desire to eat with him, though. I want to eat out here. In the open air, as far away from him as possible.'

The idea appeals to Helgi: it's not often he is invited to dine under the stars with an attractive woman. 'Did you always feel this way about Ívar or is it because you think he killed Tóti?' As far as he can recall, they had got on all right at the beginning of the trip, yet he had sensed some underlying tension.

'I just think he's a nasty piece of work. Quite apart from the Tóti business. That was the impression I got. He was really spiteful to me the first day and I've never found it easy to forgive. I know it's a flaw in my character but in this case I believe it's justified.' She falls silent, then moves to the edge of the helipad where it overhangs the cliff and sits down, letting her legs dangle. Helgi wants to sit beside her but is afraid of accidentally brushing against her. It wouldn't be the first time he'd underestimated his bulk. In his mind he's thin.

'I'm going to fetch the food and leave some behind for Ívar. If you're dying of hunger you can have some of mine. I'm not that desperate. After all, I've got more to fall back on than you.' His cheeks grow hot at the reference to his weight. Perhaps this trip will be the incentive he needs to go on the diet he has been planning for as long as he can remember. At least he knows now that hunger is nothing to be afraid of. It's really not so bad. Thirst is much worse. 'Maybe we should collect the small amount of snow that's settled and melt it inside the lighthouse.'

Heida doesn't turn to look at him but continues to swing her legs over the edge. 'Is it safe? It may have got mixed up with bird shit and you can catch typhoid from birds.'

'We can see later. I'm prepared to take the chance. You can have the water in the bottle.'

'Or we both can and Ívar can have the snow.'

Helgi has a warm feeling inside as he hurries as quickly as he dares back to the lighthouse to fetch the food. He slips cautiously through the door, taking care not to wake the snoring man. If it weren't for the ugly noises he would think Ívar was dead or in a coma. It would hardly be possible for someone to sleep any more deeply. In the cool-box he finds half a sandwich with roast beef filling and half with prawn salad. The people who put together these provisions in the belief that they would last an extra day are clearly suffering from anorexia. He reaches into the box. The layer of mayonnaise has turned yellow on one of the sandwiches so he takes the other and decides to give it to Heida. The one that's looking a bit past it is good enough for Ívar. For himself he takes the apple he has already taken a few bites out of. There are two custard creams left and he puts them in his pocket too. That's all. It's hardly a feast but even so he's looking forward enormously to the meal, if you can call it that.

He puts his ear to the door after shutting it behind him and listens for the snores that break out almost immediately. Unbelievable how the guy can sleep. What a bit of luck. It would ruin the atmosphere if Ívar blundered out and demanded to join in.

Helgi squats down far enough away from Heida to be able to manoeuvre without the risk of bumping into her, then shuffles closer on his bottom. He fishes the sandwich, biscuits and half-eaten apple from his pocket and hands her the sandwich. He places the biscuits between them. 'God, this is fantastic. We should open a restaurant.'

She makes a face at him. 'Do you seriously believe people would be interested in buying stale sandwiches?'

'No. I meant the setting. Plenty of people would be willing to dine out here. Just sitting in silence, gazing at the stars . . . Perhaps we can wait out here.' He toys with the apple but doesn't want to bite into it for fear the crunching noise will spoil the purity of the silence. You'd have thought the sea had fallen asleep too as barely a splash can be heard now from the base of the cliff.

'Maybe.' Heida takes a bite of sandwich and stares out into the gloom. 'I feel better out here than in there, anyway. Actually I feel good, believe it or not. Though my bum's cold. Weird. I suppose it's a sign our ordeal's nearly over.' She glances at Helgi and smiles, then repeats her words as if this will make them come true. 'Yes, it's nearly over.'

Helgi smiles back and nods. But his smile is not genuine. The night is still young. Suddenly he remembers that Tóti isn't far away. He bends forward to look down. He knows the body is floating there on the black surface of the sea and imagines the glazed eyes staring blindly at the stars that had so enchanted him and Heida. They immediately lose all their charm and Helgi jerks back, his face as pale as hers.

His worries are building up inside him like a boulder in his chest. This is going to end badly, he knows it.

Chapter 27

26 January 2014

At this hour of the night the police station reminded her of a noisy children's toy whose battery has run down. Where before there had been a din and bustle, now there was deathly silence. Everything seemed to be on hold: the printers were quiet, the coffee machines deserted. Nína walked along the empty corridor, relishing the sound of her footsteps, relishing not having to encounter her colleagues. But that wasn't why she was here in the early hours. She had started awake in the middle of the night and been unable to get back to sleep. It wasn't particularly surprising as there was no real way of making oneself comfortable in the armchair in Thröstur's room. It was so long since she had slept in a bed that she was beginning to forget what it felt like.

Yet it wasn't the discomfort that had woken her so much as the thoughts that had made it hard for her to get to sleep in the first place. When she finally dropped off they had infiltrated her dreams so thoroughly that she had jerked awake, still tired, with a stiff neck. There were too many unanswered questions, and patience had never been her forte. If the answers were out there somewhere she had to track them down, and that wasn't going to happen in her sleep. Dreams were too unreliable for that. After twisting first to the right, then to the left, she tried putting her legs up on the arms of the chair, then resting them on the edge of Thröstur's bed, then tucking them beneath her and even putting them down on the floor as if she were sitting on a bus. Nothing worked.

So she had splashed some water on her face and kissed Thröstur's cool cheek. It felt clammy to the touch and there was a smell of plastic from the tube in his mouth. He lay there as motionless and remote as ever; her kiss meant nothing to him. She hurried from his room, painfully aware that it was becoming easier to leave him in the mornings. This evoked mixed feelings; sadness but also relief that she was gradually beginning to accept the inevitable – which was uncomfortably near at hand. Shamefaced, she sneaked out of the ward so the staff wouldn't chase her about fixing the fateful day. Now that the chances of her finding an explanation for what Thröstur had done were looking more realistic, she wanted to put the brakes on and deeply regretted having made a decision about his future. When the moment came to say goodbye, she wanted at least to have an inkling of why he had acted as he had. But she couldn't expect anyone else to understand this. The ward would probably send a member of staff to ambush her if she didn't present herself within the next couple of days. Hospital beds were precious; Thröstur wasn't. Not any more.

Nína had unconsciously sped up as she walked down the empty corridor of the police station, but now she slowed down a little. There was no rush, yet she felt as if she were in a race against time. As if somewhere there was an egg timer with her name on it in which the sand was running out – ever faster. She opened the door to yet another corridor, which led to the small room used by the night shift. There she hoped to find the policewoman who apparently had the file open that Nína wanted to read. She wasn't going to ask her to close it – there was no need. She was simply curious to know why the woman had been looking at it in the first place.

It was the report on Lárus Jónmundsson's suicide, which was ancient history by police standards. At least it wasn't at all clear why someone would want to read a month-old incident report in the middle of the night.

Inside the room sat three police officers, two men and the woman Nína was looking for, holding steaming mugs of coffee. All three looked shattered, their eyes glassy, their cheeks a hectic red after coming in from the cold. Nína recognised the atmosphere; the Saturday night shift was never an easy one. The city centre resembled the set of a disaster movie in which the revellers were zombies and the police officers the army that had been sent to the scene in a forlorn attempt to hold back the tide.

'Is it eight already?' One of the men sat up, surprised but pleased. His trouser legs looked as if they had been splashed with vomit, which would explain the bad smell in the room. When she shook her head, he slumped back in his seat. They were obviously too tired to give her the cold shoulder.

'I came to find Aldís.' Nína smiled at the woman who looked exhausted and didn't return her smile.

'What?' In different circumstances the response might have seemed brusque but no one could expect politeness at this hour. Not from people stinking of vomit, courtesy of some wasted partygoer. In fact, it was one of the friendliest greetings Nína had received since she'd lodged her complaint. Perhaps she should apply to work the night shift.

'I need to look at the case of Lárus Jónmundsson who committed suicide in December, and I saw on the server that you've got the original report open.' Nína hesitated, wondering if she should sit down as well, but decided to remain standing. Tired as she was, she didn't belong with this exhausted trio. And you never knew, they might suddenly recollect that she was a pariah and get up and walk away. Though that was unlikely; none of them looked as if they could so much as stand unaided.

'Oh. I must have forgotten to close it earlier. We were called out to Ingólfstorg Square to help the city-centre shift.'

'Do you mind my asking why you had it open? Isn't the case closed?'

'Yes. I wasn't working on it directly but I was involved in a call-out earlier tonight that may be connected. I didn't have a chance to read it properly, though, so I've no idea how.' Aldís drank some coffee and made a face as she swallowed. 'I'd forgotten all about it. It feels like it happened days ago. Do you want me to go up and close the file?'

Nína wasn't about to ask this woman to stagger upstairs to her office; she would barely make it to the first landing. 'No, thanks. I just wanted to know why someone other than me was interested in it.'

Aldís wrinkled up her nose again at the bitter coffee. 'Why did you want to look at it? Are you involved with that strange case in Skerjafjördur?'

'Skerjafjördur? No, I've not heard any mention of that. I've been working with old files down in the basement recently. I've been taken off the beat temporarily, as you may know.' The men exchanged glances and at the sight of their expressions Nína lost the thread.

Aldís noticed her consternation. She stared down into her cup. 'I've never understood why that's supposed to be a punishment. If someone took me off the beat I'd welcome it as much as a pay rise. If people caught on, we'd all get ourselves punished and crowd out the basement.' She pushed away her mug and stood up. 'If you don't mind tagging along, I'm going to get some fresh coffee.'

On the way out they walked past the coffee machine but Aldís's companions were too tired to comment, and, anyway, why point out the obvious? Aldís wanted to give Nína a chance to talk to her in private. 'Sorry. I thought you might find it easier to talk one to one. Gunni and Thór are OK, but they're fed up right now and they might start butting in.'

'Thank you.'

Aldís closed the door and they stood outside in the corridor. There was no coffee machine in sight. Aldís leant against the wall, knocking a framed fire-safety certificate askew. She came straight to the point: 'What's your interest in this Lárus?'

Nína decided she would cut to the chase, too. The woman was obviously too exhausted to take in all the details. 'I found his name noted down among my husband's papers. There was no explanation but since my husband and Lárus suffered more or less the same fate, I wondered if they had anything else in common. Anything that could explain what happened to my husband. And maybe what happened to Lárus too. I'm trying to find a link between them, in other words.'

Aldís nodded and Nína silently thanked her for not pasting on the dreaded expression of sympathy that people generally adopted when they heard any mention of Thröstur in her presence. Not that she had encountered much sympathy in her colleagues' faces lately. Perhaps they thought it served her right for causing trouble.

'You know Lárus took an overdose? But your husband tried to hang himself – have I got that right?' Straight to the point again; no beating about the bush.

'Yes.' Nína restrained an impulse to reach out and straighten the framed certificate. The world was enough of a mess without things being allowed to hang askew. 'I wasn't suggesting they were murdered, so the different circumstances come as no surprise. It's just that I don't like coincidences.'

'When did he note down Lárus's name?'

'I don't know exactly. Probably in November or maybe even earlier. Thröstur's been in a coma since the beginning of December, so of course it would have to have been before then.'

'So he was interested in Lárus for some reason before he tried to kill himself?'

Nína nodded.

'And they both resorted to suicide in the same month?'

Again Nína nodded.

'Extraordinary. Did they know each other?'

'No. Not to my knowledge. At least I don't remember Thröstur ever mentioning him. Perhaps their paths crossed in connection with work but Thröstur very rarely discussed the stories he was working on and I didn't talk to him about my job either. In spite of the rumours doing the rounds here.'

Aldís shrugged and the certificate on the wall was knocked even more crooked. 'I don't know if you've looked at Lárus's file but some people thought his death was suspicious.'

'I remember.' Nína gave a wry smile. 'I was aware of the

case though I wasn't allowed anywhere near it because of my situation. It was considered inappropriate.'

'Understandably.' Aldís did not return her smile.

'But I didn't hear how it ended, for example what happened about the visitor who was supposed to have been with Lárus that evening. If I'd known Thröstur had some connection with Lárus I'd probably have taken more interest. Was the visitor ever found?'

'No. All we know is that there was somebody with him that evening. His wife was away but the neighbours said they'd heard talking and there were signs in his flat that more than one person had been drinking there. They concluded that the unknown individual had probably left by the time Lárus took the overdose. At least there was no evidence that he'd been coerced into taking the pills.'

'What's the link to the Skerjafjördur business you mentioned?'

'Had you stopped following the case by the time Lárus's widow brought in the letters she found in his office?'

'Yes. I expect so. I don't remember hearing about them, anyway. What were they?'

'Cryptic messages that we never got to the bottom of. Short sentences, one per sheet of paper, which had been folded to fit inside an envelope. No one knows if the letters came in the post or if Lárus wrote them himself intending to send them to other people. His wife had no knowledge of them. She vaguely remembered Lárus receiving letters but had the feeling he'd told her they were junk mail from the bank. Advertisements for investments, that sort of thing. But she was adamant that she had seen no logos on the envelopes. She was convinced the notes were proof that Lárus had been murdered. She started laying into us when it sank in that we didn't consider them sufficient evidence to justify reopening the case.'

'Just what did these letters contain?'

'That's the weird part, and that's where the Skerjafjördur business comes in. Notes were found there containing exactly the same kind of messages. At the family's summer chalet. Then another note was posted through their letterbox late yesterday evening.'

'What is the Skerjafjördur case precisely?'

'What isn't it?' Aldís made a face. 'The husband called us yesterday afternoon because he'd found a dead cat on the barbecue at their summer chalet.' She looked wearily at Nína. 'Don't ask. They wanted to report some Americans they'd done a house swap with, who they believed had disappeared off the face of the earth. Or something like that. The whole thing's far from clear and although I've read the first report several times I'm still none the wiser. But among the evidence they handed over to the police were these notes. Something about liars getting their come-uppance. Then just before midnight last night the wife was knocked down by a car and I was sent round to break the news to her husband. He was initially regarded as a suspect. Then it emerged that another note had arrived. The husband said he didn't know Lárus Jónmundsson and his wife is so mashed up that we won't be able to get a word out of her till later today. Maybe even tomorrow.'

'Who was the driver?'

'We don't know. It was a hit and run.' Aldís kicked her foot against the wall, leaving a dirty mark on the discoloured paint. 'Did you two receive any notes like that?'

'No. Definitely not. I've just been through all our stuff because I'm selling the flat, and there were no messages like the ones you've just described.'

'It seems Lárus didn't tell his wife about the notes, and the husband in Skerjafjördur was equally in the dark. He didn't know how the letters had reached the chalet. One of the officers who went to see them originally said the wife started acting very strangely when the subject came up and he thought she might know more than she was letting on. Is it possible your husband could have kept the notes secret from you? Read them, then thrown them away?'

'Not if they came in the post. He was at work until evening, so it was usually me who picked up the post. I don't remember any strange letters.'

Aldís shrugged. 'Perhaps it's all completely unrelated. Stranger things have happened. Do you know a man called Nói or might your husband have known him?'

Nína shook her head and the bones of her neck clicked. 'I'd recognise the name. It's not that common.' She sensed the conversation was coming to an end. Aldís obviously wanted to get back to the others, take the weight off her feet and let her fatigue slowly dissipate over a bad coffee. 'Will you be involved any further in the Skerjafjördur case?'

'Yes, I expect so.' Aldís frowned slightly. 'Why?'

'I was wondering if I could have another word. Not today but maybe next time you're on duty.' Nína was quite prepared for her to say no. Word at the station was that Aldís would go far. Though she was still forced to take the occasional night shift everyone knew this would soon be a thing of the past. Nína, on the other hand, was on her way down. Or even out. So it would be only natural if Aldís didn't want anything to do with her during daylight hours. 'I won't get in your way – I'm down in the basement most of the time. I'd just like to keep in touch about what happens.'

'If you like. I'm not sure there'll be much more to hear. With some cases you know from the moment they're reported that they'll hang around for a while, then sink without trace. The Skerjafjördur business is one of those.'

'What about the Americans they did a house swap with? Have they been found or is the suggestion that they're missing actually a possibility?'

'We haven't established that yet. Hopefully things'll be clearer on Monday or Tuesday when they've checked the passenger lists at Keflavík. It complicates matters that they were apparently travelling onwards to Europe and we don't know where they were heading or which airline they were flying with. Though we do have the date of their flight.' Aldís yawned without opening her mouth, her lips barely parting. 'But I don't suppose much'll come of it. If they haven't left the country they've probably got lost in the highlands on one of those crazy hiking trips that can only end in disaster at this time of year. An appeal will be put out for them and someone'll phone in to say they were spotted at a petrol station in the countryside, buying supplies from the shop. They'll turn up when the snow melts.'

'I suppose so.' There was nothing more to say. Aldís's assessment of the situation was only too plausible. 'But maybe I could talk to you later in the week. Send you an e-mail or ring you if I don't run into you.'

'Sure. E-mail me. That'd be best.' It didn't surprise Nína that Aldís should choose a private method of communication over a conversation in the middle of the corridor for all the world to hear. Aldís went back into the room, leaving Nína behind on her own. She longed to keep talking but checked the urge to follow Aldís. If the woman was going to be given a major role in this investigation, Nína felt annoyed with herself for not having pressed Thröstur's case harder.

She went back to her office. Pity it was still too early to make any phone calls. It had occurred to her that Lárus's widow might be able to shed light on her husband's connection with Thröstur. There must have been one, given that Thröstur had noted down his name. Perhaps he had been abused in his youth and Thröstur had interviewed him about it. Larús might have been the main subject of yet another series of articles about historical sex abuse cases. For all she knew, raking the whole thing up might have thrown his mind into such turmoil that he had felt unable to go on living. But that didn't explain why Thröstur had resorted to the same way out. And done so first.

Nína sat down in front of her computer but instead of poring over the report on Lárus's suicide she decided to examine what had been entered into the database about the Skerjafjördur case. She looked up the husband Nói's address in the phonebook. He turned out to be the only person with that name in Skerjafjördur, which would make it easy to find the evening shift's report on the server. But it was unlikely that Aldís and co. would have finished their incident reports for the night yet, so Nína would have to be patient.

She checked the earlier report and hadn't read far when she came across the name of Nói's wife. Nína leant back slightly from the computer. Vala Konrádsdóttir. The woman the police thought had something to hide.

Chapter 28

26 January 2014

The light was on over the kitchen table. Apart from that the house lay in darkness. The open doorways leading to the sitting room and hall yawned black and silent, and an air of lonely melancholy lay over everything. As Nói contemplated the dimly lit kitchen, for the first time he saw through the illusion he had created. The perfect family life that he had dreamt of and taken such immeasurable pains to construct was really as flawed as everything else in this world.

It was rather late to come to this realisation now that their life was lying in tatters.

There would be no chance to start afresh and undo the past: take the pressure off Vala and Tumi, cease the perpetual nagging that they had complained about so bitterly over the years. He had always known that a shiny fitted kitchen and soft leather sofas weren't everything, so he had stressed the importance of cultivating family life. Felt that he had achieved the only things that really mattered: that Tumi and Vala should be perfectly happy and healthy; that Tumi's childhood should be different from his own upbringing; that his son would never have to be ashamed of their house or hesitate to invite friends home for fear that his parents would be drunk and embarrassing; that his clothes wouldn't be full of holes and he would never have to resort to pulling things out of the dirty laundry basket to find something to wear; that he would never have to lie about the gifts he had received in his shoe in the run-up to Christmas because it had always been empty in the morning. His son deserved a perfect existence on which nothing cast a shadow.

Therein lay the problem. Nói had aimed too high. He had never known what was normal or realistic, had failed to grasp that it was possible to go too far the other way. Nobody lived a perfect life; by refusing to adjust his expectations he had ended up even further from his goal. Although he meant well, he had forced his family to act out some sort of utopian fantasy. Tumi and Vala – but especially Vala – had chosen to hide from him anything that didn't fit in with his vision.

On the kitchen table lay the notes Vala had concealed from him. He was still ignorant of their origin and purpose, and endlessly poring over them was futile. All he had gained by this was to sense the anger of the person who had written them. He couldn't exactly read between the lines, since each note consisted of only one line. No, the thoughts that had flown through Nói's mind had been of Vala. Why hadn't she confided in him? Why had she hidden the vile threats, which, it was now clear, were far from empty?

Of course she couldn't have known at first how serious this was, but why hadn't she shown him the letters, shaken her head over them, laughed them off as nonsense? It was impossible to tell what order the threats had arrived in, so he was in no position to decide what a normal reaction would have been in the beginning. They were undated and although every note showed signs of having been folded to fit in an envelope, they could just as well have been delivered by hand, pushed through the letterbox like the one yesterday evening. There were no envelopes in the box where Vala had hidden them.

No, there must be more to it than these sinister notes. It didn't make sense otherwise. How would she have known the threats were meant for her? Surely, they could just as well have been for him? Or Tumi? If he had found a letter like this in the post he would immediately have assumed it was something to do with their son; that it was teenagers fooling around. If he had received letters like this and had no idea why, it would never have occurred to him to conceal the fact from Vala and hide them in a box of old trainers. Vala must instantly have connected them with some event from her past that she was unwilling to reveal to her family. To him. Something to do with a lie she must have told, if there was any truth in the repeated references to lies or liars. But who had she lied to and what had she lied about?

Nói rubbed his dry eyes, which only made them feel worse. So many questions but no answers. Why hadn't Vala simply thrown the letters away? Was she expecting to have to bring them out later if the situation turned out to be serious? Probably. But *probably* wasn't a good enough answer.

Nói didn't want to face up to the hardest question of all: was Vala mixed up in something so bad that it wouldn't merely shake the foundations of their marriage but destroy it completely? He could only think of two alternatives. One was that she had cheated on him and the letters were from her lover's wife. The other was that she had been involved in something illegal and the victim was out for revenge. The first theory seemed far more plausible. He simply couldn't imagine Vala committing a crime. The idea was absurd. Yet he couldn't entirely dismiss it: after all, what seemed absurd sometimes turned out to be the bitter truth.

And which was worse, when it came down to it?

That she had cheated on him or broken the law?

Cheating, he thought. That affected him personally. Breaking the law affected others. But like every aspect of this miserable bloody business, the choice wasn't that simple. How would he like to visit Vala in prison? Would he allow Tumi to go? Would that be easier for their son than if they divorced because Vala had been unfaithful? In that eventuality, which of them would Tumi live with? Which of them would stay on in the house? However hard Nói wrestled with the problem, the answer eluded his grasp. On second thoughts, it might be easiest for everyone if Vala went to prison, however implausible the idea. If only he knew what was behind all this.

He would have his answers when Vala woke up tomorrow morning, so there was no point losing his mind just yet. He had stopped himself from asking her any questions when he found her in the utility room, just dosed her with painkillers and helped her back to bed. He had given her some sheets of paper and a pen and told her to write it down if there was anything she needed. He could fetch water, a blanket, whatever she wanted.

She had taken them and turned away, avoiding his eye. Nói thought it best to leave her in peace. She could do with some rest if she was going to be fit enough to provide him with an explanation tomorrow morning. He didn't care if it took the whole of Sunday, from sunrise to the following night, to drag the truth out of her.

Vala would be up in a few hours, but even so he couldn't stop brooding.

He ceased rubbing his sore eyes and blinked a few times in the hope that they would recover. They didn't. Instead, it felt as if he had dislodged grit from his lashes and forced it under his lids. Every time he blinked it hurt. He got up to fetch some eye drops and noticed that his neighbours' kitchen light was on. Clearly he wasn't the only one with insomnia.

Forgetting the eye drops, Nói went over to the window. He was curious to know which of them was up and about. Not that it mattered but at least it would be a distraction from his worries. No movement was visible in the brightly lit kitchen windows. It used to irritate him when he was loading the dishwasher after supper that he risked glancing up to see the couple opposite doing exactly the same thing at exactly the same time. Whenever it happened, it was hard to tell who was more embarrassed, him or his neighbours. Sometimes they exchanged waves, at other times they pretended not to notice one another.

Now, unable to see either of them, Nói concluded they had forgotten to switch the lights off. He was turning away from the window when he caught sight of a movement in the garden behind the neighbours' house. He strained his eyes but could hardly see a thing in the darkness, let alone tell who or what was there. Nói felt his tiredness receding as the adrenalin began to pump through his veins. Part of him hoped it was the perpetrator prowling around out there. If so he would reduce him to the same state Vala was in. It would be infinitely sweeter than any justice administered by the courts. If the driver was found, it would take years for the case to pass through the system, no doubt deliberately to ensure that all the wind had left the victim's sails by the time the suspended sentence was finally passed. No, thanks. An eye for a fucking eye and a tooth for a fucking tooth. He may have buggered up many aspects of their family life over the years but no one would be able to say that he had sat idly by while his wife suffered an injustice.

He was surprised at how easily he slid into the role of primitive man of violence who longed to redden his hands with another's blood. He certainly had enough pent-up rage. Well, here was his chance. He shoved his feet in his clogs as fast as he could and dashed outside onto the decking.

His primitive instincts were immediately checked by the cold. Gooseflesh reminded him how inadequately he was dressed and how ill equipped he was for any kind of struggle if it came to blows. If this was the man who had knocked Vala down he was almost certainly armed with a blunt instrument, a knife or worse. Nói was empty-handed. He wondered if he should go back inside, fetch his jacket and something to defend himself with, then realised that it was the woman from next door who was standing there, gazing out to sea. She was clutching a thick towelling dressing gown around her and had on a large pair of boots. The wind whirled her hair, making her look half crazed. Nói turned back to close the door, noticing too late that Púki had slipped out. His pawprints led away across the snow. Damn. Nói walked over to the boundary between their properties and called out in a low voice: 'Hi, Bylgja. Is anything wrong?' Perhaps she had seen a man lurking out here. If so, he would urge her to go straight back inside.

The woman turned to Nói, apparently unsurprised at encountering someone in the garden in the middle of the night. 'I couldn't sleep.'

'Same here.' Nói hugged himself in a losing battle against

the cold. It was hard to stop his teeth chattering. 'I thought I saw a movement and wanted to check what was going on, but I expect it was you.'

The woman glanced around as if she had only just realised where she was. 'I didn't see anything.'

'Good. I'm a bit twitchy at the moment. All the bulbs in our outside lights have been smashed twice and I thought I might finally get my hands on the vandal.'

'Well, it wasn't me.'

Nói smiled and his teeth ached with the cold. 'No. I realise that.'

The woman turned back to the sea, staring as if she was expecting something to rise up out of the choppy, black expanse. 'It's so strange. I've been waking up every night with a powerful urge to go and watch the sea. I've never experienced anything like it before, though we've lived here nearly fifteen years. I'd understand if we'd only just moved in.' She pulled a strand of hair out of the corner of her mouth. 'It's a very odd feeling.'

Nói turned to the sea too, as if he expected to find the explanation there. 'I've caught myself standing staring at it several times too. When they're searching for people who've walked into the sea to commit suicide, I can't stop myself – I keep expecting to see their bodies floating out there.'

She looked at him, smiling sleepily. 'I know what you mean. Now you come to mention it, the feeling's not dissimilar. Perhaps, without realising it, I've heard there's a search under way. It's probably my subconscious at work.' She gazed out to sea again and Nói followed her example. Somehow, though he was still freezing, the cold no longer bothered him.

'I told the police about your satnav.' Nói didn't know why

he had brought this up now. It wasn't as if they were standing awkwardly at a party, trying to make small talk. He ought to hurry back inside.

'Oh. I've given up worrying about it. I wrote it off after Steini noticed it was missing and spent the whole evening going on and on about it. Do you think it'll ever turn up?' A small laugh escaped her. 'Not that I care. But it would serve Steini right because, if I know him, he'll be planning to give me a new one for my birthday next month. It would serve him right if ours was found and it ruined his idea. I've had it up to here with his moaning.'

Clearly Nói wasn't the only husband who liked to nag. But he didn't laugh; he wasn't particularly keen to end up like Steini. If he didn't get a grip on himself he would end up a grumpy old git like him in ten years' time. 'I wouldn't get your hopes up. I'll be interested to see if they find the couple, let alone the satnav.' Or the keys to the chalet. 'When the police came round they mentioned that someone had reported hearing a shot down here one night while we were away. That wasn't you, was it?'

'No.' The woman didn't seem surprised by the question. 'It was the people on the other side.' She pointed to the house beyond theirs. 'Steini and I never wake up.' She rolled her eyes. 'Says she, standing out here in the garden in the middle of the night. But I gather it turned out to be a false alarm. At least nothing came of it. Perhaps they imagined it. Why do you ask?'

'Oh, it's just that I keep wondering about the Americans. There's been no news of them. It occurred to me that it might have been them messing around, shooting at birds.'

'Better that than somebody shooting at them.' A sharp

gust of wind buffeted them and the woman took a step backwards to keep her balance, still without taking her eyes off the sea. 'I do hope nothing's happened to the poor things. That would be terrible. I've always thought there was something so sad about dying on holiday. You feel people could at least be spared that when they've gone and paid for a trip. Like the way I feel I shouldn't need to wear a seatbelt in a taxi.'

'Sadly that's not the case. People drop like flies on holiday. It's probably the stress of coping with airports.' Nói was feeling so light-headed he might have been on drugs. He was prepared to say any old nonsense for the sake of being allowed to stand here beside her, watching the waves rising and falling in the gloom. It must be fatigue. Apart from his nap yesterday evening he hadn't slept for nearly twenty-four hours.

'I've never been stressed by airports. There's no point. If I miss my plane, I miss it. That's all there is to it.' Her dressing gown flapped, revealing a gleam of white knees. 'But what do I know? I never fly out to attend business meetings or anything like that. Whether I arrive on holiday a day earlier or later makes no odds.' She turned to Nói. 'I don't know why I'm talking like this. I'm not interested in flying. I'm probably just tired and need to get back to bed. I hope everything will turn out OK for those poor Americans. They were a nice couple.'

Nói watched the woman pick her way over the snow to the back door. Before going inside she turned and scanned the sea one last time, as if to reassure herself that she hadn't missed anything. Then she disappeared inside and the light over the door went out. Nói was left standing in the same spot, shivering, though not from cold. This was silly, he knew, but he wasn't in a hurry. He decided to make sure all was well. If he found so much as a footprint in the newly fallen snow near their garden he would call the police and demand that a guard be stationed outside their house.

The snow creaked underfoot but the only tracks he could find were Púki's. They led down to the coast path and from there doubtless down to the beach. He opened the garden gate and walked a short way beyond their property. There was no sign that anyone had been loitering there this evening. Relieved, Nói suddenly became aware of the freezing temperature again. But instead of hurrying back inside he told himself he should follow the cat down to the shore and persuade him to come inside. It wouldn't be a good idea for Vala to find a dead mouse in the house tomorrow morning. She was in such a fragile state already and nothing – absolutely nothing – must happen to prevent her from telling him everything. Or rather, writing everything down for him.

'Here, kitty,' Nói whispered, pausing before the glistening belt of seaweed at the top of the beach, which suddenly struck him as disgusting, slimy and malodorous. He visualised his foot sinking deep into the decaying pile. 'Púki! Kitty, kitty. Come here, boy.' He listened for the bell and thought he heard a faint sound nearby, though he couldn't work out where it was coming from. Could the cat be trapped or tangled up somehow in this rotten, salty mess of weed? He called again, slightly louder this time. Now the jingling of the bell was unmistakable and he could turn back; confident that Púki would run after him in the hope of a decent meal.

The sound of the waves intensified when Nói turned his back to the sea and he looked round, his heart beating faster, as if he expected to see a tidal wave rearing up on the horizon.

But as he suspected, nothing had changed; the breakers were no bigger or smaller than they had been before. Yet he felt uneasy as he walked home, conscious of the sea behind him and everything that lurked in its depths. He drew some comfort from the faint mewing that pursued him all the way back to the house, though the note seemed a little plaintive. He was fairly sure that if the cat could talk it would be complaining. Or warning him.

Nói followed the woman next door's example and stopped in the doorway for one last look around. He was too far from the shore to be able to make anything out, which probably made matters worse. Imagination was far more powerful than reality. Despite this, Nói continued to stare down at the shore while the cat wandered slowly across the garden. Eventually, Púki made up his mind to come in and Nói closed the door on the cold and dark, and pulled the curtain.

Only then, when he was no longer tuned into the sights and sounds of the night outside, did he sense that something was wrong.

The kitchen lay in darkness.

But he hadn't turned the light off when he went outside. And even if Tumi had been up and about, instinct told Nói that this was not the explanation.

There was something evil in the air. A floorboard creaked overhead and the hairs prickled on the back of his neck.

There was an uninvited guest upstairs.

Chapter 29

26 January 2014

Time seemed to pass more slowly at night. Nína felt as if she had been sitting in her office for an eternity. Her impatience for the day to begin only seemed to slow time down even more. Perhaps that was why she felt the years were passing more quickly as she grew older; she had nothing special to look forward to any longer. Before, there had always been something: she was waiting to be six so she could start school; she was waiting to be ten and into double figures; she was waiting to be confirmed, to start sixth-form college, to take her driving test, to be old enough to buy alcohol. After that few goals remained. It wasn't that life had suddenly lost its meaning, it was just that there was nothing specific to look forward to. Every passing year merely shortened your life by exactly twelve months. Mathematicians still hadn't developed an equation to express this truth: when you want something to happen, time slows down; when you'd like it to put on the brakes, it speeds up. The theory of time's intransigence – which she was now experiencing firsthand.

At long last her wait was over. At exactly quarter to eight, Nína picked up the receiver and dialled. She had chosen the time with care. She didn't want to ring too early and wake the woman; nor did she want to catch her after she had left the house, when she might not be able to speak freely.

Instead of a conventional ringing tone, Nína was forced to listen to a few bars of a pop song, endlessly repeated, which had been popular over a year ago and quickly forgotten. By the time the woman finally answered, Nína was on the point of hanging up to be free of the wailing in her ear. She was dreading this phone call; despite her impatience to ring, she felt her nerve going when it actually came to the crunch. There was something so awful about having to talk to Lárus's widow in light of her own predicament: she was in limbo, neither married nor widowed. She felt much worse about this than she had about talking to Thorbjörg, perhaps because Klara's loss was more recent.

'Hello?' The woman's voice was muffled and a tap was running in the background.

'Hello. My name's Nína Kjartansdóttir and I'm calling from the Greater Reykjavík Police. I'm sorry to disturb you so early.' She had no compunction about referring to the police. She wasn't lying, though this wasn't official business; she was quite literally calling from the headquarters of the Greater Reykjavík force.

'The police?' The woman made a spitting sound and when she spoke again her voice was much clearer. 'Is something wrong?'

'No, not at all. I'm calling about an investigation in which your husband's name has cropped up. I should make it absolutely clear that he's not suspected of being involved in anything criminal.'

She could hear the woman breathing. When the reply finally came it was curt. 'I think you've got the wrong Klara. My husband's dead. You should take more care next time. What's your name again?'

'Nína Kjartansdóttir.' Afraid the woman was going to hang up, she added quickly: 'I know your husband's passed away. That's why I wanted to talk to you – I was hoping you might be able to provide me with some information.'

'I'm late for swimming.' The woman sounded awkward, as if she was aware this was rather a lame excuse.

'It shouldn't take long.' Nína grimaced inadvertently as she waited for an answer. Now she had begun the conversation, she wanted to see it through. 'I should make it clear that I have a personal connection to the investigation. My husband. Let me stress again that it's nothing to do with anything criminal.'

'Are you lot off your rockers? Are you telling me that you're investigating your own husband on behalf of the police? And you expect me to help you? I can tell you, and the rest of that bloody useless police force, that I'm barely keeping it together at the moment. If you had any consideration at all you'd leave people like me alone. You refused to help me, so I'm certainly not going to help you. You've got a bloody nerve asking. I'm speechless, quite frankly.'

Nína thought she was doing pretty well for someone who was speechless but kept this observation to herself. She was merely grateful the woman hadn't hung up on her. 'Klara, my husband tried to kill himself at the beginning of December. He's lying in a coma and isn't expected to live. I'm in a similar situation to you.'

Silence at the other end. Nína felt instinctively that the woman was fighting back tears. 'What do you need to know? Make it quick.'

'I found Lárus's name on a piece of paper among my husband's belongings. He'd written it down but there was no explanation why. Given that their fates were so similar, I wanted to find out if they knew each other or how they could conceivably be linked. That's all.'

'I can hardly be expected to answer that if you don't tell me what your husband was called.' The woman either hadn't taken it in when Nína said Thröstur was still alive, or she considered him as good as dead.

'His name's Thröstur. Thröstur Magnason.'

'Never heard of him.' The answer came back instantly – too quickly, Nína thought. But then the woman continued and it turned out that there was an innocent explanation for this. 'Which doesn't necessarily mean anything. I didn't know all Lalli's acquaintances. We'd only been together just over a year when he died.'

'Thröstur worked as a journalist. Is it possible that he got in touch with your husband about an article he was writing?'

'Did you say journalist?' From Klara's voice it sounded as if Nína had struck lucky. 'A journalist did ring Lárus at the end of November or beginning of December and had a long conversation with him. I don't know his name, though.'

Nína felt her heart beginning to pound. 'I expect that was Thröstur. Do you have any idea what they talked about?'

'No. Lalli wouldn't discuss it. When they started talking he shut the door of his room. All he'd say afterwards was that it had been a journalist and he couldn't discuss it. I tried to get him to tell me but I gave up in the end and assumed it was work related. Lalli was a lawyer so he could well have been handling a case that had attracted media attention, though I don't remember anything like that happening while we were together. But then he didn't really talk to me about his cases, unless he wanted to try out some clever angle on me. He used to bounce ideas off me and I'd tell him what I thought.' Klara sniffed loudly. When she spoke again her voice was harsher, as if she wanted to push these pleasant memories to the back of her mind. 'He acted very oddly after that phone call, though. Until you mentioned it, I hadn't made the connection. But yes, he seemed irritable and anxious.'

'You don't happen to remember any of the conversation you overheard?'

The phone crackled as Klara exhaled thoughtfully. 'Hmm. Let me think. Naturally I only heard the beginning but I got the impression the caller was trying to help Lalli remember him. As if they used to know each other, but Lalli was having trouble placing him. Then he seemed to twig and reacted very oddly – like I said, he went into his room and closed the door. I didn't hear any more.'

'So he didn't mention afterwards how they knew each other?'

'No. He wouldn't discuss it. Not at all. He was very pale and preoccupied.' Klara sniffed again. 'By the way, it wasn't your husband who sent Lalli the letters that you lot refused to take seriously?'

Nína was thrown. The possibility hadn't even entered her head. If Thröstur was linked to Lárus and the family in Skerjafjördur, it was conceivable that he hadn't received any letters because he was the one who had sent them. 'No. I doubt it. Though I have no proof apart from the fact that he just wasn't the type. *Isn't* the type, I mean.'

'But you can't be sure?' When Nína admitted as much, Klara went on: 'If your husband sent those letters, I've got nothing more to say to you. I believe someone forced those pills down Lalli's throat and I reckon it was the person that sent those letters who did it. Lalli had no intention of killing himself. He lived too fast for that. He drank too much, smoked too much, ate too much unhealthy food. People like that want to live, strange as it may sound.'

Nína wouldn't argue with that.

'Look, I've got to go. I'm late and I have nothing further to say to you.' Instead of hanging up, Klara added, in a rather more conciliatory tone: 'If you find out something about Lalli that could explain this to me, please call again. Otherwise don't bother.'

'I promise I will. Thank you so much—' But Klara had hung up.

For once there were sounds of movement in the basement. The noise was coming from the corridor leading to the archives. Nína walked past piles of dusty boxes, tools, bicycles and obsolete safety equipment, which would only ever see the light of day again on their way to the tip. She averted her eyes from some broken-necked floor lamps that were lined up like a guard of honour. They reminded her too much of Thröstur, silent and lifeless in the shadows, their heads lolling. She didn't want to think about him right now; the basement and archives were supposed to be her refuge.

After the phone call she had sat staring at the blank wall in front of her. At that moment she would have been grateful to be able to look out of a window and watch the morning traffic. Then she had stood up, smoothed down her crumpled clothes and hurried out of her office. It was just after eight and the working day was beginning. Again she reminded herself that it was nobody's business what she did in her spare time – short of running a brothel or a crackhouse – but in work hours she had better get on with the job she was paid for: to sift through old sins and decide which should be preserved and which could safely be destroyed. As if she hadn't had a hard enough time making that decision in relation to Thröstur.

'You're doing pretty well here.' The caretaker was standing by the open door to the archives; a man no longer young, with strong, work-worn hands protruding from the slightly-too-short sleeves of his overall, which looked almost like a uniform, the blue denim covered in pockets, not all of which appeared to have a function. 'There's so much crap in those storerooms. Throw out the bloody lot like they originally intended, that's what I say. Who's interested in all that paper? Not the criminals, that's for sure. I just can't understand why they've lumbered you with this.'

Nína liked the man, who generally had a warm smile for her. Shortly after she'd joined the police, they had both arrived at the door to the station yard at the same time. He'd had his arms full of clean mops and she had waited for him, holding the door open. Ever since then he'd had a soft spot for her.

'It's all right. I'm not up to much at the moment so it suits me fine.'

'It's not exactly a cheery place to be. If you're having problems you shouldn't be locked away down here, you should be upstairs with your colleagues. I know people can be so and so's at times but we all need company. You won't get much of that from old documents.'

'Maybe – but it can be good to have a bit of time to yourself. I'm not complaining anyway.' She smiled dully at him. He was right in a way; certainly she was in no hurry to end this conversation. It was so comforting to have a normal chat with someone at work that Nína felt almost humiliatingly grateful for the man's kind words. Being ostracised had obviously affected her more than she had realised or been willing to admit. She resolved to hold the door open for people whenever possible from now on.

The man shook his head, frowning. 'It's daft, if you ask me. Nobody's set foot in these archives since they filled up. I should know – I used to look after the keys until we opened them up for you. Chuck the lot, I say. No one has any use for this junk now.' Suddenly, however, he seemed struck by a thought. 'Though I do remember one time when they needed something from down here. Not that long ago either. But that's once in more than twenty years. Chuck the lot, then you can slip off home and take a little holiday. I won't tell on you.'

Nína's mind flew to the missing reports. 'You don't happen to know which documents they fetched?'

The man looked amused. 'No. I may know this building better than anyone else but I haven't a clue what goes on in here. Nobody ever tells me a thing about the cases you're investigating or who you're arresting. Not that it usually matters – it's none of my business, apart from that one time I was here over the weekend and had no idea that my son was locked in the cells the whole time. So no one would dream of telling me what files they were fetching from down here. Especially not the top brass. I'm invisible to them.'

'Was it a senior officer then?' Nína pictured the folder lying open on the shelf the first time she came down to the basement. Little dust had settled on the open pages and it was obvious now that whoever had gone down there had removed the reports she so desperately needed. If she'd known that the archives were usually locked, she would have gone to the caretaker straight away to ask who'd been in.

'Yes. *Your* boss, as a matter of fact. I reckon he should try his hand at this himself.'

The lights seemed to dim momentarily. 'Örvar?'

'Yes.' The caretaker hesitated. 'Anything wrong?'

'No. Not at all.' This was no lie. Nína suddenly felt alive, her tiredness forgotten. 'Did you see what he took upstairs with him? Was it a whole file or a box maybe?' She remembered seeing a dust-free space on one of the shelves where a box might have stood. Perhaps she was hoping for too much.

'No, it was just a few pages. Not a thick bundle. About ten pages or so. I was pottering about waiting to lock up after him. That's how come I saw him leave, though he didn't notice me.'

'Do you remember when this was?'

He wrinkled his brow. 'Before Christmas. The beginning of December or thereabouts. I can never remember dates, I'm afraid. I never give any thought to what day it is. For me it's either a weekday or a weekend. I generally take weekends off but I've had to make exceptions recently because of the move. The overtime comes in useful, though, so don't think I'm grumbling.'

Thröstur had tried to kill himself at the beginning of December and he had probably phoned Lárus shortly beforehand. She had to get hold of those papers. 'You know what, I'm going to follow your advice and take a break from the archives today. Find something to do upstairs.'

The caretaker's face lit up. 'Good for you! You know where I am if you need any help emptying those rooms. I'd have the whole lot down at the dump in an hour.'

'Amazingly enough some of this stuff still matters. I'll tell you about it later.' She smiled and set off upstairs. She was going straight along to Örvar's office and wouldn't leave until she had the missing reports in her hands. He should be at work today; she'd seen the duty rota. The bastard. She had only taken a few steps when she turned. 'Is it possible he took a box too? Came back to fetch it, I mean?' Perhaps there had been more information about the case than just files. There was no telling what it might have been, but if Örvar was the only person who had been down here for years, the large, dust-free gap on one of the bottom shelves must be his doing. Nína knew it was optimistic of her but she had the feeling that her luck had suddenly changed and that now anything was possible.

'No.'

She tried and failed to hide her disappointment.

'You're not looking for the videos, are you?'

'Videos?' She realised the misunderstanding. 'Oh, no. It was me who took that box. The one I'm trying to trace could have contained just about anything. All I can tell is that a box is missing from the shelves and I was wondering who'd taken it and what might have been inside.'

The caretaker walked over to her. 'I don't know if we're talking about the same thing but I took a box of videos off one of the shelves when I heard they were planning to go through all this stuff. That was before I knew you were being given the task – when I thought it would land on me. I assumed they were planning to bin the lot. I forgot to put it back.'

'So you didn't get rid of it?' Her luck hadn't deserted her after all.

'No. It's in a heap of junk I'm collecting to take to the dump. But it hasn't gone there yet.' He led Nína over to a pile that looked no different from any of the others. She would have liked to ask the caretaker how he went about deciding what to keep and what to throw away, but didn't want to hang around down there any longer than necessary. So she accepted in silence the dirty, battered cardboard box that he dug out of the heap, and carried it upstairs. Despite the heavy weight in her arms she felt as if she were walking on air, for the answers she was desperately seeking might finally be within reach. Now, at last, she could say goodbye to her old life and begin a new one. Not as Nína the widow, but simply as Nína. Nína, who had lost her husband but who wasn't going to let that rule her life. Ahead was some sort of closure, or at least a turning point.

Chapter 30

26 January 2014

The fan in the old video player whirred and groaned horribly but Nína ignored its protests. If she fetched the technician he was bound to confiscate it and put it in intensive care and she didn't know where she could lay her hands on another.

When she'd signed for the machine she'd noticed that no one else had used it since her last week. Before that it hadn't been taken out for three years. So any damage it might incur would be understandable. Inevitable, really. This excuse reminded her of the times she and Berglind had got up to mischief as children. She had usually known better but been unable to help herself; either because the forbidden activity had been too much fun, or because she'd thought they would get away with it. Berglind hadn't suffered the same twinges of conscience because she'd put all her faith in her elder sister. When they were caught she would howl, having more often than not been Nína's innocent sidekick.

Nína missed her sister's company as she sat there alone, wrestling with her conscience and trying to ignore the machine's screeching complaints and the faint smell of burning. It would have been easier to assuage her guilt over the mistreatment of the VHS player if Berglind had been beside her, since guilt shared is guilt halved.

Nína fast-forwarded and the burning smell intensified. She still hadn't come across any interviews from the case Thröstur had been linked to. She only hoped the fan would last until she had gone through all the tapes.

Suddenly a child appeared on the screen. Nína paused the video, fire hazard and protesting shrieks forgotten. She was drawn into the interview room, her entire mind focused on the events of thirty years ago. She rewound a little, then watched the playback at normal speed. A handwritten notice was held up to the camera and on it Nína read the familiar case number and learnt that they were about to question the witness Lárus Jónmundsson.

Nína felt uncomfortably hot; there was a humming in her ears. With trembling hands she put on the headphones. Here was the link. Lárus and Thröstur had both been called in for questioning as part of the inquiry into Stefán Egill Fridriksson's death. Nína leant back. Lárus must have been one of the children who sat on the wall with Thröstur, collecting car registration numbers. That had to be it. Thröstur's phone call to him must have been about this case. What else did they have in common? Nothing, probably. That would explain why Klara said her husband had taken a while to work out who the caller was. They had known each other as boys but their friendship had ended when Thröstur moved away from the west of town shortly after the incident. Thröstur's scribble, *Lalli? Lárus – Lárus Jónmundsson?*, must be evidence of his attempts to dredge up the man's name.

Nína concentrated on the screen, dismissing all pointless, premature speculation. Once she had watched the recording and tracked down the reports it would be easier to figure it out. She pressed play again. A skinny, mousy-haired boy came in, accompanied by a man in an overcoat, who seemed anything but pleased to be there. As he entered he announced irritably that he was extremely busy and didn't have time for this nonsense. His hands were buried in his coat pockets and Nína guessed his fists were clenched. This must be the boy's father, though he looked more like his lawyer. Under the coat was a glimpse of suit and tie. But surely Lárus's parents wouldn't have sent him to see the police with only a legal counsel for company? The boy looked cowed as if he had been forced to listen to a tirade from his father on the way to the station. Remembering what it used to be like sitting in the back of her own father's car after she and Berglind had committed some childish misdemeanour, she pictured the boy staring out of the window all the way to the station, gazing enviously at the passers-by who weren't being subjected to a scolding.

The police officer indicated some chairs and the boy's head drooped dejectedly as he walked over to one of them. The officer was the same man who had interviewed Thröstur, exuding the same air of calm. Ignoring the father's grumbling he focused his attention on the son.

When the boy sat down, his stiff anorak rode up. He seized the opportunity to bury his chin in the neck so his mouth and nose were hidden. Only his large eyes were visible above the collar, staring down at his zip. He stuck his hands in his pockets like his father. It was as if he wanted to disappear inside the bulky jacket. But his wish was not granted. When his father sat down beside him, he nudged the boy sharply and told him to sit up like a man. From his expression, it was plain that the child wasn't sure what this entailed.

The first questions were more or less the same as those that had been put to Thröstur. The answers were similar too, the main difference being the behaviour of Lárus's father, who constantly interrupted his son. He invariably began by pointing out that he was a lawyer, as if the police officer had no short-term memory. Or perhaps he expected the man to fall to his knees in awe? Rather than being annoyed by the father's high-handed behaviour, Nína felt smug that she'd interpreted his appearance correctly. She wondered which was better for a child: to be accompanied by a parent who never uttered a word, like Thröstur's mother, or one who behaved as if his child was about to be charged with treason. As a police officer, she would prefer the former; as a child, the latter. Lárus seemed to be getting away with much briefer answers than Thröstur had, in any case, and was subjected to fewer questions. The replies he did give were short and childish: he had told the truth, he hadn't seen anyone go inside the garage. No one at all. Nína thought it obvious the boy was lying, like his friend Thröstur. He never met the policeman's eye, squirmed in his chair every time he repeated this mantra, and looked relieved whenever his father intervened.

This time the interview was not cut short by the tape ending, as it had been in Thröstur's case, but nothing emerged that she didn't already know; the boy's name and his connection to Thröstur were what mattered. Nína watched the father jerk his son roughly from his chair and march him out of the room. The boy's short legs were unable to keep up and as he disappeared through the door he looked back despairingly at the policeman. The overhead lights drew a glitter from his eyelashes where he had shed a tear. Perhaps it was simply a reaction to his father's harsh grip.

Then father and son were gone and the recording ended.

Nína paused the video and sat pensively, still with the headphones on. They were so effective that she might as well have had no ears, which suited her fine since she needed peace and quiet in which to consider this latest development. It didn't help, though: she found it impossible to piece it all together. Lárus and Thröstur had had a grandstand view of what had happened in front of the garage while Stefán was hanging himself inside. It was only natural to suppose they would have noticed any comings and goings, so the police had questioned them at the scene. Presumably it would have been regarded as a mere formality until it emerged that the boys flatly denied having seen anybody enter the garage, including Stefán himself. Since it was known that he had gone inside while the boys were sitting there, this had aroused suspicion that all was not as it seemed, and the widow had added fuel to this fire. So the boys had been summoned to the police station and interviewed again. But in vain. They had stuck to their story and claimed to have seen nothing. An odd anomaly in an otherwise straightforward incident. Case closed.

Nína was convinced they had been lying. The question was why. She was equally convinced that such young children could not have played any part in the man's death; the idea was too absurd even to consider, surely? Was there even a remote possibility that they could have gone inside the garage and bumped into the man as he was standing there, head in a noose, preparing to step off the stool? Or even just gone inside, seen him dangling from the ceiling and thought it was their fault or that they would be blamed if the fact came to light? Children have a tendency to misinterpret the adult world and the boys had been so young they could hardly have been expected to think rationally.

But even if her conjecture turned out to be right, it was only half the story. An explanation was still needed for why Lárus and Thröstur had decided to kill themselves in the same month all these years later, shortly after talking to each other on the phone.

It sounded from Klara's description of their conversation as if they hadn't spoken since they were children. Something had prompted Thröstur to ring Lárus, but there was no telling what it had been. Perhaps he just wanted to hear his old playmate's voice and find out how he was doing. Find out if his guilt about their long-ago lie made it hard for him to sleep at night. Neither of them was able to tell the tale. Nína's only hope was to trace the third child and demand some answers, assuming he hadn't also committed suicide. That would be bloody typical. She thought about the family in Skerjafjördur and the connection Aldís had thought they had to Lárus. She hoped fervently that the husband was the third boy because he at least was still alive. Perhaps he held all the answers.

Nína fast-forwarded but found nothing but a long interrogation of a drunk who kept sliding off his chair. Speeded up, it looked like a comedy, until he threw up all over the table. The policeman's leap out of the way was worthy of a farce. Nowadays the clip would have been a big hit on YouTube. Nína didn't waste time enjoying it but ejected the tape when snow filled the screen and inserted the next. Halfway through it she decided to fetch herself a coffee. The small of her back ached and there was an ominous burning in her shoulders. Perhaps she could trick her body into staving off the stiffness by moving about a bit now. A short break would be beneficial for the video player too. She turned it off and her own face met her, reflected in the black TV screen. It wore an astonished expression, the eyes huge above hollow cheeks. She ran her fingers through her hair and straightened her shirt on her shoulders; there was no need to look as if she'd spent a night in the cells.

When she emerged from the poky storeroom, the tech guy was still in his spot outside, perched on a high barstool, holding a mini screwdriver and inspecting a heap of screws, wires and metal parts on a round table. It looked like a repair job that had got out of hand. She hoped it wasn't somebody's new iPhone. Hastily closing the door behind her so the burning smell wouldn't follow her out, she told him she would be right back. He nodded without comment. The pile of parts held all his attention.

The corridor was empty but the tranquillity of the night hours was gone. She could hear muffled conversations and somewhere the staccato beat of a printer spewing out paper. At the nearest coffee machine she filled a cardboard cup, too lazy to go and fetch her own mug which had 'Cop Fuel' printed on it. Thröstur had given it to her after attending an NBA game in the States with his friends and, unbelievably enough, many of her colleagues were envious.

She slurped down the hot coffee, standing by a window that faced onto the back yard. There was an unusual number of police vehicles in the car park this morning as Sunday was the quietest day of the week. The day no one could be bothered to cause trouble: the violent thugs were generally too hungover to resort to their fists and the criminals were probably lying on their sofas in front of the football. Even dangerous drivers generally behaved themselves on thc day of rest.

Nína shrugged her shoulders and rolled them backwards

and forwards, which alleviated the stiffness a bit. She stood tall and the pain in her back seemed to diminish as well. Feeling her phone in the pocket of her jeans, she thought of ringing Lárus's widow to tell her what she had discovered. But on second thoughts she didn't think she had enough to report. Not yet. If she kept pestering her, the woman might start screening her calls. Aldís would be interested, but she had knocked off and gone home, and was probably sleeping like a baby by now. Besides, she hadn't given Nína her number and although Nína could dig it up, she doubted Aldís would want to hear from her.

Nína realised that she was longing to talk to another human being about her discoveries; to focus her mind by putting her thoughts into words. Since she'd started spending every free moment at the hospital she'd had almost no interaction with anyone except about work or Thröstur's health. She missed chatting, hearing news of friends and relatives, bitching about politics, gossiping, airing her opinions of actors, moaning about the weather. She couldn't remember the last time she had let rip about index-linked mortgages. Not that she missed that in particular, but she felt a powerful need for idle chatter. She wanted to fill the corridor with pointless words.

Berglind was the only person she could ring. It was so long since she had been in touch with her friends that she would be forced to begin with a detailed update on Thröstur's situation. If she just called them for a friendly gossip they would think she was either heartless or crazy, or both.

Rather than phoning Berglind, Nína decided to finish watching the videos. According to the duty rota, Örvar wasn't due in until midday and she wanted to go through all the material before tackling him. He wouldn't get away with blowing smoke in her eyes again. This had to stop.

The technician was still sitting there, the heap on the table no smaller. She didn't bother to greet him but walked straight in, sat down and finished the coffee that tasted of cardboard. She threw the cup at the waste-paper bin but it missed and bounced into the corner. Ignoring it, she put on the headphones and resumed watching.

There was only one VHS left and at quarter to twelve her efforts finally paid off. A little girl walked into the interview room and Nína paused the tape as the child looked up in the doorway. She rubbed her dry eyes. The girl was doll-like with curly hair and an unusually straight back. She looked as if she'd wandered in by mistake and should have been next door at a photo shoot for the children's clothing section of the Hagkaup catalogue. Nína rewound to the beginning so she could read the handwritten notice. It was the same case number as Thröstur's and Lárus's interviews. The girl's name was Vala Konrádsdóttir. Nína exhaled. The wife of the man called Nói who lived in Skerjafjördur. The one who appeared to have something to hide. Quickly she pressed play and received confirmation that this was indeed the third child on the wall.

When she tried to call to mind what Örvar had said, she couldn't remember if he had mentioned the sex of the children. Had he talked of three boys sitting on the wall or had she herself merely assumed that? She had the feeling he had said 'kids', and, like an idiot, she hadn't asked for any details. But she couldn't be sure.

The little girl repeated the same mantra as Thröstur and Lárus. She hadn't seen anyone go inside. No one, no one at all. Like Lárus she had come with her father. He interfered less than the lawyer had done, but never took his eyes off his daughter and occasionally stepped in when he felt the policeman was putting too much pressure on her. He was restrained, barely raising his voice, but was solicitous of his daughter. And she got away with a blatant untruth. The lie.

The recording ended but instead of watching it again Nína decided to storm into Örvar's office to make sure she didn't miss him. She took the two tapes with her, after replacing the rest in the box. She informed the tech guy that she would be back to tidy up and, without waiting for an answer, marched off to her boss's office. Before she got there she walked straight into him, on his way out, wearing uniform and an anorak.

Nína let rip before Örvar had time to realise who she was. 'A man called Lárus, who killed himself in December, was a witness in the journalist Stefán's suicide case. The third child was a girl. Her name's Vala Konrádsdóttir. She was knocked down by a car last night and—' She was given no chance to finish.

'I haven't got time for this. You'll have to tell me later. There's been a serious incident in Skerjafjördur. A man appears to have murdered his wife, then taken his own life.'

Could the wife be Vala? Suddenly Nína's ears were ringing; all hope of talking to Vala faded. 'I'm going to get changed. I'm coming too.' She ran off before Örvar could forbid her. She called to him as she ran, without turning her head: 'I'll meet you in the yard in five minutes. If you leave without me I'll set fire to your office.' She wasn't joking.

Chapter 31

26 January 2014

Nói couldn't stop thinking about the keys. The keys to the chalet and – what was worse – to their house. He had locked the front door when he brought Vala home from the hospital, feeling that here at least they were safe. Nothing bad could happen to them in their own home as long as they remembered to lock up. That's how it was supposed to work; that was the basis for the ordinary citizen's sense of security. Those who left their doors open were inviting disaster, whereas careful types locked them and were rewarded with safety. It had never entered his head that there could be exceptions to this rule. Like now. An individual in possession of a bunch of keys could come and go from their house at will, and the lock in which Nói had placed all his faith was useless. He would have been better off giving in to his impulse to barricade the doors with furniture.

Nói felt his way cautiously from the back door towards the front hall. He took care not to bump into anything, grateful that his eyes had grown accustomed to the darkness outside. The gloom was even more impenetrable in here, without the benefit of the dim lamp over the neighbours' back door. But he didn't want to turn on the light in case he attracted attention. It was bad enough that he had opened the door noisily; the intruder, if there was one, must have heard him. He had closed it incredibly quietly behind him but now realised how pointless that had been. The damage had already been done.

A faint but cloying smell of cheap aftershave hung in the air. There was somebody inside. But who? Was it the person who had sent those vile letters?

Nói's attention was caught by a small red light under the kitchen counter, and he remembered the robot vacuum cleaner that seemed to specialise in starting up at the worst possible moment. He bent down to switch it off and saw the glow of Púki's eyes. The cat hissed as Nói reached for the vacuum. There was no malice in the hiss; instead the cat seemed to be warning Nói or inviting him to crawl under there and join him.

He straightened up and the cat uttered a low mew. Nói strained his ears but could hear nothing out of the ordinary. The fridge emitted its familiar hum and the clock on the wall ticked with quiet clicks.

Otherwise silence.

There was no creaking of floorboards upstairs, no squeak of a door. The intruder seemed to be keeping still. Nói pictured him standing beside Vala's or Tumi's bed, with evil intent. One of those unanswerable questions sprang into his mind: who would you rather save, Vala or Tumi? He couldn't say, and anyway it wasn't up to him. He pushed away mental images of his loved ones' mangled bodies. What kind of person would even think like that?

It was almost pitch black in the hallway by the staircase where there were no windows and the walls were painted dark green. He regretted now that he hadn't gone with the pale yellow shade that Vala had wanted.

But then he regretted so many things.

Reminding himself of the furniture layout between door and stairs, he took a quick breath and started edging his way forwards. He kept expecting the intruder to be lying in wait, ready to hit him over the head with a baseball bat or stab him with a knife.

Again his mind set him a quick test: would you rather be bludgeoned or stabbed? The answer came straight back, without pause for thought: bludgeoned. At the thought of a shining, lethally sharp blade piercing skin, muscle and internal organs he instinctively clutched at his stomach to deaden the hot pain that his imagination conjured up. But his resolve did not falter. He was going to drive this man out of his house, whatever the cost to himself.

Nói breathed more easily when he felt the bottom step and began to tiptoe up the stairs. He mustn't make the slightest noise. He had broken out in a cold sweat and his hands were damp as they brushed along the walls.

The whiff of cheap aftershave grew more noticeable the higher he climbed. Nói wondered what kind of person would bother to put on that noxious stuff before breaking into somebody's house. He recognised the pong; it reminded him of the sleazy blokes who used to visit his mother in the bad old days. It was the sort of aftershave men buy from the corner shop, aimed at those without money or taste. Could it be a smokescreen? Perhaps it wasn't a man at all but a woman who was trying to disguise the fact to make herself more menacing? That was a long shot. The alternative was more plausible and far worse – that this was a man who had made an effort to smarten himself up in excited anticipation of what he was about to do.

Nói almost lost his nerve. Warily he took a deep breath and his courage returned. But only for a second. It dawned on him that he was empty-handed. If only he'd had the presence of mind to grab a knife instead of wasting time posing himself questions. There were enough sharp blades in the kitchen. But it would be unthinkable now to creep back downstairs, fetch a weapon and climb up again. There was too great a risk that he would be heard, and time was running out. He couldn't afford any delays. And Vala and Tumi certainly couldn't.

It was perceptibly lighter upstairs. There was a skylight over the TV alcove, which he used to curse because it caused a reflection on the screen. Now he thanked God he had never got a builder to block it off as he'd often planned to. The grey illumination was enough to show him everything.

Four doors opened off the upstairs landing, all of them closed. They led to his and Vala's bedroom, Tumi's room, the bathroom and the stairs to the loft. The choice was between the two bedrooms.

Tumi – Vala, Vala – Tumi?

Which room should he check first? Which of them could he bear less to see harmed – suddenly the question was no longer hypothetical. He couldn't hear anything to hint where the danger lay. The silence was absolute; no sound but the odd plink from the bathroom tap.

Vala – Tumi, Tumi – Vala?

This was no time to hesitate, so he chose his and Vala's room. If it was the person who had sent the letters, he was probably the very same man who had knocked Vala down. She was the one he was after. It was unlikely that he would be interested in Tumi. Nói moved towards the master bedroom, taking care not to tread on the floorboards that he knew squeaked. He made it noiselessly all the way to the door and laid his ear against it. He thought he could hear Vala breathing deeply inside but he wasn't sure. Perhaps it was only the wind. But there was nothing to suggest that she wasn't alone. Nói gripped the handle and opened the door. There was no point trying to be quiet; he knew the worn hinges too well.

It opened with the loud creaking that had always filled him with a cosy sense of home but now sounded worse than nails on a blackboard. He flung it back against the wall inside. That way he could see the whole room and simultaneously reassure himself that the man couldn't be hiding behind the door.

The curtains were drawn back. Outside the black clouds had parted and a delicate, silvery radiance flooded into the room. Nói decided to switch on the light anyway. If someone was in there, hiding behind the curtains or in the cupboard, he would have to be deaf and blind not to be aware of Nói by now.

There was a view of the dark sea through the window and his eyes automatically searched for whatever it was that had drawn his attention to the beach. He thought he could see something pale floating just below the surface, but then it was gone and he assumed it must have been the moon gleaming on the waves. When he switched on the light the window glass went black, as if a screen had been turned off.

Vala was lying in bed and showed no sign of having been harmed beyond her existing injuries. She had kicked off the duvet, and Nói's baggy T-shirt had rucked up under her breasts. Her bare belly and what could be seen of her limbs were blue with bruises, but there was no blood on the white sheet and she seemed to be breathing normally. He couldn't see her face but sensed that all was as it should be.

Then Nói spotted the sheets of paper he had given Vala lying on the bedside table with the pen resting on them. For an instant he forgot the imminent danger. It looked as if the top sheet had writing on it, perhaps the others too. He stepped into the room, compelled by the longing to read what she had written, but had the presence of mind to check first that no one was hiding inside. Full of trepidation, he whipped the heavy curtains back from the sides of the window and his fear intensified as he opened the wardrobes one after the other. Each hiding place that turned out to be empty only increased the odds that the intruder would be lurking in the next. It was like Russian roulette. His fear peaked when he opened the door to their en-suite. There was nowhere else to hide and he felt an overpowering certainty that this was it.

There was no one in the bathroom, no one behind the door or in the shower. He sniffed the air for traces of after-shave but could no longer detect it with any certainty. Perhaps he was inured to it by now. Unless he had imagined the whole thing. Perhaps there was no one in the house but the three of them and poor old Púki. The smell of aftershave might be emanating from Tumi. Who knows, he might finally have fallen for a girl and be trying to impress her – or maybe girls in general. It was possible that he had invested in a bottle of cologne from the local shop; after all, he was hardly old enough to know that the brands sold there were mainly bought by alcoholics as a cheap tipple.

Relief flooded Nói: the danger was over, if it had ever existed. He decided to check the other rooms upstairs, but there was nobody in the family bathroom or in the loft or in Tumi's room. There wasn't any hint of aftershave either, which bothered Nói. He would gladly have suffered a migraine from a thick miasma of the stuff in exchange for an innocent explanation for its origin. But Tumi's room was merely stuffy. Nói opened the window to let in the pure night air, daring now to relax and linger to tuck his son in properly. Perhaps the intruder had left via the window in the master bedroom when he heard someone coming upstairs. It was far from easy to climb down the fire escape but a piece of cake compared to dropping to the ground.

Had Nói been completely mistaken? Was there no intruder at all? The creaking he heard could have been Tumi or Vala. It wasn't unheard of for them to nip to the loo in the night. But that didn't explain the smell of aftershave or the fact that the lights were off downstairs.

There was little point tucking the boy in; he had already kicked off his duvet again. Pausing in the doorway Nói surveyed the chaos in his room and the shelves that had once held Lego creations of all shapes and sizes. He had bombarded the boy with the sets, remembering how he himself had hankered after Lego when he was little. Now that they had gone from the shelves, he felt sad that he hadn't allowed Tumi to play with the models once they had finished making them. It would have made more sense than putting them on display like a hunter hanging trophies on the walls. Well, it was too late now.

Vala was still lying in the same position. Nói pulled the crumpled T-shirt down over her stomach, then began to draw up the duvet. His gaze became fixed on a bead of blood in her belly button. It must be connected to the accident; it could hardly be a sign of internal bleeding. Although he knew nothing about medicine, he was pretty sure you couldn't haemorrhage through the navel. To double-check, he fetched some loo paper and dabbed gently at her stomach. Vala didn't stir, so it could hardly be a wound that the doctors had overlooked. Unless the painkillers were incredibly effective. Nói raised the paper to the light and saw that the blood had spread out slightly. He looked back at her navel, which now appeared perfectly normal, with not a drop of red to see. He vacillated, wondering if he should wake her or call A&E to ask what it might mean, but decided to leave it. Vala seemed fine, so he made do with covering her up, then reached for the sheets of paper on the bedside table.

He began to read as he stood by the bed. Her handwriting covered two pages. Clearly she had meant to give them to him in the morning so she wouldn't have to speak. Perhaps she had found it easier to write the whole thing down, alone in bed, than to have to explain it to his face tomorrow. He didn't blame her. It was obvious that she had seen through him when he escorted her back upstairs. She knew he wanted answers, however much he pretended it didn't matter. Before reading the letter he checked to see if she had finished it and thought she had. It must have been a real effort to use her right hand when her arm was in plaster and sore from the accident, but she must have started the moment he went downstairs, and fallen asleep straight afterwards.

At first Nói had difficulty working out the context because Vala had written as concisely as possible, often using abbreviations. But then his eyes opened and he raced through the rest as fast as he could. Afterwards he lowered his hands and stared at his wife's averted head in a feeble attempt to grasp how she could have misunderstood and underestimated him so badly. But the longer he reflected, the more the truth dawned on him and he was forced to admit that there had been no misunderstanding. This handwritten account had no place in the sterilised world he had created for his family. Had she told him when they first met, he wouldn't have considered her a suitable candidate to be his wife and would have continued his search elsewhere. There had never been a right time to tell him. Some things have to be revealed at the beginning of a relationship. Later, the time that has elapsed becomes its own kind of betrayal. When was she supposed to have told him this story? On their wedding day? When she had just given birth? In front of the telly one Tuesday evening? He knew himself well enough to recognise that he would never have been able to accept this. Vala had been right to keep quiet about it.

Nói bent down to whisper to Vala that he realised he was emotionally constipated. It was his fault she hadn't dared confide in him as soon as the letters started arriving, as soon as she received the phone call warning her that her past was about to catch up with her. He meant to tell her that the man named in the letter would get his just deserts; he would see to it personally that he never walked free. If the justice system let them down, he would find a way to rid them and society of this vermin. That was a promise, and hopefully it would go some way to making up for all his mistakes. But as he bent down to kiss her, Vala emitted a strange rattling sound. Stiffening, he turned her head carefully towards him. Her eyes opened but he could see nothing but the glazed whites. Foam oozed from the corner of her mouth and her whole body started to shake.

Everything was far from fine.

Nói flung down the sheets of paper, wondering frantically what to do. Ring for an ambulance or start mouth-to-mouth resuscitation? Which came first?

He got no further. From under the valance around the bed two strong hands shot out, grabbed hold of his ankles and jerked so that he toppled over backwards. The world spun before his eyes, and he gasped and groaned weakly as the intruder crawled out from the one hiding place Nói had overlooked: the most obvious.

Everything went black.

When Nói recovered consciousness, it was not due to the mercy of the powers above. He was freezing and couldn't see a thing. His ribcage felt as if it were bursting and there was only one thought in his mind – that he couldn't breathe. He became aware of the throttling grip on his throat that was holding his head down. A great weight was pressing on his back, making it impossible for him to turn.

He was drowning.

The taste of salt told him he was in the sea. Probably off the beach below the house. His lungs sent a warning that they couldn't hold out any longer. He should prepare for them to fill with icy seawater. Instinctively Nói opened his eyes wide and struggled but found he had no strength left. In front of him was something lighter in colour than the surrounding murky gloom. It spread out as if to engulf him. Perhaps this was the afterlife welcoming him. He remembered hearing stories of a white light. This was merely pale but even so it gave him hope that what was to come would not be so bad. Not so bad after all.

Nói gave up fighting and filled his lungs. His death throes did not last long and during them he comforted himself with the thought of Vala's letter. With any luck it was still lying on the bed and would ensure that justice triumphed in the end. As long as the man hadn't spotted the pages and shoved them in his pocket. That would be so unfair.

The pale colour vanished and everything went black.

Chapter 32

26 January 2014

There was such a throng of vehicles at the end of the street that anyone driving into the cul-de-sac would be forced to reverse out again. Örvar parked the police car in the drive of the neighbouring house, ignoring the man watching them angrily out of the window. Beside him stood a woman who clearly couldn't care less about the parking place but was anxiously following what was happening next door. As Nína and Örvar walked away they heard a furious banging on the glass behind them but neither looked round. Instead they quickened their pace to make sure they were out of reach by the time the man stormed outside.

They hadn't spoken much on the way. Örvar had been on the phone most of the time, talking to officers on the scene, and Nína had only managed a couple of quick questions when they first got in the car. She had asked about the files from the archives: why had he fetched them and where were they now? She had bitten back the urge to berate him for keeping silent when he knew all along that he had the reports she was looking for. That would have to wait. But she had received no answers. Örvar had said there was no time to discuss that now, then put on his headset and started talking on the phone. Nína had a hunch that there was no one on the other end.

It looked as if someone had set up a huge open-air casino in the cul-de-sac. The flashing lights of the ambulances and police cars hurt their eyes and Nína almost expected to hear someone celebrating the fact that they had won the jackpot. There was even a fire engine. Surely that was excessive.

All kinds of uniforms were milling around – doctors in white coats, divers in black drysuits, members of the rescue team in luminous jackets, paramedics, police. They moved briskly in and out of the house, crisscrossing the gardens both front and back, and a couple of police officers with a dog on a lead were walking the boundaries. The lights had attracted curious passers-by and two officers had their hands full trying to keep them out of the way.

Örvar banged irritably on the roof of a car belonging to an elderly couple who had become stranded in the middle of the road, and were sitting there, rigid with fright at their predicament. He waved them away, then sent some officers to the end of the street with orders to let no one through unless they could prove they were residents or had urgent business there.

Flickering blue light played over an attractively renovated wooden house that would have looked at home in the playground of a fairytale princess. Its innocent appearance was completely at odds with the gruesome crime that had been committed there.

When they entered, the floor creaked loudly as if the house were wincing under the strain of all this activity. Apart from that it was oddly quiet. The strange sense of unreality extended to the interior as well: the paintings on the walls hung with perfect precision, every object seemed handpicked for the setting, as if the family had shed all their old belongings when they moved in. There were numerous people indoors as well but they spoke in an undertone and their movements were slower and more methodical. Everyone seemed to have a role to perform. Nína followed Örvar in silence, trying not to let it show that she had no appointed task. He seemed to have forgotten her presence as he surveyed the interior of the house and pulled on a pair of latex gloves. She copied his example – with the gloves on she hoped she would look like a fully paid-up member of the investigation team.

In the kitchen they came across a teenage boy sitting bolt upright in spite of his gangling frame. He had a tabby cat in his lap, which stared at Nína and Örvar with half-closed eyes. One of the boy's feet was twitching continually up and down and his hands kept wandering to his neck or forehead but finding nothing to do there. They fell straight back to his lap, stroked the cat briefly, then sought out his face again or fiddled with the table top. He didn't seem to have been crying but his blue eyes fluttered around constantly as if he had been injected with a stimulant, as if he were searching for something to mitigate the unbearable pain.

Of course it was futile. All around him were reminders of his parents who had left this life while he was asleep. His curly hair was in a wild tangle and kept flopping over his wide, staring eyes. He let it hang there for longer than seemed natural, perhaps grateful to be able to draw a veil over his surroundings, then tossed his head back, flinging his fringe out of his eyes again. Beside him sat a woman Nína knew to be a psychologist from the police commissioner's office. She was talking to the boy in a low voice and tried to take hold of his hands as his trembling fingers paused on the table but he snatched them away. Opposite them a plainclothes detective was sitting as if turned to stone, presumably waiting for a chance to interrogate the boy. Nína hoped he wasn't waiting for the boy to recover. If so he might as well sit there for the rest of his life.

'What a bloody nightmare.' Örvar looked round at Nína. She saw his shoulders sag as the scale of the tragedy sank in.

Nína merely nodded, feeling she had nothing to say, and was profoundly relieved when Örvar turned on his heel and walked over to the staircase. She was having a hard enough time dealing with her own grief without taking on somebody else's.

Upstairs, plastic sheeting had been draped over an open doorway. Nína saw two men from forensics busy at the end of the bed inside. As they moved nearer she spotted the pathologist behind them, bending over the bed with a cotton bud in her hand. Nína had communicated with this woman several times in connection with work and although her manner was rather chilly, she liked her. A body was lying motionless on the bed, the tanned legs looking uncannily healthy and alive. Vala. The third child witness. There was no one left to tell the tale.

Örvar tapped awkwardly on the plastic. It rustled a little but no one seemed to hear him. He coughed and finally the forensics technicians looked up. One of them came slowly over to the doorway, dressed in a paper overall that resembled a child's fancy-dress astronaut costume. 'How's it going?' Örvar was standing so close to the plastic that steam condensed on it as he spoke, like a faint shadow of his words.

'Fine. They'll be able to move her shortly. Within half an hour, at a guess.'

'What does she think?' Örvar looked over at the pathologist. 'Is the cause of death obvious?'

'An overdose of painkillers, she reckons. There are some empty bottles in the kitchen. We found what looks like a suicide letter too. It's written in a clumsy feminine hand, which would be consistent with the fact she's in plaster.'

Nína pricked up her ears and had to dig her hands into her pockets to prevent herself from tearing down the plastic to get at the letter. She hadn't been expecting this and felt new hope quickening in her breast. The letter would doubtless explain why Vala had taken her own life, and the same explanation could very probably be extended to Lárus and, more importantly, Thröstur. It couldn't be a coincidence that all three of them should have resorted to the same desperate measure, at virtually the same time. The odds against it were too great. It must have been a joint decision taken by the three of them or else they had somehow ended up coming to the same conclusion. A triple coincidence would be more than a little suspect.

'What does the letter say?' Örvar craned his head to see further inside.

'We've sealed it in a plastic bag. There are two closely written pages. She's going to read it later.' He indicated the pathologist behind him. Nína would have given anything to be in the woman's shoes. The man shuffled his feet, his overall crackling. 'Konni and I already have more than enough on our hands. We're in a hurry to finish up here.'

Nína and Örvar went back downstairs. On their way out they passed through the kitchen, where the situation remained unchanged: the cat restless, the boy distraught, the psychologist patient and the detective champing at the bit.

When they re-emerged into the open air they found the same chaos, only now the bystanders' cars had gone; the show was over for the moment.

'Who reported it?' Although Nína had picked up the gist by eavesdropping on the telephone conversation Örvar had had – or pretended to have – in the car, she was still largely in the dark.

'Some joggers spotted the husband floating down by the shore. A team had no sooner set out to deal with that than the poor boy called. He'd woken up and found his mother in bed. He thought she was in a very bad way and requested an ambulance. With a defibrillator.'

'Oh, God.' The impacted snow squeaked beneath their feet. Nína assumed the garden had already been fine-combed. 'Are we absolutely certain that it's the father? Has the boy identified him?'

'No. But it's him.' Örvar didn't reveal how he knew. He scanned the garden, then headed for the back gate. Beyond it they could see more police officers and divers busy on the stony beach. Suddenly another diver's head emerged from the waves. He waved vigorously, then started swimming to shore. The other people on the beach ran over to meet him. Nína followed hard on Örvar's heels so she could keep plying him with questions. 'Do they think he walked into the sea?'

'Initially they did, yes. But it turned out there were injuries on the back of his neck that indicate the use of force. It'll all become clear in due course. No point speculating at this point.' Örvar was so breathless he could hardly get the words out. His strength seemed to have waned over the last few days.

Nína was relieved to see they had removed the man's corpse from the beach. It must have been done as quickly as possible due to all the traffic along the coast path. She and Örvar had already passed a couple with a pram watching what was going on; further off a jogger was standing with his hands on his knees, his whole body heaving as he tried to catch his breath, his attention fixed on the activity below. Unless they were moved on, these people were likely to see more than was appropriate since the diver seemed to be indicating that another body had been found. Two, in fact. Nína turned and began to herd the members of the public away, much to their indignation. Someone had to do it and everyone else on the beach seemed too busy. No one thanked her when she returned from this self-appointed task and she was glad: it meant they regarded her as one of the team. It wasn't the custom to praise fellow officers for performing routine tasks at a crime scene. She sensed a lessening of hostility towards her; people obviously had more important things on their mind right now than cold-shouldering a colleague.

At the top of the beach, just above the belt of seaweed, lay a deflated bright yellow rubber dinghy. Nína tapped the arm of the nearest policeman and asked how the boat was connected to the case. He turned his head and didn't look best pleased when he saw who had posed the question. Clearly she hadn't entirely come in from the cold.

'The man was found tangled up in it. At first they thought he'd gone out in the dinghy but it appears to have been in the sea for some time. Longer than the bloke, anyway.'

Nína had no experience of drownings or bodies washed up by the sea, but she'd heard enough stories at the station. She remembered one of her older colleagues teaching her that you should always treat people's physical remains with respect, even if there was nothing left but a heap of ashes.

The commotion on the beach as the diver went back out, accompanied by another man armed with a camera, did nothing to suggest that this piece of advice was being followed.

'I think I know who they are.'

Örvar, who was standing nearby, started. 'What do you mean? The bodies?'

'Yes.' Nína felt like issuing an ultimatum: she would share the information with him on condition that he told her about the reports he had removed from the archives, but she knew that if she tried anything like that he would send her away. 'I met Aldís last night and she gave me the lowdown about what's been happening here over the last twenty-four hours. The couple contacted the police and one of their concerns was that something might have happened to the foreigners – an American couple – who'd been staying at their house. The case was given routine treatment but then yesterday evening the wife was knocked down by a hit-and-run driver and that put a different perspective on things.' She wondered if she should tell him about the notes they had received but decided against it. He would find out soon enough and it was better not to remind him of Thröstur's possible connection to the case. If he stopped to think, he might send her straight back to the station. It was unethical to allow people who had any link to the case to be present at the crime scene. The fact that he hadn't twigged after she blurted out the connection between Vala and Thröstur suggested either that he hadn't understood her or else that he was preoccupied with trying to conceal something from her. She was inclined to believe the latter.

'Why were you at work last night?' He didn't seem to have taken in what she said. 'And what are you doing here now? You're not supposed to be working weekends.'

'Don't you remember? I'm making up for my day off last week. I'll need to take another day off in the middle of next week, so I wanted to make up the hours. They're going to switch off Thröstur's life support.' She was ashamed of herself for using her dying husband as an excuse. 'I thought it would be OK. It's not as if you can tell the difference between a weekday and a weekend down in the basement.'

'You don't need to make up the hours, as you well know. I've repeatedly invited you to take leave.' Örvar struggled to hide his anger. Before he had fallen ill and lost so much weight, he had been better at maintaining a poker face, but now he lacked the flesh to mask his feelings. 'I've half a mind to send you home on leave whether you like it or not. Compassionate leave's not the only kind, you know.'

There were times when not caring came in useful, allowed you to be selective about what you heard or chose to discuss. 'Örvar. Are you listening? The two bodies in the sea may be the foreign couple who'd been staying at the house. I'd warn the team; they're going to have to answer to the American police about the way they conduct the inquiry. Or to the ambassador, at least.'

'What?' Örvar's anger faded. He opened his mouth to say something, then started talking to the man in charge of operations on the beach. Nína stood back and smiled at the men when they looked round at her.

They turned their attention to what was happening in the sea. Camera flashes lit up the water from below. Then the divers' heads broke the surface. One of them tore off his mask and clumsy mouthpiece, and called to land that they had finished photographing the scene and were ready to bring the bodies ashore. He put his equipment back on and the two of them submerged again. Catching a glimpse of patterned material that no doubt belonged to one of the bodies, Nína hurriedly set off back towards the house.

There were enough witnesses to this horror without her adding to their number.

As she crossed the garden she came face to face with the pathologist. The woman was inadequately dressed for the cold, as if she hadn't had time to pull on a coat. Their eyes met but instead of returning Nína's greeting the woman averted her gaze and half ran down to the beach. She must have been informed about what to expect and wanted to be on the scene when the bodies were brought ashore. But she could at least have said hello. Still, it wasn't really fair to judge people at times like this; some became taciturn and irritable; others talked non-stop. Few maintained their usual disposition. But it would have suited Nína better if the pathologist had been friendly since she was desperate to get hold of a copy of the suicide note. She didn't believe for a minute that the woman's standoffish behaviour was connected to her complaint since it was unlikely to have filtered through to the police commissioner's office yet. Besides, the woman would be far more likely to put the blame firmly where it belonged – on Nína's colleague, for dereliction of duty. Or so Nína believed, though of course one could never be sure. This was Iceland, after all, and for all she knew the pathologist might turn out to be the bastard's wife or sister.

Rather than go inside, Nína decided to wait in front of the house. She didn't want to risk encountering the son again. Presumably he would be taken away sooner or later, to the police station or hospital or to stay with relatives.

Here, she could melt into the shadows the moment she saw him come out. She didn't want to be confronted by his inconsolable grief. Didn't want to be faced with the dilemma of whether to lower her eyes or acknowledge him. She remembered how people had reacted immediately after Thröstur had been taken to hospital. An old friend of her mother's had been so flustered to meet her that she had crossed herself. But although the experience had taught Nína a thing or two about what was not appropriate at such moments, she was still none the wiser about how one *should* behave.

An ambulance drove off down the street. No siren or flashing light. The lack of urgency suggested that it was carrying Vala. Nína watched the vehicle disappear round the corner, her heart sinking. She didn't want to think about the orphaned boy. Her own grief was nothing compared to his. He was only a child and his entire world had been obliterated. What were the chances he would ever get over it?

The front door opened and Nína retreated into hiding. As she skulked by the wall of the house she heard quick footsteps approaching over the snow behind her. It was Örvar, crimson in the face and even angrier than before. Though Nína didn't know why, she knew his anger was directed at her.

'Nína!' He slowed his pace and, panting, hobbled the last few steps towards her. 'For fuck's sake.'

'What?' Nína had no need to fake surprise. She realised she was about to receive a bollocking but had no idea what for.

'You're to get out of here this minute.' Örvar stood, bent double, with his hands on his knees like the jogger on the footpath. His face could hardly be seen for the clouds of steam.

'Me? Why? What have I done?' There must be some misunderstanding.

'Stay here and don't move an inch while I find someone to drive you back to the station. You're to wait for me there. And don't count it as work time.' Örvar straightened up and limped round to the front of the house.

Ignoring what he had said, she hurried after him and seized his arm. 'What's wrong?'

Örvar rounded on her, his expression furious. 'The pathologist read the letter the woman left behind.' He broke off to catch his breath. 'You're connected to this case.'

'I'm not!'

'Not directly. But your husband's named in the letter. I'm not saying another word now. I'll deal with you later.'

He shook off her hand and kept walking.

Instead of chasing him she was distracted by the sight and sound of the coastguard helicopter taking off from Reykjavík airport. It appeared to be heading south but then swung round towards them. It hovered for a while above her head as if those on board were curious or taking photographs of the activity below. She wondered if she would be visible in the pictures, loitering round the corner of the house. She felt a flash of envy for the people on board. To distract herself, she wondered where they were going. It must be a leisure trip since they'd allowed themselves this detour.

Then the helicopter flew off in a south-easterly direction. How lucky the passengers were.

Chapter 33

26 January 2014

Word had leaked out at the station. Her colleagues stole surreptitious glances at her, only to drop their eyes if she met their gaze. The change was subtle, and yet . . . People whispered, and one jerked a furtive elbow in her direction. When she went into the coffee room to kill some time and satisfy the worst of her hunger, everything went quiet and people stared down into their cups. She could feel her cheeks burning, but although she wanted to turn back in the doorway, she forced herself to walk, her head held high, over to the small fridge. She could feel everyone's eyes on her as she chose something at random. She'd hoped the fridge would cool her cheeks, but when she closed it they felt just as hot. As she walked out again with a bruised banana in her hand she felt a momentary urge to scream at them that it wasn't as bad as they thought and they shouldn't be so quick to pass judgement.

But that would only increase their embarrassment and give new life to the gossip. Resisting the temptation to pause and eavesdrop on the whispering after the door had closed behind her, she went in search of a bin where she could dump the blackened banana.

Then she sat in her office and waited.

Time crawled by and she kept wanting to thump the computer monitor in case the onscreen clock had frozen. Browsing the web didn't appeal; all the news seemed dull, even the first tentative reports of the police operation in Skerjafjördur. From the vague wording it was clear that the reporters had failed to penetrate the tight control at the end of the street.

After slogging through all the Icelandic news outlets, she checked her e-mail in a vain quest for distraction. She wasn't even cheered by the message from her estate agent that an Icelander based abroad was going to put in an offer on her flat, though she did at least send a reply that was terse and to the point: *Fine – I accept.* Only after the message had been sent did she realise that no offer had actually been made yet.

At last the phone rang and a number flashed up onscreen: Örvar calling from his office. She leapt to her feet and ran downstairs. Outside his door she braced herself with the thought that there were countless other jobs she could do if she was given her marching orders, though none came to mind when she tried to list them. Anything had to be better than this.

Örvar was engrossed in reading a document and ushered her silently to a seat while he finished. Then he slapped his hand on the desk and turned his attention to her. She sat bolt upright, her eyes roaming round the room.

'You've got a real knack of getting yourself into trouble.'

'That's not fair.' While he was ignoring her, Nína had decided not to make this easy for him. She had nothing to lose. Well, not much.

'We'll have to agree to disagree about that. Anyway, it

makes no difference.' Örvar wasn't going to let her divert him from his purpose.

Nína wondered which of them was finding this more uncomfortable, and decided that on balance it was probably him. Buoyed up by the thought, she lifted her chin defiantly.

'What happened earlier was entirely unacceptable and the only possible argument in your defence is that you had no idea your husband was connected to the case. The thing is, I suspect you did know.'

'That's right.'

'What's right? That you knew there was a link?'

'Yes. Though not until last night – after I'd spoken to Aldís here at the station. Before that I hadn't a clue that the couple in Skerjafjördur even existed.'

'That's no excuse, Nína. If you knew, you knew. The point is that you knowingly compromised the investigation.'

'I'm not going to try and make excuses. I worked out the connection between Thröstur and Vala about five minutes before I bumped into you on your way out. I was coming to tell you but I changed my mind.' Nína shifted in her chair. She wasn't used to being the subject of serious accusations and she didn't like it. It was extraordinary how decisions that had seemed self-evidently right at the time proved to be so obviously wrong once you were forced to analyse them out loud. 'If I was going to make excuses I'd point out that I couldn't trust my boss to tell me the truth. I had no choice but to go along myself if I wanted to know what was happening. On top of that, I believe it's essential that I'm included in the consultation. I know more than anyone about Thröstur's case.'

'May I remind you that we're not investigating what happened to your husband. That case has been closed, so you could have shared your findings with us without going to the crime scene.'

'What was in the letter, Örvar?'

'Why should I tell you? You're in no position to make any demands.'

'Because it's vital. Both for me personally and for the investigation. If my husband's mentioned in the letter I might be able to shed some light on what it says. And it might also help me to accept what's happened.'

'I can't allow you to read it.' Örvar raised his hand before she could protest and continued: 'But I can paraphrase its contents for you – though it won't help you with the grieving process or whatever you're hoping you'll achieve by reading it. You'll be as distressed afterwards as you were before. In case you hadn't realised, this is a disciplinary interview and you should be grateful I decided to keep it informal or your conduct would have been brought to the attention of my superiors. I needn't go into the effect this could have on your future prospects in the police.'

Nína's expression didn't change. Judging by the speed at which the tale of Thröstur's connection to the case had reached the station, it was unlikely another day would pass without someone in the upper echelons of the police getting wind of it. Örvar was merely protecting himself. In a formal interview she would have had an opportunity to mention the missing files and even if he had chosen to leave her comment out of his notes, he knew her well enough to realise that she was perfectly capable of adding it beside her signature. A formal interview and discussion of Nína in the commissioner's office would also bring to light the manner in which her complaint had been handled.

'What did the letter say?'

Örvar frowned, the wrinkles deepening round his eyes. They reminded Nína of the rays she used to draw around the sun when she was a child. Then his face relaxed and pale lines remained. When he spoke again it was in a different, less combative, tone. 'It wasn't a suicide note. Not from what I can tell. And the pathologist agrees with me.'

'Was it her who reported me?' Nína asked, curious rather than bitter.

'Yes.' Örvar made no attempt to hide the fact. 'She knows who you are and when she spotted Thröstur's name in the letter she took appropriate action. I hope you'd have done the same in her shoes.'

'Maybe.' There was no way she was going to give him the satisfaction of agreeing with him.

'The letter's a sort of summary intended for her husband, Nói, who was found dead on the beach. Of course all suicide notes are different, but this would have to be among the oddest I've seen. Unless she didn't mean to end it all as quickly as she did but the drugs took the decision out of her hands.'

'Is it possible that she didn't swallow them voluntarily but was forced?'

'They don't think so but it complicates matters that the woman was covered in bruises from her accident. Tomorrow they'll start comparing photos taken at A&E with the injuries on her body. At first sight none of the bruises appear to have been made by force – there are no signs that she was strangled or anything like that.'

Nína nodded, grimacing. 'Could she have drowned her husband, then taken her own life?'

'No. She hadn't been anywhere near the sea. Her plaster cast was completely dry. So were her other dressings. They would have been soaking if she'd been on the beach. Besides, he could easily have fought her off given the state she was in. No, some other person was at work there – almost certainly the same person who killed the other two people who were found in the sea.'

'The Americans?'

'No one's sure but they think so. We found a phone at the bottom of the garden, which is believed to have been theirs. Our first priority was to check the passenger lists and it appears the couple didn't leave the country as planned. Their onward tickets to Europe haven't been used and there's no evidence that they took a different flight. So it seems likely to me that it's them. No other people have been reported missing, apart from some young drug addicts, but these bodies are adults.'

'Is there nothing about them in the letter?'

'Nothing that would explain their deaths. Vala wrote about herself for the most part. She described an incident from her childhood that she believed had brought down disaster on her family.'

Nína pricked up her ears. 'I know what it was. When I met you on your way out earlier I was going to tell you that she was one of the three child witnesses to the 1985 case, along with Thröstur and Lárus Jónmundsson. Now they're both dead and Thröstur's as good as.' She took a deep breath. 'One thing's been seriously bothering me ever since I found out that Vala was one of the children, and that is that I can't remember if you told me it was three boys or if you didn't specify their sex. I've decided to give you the benefit of the doubt.'

Örvar pretended not to hear this. 'Why didn't you say anything? You had plenty of opportunity.'

'Yeah, right. Earlier in the car, when I asked you about the files, you didn't answer, just started talking on the phone. That gave me time to think and I decided not to mention it until after the examination of the crime scene. Anyway, I suspect it wasn't really news to you. If you removed the evidence, you must have been aware of the woman's name.'

Örvar stared at her in silence. Nína met his eyes levelly. Then he turned his head away and looked out of the window for a while as if giving all his attention to the weather. Then he looked back at her. 'When I set off I hadn't a clue who the woman was. Someone mentioned the man's name when we were on the beach, but not his wife's. It wasn't until the pathologist chased after me that I heard it was Vala, or I'd never have agreed to take you along.'

Nína didn't comment on this. After all, she had forced herself on him. 'What does the letter say about Thröstur?'

Örvar leant back in his chair and stroked his chin, as if pretending to ponder whether he should confide in her or not. Which was pointless, as they both knew he would in the end. Then he leant forwards over the desk again. 'According to Vala's letter, he rang her about an article he was intending to write. He wanted to warn her it was coming out but also to ask if he could quote her. Lárus too.'

'About the old case?'

'Yes. Originally the article was supposed to be about historical child-abuse cases – cases that had been hushed up and shelved at the time. He'd been through the newspaper archives and found among others a case that had been dropped when the journalist who was working on it died.'

'Stefán Egill Fridriksson?' Nína was impatient for him to get to the point.

'Yes. It sounds as if you know all about it. Perhaps I shouldn't be wasting my time telling you if you're already up to speed.'

'I don't know all about it. But the journalist could hardly be anyone else. I found some documents belonging to Stefán among Thröstur's papers. Now I understand why they were there. Go on.'

'From what Thröstur seems to have told Vala, he realised that his house was connected to the case Stefán had been intending to write about. There was a picture of your garage among the files. Afterwards Thröstur discovered that the journalist had killed himself. At that point it dawned on him that he had been sitting outside the garage as a child, with Lárus and Vala, while Stefán was hanging himself inside.' Örvar gave Nína a moment to digest this.

'So Thröstur didn't remember the garage when we bought the flat?'

'Apparently not. Which is understandable. How much do you remember from when you were that age? I can't even describe the house I was living in when I was seven.'

'Why did he want to quote Vala?' Nína asked. 'What did she know about historical paedophiles?'

'After he made this discovery, Thröstur decided to change his angle; to write about Stefán's suicide and mention the part played by the three of them.'

'What do you mean?' Various ugly versions of what might have happened ran through her mind: three skinny little kids knotting a noose; one of them Thröstur.

Örvar's computer bleeped. He turned to the screen to check his e-mail. It only took a moment but felt like a lifetime to Nína. She had been waiting so long for this information that it wasn't fair to have to wait any longer. She had to stifle a sigh of relief when Örvar finally turned back to her. 'Apparently the kids saw a man enter the garage and come out again shortly afterwards. In other words, they lied when they repeatedly insisted they hadn't seen anyone. The man noticed them as he was about to make off and came over. He grabbed Vala's arm and told them that if they ever told anyone they'd seen him come out, he'd murder them. But first he'd kill their mothers, cut off their arms and legs and drown them in the sea – in front of the children. Then he'd do the same to them. He frightened the life out of them so they didn't dare disobey. They promised to say they hadn't seen anyone going in or coming out. And they kept their word.'

Nína felt dizzy. The moment when the policeman in the video had told Thröstur he mustn't hurt his mother suddenly acquired a whole new meaning that the officer hadn't intended. 'How could the man have dreamt that they'd keep quiet?'

'Because he knew from experience that children don't open their mouths if you threaten them badly enough. He'd been sexually abusing children for years, so these kids got off very lightly compared to some of the others who crossed his path. Think of all the people who are coming forward now and opening up about abuse they suffered thirty, forty years ago; people who've kept quiet about much uglier secrets than this, just because their abuser convinced them that something terrible would happen if they opened their mouths.' Örvar fell silent and looked at her, puzzled. 'Why do you think Thröstur didn't tell you any of this if he was planning to make it public anyway? You were pretty close, weren't you?'

'Of course. We were married. *Are* married.' It wasn't only the patronising tone of his questions that aroused her resentment. She was also unhappy about the implications they contained. Why *hadn't* Thröstur told her? Did he think she wouldn't understand? She was his wife and best friend first; a cop only a poor second.

'Calm down.'

These words really made Nína's hackles rise – whenever she heard them. She'd often wondered if people realised how counter-productive they were. But she remained silent and allowed Örvar to continue.

'I'll tell you what the letter said about that. It seems that Vala had been longing to explain to her husband why she hadn't told him. She mentioned that Thröstur had kept it quiet too, so she hadn't been alone.'

'Why did they?' Nína wanted Örvar to tell her, even if the answer proved to be humiliating for her. She knew nothing about his relationship with his wife but could only hope they fought like cat and dog. Perhaps that was why he was always at work. The thought made her feel a little better.

'Vala didn't want to confide in her husband because he was a control freak when it came to his family. He wanted everything to be perfect: their home, health, their whole life together. The fact that she'd lied to the police as a child would in no way fit in with that picture. She wrote that she'd buried the incident at the back of her mind and avoided thinking about it, so she hadn't unburdened herself to him at the beginning of their relationship. As the years went by it grew more and more difficult to bring up the subject, especially as there was no reason to. Then Thröstur rang. You can imagine how shocked she was when he said he wanted to quote her in the article. She also wrote that Thröstur had told her he was in the same position: his wife didn't know anything; she was a police officer, so it was a sensitive issue. But he was going to come clean before the article appeared. Does this sound familiar at all?'

Nína shook her head. 'No.' Her voice was high and brittle as glass. She felt as if she were crumbling into little pieces. 'He never told me.'

'No. I couldn't be sure.' At last there was a trace of sympathy in Örvar's voice. 'Did you receive any letters at all – strange, threatening notes?'

'No. None.' Nína was reduced to monosyllables. Every word stung.

'Vala did. And Aldís informed me earlier that Lárus did too. She'd just woken up and saw the news about the events in Skerjafjördur. She told me everything that she presumably shared with you last night.' Örvar gave Nína the chance to add something but she merely nodded warily. 'Vala hid the letters,' Örvar continued, 'like Lárus. I imagine that as a lawyer he wasn't keen for this to leak out. But Vala didn't throw the letters away because she was afraid the threats might be serious and she wanted to be able to bring them out if anything happened. But she failed to do so when it appeared that the people who were staying in their house had vanished. She closed her eyes to the obvious explanation. The first notes had arrived before they did their house swap and Vala had hoped things would die down while they were abroad. She can't have realised the danger she was putting their guests in.'

Nína sat up. Her self-confidence revived a little. 'Could she have made the whole thing up? I doubt Thröstur would have got an article like that published in the paper. It has no substance. It doesn't prove anything, be it child abuse or anything else. Three children told a lie – that's not news.'

'No, but Thröstur uncovered the identity of the man who threatened them. There was a picture of him among the old documents. He tracked him down, confronted him and told him he was going to tell all.'

'All what?'

'That he'd dug up enough evidence to expose him. This was the man Stefán had been planning to write about. Thröstur added that he was going to put forward the theory that this man had been involved somehow in Stefán's death. And I'm fairly sure he was right. Why else would it have been so vital for the man that the children didn't let on they'd seen him?' Now it was Örvar's turn to sag in his chair. He seemed to have shrunk all of a sudden. 'I should have followed my own conviction at the time. I sensed that Stefán's widow was onto something but I didn't do enough. I was so young and new to the force. She ended up in the gutter and her son was a more pitiful sight every time we went round. It's weighed on me ever since. I've seen worse, but this was the first human tragedy I witnessed. You don't forget something like that.'

'Why did you take the reports?' Nína was exhausted. She couldn't bear any more. She had her explanation but she felt just as awful as before.

'I heard someone say that they'd received a call from one of the papers about an old case involving a suicide in a garage. I hadn't a clue it was Thröstur who'd rung; his name wasn't mentioned and the person who took the call obviously didn't connect him to you. I said I'd deal with it next time the paper called and went down and fetched the file. But the call never came. This was at the beginning of December. We both know why no one rang back.'

'Does that mean you still have the file somewhere?'

'No. I can't find it. Perhaps it got thrown out by accident.'

Nína knew Örvar was lying and he seemed to sense the fact. He didn't give her a chance to speak: 'I suggest you take some leave. Thröstur's case will be reopened and Lárus's too. It would be best for everyone, you most of all, if you stayed away from the station while this is going on. We believe the man who killed Stefán may have been involved in Lárus's death and possibly Thröstur's too. The plan is to gather evidence and arrest him as soon as we've put a case together and can be sure we've got the right man. At the moment we only have his first name. But the investigation's only just been launched and there's no reason to believe we won't have all the necessary information very shortly. We could even arrest him as early as the middle of this week. Until then it's vital that you keep away. You mustn't under any circumstances try to make contact with the man. If you don't think you can stop yourself, I'll have you locked up in the cells.'

There were plenty of things he could do as her boss but throwing her in the cells wasn't one of them.

'I have no desire to meet this man. Not now.' Nína stood up. 'I've got to go over to the hospital. I won't be going in tomorrow or the next day. Or ever again, probably.' There was no pleasure in knowing that Thröstur might not have intended to kill himself after all. She had persuaded herself that the only thing that mattered was to find an explanation; that it would be easier for her to cope if she only knew why. Now she was close to knowing but felt just as bad. Thröstur had gone and would never come back.

Before opening the door she turned round. 'What's his name? I need to know so I have a name in mind when I curse him and gloat over what's in store for him. Not for any other reason. You can be sure I won't discuss it with anyone – not the business of the files or our conversation just now.'

Örvar studied her and seemed satisfied from her expression that she could be relied on. She was obviously too tired for pretence.

'His name is Ívar.'

Chapter 34

28 January 2014

It is still pitch black in the lighthouse. The only light emanates from their torch beams, which are becoming worryingly yellow and weak. Fortunately, however, there is a promise in the air that the winter dawn is not far off. Helgi and Heida retreated indoors when they could no longer withstand the bitter cold outside on the helipad. It is freezing inside as well and they are sitting huddled in their sleeping bags again. They long ago ran out of things to say. Heida's eyelids are beginning to droop and Helgi sees her head nodding onto her chest.

Ívar is the only one who has managed to sleep properly, though even he has stirred regularly. Once he sat up and ate half of the unappetising prawn sandwich that Helgi had left him. Heida had been fully awake at that point and they had both sat watching him in silence while he wolfed down the sandwich in two large bites. Heida's face contorted in disgust when Ívar belched before lying down to sleep again. Helgi thought he himself had probably looked pained as well.

Now there is no way of telling how Heida is feeling; sleep has obliterated all expression, her mouth hangs slackly open and by the waning torchlight there is no colour in her face apart from two red blotches of cold on her cheeks. She reminds him uncomfortably of a blow-up doll.

Ívar has turned to face the wall but Helgi has no wish to see him anyway – his snores are bad enough. It has occurred to him to pull the sleeping bag over the other man's mouth but that might wake him.

Suddenly a blue light illuminates the shiny fabric of Heida's sleeping bag. A shockingly loud, cheery ringtone fills the tiny space and Ívar's snores fade as if out of courtesy. Heida is jolted awake, her hair flying back, and stares around in bewilderment.

'Your phone was ringing.' Helgi points to the flat object in her lap. It lights up and starts ringing again.

'What time is it?' Her voice is despairing, like someone afraid they've missed a flight.

'Why don't you answer?' Helgi's keen to stop the noise as Ívar has begun to stir. He hasn't opened his eyes yet but they seem to be moving under their lids.

'Hello.' Heida's voice is husky from sleep. 'Yes, that's me.' A look of astonishment crosses her face. 'Yes, there are three of us.' Again she falls silent. 'In the lighthouse.' She looks at Helgi and frowns, then puts her hand over the phone and whispers to him. 'It's the coastguard.' Then she concentrates on what the person at the other end is saying. 'What?' She wrinkles her brow, perplexed. 'I don't understand. Aren't you coming?'

'Don't say that!' Helgi blurts out, louder than intended. Ívar opens his eyes and seems to be trying to work out where he is.

Heida's gaze is lowered. She strokes the shiny material as if picking up pieces of text message that have fallen from her phone. 'OK. We're ready.' She looks up and smiles at Helgi. 'Should we wait outside or inside?' It's a stupid question, as she seems to realise. Even if they cut up their sleeping bags and stuffed the down into their ears, they still couldn't fail to hear the helicopter arriving. 'What?'

Ívar rises on his elbow. 'Who's she talking to?' He speaks loudly and Heida turns away, trying to hear what's being said on the phone.

'Coastguard,' Helgi whispers but Ívar answers as loudly as before.

'What? Has my battery died or did I sleep through the ringing?' He roots around in his sleeping bag, pulls out his phone and checks the screen with a disgruntled look. Up to now the coastguard has called either him or Helgi, who can't help smiling at this latest development.

Heida raises her voice and Helgi's smile fades. 'Can't you come at once? Now, I mean. Straight away. We can't stay here with this man. I knew it. I knew it. I said so all along.' Her eyes are stark with terror. 'I can't stay here any longer. You've got to get me out of here. Now. At once.' She scrambles out of her sleeping bag, her movements violent.

'What on earth's wrong?' Helgi can't believe Heida's losing control now, when it's so nearly over. She is staring rigidly at Ívar, her breathing ragged. Helgi gets up and says firmly: 'Heida, give me the phone. I'll talk to him.' Heida backs into the corner, as if she wishes she could escape through the wall. 'Give me the phone.' To his astonishment, she obeys.

'Helgi here. Anything wrong?' The question is redundant but he can't help hoping that the answer will surprise him.

The man at the other end speaks with the calm deliberation of a person telling someone that a tiger is standing behind him, baring its teeth. 'Your phone's dead.'

Helgi fishes his phone out of his anorak pocket and sees that it has switched itself off. 'Oh, I didn't realise.'

'Never mind. Listen to me. There's no reason to think anything bad's going to happen to you.'

'No. I didn't think there was.' Helgi tries in vain to keep his voice equally level. He licks his lips, his eyes wandering around the interior of the lighthouse without fixing on anything. He finds the other man's calm manner provoking.

'There's a man with you called Ívar. We've been told to pass on a message from the police that you're to stay as far away from him as possible while you're waiting to be evacuated. We're not talking about a long time because they're getting the helicopter ready now. We'll be with you as soon as it's light enough to operate the winch.'

Helgi can't stop himself from staring at Ívar. The man is frowning, apparently aware that they're talking about him, though he can hardly guess what's being said.

'Excuse me? You do realise where we are?'

'Yes. I know.' The voice on the phone is still irritatingly composed. Helgi has begun to suspect that it's a computer.

'Then you'll realise there's nowhere for us to go. It's not as if we're each sitting here in our own private corner, if you see what I mean.'

'I'm well aware of the fact. Nevertheless you're to keep as far away from him as possible. For example, you two could climb out onto the crag if he follows you outside, or wait on the helipad if he can be persuaded to sit tight in the lighthouse.'

'Why should we?' Helgi's eyes are fixed on Ívar, who is looking back with a puzzled expression. Helgi forces himself to smile at him but can tell he's not very successful.

'The man is believed to be dangerous. A police officer is being sent out with the chopper, to be lowered after our man. You and Heida are to keep your distance while Ívar is arrested and try not to draw attention to yourselves. I repeat that you're to retreat to a safe distance.'

Suddenly Helgi feels overwhelmed with exhaustion. He hasn't slept for twenty-four hours and is in no fit state to get into a fight or resort to any complicated measures. He knows it's vital to fob Ívar off with a convincing lie once the phone call is over, but he can't for the life of him come up with anything plausible. He wants to burst out laughing at the absurdity of the situation. 'Thank you. We'll be packed and ready.' He says goodbye, hangs up and forces out another smile.

'What was that all about?' The glow of the torch casts a strange shadow on Ívar's face. His cheekbones are thrown into relief and dark semi-circles spread under his eyes like grotesquely distorted bags.

'They just wanted to let us know that they're getting ready.' Helgi can see that Ívar has worked out there's more to it. 'They're having problems with the winch and told us not to stand underneath while they're lowering their man. And they're worried about us because of the long delay.' He falls silent, congratulating himself on having come up with this lie.

'What was that stuff about having nowhere to go? And why's she behaving like she's off her rocker?'

Although Helgi doesn't have eyes in the back of his head, he senses that Heida is close to breaking point. He wishes he could lean back and wedge her into the corner to prevent her from putting them into even more danger. It's vital that Ívar should believe him. 'I wanted to know how far we should be from the helipad while they were winching down. Heida's in a state because she misunderstood the guy and thought they were postponing again.' It's tempting to turn and say: 'Right, Heida?' But Helgi doesn't trust her to play along.

'Why didn't they ring me? I'm the contact.' Ívar sounds as if he's been badly let down.

'I don't know. Perhaps they couldn't connect because your phone was inside your sleeping bag.' Helgi swallows.

'Bullshit.'

'I don't know. I'm only trying to answer your question.'

'I can't stay here!' Heida shrieks this so loudly that the new radio transmitter resounds. To sit here any longer would be to invite disaster. Assessing the situation, Helgi decides that it would be impossible for him and Heida to go outside and leave Ívar in the lighthouse. He'd be stepping on their heels like a street hustler. There's only one course of action.

'Come on, Ívar. Let's shift the stones off the gear outside and get everything ready. That's what they asked us to do. Heida needs to be alone.'

'She needs tranquillisers, that's what she needs. Women are such fucking idiots.'

'You bastard.' Heida's voice rises to a shriek again and Helgi hastily drags Ívar outside with him. He closes the door behind them but, alas, there's no way of locking the lighthouse, so there's nothing to stop Heida from following them.

The cold saltiness of the air is strangely invigorating. Now all Helgi need do is spin out the preparations for as long as possible. The chopper should be there in less than an hour, but even so it seems like an eternity to wait and the thought of it saps his energy again. Suddenly the cold filling his lungs has a soporific effect and the taste of salt makes him want to retch.

He mustn't fail now.

'There's something going on. You can't fool me.' Ívar is standing beside him, zipping his anorak up to the neck. He pulls his hood over his head but Helgi hasn't the energy to copy him, in spite of the biting breeze.

'I'm not trying to fool you. Come on, let's get cracking.' Helgi's voice is threadbare with tiredness now, which has the effect of making him sound sincere. At least Ívar seems to think so because he hesitates, and Helgi seizes the opportunity to pick his way round the corner to where their gear is piled in the narrow gap between crag and lighthouse. It means turning his back on Ívar but it can't be helped. If he shuffled along in reverse, keeping his eye on the other man, that would give the game away immediately. 'We need to shift this stuff onto the helipad. All the loose items are already packed in the boxes.' He doesn't know how he's supposed to achieve this; he barely has the strength to lift a matchbox right now.

The door creaks as Heida comes out, and as his eyes meet Ívar's Helgi is unable to disguise his fear any longer. Now Ívar knows for sure that something is wrong. He reaches quickly into the box that he has dragged out of the pile and whips out an object that flashes in the faint moonlight. Helgi can no longer think straight; all that occurs to him is to shut the door on Heida; make sure she doesn't witness what is about to happen or put herself in danger.

'Get inside. Don't open up until I tell you. Hold the door shut.' He shoves her back into the lighthouse, reaches for the door and slams it. Then he turns to confront Ívar and what is to come. Despite his overwhelming fatigue, he is looking forward to this. It's nearly over. It's all got to end, one way or another.

The heavy throbbing of the engine is a joy to the ears. Helgi is lying on his back on the rocky ground, his shoulders propped on the bottom step of the lighthouse. Above him is the small whitewashed tower with its red lantern casing, like a wedding cake plonked down incongruously in the middle of the ocean. His eyes close again and he hopes this is the image he will take with him into eternity. His throat rattles as he makes one final attempt to coax Heida outside. So far his feeble cries have had no effect and the closer the helicopter approaches, the less likely it is that she'll be able to hear him. The sensation of cold seems to have gone; one minute he thought he was dying, the next he couldn't feel anything. He doesn't need a doctor to tell him what this means. Heida will have to come out and help him staunch the bleeding. He can't wait for the chopper.

'Heida!' Helgi coughs and tastes iron. 'Heida!' He makes a desperate attempt to crane his neck to see the door and almost weeps when it moves. Only a tiny crack at first, but then Heida's head appears. He realises that she has caught sight of his outstretched hand, which looks ready to grasp at whatever might fall from the sky. But his strength is waning and his head falls back on the hard step. Yet he can't feel any pain.

He hears her gasp, then footsteps, and when Helgi opens his eyes again she is kneeling over him, gazing into his face. 'Oh, God!' She breaks down in tears. 'What can I do? Please don't die.'

Helgi coughs again and she flinches away. Blood must have come out of his mouth because Heida is trembling like a leaf and glancing around frantically, up into the air and out to sea. 'Has Ívar gone?'

Helgi replies to the tremulous question with a weak nod.

'I knew I should have opened at once to find out if it was you groaning out here. But I didn't dare. What was I supposed to do if it had been . . .?'

Helgi doesn't have the energy to answer this; he senses he had better not waste words.

'Even when I looked out now I wasn't sure. I had a crazy idea that Ívar might have put on your clothes to confuse me. But then I recognised your hair and saw you were bigger than Ívar. Oh, God, oh, God.'

Helgi is having trouble keeping his eyes open. More than anything he longs to close them and go to sleep. Just for a little while. Before his lids droop he sees again the words written in marker pen on the wall. *Stefán Egill Fridriksson 1985*. With all the strength he has left he gasps: 'Did you hear what Ívar said?' Of course the shouting and sounds of the struggle must have carried to her on the wind but he doubted she could have heard the actual words. That was what mattered.

'No. I had my hands over my ears, I was so terrified. I closed my eyes and tried to think about my little girl. I thought I'd never see her again.' Heida's nose is running and she sniffs. 'When I listened I heard such horrible yelling and screaming that I put my hands over my ears again. But I heard enough to realise that one of you was injured, maybe even dead, and the other had fallen off the cliff.'

The noise had been anything but pleasant: Ívar had uttered a bloodcurdling scream as he plummeted, howling so the rock echoed every time he crashed into a sharp jutting stone. If Helgi had been able to he would have covered his own ears. He closes his eyes. He wants to sleep. Just for a moment.

The racket of the rotor blades draws closer and he senses that Heida is smiling, although she's still in shock and must be as weak with exhaustion as him. 'What will the men in the chopper think of me when they hear I did nothing to help you?'

Helgi tries to groan out a few words, though he has resolved to spare his energy. It's not her fault. Quite the opposite. 'You did nothing wrong. Everything's OK.' Opening his eyes, he peers up at the lighthouse, as if expecting to see a figure standing on the little gallery, waiting to accompany him. Perhaps the apparition he thought he'd seen in the fog: the harbinger of doom. But there's nobody there; he's not being pursued by any mysterious shadows, only a growing lassitude. He must close his eyes. 'Did you hear what Ívar said? Any of it?'

'No. I heard nothing.' She bends over him, stroking his forehead gently. 'It doesn't matter. You can tell the police yourself. The chopper's coming. Everything's going to be OK.' Heida looks skywards and sees the helicopter approaching, shining and beautiful in the pale morning light. Helgi's eyes close and he feels her warm hand stroking his face. Then she whips back her hand and he wonders if it's because she can't bear to touch him.

'Helgi,' Heida whispers, as if she thinks he's asleep and doesn't want to wake him. He can't move, though he wants to. Finally he summons the tiny amount of strength he has left and fumbles for the knife sticking out of his side. He hears her cry as he gropes with his fingers at the bloodstain surrounding the blade. His anorak is already soaked through. He feels blood welling up the handle from the wound.

'Oh, no! Oh, no! Oh, no!' Heida's cries do nothing to help. 'What should I do? What should I do?' The events of the last twenty-four hours seem to have addled her brain. 'Should I pull it out?'

Helgi tries to protest but can't utter a word. The knife is at least blocking the wound; it'll open if she pulls it out. Then he hears a sucking sound, feels a tremendous pressure in his side and his mouth gapes in a silent scream. He opens his eyes wide and stares into Heida's face. She looks bewildered; Ívar's bloody knife is in her hand. Helgi's head falls sideways and he sees blood pouring from the wound, shiny red and viscous. With a desperate effort he manages to turn his head back and look up; he doesn't want to see what's happening. The rock mustn't drink his lifeblood.

As his lids droop once more he sees Heida open her mouth and lean backwards. Knife in hand, she shrieks as loudly as she can in a desperate attempt to be heard above the thunder of the helicopter.

He sees two faces staring down at them from under white helmets. One of the men seems to be speaking to them and Helgi smiles at the idea that he should think they can hear. Then the long-desired sleep overwhelms him.

Chapter 35

31 January 2014

The vending machine refuses to accept the fifty-krónur piece. Whatever Nína tries – force, cajoling, indifference – nothing works. She could kick the machine or shake it, but she's not *that* angry. Besides, there are too many people around in visiting hours and she doesn't want to attract any attention. She feels conspicuous enough as it is, dolled up in a red dress and high heels in honour of the occasion. It had seemed wrong to turn up looking as if she were going straight home after this visit to flop on the sofa and watch a film. But the only dresses she owns remind her of cocktails and dancing. The red one seemed the least inappropriate; it's not low cut, at any rate, and almost covers her knees. Even so, Thröstur's sister couldn't hide her disapproval when they ran into one another earlier; she herself had been wearing a grey suit that might have been designed with a deathbed in mind.

Instead of beating up the vending machine, Nína sits down on a bench and watches time passing on the clock on the wall. Thröstur's father and sister asked to be alone with him for an hour – their last hour with him in this world. She is intending to give herself slightly longer. The doctor who's going to switch off his life support is not due until eight, so she will have plenty of time to cry her eyes out at Thröstur's bedside. She suggested the hour herself, because she doesn't want it to happen during daylight. She feels the process should be as much like going to sleep as possible. That way she can convince herself that Thröstur is following his dreams into an everlasting night, rather than being obliterated like a text being deleted. The doctor wasn't particularly pleased at having to do it in the evening but was too kind to object.

Nína puffs out her cheeks and exhales slowly. The action seems inappropriate in a woman dressed up like this and she's glad no one can see her. Before choosing the date she had checked that it held no special significance for Thröstur's family; she didn't want to spoil some relative's birthday or wedding anniversary by associating it with the day Thröstur died. But it turned out that today's date belongs to no one, and now there's no turning back.

'Hi! It's Nína, isn't it?' The voice is familiar but Nína can't immediately place it. Lowering her eyes from the clock, she sees that it's a journalist who used to work with Thröstur. He beams at her, running his eyes over her party dress. 'Fancy bumping into you here. What are you . . .?' The man suddenly twigs. 'Sorry. God, of course. What news of Thröstur? Any change?'

Nína prepares to lie. She can't tell the poor guy that after today Thröstur will finally be at peace. She wishes she could, if only to explain why she's got up like a dog's dinner, but resists the impulse. It would be too embarrassing for them both. 'No. No change, I'm afraid.' She adds hurriedly, to change the subject, 'Were you visiting someone? Nothing serious, I hope.'

'Oh, no. Not really. I was visiting a photographer who's done a bit of work for the paper. Did an interview with him and got some of his pictures. He was in the lighthouse with that bloke. He's the one who was very nearly killed. Luckily for us he survived. It'll be an exclusive.'

Nína isn't particularly interested in the case, so merely nods as if she agrees that it's a mercy their photographer escaped with his life so they can interview him for their paper. The man, insensitive to her indifference, carries on regardless. 'It's a shocking story. Have you been following the news?'

'Er, yes. A bit.' Nína hopes he won't start testing her. She hasn't been able to make herself follow the coverage ever since she read the first article in which Thröstur's name cropped up uncomfortably often. New revelations have been splashed across the front page of his old paper every day. His former colleagues have firsthand access to the story since their own office was involved. She particularly avoided the issue with the photo of Thröstur on the cover. The editor obviously didn't have a very clear eye as to what would sell the paper as you could hardly see Thröstur for the headlines, which was some compensation.

'It's a shocking business – and the story's ours, of course. Two of our own guys! We've trampled all over our competitors, as you can imagine.' The flow of words stopped abruptly and he looked at Nína as if seeing her for the first time. 'Hang on a minute! Would you be up for an interview?'

'Me? What about?'

'This business with Thröstur. I never believed he could have done something like that. There had to be an explanation.' He smiles expectantly. 'Plenty of people would be eager to hear your side. Suicide that turned out to be murder. Sensational stuff.'

'Er, no, thanks.' Nína regrets not having told the man what is happening today. If she had, it wouldn't have occurred to him to ask – though you never knew. 'I don't want to discuss it in public.'

'We can close it to comments if that's what's worrying you.'

Nína shakes her head. That doesn't bother her; the whole thing is too awful for other people's comments to change anything. But the man is only fishing. He smiles again. 'Think about it, anyway. Though not for too long. People have a limited attention span when it comes to news.' He seems undeterred by the fact that Nína doesn't answer. 'What can you tell me about the investigation? Have they managed to confirm that Ívar murdered Throstur? It would be fan-bloody-tastic if we could break the news.'

'Actually, Thröstur's still alive.' Casting round for an escape route, she stands up. Anything she says about the investigation will find its way into the paper: *according to a source close to the events* . . . 'I've got to go. I know nothing about the investigation as I'm on leave, and I don't hear anything.'

'I understand.' The man can't hide his disappointment. 'One more thing before you go. We were talking about how terrible it was when this whole thing came out. I just wanted you to know that it never occurred to anyone at the paper that Thröstur's article might have these kinds of repercussions. He kept the contents to himself and the editor was ready to do his nut when Thröstur refused to discuss the piece before it was finished. He should have forced it out of him. But it's easy to be wise after the event.'

'It wouldn't have changed anything.' Nína picks up her bag. 'Say hello to everyone from me. I've got to go – someone's waiting for me. And good luck with writing up the interview with the photographer.' She says goodbye and walks off. She's only taken a few steps when it occurs to her to turn and ask him something that's been bothering her ever since she learnt about Ívar and his probable responsibility for the death of all these people. But the information she wants may have already appeared in one of the articles she has avoided reading. She doesn't like to reveal to the journalist that she hasn't actually read any of the coverage. She'll follow it up later; she can't be the only person who has wondered how Ívar got hold of the names of the other two witnesses, Vala and Lárus. She knows Thröstur well enough to be certain that he would never have revealed them. She just hopes no one will think he blabbed. If so, she'll make damn sure she corrects that misapprehension.

Nína wonders where to go. It's too cold to wait out in the car and she doesn't want to sit alone among the patients and visitors in one of the hospital lounges. Then she remembers Thorbjörg. She will have heard by now that they believe her husband was murdered. It must have meant a great deal to her to receive confirmation at last that she was right. Even though the knowledge has come thirty years too late, Nína wants to congratulate her. Probably nobody else will bother; certainly no one has patted Nína on the back yet. She would also appreciate a chance to talk to the woman, even if only briefly, since she doubts anyone else understands her as well at this moment. And it's mutual.

In the corridor outside Thorbjörg's room, Nína encounters a nurse who apparently recognises her from her previous visit. She comes over to inform Nína that Thorbjörg has a visitor and asks her to wait a moment. The woman's estranged son, who she hasn't seen for years, is in there with her now, and it would be a pity to interrupt their reunion.

Thorbjörg's head is spinning. It's not unlike the feeling you get when you lie down on a pillow and sink into alcohol-induced oblivion. She should know. But this time the world is not receding; this time, unfortunately, she's completely with it. She doesn't want to think about what her son has just told her; doesn't want to wonder if he could have invented the whole thing or if she's experiencing the DTs. The happiness she felt when he walked in was short-lived. It was fantastic that he had come to see her. Did it mean he had finally forgiven her, little though she deserved it?

She had been overwhelmed with self-pity at the time of Stefán's death; she hadn't been able to see what was under her nose – the little boy whose suffering was even greater than hers, who had no one else to turn to but his wreck of a mother. A tear runs down her cheek and she catches it with the tip of her tongue. The visit had begun well; Helgi was just like he always used to be, placid and likable. Perhaps he hadn't completely forgiven her but at least he didn't snap at her or make any snide remarks. Then all of a sudden he changed. Said he wanted to tell her a secret. His voice had taken on a mechanical quality and all feeling vanished from his face, as if Helgi the person had been switched off. She doesn't know what replaced him and isn't sure she wants to know. 'Could you repeat that, please, Helgi dear? I'm not sure I understood.'

He doesn't sigh or show any other sign of irritation, merely begins his account again in an emotionless monotone. 'At the end of November a journalist called Thröstur asked me to go round and see him. He wanted me to take some photos for an article he was writing. I sometimes work for his paper, so I agreed. The address was pretty familiar – our old house in the west end. He even asked me to meet him in the garage where Dad was supposed to have hanged himself all those years ago. I didn't say anything, just turned up at the appointed time, feeling very curious. Thröstur was waiting inside the garage and he began to tell me all about the article in the hope that it would give me ideas for suitable pictures.'

Thorbjörg sits up a little more so that she can see out of the window. It feels better to have life before her eyes while she is listening to this tale again. She can't bring herself to look at her son. 'Go on.'

'Thröstur told me the article was about a journalist who was thought to have committed suicide in the garage.' Helgi hesitates a moment, then carries on. 'He said he had a theory that he'd been murdered, just like you always thought. He said he'd come across an article in the newspaper archives that Dad had been writing, about a paedophile. I didn't mention that I was connected to the case – I was speechless. And at that point I didn't mean to do anything bad.

'Bad things have a way of creeping up on you,' says Thorbjörg consolingly. Outside it has begun to snow and she can't see anything but the huge flakes floating down past the window.

'It turns out the paedophile rented the garage from you to run a bike repair shop.'

Thorbjörg closes her eyes. In those days only children and teenagers had ridden bikes, so the customers of the repair shop had mostly been innocent little things. They must have brought their buckled mudguards, tangled chains and broken gears right into the monster's lair. 'We didn't know,' she said. 'The man came with the building when we bought it. I remember how surprised I was to come across some children's bikes he'd left behind when he moved out. No one fetched them. Now I understand why. The poor little souls who owned them!' The snow is coming down heavily now. 'I remember him well. A young man, bit of a loner, didn't talk much. His name was Ívar, I think.'

'That's right. He doesn't talk at all now.' Helgi's voice is as monotonous as when he embarked on his account. As if he were reading announcements from the Directorate of Fisheries. 'Thröstur told me Dad had almost finished his article and that it would have been groundbreaking because no one wrote about child abuse in those days. But it never appeared because the editor thought the suicide indicated that Dad hadn't been in his right mind. What if the article had been wrong? So it never appeared in print and the paedophile got away with nothing but a fright.' Helgi pauses in his account. 'But Thröstur told me that Dad made the mistake of confronting Ívar, who naturally packed up and disappeared off the face of the earth. Almost.'

Thorbjörg tries to connect this with what she remembers from those days. When Ívar had announced out of the blue that he was leaving and then decamped, she had been livid, grumbling about it endlessly, unaware that her Stebbi had been the cause. They couldn't afford to lose the rental income, so her fury was understandable. But could she have been so unreasonable that Stebbi didn't dare tell her what lay behind it? From what she remembers, she doesn't think so, but perhaps she has glossed over the memory. Would it have changed anything if he'd told her? The story would probably have ended the same way, but the police might have listened to her if she could have pointed the finger at Ívar. Still, there's no point wondering what might have been. It's hard enough for her to take in what actually happened.

'Then the thunderbolt struck. Thröstur told me he'd found a photo of Ívar among the old papers and it had jogged his memory. He realised that the man in the picture was the same guy who had threatened him and his friends when they were kids, sitting outside the garage, writing down car numbers. They'd seen the man in the picture go into the building and come out again looking shifty. Ívar had clocked them, gone over and threatened them with dire retribution if they told on him. So they'd kept quiet, even when the police interviewed them all separately. They were too scared to tell.' Helgi clears his throat. 'I just saw red. In front of me was a man who'd held our future in his hands but was too gutless to do the right thing. If he'd told on Ívar I wouldn't have grown up as the son of the man who hanged himself and the woman who almost drank herself to death.'

'What do you mean *almost*?' Thorbjörg turns back from the window and stares blankly at the wall opposite her bed.

'Thröstur told me he wanted to write the article to make up for the fact that he hadn't told the truth. He'd suppressed the memory and even bought the same flat without realising that it came with the garage he'd been sitting outside as a boy.' Helgi snorts. 'He said he realised now that Ívar had played a part in Dad's death and wanted to make up for having perverted the course of justice. He was planning to expose Ívar and let the court of public opinion tear him apart. As if that would make everything all right again. He seemed to have no idea of what he and his friends had done to us, to me and you. He didn't even mention us. If he had, maybe I'd have reacted differently.'

'The police didn't tell me about those witnesses.' It was easier to remember that than think about what Helgi was telling her. 'I bet I could have forced the truth out of the little wretches.'

Helgi doesn't listen. He continues his account as if his mother hadn't spoken. 'I suggested we stage the hanging, so I could take a picture of the moment before the stool was kicked from under him – and the idiot agreed. He knotted a noose and climbed up with it round his neck. He had his back to me so his face wouldn't show in the pictures, so all I had to do was kick away the stool. And that's how it ended. I left and no one got in touch or asked me anything.'

'And the others?' Thorbjörg sounds even hoarser than before. She longs to ask Helgi for some water but doesn't want to interrupt his story. She's desperate to hear it again to make sure she hasn't misunderstood.

'I didn't mean to hurt them. Not at first. Of course they were all equally guilty, the other two even more than Thröstur, in fact. He said they'd refused to comment or even acknowledge what they'd done for the article, whereas he was intending to admit it publicly.' Helgi shrugs his shoulders casually, as if they're discussing the weather. 'I just meant to remind them and give them a chance to correct their past mistake. I sent them some letters I knew they'd understand, but nothing happened. No news, no investigation. Nothing. They were completely unrepentant. Then I began to see things in the right light. Although the business with Thröstur was a mistake, I soon realised that it was fated to be. You can't go around destroying other people's lives without suffering the consequences. It shouldn't work like that. So I saw that it was wrong to let the other two escape scot-free when Thröstur had got his just deserts. After all, he was more like a repentant sinner. The only problem was that Thröstur hadn't mentioned their names.

'How did you find them out?'

'Do you remember the good cop who sometimes came round to visit us? That guy Örvar?' Thorbjörg nods. 'I went to see him and said I'd really like to read the reports about Dad. I asked him very nicely and thanked him sincerely for how kind he'd been to us at the time, when nobody else would listen. He fell for it. Asked me to come back the following day as he'd have to search for them in the archives. When I arrived he handed me the reports and said I could have them. Most of the old files were about to be thrown away so it was lucky I'd come when I did. But he told me to keep it to myself. He wasn't really supposed to hand them over unofficially like that but in the circumstances – since they were about to be chucked out anyway – it would be simplest for everyone if I just took them. That's how I found out the names of the other two witnesses, and it wasn't hard to track them down. He doesn't seem to have told anyone. Not yet, anyway.'

Thorbjörg wants to swallow but her mouth is dry. Alas, she didn't misunderstand anything. 'There's no point going on with the story. It's too late now.'

'I'm going to tell you anyway. I want to; I need to talk about it and you're the only person who understands. After that I promise never to mention it again.' Helgi continues his account without giving her another chance to object. 'As you of all people should know, I'm used to handling alkies, so I went round for a drinking session with Lárus. I'd made contact with him, pretending to have received the same kind of letters as I'd sent him, and that his name had come up in one of them. He was eager to meet me and I made sure he knocked back a hell of a lot of booze. We talked a load of nonsense; he was almost incoherent and all I had to do was put forward the odd stupid theory about where the letters might have come from. When he passed out, I injected a solution of pills dissolved in spirits into his abdomen through his belly button. Then I waited till he croaked. No one caught on, and I suppose that may have made me a bit careless. Two dead and no repercussions. I should have been more careful.' For the first time since Helgi began his tale, there is a shade of regret in his voice. 'I killed the wrong people. A couple of foreigners. I'd been watching them from a distance for several days and I wasn't to know they weren't the right people. How could I have known?'

'I don't know, Helgi dear. I don't suppose you could.' Thorbjörg is beginning to wonder if this is a dream. Or a nightmare. Soon she'll wake up and find nobody sitting in the chair and her son still estranged from her. It would be the better of two evils.

'I waited for my chance, hung around the neighbourhood for several evenings and followed them up to the holiday chalet where they spent three days. Teased them a bit by catching a cat near where I lived that looked like their pet, killing it and putting it on their barbecue. Unfortunately their own cat was always inside – it would have been better to have used the real one. I didn't get to witness their reaction, as I'd hoped, but it had the desired effect because they fled back to town. I passed them coming from the opposite direction, turned round and followed them home. When the bloke went out again shortly afterwards I seized my chance, rang the bell and the woman opened the door. Before she could say anything I shoved her. She fell, hit her head and was dazed. It didn't really matter because I'd decided to make it look like she'd fallen downstairs. It's a two-storey house, you see. After I'd dragged her up to the top and pushed her down a couple of times the bloody man came back. He'd only gone out to fetch a pizza. And he spoke English.'

'Those poor people. I do hope they didn't have children. You could have done the same to a foreign child as Ívar did to you. Do you realise that?'

Helgi clearly doesn't want to hear this, as he ignores his mother's interruption. 'I ended up having to kill him too. With some scissors I found in a bathroom upstairs. I dragged the woman into the bedroom and laid her on the bed, then hid behind the door. The man searched the whole house for her then finally came into the bedroom to see what was wrong with her, and I stabbed him in the back. Again and again, until finally he stopped breathing. I left them there and pulled the curtains so nobody could see in. Then I took the house keys away with me and came back that night to get rid of their bodies and remove anything that appeared to belong to them. I didn't want the owners of the house to suspect anything. Luckily it was near the sea. I brought an old rubber dinghy and my rifle from home, lugged their bodies on board in the dark and tied a few rocks to them to make sure they wouldn't float. When the dinghy had drifted far enough out I shot a hole in it and it sank. Did you know I was a hunter?'

The question is bizarrely ordinary compared to all that has gone before. Of everything he has poured out it's the only detail Thorbjörg would have liked to hear. If only he had come here and told her about himself, what he'd been up to for the past few years and what he did for fun. He could have left out the rest. Every sentence, every syllable. 'I just can't listen to any more of this, Helgi dear. I feel so bad when I do because I'm terrified you're going to be found out.'

'I won't be. Weirdly, no one seems to suspect me. Everyone's so satisfied that Ívar's the bad guy that they have no reason to consider any other angles. No one's put two and two together and worked out that I'm Stefán's son. They all just see me as the victim who was lucky to escape with his life. You're probably the only person who could give me away. And I'd understand that. I never really meant to get away with it. There wasn't any plan as such. You just have to play some things by ear.' Helgi smiles at her but his eyes are dead. 'Of course it's a pity that four people died who didn't deserve it. The foreign couple, the husband and the carpenter at the lighthouse. I thought he was Ívar. They'd swapped places in the night. That was me being careless again. I was stressed because I thought we were going to be lifted off shortly. I'd sent the guy some letters and tormented him slowly but surely about what was to come. He was the only person I seriously wanted to kill. But not by pushing him over the cliff. That was too good for him.'

'He was the only one who deserved it, Helgi. Those other people were different. Do you understand that?' Thorbjörg doesn't know why she feels this matters. It's too late now. But he doesn't hear what she says; catches the words but not their meaning. When he resumes his account it's as though there has been no interruption. As though he had merely paused to draw breath.

'When I first tracked Ívar down I stalked him for a while and even struck up conversation with him in a bar when I saw that he was drunk and off his guard. He told me he was going out to a lighthouse to do some maintenance work and like a typical drunk he started insisting I come along. He was supposed to be going alone and when I was given permission to go too, I thought it would be no problem. Once we were out there on the rock I could overpower him and force him to pay for what he had done to us. With interest. But it didn't work out like that. We weren't alone after all, and I made a mess of things.'

'Yes.' Thorbjörg has almost lost the power of speech. All she can say is 'yes' or 'no'. She can't begin to form a coherent sentence.

'But because the idea was to throw myself off the cliff once I'd tortured and killed Ívar, I had to deal with the third witness the evening before we went out to the lighthouse. I only had Saturday to do it, and it didn't turn out too well. Not at all the way I'd planned. I'd been watching the house in the hope of finding some clever solution to the problem of catching her alone but that didn't work out. Luckily I still had the keys to the house, though, so that made things easier.'

Spare me, thinks Thorbjörg and her wish is granted. When Helgi starts speaking again it is about Ívar.

'I took a satnav to the lighthouse with me, which I'd taken from the house because I thought it belonged to the foreigners. The woman's watch, too, and some of the letters I'd printed out. I put them in Ívar's bag when he wasn't looking. Pretty clever. I reckon that was what finally convinced the police of his guilt.' His expression is proud, as it had been that time he came home with his school report, the spring after his father died. She had barely glanced at the string of A minuses, commented in an offhand way that she used to get straight As herself, then put down the report and lit a cigarette. He had never shown her his marks again after that and she had never shown the slightest interest in his school work.

Helgi hasn't touched her since coming into her hospital room. He doesn't do so now either when he suddenly leans close to her and whispers: 'To tell the truth, I'm a bit worried about the policewoman, Thröstur's wife, and that Örvar who gave me the reports. They might put two and two together. Everyone else is satisfied that Ívar was responsible for all the killings.'

Thorbjörg suddenly finds her voice. 'She doesn't know anything, so there's no need for you to worry about her. And surely he doesn't either – if they had any doubts, they'd have said so by now.' She tries to disguise her despair. She's had enough; this has to stop.

'I'm not so sure.' Helgi stands up, wincing as the wound in his side catches. 'I'm not at all sure.' He smiles his mirthless smile again. 'The policeman who interviewed me whispered in my ear that she's involved in some kind of dispute with a colleague she's lodged a complaint against. He sounds like a total shit. It occurred to me to find out his name, in case I need to take steps to deal with her. It's extraordinary how easy it is to make people think ill of someone. I'm sure suspicion would fall on him if anything happened to this Nína. At any rate, I can make certain it does.'

He goes to the door, then turns to say goodbye. 'Dad was

going to take me on a hunting trip the weekend he died. I haven't looked forward to anything since then. Not a thing. But I think I'm ready to now.' He stares at his mother in surprise, as if he's only just noticed the state she's in. Then he limps out, calling to her in parting, without looking back: 'Hope to see you later.' He closes the door behind him.

Thorbjörg doesn't feel able to share the sentiment. To think she had been under the impression that she had been going through hell recently. Now the day of reckoning is well and truly here. Now she will have to pay for all the tears, disappointment, humiliation and heartache she caused her son. But she can't feel sorry for herself. It's only what she deserves.

Fifteen minutes later the door opens and out comes a man of around Nína's age. She smiles at him but he doesn't seem to notice her and limps away, one hand pressed to his side. It strikes her as odd that he should be wearing a dressing gown. She raises her eyebrows, rises to her feet and enters Thorbjörg's room. The woman is gazing up at the ceiling, her belly as distended as it was the last time Nína saw her.

'Hello. Remember me?' Nína smiles awkwardly at the woman, who turns her head slowly towards her. 'I won't bother you for long. I just wanted to say a few words.' The woman's expression is not what she had been hoping for. The yellow eyes stare wildly at her as if Nína had threatened to set fire to her pillow. 'I'll come back later if it's a bad moment.'

'Yes, that'd be better. I need to be alone for a while.' The hoarse voice trembles a little and the look of terror intensifies, as if she fears Nína more than anything else in the world.

'No problem. I'll come back another time.' Nína closes

the door behind her and stands just outside, feeling mortified. God, that was embarrassing. But what had she expected? That everything would be fine, just because the truth had come to light? That the woman lying in the hospital bed would suddenly be cured? When it comes down to it, virtually nothing has changed. The woman's life is as wrecked now as it was before.

The same is true of her. Nothing has changed, really. If anything, even more pain lies in store. She can't be angry with Thröstur any more, and it's as if the anger has been holding back the worst of the sorrow up to now. Instead of feeling rage she is alive to the injustice of it all, which makes the whole thing even more unbearable. She can't even take her anger out on Ívar because he's dead.

After this evening there will be no room for any emotion but grief. She will be overwhelmed by grief for Thröstur and must be careful that it doesn't prove too much for her, doesn't blind her to all that is good and beautiful in this world. She mustn't let that happen.

She sees that it is time to head over to Thröstur's room. She wants to get there the moment the hour she allotted his sister and father is up, to give herself as long as possible to sit beside him. His death throes will not last long, according to the doctor. Thröstur will lie there motionless but alive, but a few minutes or hours later he will be lying there motionless and dead. No gasps, no rattling, no groans will mark his parting from her and this life.

Nína holds her head high as she walks out of the door to the ward. All at once the dress and heels seem perfectly in keeping with the occasion and she moves with increased confidence. She has dressed herself up for Thröstur. His last hours are to be a celebration; she is not going to weep. Instead she will whisper to him stories about all the good times they had, all the laughter they shared over the years; memories that will always have a place in her heart. Thröstur can take them with him as a parting gift when he leaves, never to return.

The door closes behind her. She walks over to the lift without noticing the man wearing a dressing gown, who is watching her with one hand pressed to his side.